Also by Maria Rose
Published by Ballantine Books:

ADMISSIONS

CHOICES

CONNECTIONS

SECOND CHANCES

SUMMER TIMES

ALL FOR THE LOVE OF DADDY

SONGS MY FATHER TAUGHT ME

MARCIA ROSE

BALLANTINE BOOKS • NEW YORK

Grateful acknowledgment is made to the following for permission to reprint previously published material: ABKCO Music, Inc.: Excerpt from the lyrics of "THE LAST TIME" written by Mick Jagger and Keith Richards. Copyright © 1965 by ABKCO Music, Inc. Rights in the U.S. and Canada administered by ABKCO Music, Inc. All other rights administered by Westminster Music Ltd. Reprinted by permission of ABKCO Music, Inc. and Westminster Music Ltd. All rights reserved.

Alpha Music, Inc.: Excerpt from the lyrics of "SOLIDARITY FOREVER." Copyright © by Alpha Music, Inc. Reprinted by permission.

Chandos Music: Excerpt from "ALL MY TRIALS", traditional, arranged and adapted by Joan Baez. Copyright © 1960 by Chandos Music (ASCAP). Used by permission.

Joan Daves: Excerpt from speech entitled "I Have a Dream" by Martin Luther King, Jr. Copyright © 1963 by Martin Luther King, Jr. Reprinted by permission of Joan Daves.

Industrial Workers of the World: Excerpt from "Mourn Not the Dead" by Ralph Chaplin from INDUSTRIAL WORKERS OF THE WORLD SONG BOOK. Reprinted by permission of the Industrial Workers of the World, 3435 N. Sheffield, Chicago, IL 60657.

Melody Trails, Inc.: Excerpt from "TURN! TURN! TURN! (To Everything There Is A Season)". Words form the Book of Ecclesiastes. Adaptation and Music by Pete Seeger. TRO—Copyright © 1962 by Melody Trails, Inc., New York, N.Y. Used by permission.

Story Songs Ltd: Excerpt from "CAT'S IN THE CRADLE" by Harry and Sandy Chapin. Copyright © 1974 by Story Songs Ltd. Reprinted by permission.

Library of Congress Catalog Card Number: 88-92807

ISBN 0-345-34537-1

Manufactured in the United States of America

First Edition: June 1989

To Sandy, Herb, Pete, and Dorothy.
Thank you.

Chapter One

Sunday, July 12, 1987   Just as she thought she might be able to take a breather, the doorbell buzzed again, insistently; and Cookie Adler, halfway across the room, cursed. Well, not to say *cursed*, exactly. "Rats!" is what she actually said. After all, she was the hostess of this shebang and the hostess must keep her cool, even if she *was* worried about her elderly parents who were late. "The door's open!" she yelled, knowing full well it was futile. No way could anyone hear her above the noise of thirty or so of their closest friends, every last one of them talking at once.

"Jonathan!" she hollered, catching sight of her son near the kitchen, pouring himself another glass of wine but who was counting. "Jon! The door! It might be Grandpa!"

"Yo!" Yo! What kind of word was *yo*? Where did it come from? The kids she worked with at the shelter—and they were from every kind of ethnic background—they all used it . . . and come to think of it, what kind of word was *ethnic*?

And where were they? Her parents. They'd promised to come early and here it was, nearly seven. Should she call? She hated to make a fuss, especially now. She didn't want Pop to think she was hovering over him. On the other hand, she didn't want them to think they'd been deserted, either. Oh, God. It was so hard, dealing with his cancer, his—let's face it—terminal cancer. After so many years of feeling close and comfortable with him, suddenly she wasn't sure how she was supposed to behave, what she was supposed to say, even how she should *feel*. She hated it, hated it!

She went to the big window that looked out on the street and leaned out as far as she could, braced on her hands. After a week of unseasonable heat, with temperatures in the nineties, it had rained briefly and was finally livable, at least for the moment. She breathed in with pleasure, smiling at herself because this was, after all, pure and fresh *city* air—45 percent carbon monoxide, 35 percent frying grease, 10 percent doggie doo, and 10 percent yuck of unknown origin.

She loved it, all of it: the noise; the dirt; the confusion; the chaos; the crazies; the street people; the yuppies with their big dogs and little babies; and, yes, even Bloomingdale's, where the message was loud and clear: Cookie Adler, pull yourself together, for God's sake! And then she began to laugh. There, across Ninety-fourth Street, in the window of the apartment opposite them, was taped a hand-lettered sign: IT'S A GIRL! RACHEL ELYSE.

Cookie turned, amused. "Hey, Dave! They had a girl!"

In a minute, a dozen people were crowded up to the window, waving and smiling. And then the woman across the street held up a finger, and everyone murmured, "Wait a minute . . . ." and everyone waited and then everyone went "Oooooh" as the woman across the street returned to her window, holding up something pink, wrapped in a pink blanket.

"Isn't that adorable! Who are they, Cookie?"

"Who are they? They're the people in the building across the street who get up the same time in the morning as we do . . . who have their dining table right across from ours . . . who prefer to keep the blinds up at all times . . . No, I'm not going to tell tales . . . ! But I will say this: when they fight and then make up . . ." and she rolled her eyes. Everyone laughed. Her friends expected her to come up with amusing comments. And she was happy to oblige.

When everyone else drifted off, she stayed by the window, scanning the street for her mother and father. She'd told them Dave would come in the car to get them but no. Pop had to walk. "It's only eight blocks, and I'm not dead yet." Tears stung at the backs of her eyes. Ever since Dr. McCormack had given him the bad news—the cancer which had gone into remission for eight years was back—her father had been matter-of-fact, accepting, and, to her surprise, talked openly about it. She couldn't get over it. Oh, he was a talker, always had been, but only about *issues*, which meant politics. Never anything personal. Never.

When she was just a little thing, the years they lived in the Coops, there was always a crowd in their living room; and in her memories, her father's voice was always the one that took charge, the one at center stage. What she remembered hearing about was the Cold War, the Soviet Union, McCarthy, HUAC, China. Or the unions, the workers, what was going to be the inevitable triumph of the working class. That's what she remembered: the talking and the marching and the piles of leaflets always stacked by the front door. And her father, discussing, arguing, giving speeches.

Pop's voice. The sound of her childhood. It was a light voice, somewhere in the tenor range, but it had great carrying power. His tone was usually even, almost soft, but you were a fool if you thought that meant *he* was soft. Once he had turned over the whole coffee table during an argument, sending teacups, books, newspapers, and eyeglasses, all flying.

After they were forced to move to Millville, it was a different story. There, he became quiet and preoccupied, usually bent over his books and newspapers, or falling asleep in his chair. Such a different Poppa. She used to go stand by his chair, diffident, hoping that this time, he would reach out and rumple her hair or even start a conversation. Sometimes he did; but not often enough to take away the knot of anxiety and loneliness in her stomach.

Well, enough of depressing memories. The past was gone. And today was a day of celebration in honor of her husband the hero. And right now, she'd better take herself back into the kitchen to get more food for her guests.

Her son appeared in the entrance to the galley kitchen, his long dark hair flopping over one eye, blue jeans low on his narrow hips, silly smile on his face, drink in hand. She wished he didn't have to drink in order to be in the same room with his father. She hoped he wouldn't get drunk and combative, like the last time. At least he was smiling, that was good. Let him stay that way.

"Need some help, Ma?"

She handed him two bowls. "Yeah. Put these on the table, would you?"

"For you, Ma? Anything!"

And unspoken, of course, was the rest of that sentence: And for Dad, nothing. She hoped he would keep his negative comments to himself tonight, especially during the TV show. This was Dave's night of glory; let him have it. And maybe after Jonathan saw the program, he'd finally realize what his father had been through these past three years. For three years, a pariah: the invisible man at his office, cut off from everyone, given no real work to do. Three years, the target of hostile investigations. Three years of frustration, worry, grief, and depression.

Cookie sighed, a heavy one from deep in her gut. Just *thinking* about that was enough to make her feel exhausted. Enough! Tonight was a celebration and she was the hostess. Of course, usually a hostess did not feel tense and uneasy on the night of her husband's triumph. A good hostess—a good wife, for that matter—would be euphoric. Well, euphoria was a bit beyond her this evening; but she could manage maybe low-level joy.

Juggling the food, she stepped into the dining area. There was a crowd around the table, of course. Their friends were eaters. And it gave her a good feeling to feed them, even though everything came from Zabar's or Balducci's. It wasn't as if she'd cooked and baked and chopped and sliced. Her only job was to point her finger: "A pound of that . . . two pounds of that . . ."

Well, anyway, it all looked wonderful, arrayed on the table: mounds of cold cuts, plates of smoked fish, a half-dozen different cheeses, every variety of bagel, hard rolls, thickly sliced rye, and raisin pumpernickel. Without thinking, she reached out and grabbed herself a piece of pumpernickel; she loved its damp, heavy sour-sweetness.

And then there was plain cream cheese, and dill cream cheese, and garlic cream cheese, and all the salads: potato salad, three-bean salad, tossed salad, Greek salad, health salad. Sauerkraut. Pickles. Olives. Jewish food, most people would call it, although it came from all over Europe. The amount, she thought with a smile, *that* was Jewish.

She loved this kind of food, loved it. Probably because when she was a kid in that outpost of civilization called Millville, New York, this kind of spread was reserved for extra-special events— and there never seemed to be any. First of all, there wasn't ever enough money; and second, you had to schlepp to Troy to get it. In Millville, Jewish food was exotic and a bit suspect. Hell, in Millville, *Jews* were exotic and more than a bit suspect!

She stood, trying to figure out how to make room where there wasn't any, when a pair of hands took the bowl from her and there was Michelle, saying, "Here, Mom, let me." Magically, her daughter created space and, while she was at it, rearranged the cheeses so they looked appetizing again. Cookie reached up and gave Michelle an affectionate pat on the cheek. A daughter was truly a blessing . . . at least a daughter like hers. As rebellious and difficult as Jon could be, that's how competent and helpful his sister was.

"Thanks, honey," Cookie said. "I'll just take some *nosherai* to those noshers in the living room."

Dave and his two oldest friends had ensconced themselves on the couch, having what they liked to call a serious discussion—

meaning everyone talked as loudly as possible and all at once—about Reagan's latest folly while eating everything within reach.

Her husband's voice could be clearly heard even above the din. "That bastard! He's not going to save us . . . he's going to *cause* World War Three!" Yes, Dave, we know, Dave, Cookie thought, just a bit irritated. For the past few weeks, ever since *City Sounds* first called him with the air date, he'd been full of himself, as if he'd just been proclaimed an expert on everything. It wasn't like him, and she didn't like it.

Now he called out, "Cookie! While you're up, get a bottle of seltzer?" Again, she felt that twinge of resentment. What was *with* him? Why wasn't he giving her a hand instead of calling for service, like she was the maid? They'd always had an egalitarian marriage—up until he became a celebrity, that is.

She came to a dramatic halt, right between the stereo and the room divider, and gave him a look. "Don't you remember where we keep the refrigerator?" And then she felt bitchy. This wasn't the time. Dammit, it was his party and he deserved to be the center of attention. And if that meant she turned and walked back into the kitchen and got out a bottle of cold seltzer from the fridge, well, big deal. It wasn't such a long walk.

"Never mind, Dave. This is your night. But starting tomorrow, buddy, you get your *own* seltzer."

"I love that woman!" Dave said, laughing, more like his usual, laid-back self. "She keeps me honest."

Cookie's eyes went to her son. Sure enough, the look of disdain was clearly visible. She didn't like that, but even less did she like him tipping his glass and draining it like it was water. She was going to have that talk with him, and soon. Cookie shook herself, impatient with her own motherly thoughts. She was tired of being a mother; and in any case, this was a party. How many times this evening had she already told herself that? Maybe *she* should take a drink.

She put the plates down in front of the men and went back for the seltzer, chatting a bit with various friends as she went. Everyone was smiling, in a holiday mood. They *all* felt vindicated by Dave's winning. Well, they should. They'd all stood by him when he got into trouble with the city. It had been a long haul. Just ask *her*. This morning, when she looked into her mirror, she'd seen the ravages of time and stress—the girlish freckles and the womanly wrinkles battling it out.

In honor of *City Sounds*, she had decided to put mascara on her pale eyelashes; and while she was at it, she gave herself the once-over. Same old Cookie: oval face, big hazel eyes, regular nose, regular mouth, lots of thick curling hair that once had been fiery red, like her pop's, but was now, what? A fading auburn tinged with gray, cut short so she wouldn't have to fuss with it. Pretty? Far from it. She'd made a little face at her reflection and applied some pink lipstick—which she'd probably eaten off by this time. But who'd notice? Who cared?

Sam, their neighbor and friend (and incidentally her boss) was giving Dave the business. "Look at all that food, man! Now I *know* this is the big time!" He laughed hugely. "When Dave Adler goes for Zabar's finest—!" And he rolled his eyes.

Dave laughed. "Cookie paid for it."

Cookie, face straight, said, "I thought *you* paid for it."

Dave looked around. "Hey, who paid for this spread? And whoever you are—where's my shrimp?" As often happened at parties, the laughter was somehow the signal for everyone to rearrange themselves into a different pattern; and Cookie took herself to the kitchen. She didn't have anything definite in mind; but her motto always was, When in doubt, feed them.

No sooner did she have her hands full of stuff when someone yelled, "Your folks are here!" and she just dropped what she was doing and ran to greet them, bracing herself as she had to do nowadays, because she was frightened of what she might see.

Six months ago, Pop had seemed much the same as always: still opinionated, definite, peppy. Six months ago, his hair was still mostly red, his shoulders square. Now, every time she saw him he looked more stooped, more tired, more faded.

This time was no different. Inside, she winced when she saw him. He looked like an old man and he *wasn't*; but, dammit, he was dying! Hoping she wouldn't cry because that would make him feel terrible, she hugged him. He felt so thin, so fragile! Her mother zipped right into the living room, talking a mile a minute, calling out to everyone she knew, giving them the big Dot Gordon hello—which was very big indeed. Her mother, while not very tall, had the presence of about ten ordinary people. She had that thing called charisma. She was a very pretty woman still, even at seventy, her skin still pretty, her color high, her eyes lively. She was still shapely, too.

Two weeks ago, when Cookie took her to the ballet at Lincoln Center, Dorothy showed up in a peasant skirt and blouse and long earrings made of tiny silver stars that trembled and twinkled with every move. Her long salt-and-pepper hair was twisted into a wonderfully intricate French knot. As Cookie approached her, unseen, she noticed several men (and not all of them elderly, either) turn to give her mother second looks. And so they should; she was what used to be called a fine figure of a woman. Much more head-turning than her daughter, Cookie thought wryly.

She had thought, walking toward her mother, that it had been years since any man had turned to give her *any* kind of look, first, second, or last.

Look at Dot now, circling the room, totally at ease, hugging those she knew, shaking hands with those she didn't, laughing, talking, already with a drink in her hand. Not a backward glance. She knew Cookie would take care of Pop.

As soon as her mother was out of earshot, Pop leaned close to her and whispered, "So? Did you hear? What did Jack say?"

Cookie laughed. "Pop! Jack hasn't said anything yet. I only called Deena two days ago! I left a message on *her* machine, and then she left a message on *my* machine . . . remember? I told you. So then, this morning I called her again and left another message. You will be happy to know that Deena's machine and my machine have now established a wonderful relationship. Okay?"

"I'm not so far gone that I don't remember what you told me yesterday. I just wondered. I don't have so much time left that I can afford to waste it, waiting around for that big *macher* to say yes or no! That's all. I just wondered. Couldn't a man wonder without you making a Federal case?"

"Well, you're going to have to wonder a little while longer, Pop. I have first to talk to Deena and then she has first to talk to Jack."

"What if he says no? You know, it didn't occur to me until just now. That so-and-so! He might just say no deal, he's such a stubborn mule!"

Cookie gave him an amused look. "Oh, really?"

"Yeah, yeah, I know. It takes one to know one! You don't have to say it!" And then he laughed.

"Anyway," Cookie said, trying to mollify him, "Jack isn't going to say no. He couldn't. I don't remember him being a mule. The way I remember him, he was easygoing, joking and singing and telling stories . . ."

"Yeah, yeah, and giving out silver dollars like there was no tomorrow! That's why you kids all liked him so much, he was always quick with the money!"

"Pop! That's not fair. He was our uncle and he was always nice to us. Weren't you two friendly?"

He shook his head. "Not me and him, never. With me and him, it was oil and water, right from the very first moment."

Cookie stood, hands on hips. "Pop! Irwin and Paul and I always thought you were really fond of each other, in spite of his politics! Dammit, Pop, you never told us *anything*!"

"It's not the kind of thing you tell young children!"

Why not? Cookie thought, but she stayed silent. What good would it do to go to war with him, at this late date? Holding tightly on to her father's arm, she went with him into the living room. As soon as they made their appearance, Ron Schwartz, who'd known their family since the old days in the Bronx, leaped up and offered his chair to Jonah. "How're you doing, Mr. Gordon?"

"Jonah. Jonah. None of this Mr. Gordon stuff. I'm doing okay—for an old man." He smiled, to show he was just making his little joke. But he almost wasn't able to cover up the involuntary groan as he lowered himself into the chair.

Cookie raised her voice just a little. "To the throngs of people who have been demanding to know when my father is going to appear this evening, here he is, fresh from Eighty-ninth Street, Apartment C."

"You cut it mighty close," Dave said, smiling. "I was beginning to wonder if you were going to show up at all!"

"Not show up! Are you kidding?" Jonah said. "How could we miss an occasion like this!" Suddenly, his voice became strong. By the second sentence, all attention was on him, all heads turned to him. Cookie marveled. All he needed was an audience.

"Dave has done a magnificent thing . . . fighting Koch's cronies. Idiots, all of them. They know nothing about the oppressed and they care even less! Only Dave. They should have given him a medal, but no! What did they give him?" He paused, arm outstretched, waiting.

"The shaft!" someone called out.

"Tsuris!" someone else added. "Trouble!"

"A hard time!"

"That's right!" Jonah was obviously in his element and enjoying himself immensely. "Dave blew the whistle, and instead of thanking him for a job well done, those bastards punished him . . . *punished* him, for being right!" His voice cracked and he stopped, reaching for a glass of water, lifting it. "A toast! Let us raise our glasses to Dave Adler and raise our fists to the crooked bureaucrats who allow innocent children to be brutalized, victimized, and murdered—'' There were shouts of agreement, which he spoke right over. ''Yes, murdered! And the real shame? The real shame''—here, his voice dropped dramatically—''that it takes a television program to tell the world what's been 'going down' . . . Oh, look there, my grandson is finally making an appearance, giving me a funny look. I can say 'what's been going down,' Jonathan. I'm hip, or hep, or whatever they're calling it now . . .'' He waited for the ripple of laughter and then continued: ''That Dave should be vindicated by the boob tube—''

''Thank God for the boob tube, Jonah!'' It was his wife, who stood up, glass lifted. ''Thank God for Dick Wallach, right? *Another* guy with guts!'' There was more laughter and a murmur of approval and everyone drank.

Cookie took a sip of her wine without really tasting it. It struck her every once in a while, when she saw her father in action, holding forth on something he cared about, how deeply the Party must have disappointed him—no, more than that, *hurt* him—to have turned him into the brooding sad-eyed man she remembered from The Bad Time up in Millville. God! Again, the memories of Millville cropping up. Why now? She'd managed to put that whole time out of her mind, for years.

One of the old gang laughed and called out: ''This is the stuff of life to an old progressive, hey, Jonah?''

Jonah laughed. ''Progressives don't have much to *kvell* about these days, not since that costar to a chimp got himself elected. Agh . . . anyway, there aren't any real progressives anymore. Young people aren't idealistic like we were.''

''Yo, Grandpa. *I'm* idealistic.''

''Yeah, yeah, Jonny. So what have you done lately? When did you last put yourself on the line for something worthwhile?''

''Yesterday, and every Saturday in fact,'' Jon said. ''Against nuclear arms. Against apartheid. Against Star Wars. You name it, Grandpa, I'm against it and I demonstrate!''

There was a great deal of laughter at this. Cookie looked at her son and marveled. He was grinning at Pop, standing with his hands hooked into his jeans belt, totally at ease. If he could do it with his grandfather, why not with his father?—who was, Cookie thought, a much easier man to get along with.

Now one of the women said, ''That's how I learned I was a Red Diaper baby: when I discovered all the other kids in my class watched cartoons on Saturday morning instead of marching on picket lines.''

Everyone laughed and applauded. Jonah leaned over and tugged on Cookie's hand, gesturing to her to bend close to him. In her ear, he said quietly, "Should she talk so openly?"

She straightened up. "Don't worry, Pop. We're all friends here."

Just then, the phone rang and Cookie ran for it. "Keep it down to a dull roar, will you folks?" Still talking, she picked up the phone, and said, "Yes?"

Her caller said, "I hope that background noise is not all coming from your children, Cookie. Because the last time I talked to you, you weren't even married."

Cookie grinned and responded without a pause, "Martin Luther King, Jr. The March on Washington. August 28, 1963. See, I remember—just like it was only twenty-four years ago!"

"Which it was, and aren't you clever, still able to subtract in your head!"

Cookie turned and yelled into the din: "Hey everyone, it's my long-lost cousin Deena, and I can't hear her!" She pointedly looked at her father, but he only looked back at her, bland as butter. Not even a smile to show he was pleased.

"It's so good to almost hear your voice, Deena. Look, there are a million people here. Let me go into the bedroom. Someone hang up this phone for me, please?"

She trotted down the short hall into her bedroom. Not hers, theirs. Correction. Not theirs, his. Correction. Now it belonged to Dave's exercise equipment. The day after they demoted him, Dave had moved a rowing machine and an exercise bike in, so he could watch television while he worked out, which meant almost all the time. Maybe now he'd move it out . . . into Jon's old room, maybe. Jon was never going to come back home to live. Thank God. And if that made her a bad mother, so sue her.

A bit breathless, she grabbed for the phone. "Deena? Sorry." She sat down on the edge of the bed, gazing out the window at the hazy sky. She was a little surprised, how calm she felt. They hadn't exchanged a word since the March on Washington. Somehow, she had thought there would be high emotion, maybe even tears. But no. "So how are you, Deena? How've you been? Do you believe what I'm saying? It's over twenty years and I'm asking you what's new?"

Deena laughed, and that sound called up instant memory. The damp and hazy heat of a Washington, D.C., August. The orderly, optimistic, determined hundreds of thousands of

marchers. Her friends from CCNY. The singing, the speeches.
Martin Luther King, Jr. God. She remembered Deena, her pretty
face shiny with sweat, her eyes filled with tears, very pregnant,
laughing because Cookie had spotted her in that mass of people.

They had embraced that day, so excited at finding each other
again, amazed that they recognized each other after so many
years—and in this place, on this historic occasion!

"Do you realize," Cookie said now, "the last time we were
together, you were pregnant with your first? And then I saw you
in the street a couple of times with a pram, then with a stroller,
then with a toddler and pram and then a toddler and a double
stroller . . ." They both laughed. "And then you moved. How
many more did you have?"

"A grand total of four. Two boys, two girls. And you?"

"Just two. Twins."

"Twins! Like your mother and Yetta! Two girls?"

"No. One of each . . . Jonathan and Michelle, twenty-one
years old. Mickey's a senior at Harvard . . ."

"Harvard! I'm impressed!"

"So is she. Surely, there's someplace else worth being, in
this whole large world!"

"It passes. My oldest went to Harvard *and* Harvard Med,
but he's beginning to adjust to the outside world."

Again they laughed and now Cookie remembered how they
had always found each other funny. It was so nice to be able to
just pick up where they had left off.

"Well, anyway, she'll be a senior next year and then it'll be
over," she said.

"And your son?"

"My son is an artist. He goes to Cooper Union, and he paints,
and he lives on the Lower East Side, excuse me, the East Village, with his *posselque*."

"His *what*?"

"P-O-S-S-L-Q. Person of the Opposite Sex Sharing Living
Quarters. Cute? Would you believe the people at our Census
Bureau thought that one up!"

"It sounds precisely like something the Census Bureau would
think up."

They laughed and then there was a long pause. Finally, Deena
drew in a deep breath and said, "I thought of you often. But, I
don't know . . . I had all those babies and Daddy was adamant
about loyalty and, I don't know . . ."

"I understand," Cookie said. "I thought of you, too, but I just didn't know how to break down that barrier."

"God, it should have been so easy. And after Michael and I moved to Brooklyn Heights, you could've come here and nobody would have known." Another beat. "By the way, I'm divorced—and I've gone back to my maiden name."

"That's all right. I never knew your *married* name!"

"And thank you for not saying you're sorry about the divorce. That's what most people say, automatically. What do they know about it? And Daddy acts as if somehow I had done something awful to *him*. Of course, that shouldn't surprise me. He always expects me to behave exactly the way he wants me to. Once, he saw me wave to you from across the street—*years* after the big hoo-ha, of course—and he couldn't bring himself to speak to me for a week and a half. And I'm his *favorite*!" She laughed, but it had a slight quiver around the edges.

"Pop was no better, believe me. And he had all that political rhetoric to call upon! Which, believe me, he did."

Deena pulled in her breath and said hesitantly, "You said in your message that your father is ill. Is it . . . bad?"

"I'm afraid so. Cancer."

"Oh, God, how awful. I'm so sorry! And it really makes me sad to think so many years have gone by and I haven't seen him . . ."

"Well, it makes me *mad*, that it had to come to this for Pop to see how stupid this feud is. But okay, better late than never, to coin a cliche. Now he's eager. Now he can't wait, he's after me every day. Will Jack agree to get together? What do you think?"

"A reconciliation!" Deena said. "After all these years! That would be wonderful! We could see each other again! But . . . why are *we* discussing it? Wouldn't it make more sense for Uncle Jo to call Daddy and they could talk to each other?"

"Who said anything about sense? We're talking about our fathers!" Again, they laughed.

"But, our *mothers* could arrange the summit!"

"Our mothers! Let me tell you what happened, Deena." Cookie said. "Pop woke up two o'clock in the morning on a Tuesday, convinced that he must make up with his brother-in-law before it's too late. So, of course, he had to wake up my mother to let her know. She asked could it wait until maybe the morning or would he like her to call her brother right then and there. You know: men have the brilliant ideas, but it's up to the women to carry them out. If you know what I mean.''

''I know what you mean.''

''Well, it seems that my mother felt funny, calling Uncle Jack without any warning. She wanted to talk to Sylvia, first. So she called *me*. What else? 'You and Deena were always such good friends,' she told me. 'You call Deena and ask her to speak to her mother to speak to her father and then call me and let me know what he says.' She didn't see anything the least bit funny about it, either! And, you'll notice, I'm *doing* it.''

''I know that syndrome.'' Deena laughed. ''Sylvia has this wonderful habit of assigning her daughters the task of talking to one another about things that are bothering *her*. But I'm not complaining this time. It's so nice to be talking to you!''

''You think he'll agree?''

''Oh, my dear Cookie, who knows what Daddy'll do! Although he's not quite the bulldozer he used to be. Lately things get to be too much for him, and he gets . . . helpless, kind of.''

''Uncle Jack? Helpless? Doesn't sound like him!''

''It's the A-curse . . . and, you know, Cookie, I've just had a brilliant thought. Facing your father alone might be too threatening . . . you know, loss of face and all that male stuff. But what about a family reunion? All of us, not just the two of them! Hell, *everybody*: children, wives, grandchildren, pozzelwhatevers. Your group, my group, all of us. Together.''

''In the same country?''

''In the same room. Kinda takes your breath away, doesn't it?''

A rustling noise behind her in the doorway made Cookie turn. It was her mother, gesticulating feverishly, pointing to her wristwatch. Oh, God! Nearly seven! Dave's interview was going to be first. ''Deena, you've just had a great idea,'' she said, talking very fast, ''but I've got to run. If you can, turn on Channel Two right this minute, and watch my husband give hell to the welfare system. But I want to see you. I *really* want to see you. I want this reunion to happen. Let's end all this *narrishkeit*!''

''You got a deal. How about dinner tomorrow?''

Deena didn't mess around, Cookie thought, anymore than she ever had. She'd always been quick to go after whatever she wanted. Well, Cookie Adler could be the same. ''Hisae's on

Cooper Square? Five-thirty?'' She was a bit surprised to discover how excited she was at the prospect of seeing her cousin again. "Terrific," she said, when Deena agreed. "And . . . Deena?"

"Mmmmm?"

"I can't wait!"

<hr>

Chapter Two

Sunday, July 12, 1987   In the living room there was an air of suppressed excitement. Everyone had taken a seat, wherever there was a space—or half a space, in some cases. Most of them were sitting on the floor. Someone yelled, "Make a space for Cookie next to Dave," but she said, "I'll have to step on ten people. It's okay; I'll just sit right here." And she plunked herself on the arm of her father's chair. He reached out for her hand. She was astonished and pleased and a little sad.

"So? What's gonna be, Cookele? That stubborn old enemy of the workers gonna come see me? But no. He wouldn't come to me, he's such a big shot. I know: I'll have to schlepp to his fancy club, am I right? And you can tell his daughter Deena that your father says he might. If Jack Strauss begs on his hands and knees. Then, maybe." He laughed.

Cookie stifled a sigh. She had a funny feeling that getting these two guys together was not going to be easy. But she was saved from having to answer him—for the moment—by a burst of applause from the assemblage as the familiar bird's-eye view of New York appeared on the screen.

Next, there was Dick Wallach's familiar face on the screen, and a big headline: BLOWING THE WHISTLE! More applause from their friends and loved ones. Then Dick Wallach said, "If you had proof that, every day, helpless children were being murdered in their own homes, wouldn't you speak out? Dave Adler had such proof and he did speak out. Dave Adler is a social worker, an administrator in New York City's Human Resources Administration—HRA—and he noticed in case after case, that reports of violence and abuse were not being followed up. Now, Dave Adler works in the system and he trusted the system. He filed proper reports to the proper authorities. Was he thanked? Was he promoted? No, he was not. He was demoted and ostracized, his salary cut in half and his career ruined. And Dave says this is what happens to *all* whistle-blowers . . .''

As the reporter's face faded from the screen, Jonah said loudly, "Huh! This is what they call news? Didn't I say that, before? Believe me, there's nothing new in this world!"

"*Shah*, Jonah. This is Dave's program," Dot said. Not exactly accurate, Cookie thought, but well meant. She looked over at Dave, ensconced on the seat of honor, in the exact middle of the couch, facing the television—really too small a screen for all these people. Dave had wanted one of those twenty-six-inch monsters; but Cookie was damned if she was going to spend nearly a thousand dollars so that a giant blind eye could dominate their nice, cozy living room with its Mexican pottery and bright Rya rug.

Dave was absolutely rapt on the screen, like a kid watching cartoons, shushing the wisenheimers who were making comments on his performance. He really looked alive tonight, and it was good to see him with his dark eyes flashing, like the first time she ever saw him. That's what she noticed right away: how dark he was, and how electric. It was on the bus coming back home from the March on Washington, the same day she'd seen Deena. They were both turned on by the magic of that most magical of days, and it was love at first sight. Or something. Well, whatever it was, they were still together.

She looked him over—it had been many a moon since she'd done that. He had aged well, Dave; there was a light sprinkling of white in his hair and beard, that's all. The thick wiry curls had thinned out but he wasn't balding, like plenty of his friends. And these past three years of working out at the health club, of running five miles a day rain or shine, snow or sleet, had tightened him up, given him new muscles.

Several of the women in the building had remarked on this. Molly Santangelo, who always had a big mouth, even said, "Jesus, it must be some turn-on, to have a husband with a great body like that."

Cookie remembered being startled. Dave was Dave. "It doesn't feel a bit different."

"Oh, sure, Cookie! Tell me another!"

She wondered what Molly would say if she had told her the truth: which was that the night Dave came home and told her he had been demoted and his pay cut in half, she had been rehearsing a speech, entitled "I Think We Should Get a Divorce." And that she still remembered every word of it, that she might still use it, she just didn't know.

Nobody in this room tonight would ever guess. And if she made an announcement right now, they'd all just gape at her. And then, they'd laugh, thinking she was making a joke. Cookie and Dave Adler were the ideal couple, sharing everything, totally comfortable with each other.

She had thought so, too—until three years ago. Well, a little longer than that. The kids had moved out and, all of a sudden, there was just the two of them. Well, sort of. Actually, they never saw very much of each other. He had board meetings, health club, his weekly poker game, and a work load that came home with him every night. She had exercise class, Community Board, her women's group, her Italian conversation class, and a work load that came home with her every night. She hardly saw him, that's what it amounted to.

And then, at just about the same time, it seemed, half the women in her group began saying, "No more of this talk about making it work. I'm getting out." One right after the other! Her best friend Lois, even!

So here she was, still stuck in the same old apartment, with her same old life, while all around her, women were casting off their shackles and their preconceptions, and taking charge of their own lives! The excitement, the freedom, the possibilities! The notion was dazzling. Maybe she had married too young; maybe she had settled too quickly because somebody said he loved her; maybe that's why she was feeling she had somehow missed out on . . . what, she didn't even know.

Romance. That was it. That's what she had never had. And never would. Never. She'd married a man because he looked good to her and his politics were correct. And mostly, because *he* liked *her*.

It was on the bus ride home after the March on Washington. August 28, 1963. A dark, nice-looking young man sat next to her and they began to talk.

Of course, everyone felt connected, that day. Cookie, who thought of herself as someone who didn't attract boys, was surprised when he wanted to talk with her: mostly about the ca-

dences of Dr. King's speech, about how the chills ran shudder-
ing down his spine at the power and beauty of the man's elo-
quence. And the crowd! The crowd! This had to have been the
event of the century!

"I've never been so excited in my entire life!" he told her,
grabbing her hand and squeezing it without even realizing it.
"History was being made and we were there . . . do you realize
that?" And they just kept talking and it was so easy, for a change!
He kept grinning at her in a certain way and her heart speeded
up. Was it possible that he found her attractive? But she couldn't
tell for sure. She knew about boys wanting sex, but this was
different.

And then he asked, "Ever hear of the Coops?"

"Hear of it? I used to live there."

"You *did*? God. I wish we could have. But my parents did
send me there for *mittel shul*." He gave her a soft sidelong look.
"I'm glad we met."

So he must be from the *real* Left. That was nice. She wasn't
going to have to tell lies, hide her background, make up stories.
She smiled at him. "But we haven't."

Consternation. "What do you mean?"

"We haven't met yet." How about that? She was doing okay
with this boy, even being a little funny. "I'm Cookie Gordon.
Karla, really, but everyone calls me Cookie."

"Hi, Cookie. I'm Dave Adler. How come I never saw you in
the Coops?"

"We moved. In 1953." Should she take a chance? She decided, yes. "My father had to go . . . away."

He took her hand and then, all confusion, dropped it. "He
was blacklisted," he whispered. "I understand."

Pop hadn't been exactly blacklisted, but it was so nice to be
with someone who knew about that time. Even though McCarthy was dead and gone, she was still scared, still felt she had to
be so careful, not to let the wrong thing slip out. It was like
having two separate lives: the one at home and one outside. She
was so tired of it.

When she didn't say anything, he reached over and took her
hand again and this time he held on to it. "I'm sorry," he said.
"We don't have to talk about it. You're too pretty to look so
sad."

Pretty! He thought she was pretty. Cookie blushed, grateful
that it was getting dark outside and he couldn't see her. Her

heart began to beat painfully. Maybe this was the boy who would truly love her.

And that was it. They began spending all their free time together, as of that moment, and the rest was history. This was love—she thought it was love, it must be love.

So often, lately, she found herself remembering that first meeting, recalling the family legend about how her parents met: "The minute we saw each other, we knew . . ." That's how it was supposed to happen. And it did, didn't it? She'd never even gotten to know him before she married him! And she was stuck! It wasn't fair! Her friend Lois was her age, her children were nearly grown, and *she* was getting a second chance. Dammit!

Three years ago. It might as well be three centuries. She had prepared her little speech, explaining very carefully that this wasn't necessarily a divorce she was talking about, but a separation, allowing her some space and some time to sort out her thoughts and feelings. All very reasonable and rational, she thought, carefully worded not to accuse or blame, simply asking for his understanding.

She started to tell him, several times, but it was never exactly the right time. And then, one Friday, she leaned on the bathroom sink and looked her reflection right in the eyes and said, "Stop stalling, kiddo. Tonight. Tell him tonight or forget it." She was all prepared: she'd even changed her clothes for the occasion; she'd even packed a small suitcase and left it in the front hall closet behind the boots. She sat in the living room, facing the door, licking her lips nervously, waiting for the sound of his key in the lock. When she heard it, she nearly jumped out of her skin.

And then he came in with a funny look on his face, his skin looking gray. And then he'd told her. His own department had turned on him; he'd been demoted; it was war and it was going to be a long tough haul.

She had put her feelings on hold, that night. She knew all about living with a man under the gun. She'd learned the hard way, up in Millville, with Pop. Dave was going to need all the support he could get. One thing he didn't need was a wife talking divorce. What he was doing was an act of conscience, an act of bravery. She was not happy, but so what? Next to what he was doing, her feelings counted for nothing. Every once in a while, though, in the small hours of the morning, lying sleepless in

their bed, weeping silently, with him snoring next to her, she
would wonder.

Now everyone in her living room murmured as Dave's face
filled the television screen. And then, of course, they all had to
kibitz.

"Dave, why aren't you smiling?"

"What was to smile about?" Pause. "Besides, I was nervous
as hell." Laughter.

"Goddammit, Dave, I never realized what a good-looking
guy you are!"

"That's Dick Wallach!" More laughter.

Dave *was* good-looking, Cookie thought, he was smart, he
was . . . *nice*. He deserved a different wife, one who would love
and adore him instead of constantly finding fault and being unhappy.

Oh, hell. She concentrated on his voice, amplified and au-
thoritative, coming out of the television set.

"I trusted the system," Dave was saying. "I was naïve. I
thought the HRA would *want* to know that there were caseworkers who were too overworked to follow up child abuse
cases."

"But you were wrong."

"*Wrong* is a mild word, Dick. No one in the HRA wanted to
know anything at all. Everyone just wanted me to shut up, forget
what I knew, and disappear."

Cookie let her mind drift. She knew the whole story, knew it
by heart. Dave, though, was the picture of total attention. How
could he enjoy reliving all that pain?

She remembered him, pounding his fist onto the dining table,
fighting tears of frustration. "Dammit, Cookie, while they fool
around and deny everything, while they look the other way and
try to pretend I'm not there, kids are *still* dying!"

That was the night he wrote anonymous letters to newspapers, to the district attorney's office, to the governor, to whom-
ever he thought might have some power to investigate. Later,
he admitted to her that it was kind of dumb to do that. "I should
have realized by then that nobody was going to pay any attention."

But they did worse than ignore him. They actually tracked
him down, through his handwriting! That shocked him more
than anything else.

Cookie had begged him to leave and go to work for a private

agency. "I could've gotten a different job," the Dave on the screen was saying, "but it was a matter of principle."

Her father leaned forward in his chair. "You tell 'em, Dave!"

"*Shah*, Jonah!"

On the screen, Dave, seen from the back, walked down the hallway of his office building, his footsteps echoing eerily in the quiet. And then, as if thinking aloud, his voice: "I don't know . . . I used to be so sure that anyone could make a difference, all you had to do was stick to it. But now . . . I don't know . . . maybe I should just quit . . ."

Cookie had been watching the screen; now she turned quickly and met her husband's eyes. He gave her that shrug, the one that said I don't want to talk about it. Dammit, how many dozens of times had Jon pleaded with him to leave, to quit, to get another job? And he'd never, ever let on that it was something he was considering. He just wouldn't discuss it, dismissing Jon with a vague, "You don't understand the complications," or an obviously false, "I'll think about it."

Dammit, after the hours she'd spent in their bed, her arms around him, fighting off the sleep that threatened to engulf her, letting him talk and talk and talk, chew it over and over, relive it, rehash it, regurgitate it! You'd think he might have mentioned a career change to *her*!

Oh, hell. What did she want from him? He always shied away from intimate talk. He would never admit to being unhappy. And if she suggested that she might be unhappy, he told her she was only bored. He'd take her out to the movies, or order up Chinese food, or make love and then say, "Feeling better, aren't you?" Anything, as long as they didn't have to *talk* about it!

Yet, this very same man would sit on the phone, in the middle of the night, discussing, listening, being ever so patient, if one of his clients called—even a client from years back. Oh, yes, she'd often been told what a sensitive and responsive man Dave Adler was!

She turned to him again, but he was standing up, stretching. On the TV, a commercial for insurance was droning on. Someone got up and turned it off. Dave Adler's big moment was over and everyone in the room was standing, applauding, and he was grinning, half embarrassed but very pleased with himself. She wished she could feel it with him.

And when Pop lifted his glass and proposed a toast to "Our hero . . . it was a lucky day when my daughter, Cookie, caught him," she had to force herself to look proud. But inside she felt only a growing sense of isolation.

❦❦❦❦❦❦❦❦❦❦❦❦❦❦❦❦❦❦❦❦❦❦❦❦❦❦❦❦❦❦❦❦❦❦❦❦

Chapter Three

Sunday, July 12, 1987   Jonah took his sweet time, getting down the front steps of the building. Dorothy watched him, longing to take his arm, to help him, maybe hurry him along a little, but he'd only get angry with her and scold. Scolding she didn't need tonight; she was tired. It was hard work, these days, being at a big party, talking, acting cheerful, putting on a show.

As soon as they began walking toward Broadway, Jonah gave her a little dig in the ribs. "You see?" She looked over at him; he was grinning like an imp. "I *knew* that old bastard would want to make up. He'd never admit it, but he knows who was right and who was wrong!"

"Excuse me, Mr. Smarty Pants, but who was it, asked for a meeting? Seems to me it wasn't anyone named Jack Strauss. And, as a matter of fact, we don't even know yet what's going to be."

"So sue me." He dismissed her words with a wave of his hand. "But look how fast Deena called back Cookie. That means something!"

Dorothy sighed. How dense could you get? "You've forgotten how Jack is, Jonah. I myself haven't seen him for a long time but, remember, I grew up with him. Jack has never said 'I'm sorry' in his entire life!"

"Sorry, shmorry! What you're forgetting is that Jack isn't getting any younger, either. Whether he says it or not, he's sorry, believe me!"

Neither of them spoke while they crossed Columbus Avenue. That made Dorothy a little sad. There had been a time, she thought wryly, when they could have crossed the street, watched the traffic, *and* had a conversation, *and* read the specials on the windows of the supermarket, all at the same time. Getting old was for the birds! She was grateful, however, for the chance to collect her thoughts before this discussion went any further. She was going to have to be very careful with this. This was risky business, very risky business.

"I don't get it," she said, once they were safely on the other side of the street. "You're the one who threatened to disown any member of your family who dared even mention 'that dirty Capitalist' . . . remember? And even when Cookie cried, you wouldn't allow her to see Deena . . . or even call her. Remember? So, what's with this making up, all of a sudden?"

"All of a sudden, I don't have so much time to waste."

"Jonah, I hate to tell you, but you and my brother are no different than you were back then. You want to know what I think? I think the minute the two of you get together, it'll be a fight. I think this whole reconciliation idea is a fantasy."

"Fantasy, shmantasy! It's two old men, willing to overlook a difference of opinion."

Dorothy stopped walking and, since her arm was looped in his, so did he. "Jonah!" she cried. "I don't know whether to laugh or cry. A difference of opinion, you call it? It was more like World War Three! A difference of opinion! And now, you expect to suddenly erase thirty-seven years of hard feelings, just like that." She snapped her fingers.

But she could see by the look on his face, the stubborn set of his lips, that he was not buying. He was set on his reconciliation, and when Jonah Gordon got set on something, it would take an atomic bomb to stop him. And then he slid a look sideways at her, the look she always called Jo's Fish Eye, and she knew she was in for it. He was beginning to suspect that she had . . . what was it the kids called it? A hidden agenda. And he was right.

"So, Dorothy? You want to tell me what's *really* on your mind?"

"What are you talking? I told you what's on my mind."

He laughed derisively. "Dorothy, Dorothy, I know you too long . . . You can't fool me."

That's what *you* think! she said to herself, nudging him a little so they could cross Amsterdam Avenue while they still had the green light. She smiled a little to herself. Jonah always assumed she was an open book to him, always had. Oh, Jo, Jo! Did I do you a favor? I wonder. She was really going to have to talk to Jack, herself, to warn him not to say too much. Just pick up the phone and talk to him . . . The thought was strange, after all the years of enforced silence. If he ever spilled the beans! That would be a fine mess! Jonah would have his reconciliation with Jack all right . . . but he'd never speak to her again.

"You know me?" she asked. "Well, I know Jack. And I'm telling you, he never forgets anything, never. He might agree to a meeting with you, but so what? He'll make sure he's in charge. He always has to be in charge . . . of everything and everyone."

"He won't get away with that, not with me!"

"Mr. Big Shot! Okay, let's say he's a pussycat. Let's say it's a regular honeymoon. What's the big deal, anyway? You didn't talk to him for thirty-seven years and you never missed it—"

He interrupted her. "Who says? Maybe I missed arguing with him. Maybe I felt bad for *you.*"

She gave him a look. "Jo, you know you and Jack didn't get along—not from the very first minute when he came to Washington to give you the once-over . . ." She paused and began to laugh. "Do you remember that day?"

"Remember? How could I forget!" He, too, was laughing. "He came into your apartment, ready to kill . . . !"

It was an unusually harsh winter in Washington, in 1942, with icy winds constantly howling and low, damp gray skies shrouding the buildings. In her little apartment on Q Street, Dorothy Strauss hung blankets over the blackout curtains at night, to keep the penetrating chill at bay. But now, it was Saturday afternoon and a pale sun was trying to shine, and Dot was looking around the living room, a little bit nervous, she had to admit.

She'd sent the letter last week, the letter that told Ma and Pa that she was going to marry Jonah Golodny, a man they'd never even met. She felt a bit breathless with her own daring, but Yetta had told her a thousand times, "You're a sissy, Dot. You worry too much about what they're going to think. Do what you want, that's the secret of life." Easy for Yetta to say. Yetta *always* did what she wanted, she always had.

They were twins, she and Yetta, and maybe that's why she was a bit of a coward, because Yetta got all the guts, like she got all the artistic talent, too. Yetta had always been the one who argued with Pa and talked back to Ma and, truth be told, if it hadn't been for Yetta, they'd still be in Brooklyn, living with their parents, still under the thumb of their strict, short-tempered father.

When she first met Jonah, at the Russian War Relief picnic, Yetta was still sharing the apartment with her. Her sister had always said it was dumb to tell their parents anything about the men they were meeting. "They don't have to know," she'd say. "After you find the man you want to marry, then it'll be plenty of time to tell them. Pa's gonna scream bloody murder, no matter *what* you do or who you do it with. So do yourself a favor and keep your mouth shut about your private life. What they don't know, can't hurt them."

Yetta had always been the daring one, the one with all the brave ideas. So Dorothy had followed her sister's lead, keeping her life to herself. And it felt good, it really did. For the first time in her life, she realized suddenly, she had privacy. And now that Yetta was in the WACs, it felt even better. Because, truth to tell, Yetta pushed her around, too. Oh, she loved her twin, loved her more than life itself. But Yetta was bossy, no two ways about it.

Well, she'd found the man she wanted to marry and now Ma and Pa knew all about it. And now Jack was coming to see for himself. She had the telegram memorized:

ARRIVING UNION STATION I2:I5 SAT. STOP. MUST TALK TO
YOU STOP. LOVE JACK.

What did it mean, though? She had no idea. You never knew, with Jack. Most of the time, he stood up for his sisters, jutting out his jaw, just daring Pa to make trouble. He'd done it when they came down to Washington to work. He roared right back at Pa. "You want them to run away from home one night and you, not knowing where they are? Is *that* what you want?" When Jack yelled, Pa knew he was beaten. He had to let them go.

On the other hand, Jack could be *like* Pa, scowling, hollering, insisting that you do it his way. She hoped to God he wouldn't be like that today, when he got here. Today, she needed him to be her wonderful brother, Jack, the one who understood.

It was one-thirty. Even with the streetcars so crowded because of the war, Jack should be here any minute. Jonah had promised to be here at noon, to be standing by her side when her brother arrived. As usual, he was late. A couple of his buddies from the Lincoln Brigade were in town and he had gone to meet them this morning. She made him swear on his mother that he wouldn't forget Jack was coming, but she knew darn well what happened whenever he got together with his old comrades. It was talk, talk, talk, refighting the battles, telling themselves over and over how the world had been too stupid to help them, when Franco had only been the dress rehearsal for Hitler. It was all true, of course, and they were all idealists and heroes. Still, she'd really like Jo to be here when her brother came.

Like the deed following the thought, her bell rang and it was Jonah. At last. She gave him a really big hug, clinging to him until, laughing, he asked her, "What? What? Why all the passion, all of a sudden?" And then he kissed her quickly, to show he was just kidding. He smelled of wine. They always drank a lot of Spanish red whenever they got together. "So?" he said, looking around the room, "I thought I'd find the big brother here."

"Any minute," she said.

"Am I going to have to tell him my prospects? My intentions?" Jo laughed but she didn't. Jack was likely to be very serious. She knew when she wrote the letter that Ma and Pa weren't going to take kindly to an announcement that she was going to be married soon, down here. She was expected to come home, bringing her fiancé with her, and go through all the usual motions: the announcement, the dinners with relatives, the talk with the rabbi, the wedding. She could just imagine her father's reaction to her letter.

"Jo, promise me . . ."

"What now?" He softened his tone, putting a finger under her chin, tipping her head up to look into her eyes. "I've already promised to love you forever. Isn't that enough?"

Dot looked into his green-gray eyes, the soft pale eyes surrounded by the soft pale lashes. She loved his face, fair and freckled, the red-gold hair, the deep-set light eyes, the quick smile and the one dimple right next to his mouth on the left side. He was tall, tall and slender. So different from the dark, vivid coloring in her family, so different from the muscular blocky build both Pa and Jack had. So different, so dear. She sighed and smiled up at him. When he met Jack, then he'd understand better.

But, of course, it began the minute Jack came in the door, his soft woolen overcoat flung casually over his shoulders, everything he had on so carefully chosen: gray trousers, white shirt, red tie, gray-and-red argyle sweater, a new gray fedora in his hand. He looked like a picture from the *Saturday Evening Post*. Dot was suddenly aware of Jo's red plaid shirt and worn green tweed pants and his scuffed brown shoes. She was also aware of how Jack took him in, in one cool sweeping glance;

and of how Jonah bristled and got that little sneer on his face; and she thought to herself, Uh-oh.

She made introductions—she thought she did, later, when she tried to remember exactly what had happened—and then, even before he sat down, Jack said, "So you're the fellow who's planning to steal my little sister!"

"Not exactly *steal*." Jo stood his ground, leaning against the doorjamb as if he hadn't a care in the world, arms folded across his chest, while Jack sat back in her one easy chair, legs crossed, hands relaxed on the big round arms. "Dorothy and I love each other." The two men looked at each other, each with a small superior smile. Dorothy thought that if they pretended to be much *more* relaxed, they'd both fall asleep.

"Well . . ." And Jack reached ever so casually under his sweater, bringing out a pale blue envelope Dot recognized only too well. "This letter says you two plan to get married down here, instead of coming home and doing it properly with Rabbi Friedman, like everyone expects."

"That's right." Dot could tell by Jonah's voice that the word "properly" had got to him, not to mention "like everyone expects" and "Rabbi." Jack had really done it! "That's what we plan and that's what we're going to do."

"Dorothy's parents want her to come home to get married. By a rabbi. Under the canopy."

"By a rabbi? Never!"

Dorothy quickly interposed. "Jack, Jack, let me explain. Jo's a nonbeliever."

"He's a *what*?"

"Let's stop beating about the bush, Strauss. I'm a Marxist, a member of the working class, and I don't believe in organized religion or any of its outdated ceremonies."

Dorothy could not look at Jonah; her eyes were glued to her brother's face as it paled and then reddened and once again drained of color. His mouth opened and closed, with no sound, and then he spat out: "A Red! You're a goddamn *Red*!"

"Damn well told. And goddamn *Reds* don't get married by a rabbi!"

"Well no Red marries my sister at all!"

"Says who?"

"Says *me*." Jack's jaw shot out pugnaciously and his eyes narrowed into little slits. Dot's heart began to beat heavily in her chest. No trouble! Please, no trouble! She didn't want to have to choose between them. Jack was her big brother—her protector from as far back as she could remember . . . the one who walked her and Yetta to school when they were little; the one who threatened any bully in the neighborhood; the one who, in fact, had saved her life.

But Jo—Jo brought her heart into her throat whenever he touched her. Jo was heroic and exciting. He had the tiniest little limp from a war wound he got fighting in Spain. Fighting in Spain! She, little Dot Strauss from New Lots Avenue in Brooklyn, walked down the street in the nation's capital, holding hands with a man who had fought fascism in Spain! Her heart filled every time she thought of it.

"Our father," Jack was going on, "will have a *fit* if Dot isn't married by a rabbi. Our father is an immovable man. And then our mother will probably have a heart attack. No, no, it's impossible."

"You want to match fathers? Let me tell you about *my* father! When he was a young man, fourteen years old, he was coming home from school, crossing a bridge—this was in Dneiperpetrovsk, in Russia—and two soldiers, bored, with nothing better to do, grabbed him. 'How about a swim, Jew boy?' they said, and together they hoisted him over the parapet.

"My father was not about to allow himself to be thrown into the Dneiper River in the middle of winter. He fought like a lion and then, he grabbed on to the edge of the parapet and he hung on like a leech! The soldiers began to kick at his hands, to make him let go. But then, some men came by in a wagon and they saw what was happening and they chased the soldiers off.

"So don't threaten me with your stubborn father. Nobody in this world could hang on like my father. And I take after him!"

Jack kept shaking his head. "You don't know Saul Solomon Strauss, Golodny. If you doubt he'll make trouble, ask Dot."

Now Jo began to smile. "Hey! It could be worse. We don't have to get married at all. You know us Reds . . . we believe in free love!"

"You—*what?*"

This had gone on just about long enough, Dorothy thought. "That's enough from *both* of you," she said sharply; and they were both so intent on each other that her voice shocked them into silence.

"That's right," she went on. "I'm in this, too, you know. It isn't up to you to decide my life." She couldn't believe she had the courage to say this to Jack and, as he glowered at her, she felt her mouth going dry. Oh, no, she wasn't going to let *that* happen.

If it was Yetta standing here between these two, she'd just tell them what was going to be and how it was going to be . . . and then she'd march right by them and pour herself a shot from the bottle of Seagram's Seven on the gateleg table. So, let her pretend. For the duration, she wasn't dull dopey Dot, she was devil-may-care Yetta.

Just as Yetta would have, she stood up straight. "They can have all the fits and heart attacks they want," she said in a clear ringing voice, "I don't care. I'm marrying Jonah any way he wants and that's the end of it. Rabbi, shmabbi!" she said, giving Jo a wink as she imitated him. "What difference does it make, so long as we're together?

"So he's on the Left! I'm proud of that and proud of him, too! The Reds at least are doing something for the working class—and that includes Pa, in case you'd forgotten, Jack! When this war is over, you'll see: it'll be the Communists who'll be there with all the forward-looking ideas! Just like they always have! Who do you think thought up Social Security? Who do you think fought for the unions in this country!" She stopped, a bit breathless at her own audacity. She had no idea she could be so articulate. Look at that! she said to herself. You had it in you all the time! Well, well, well.

As for Jack, that Saturday afternoon so long ago, he had been struck dumb—something that rarely happened to him. "Remember my speech?" she reminded Jonah. "Remember the look on Jack's face?"

Jonah gave a laugh. "For once in his life, he was without an answer. He couldn't believe his ears, that his little sister, so sweet, so innocent, so pure, so Capitalist, had picked up evil left-wing ideas."

"No," Dot disagreed. "He was only surprised I could talk so fast. Poor Jack! He thought only Yetta had a mouth."

"If he'd known what Yetta was up to," Jonah said with a laugh, "he wouldn't have wasted his breath on us."

Dot had to laugh, too. Yetta! Yetta had joined the WACs and gone to Europe and had never come back home. Forget Brooklyn, she'd only been back to the United States two or three times since 1945. Paris. London. Majorca. Even a two-year idyll in Ljubljana, Yugoslavia. And for each place, a child. Never a husband, but plenty of kids. That Yetta!

Dorothy sighed noisily. Every once in a while, she missed her twin terribly. It was seven years since Yetta's last flying visit. She wondered if her sister had aged. Probably not; Yetta would never allow the mere passage of time to dictate to *her*. When they were little girls, they had looked identical—people couldn't tell them apart—and one of their favorite jokes was to keep changing who they were. "You're Dorothy." "No, I'm Yetta." "Hold on. A minute ago, you said you were Dorothy." "No, I didn't." They both found that so hilarious. But that was a very long time ago, a very long time. She sighed.

"There's Annie," Jonah said. "You got a quarter for her?" Annie was one of his street people, a bag lady who some days was so garrulous you had to walk away while she was still talking; and on other days, would wrap herself up in her tattered blanket if she saw you looking at her. Jonah always gave her some money. He called her Annie, and on her good days, she called him Jonah. On her very best days, they would talk, exchange a few sentences.

She dug into her bag and came up with a handful of coins, and Jonah walked over to the woman. Today was not a good day, apparently. Annie ducked her head, refusing to look at him, or even to hold out her hand for the money. Carefully, he bent and put the change on top of one of the stuffed plastic bags, and when he rejoined Dot there were tears standing in his eyes. She hated that! Ever since the cancer came back, he gave way to sentimental tears often. Too often. Just because he was elderly and ill, that was no reason to lose his dignity.

"It's horrible," he said. "Horrible, that we should let people live like that, huddling in filthy blankets on the streets, prey to every hooligan who comes along. In the Socialist countries, they don't allow their poor sick people to live in doorways and alleys. In China, everyone is cared for. In Cuba—"

"Stop with the politics, would you, Jo? What do China and Cuba have to do with Mayor Koch? He makes all the decisions around here. What good does pointing to China do Annie? I ask you! It would be far better for her—for all of the homeless—if we all got mad enough to *do* something, right here in New York! Anger and action, Jo, that's what we need to make a just world, not a lot of sentimental talk about how wonderful life is in China!"

Once he would have agreed. Now, though, he just shrugged and said, "Dorothy, you've become so harsh. What's happening to you?"

After a minute, she answered, "Those were your own words, you know. 'Anger and action.' Your own words."

"So," he said. "I'm getting old. So sometimes I forget. So sue me." With the last three words, he gave her a smile. It had been a code with them from the first, a way to say "I'm sorry."

"Oh, Jo, you were such a firebrand," she reminisced. They were at their building and she unlocked the big front door, waiting very patiently while he negotiated the four shallow steps. "I can see you now, out on the street, handing out leaflets, giving a speech to every person. It was in '62. 'Help our brothers and sisters in the Deep South, help them get their freedom one hundred years after it was promised.' Oh, I remember *that* day, like it was yesterday. 'But even late, it's better than slavery, better than prejudice, better than slavery that hides behind prejudice!' Oh, you could always talk, Jonah, when you were at a meeting or arguing politics or out in the street. It was only with us . . ." She let her voice trail off and then held the elevator door open for him.

As it creaked up, she regarded him. In the cold fluorescent light, he didn't look so good. "Are you all right, Jonah?"

"Of course, I'm all right. A little tired, maybe, a little tired. You know, Dot, when you were talking before, about me handing out leaflets on the streets, I had a picture all of a sudden, of you, of piles of pink leaflets . . . I don't remember what they were about or what year it was, but it must have been the late forties . . . you and two kids, Cookie a toddler with those bright red curls and Irwin sitting in a red wagon, handing out leaflets. Just a baby but already involved."

"There were a lot of times like that, Jo," she said dryly. "A lot of them."

"I know, I know. But I remember this one time, because when I started to make a speech, Irwin yelled bloody murder, remember? He wanted his papa! Agh! A long, long time ago, Dot. And now? Now he sits up there in Boston, a so-called artist, borrowing money from his brother and sister, and you, too—oh, yes, I know all about that—lying about his background, ashamed of his family, calling himself Win! *Win!*"

Jonah's voice was so disgusted as he said the name, she couldn't help laughing. "Irwin never did like who he was. Remember the year he was Orthodox?" The elevator door opened and they stepped out, she leaning against the edge so it wouldn't close. "Remember the year he spent in a kibbutz? Remember the guru in India? Remember when he worked for *Reagan*?"

She unlocked their apartment door and flicked on the switch. "Poor Irwin, he's always had a problem with his identity."

"Let him get an identification bracelet; then he'll know," Jonah grumped. Then suddenly his eyes filled, and he said, "Dorothy, what did we do wrong with our boys? One thinks of nothing but money, the other of nothing but himself. Is either one of them political? I ask you, is either one of them a real man, ready to fight for anything really *important*?"

She wanted to say, What do you mean: what did *we* do? She wanted to say, You're the one who was withdrawn for seven long years, when they really needed a father, and you weren't there for them. I did it all, she wanted to say. I held the whole thing together while you mourned the death of the Communist dream in America.

But, of course, she said none of it. She never mentioned those seven years in Millville anymore. He had always brushed it aside, as if it didn't deserve to be remembered.

She put a hand on his arm and said, as gently as she could manage, "Jo, just listen to yourself. When you talk about your sons, there's never a good word. When you were younger, you could always see the other fellow's viewpoint, even if you didn't agree. You weren't a grouch. That's why I liked you, when I first met you. And now . . . nothing's ever right, by you!"

He looked at her, utterly stupefied, and said: "You know what, Dorothy? I don't know what you're talking about!"

❧❧

Chapter Four

Saturday, August 16, 1941   The lanky young man with the Clark Gable mustache whirled her around. She was so dizzy, so breathless, so hot! They were doing some kind of Russian folk dance with an unpronounceable name and an intricate set of steps, and she had to concentrate very hard. But it was fun, Dorothy loved to dance. She could never hear music without her foot starting to tap. The young man twirled her the other way around. "You learn quickly, don't you?" he laughed, flirting a little. So, of course, the minute he said it, she stumbled. "Too quickly," she shot back, and he gave her a wink.

She was glad now she had allowed Yetta to persuade her to come. It was a beautiful, bright day—terribly hot, of course, and terribly muggy, of course. Typical Washington weather. When Yetta said, this morning, that Dorothy ought to come to the picnic, Dorothy said, "For the tenth time, Yetta, your friends from the Russian War Relief don't particularly interest me. They're always talking politics and you know how that bores me."

And Yetta said, "Well, it's not going to be that way today. This is for fun. There are some cute fellows . . ."

Dorothy shook her head. "Nothin' doin'." It was too darn hot to do anything that required more exertion than turning on the electric fan. And, in spite of what her sister said, Dot knew this group, and they were all loud and argumentative. The picnic might be for fun but sooner or later—and probably sooner—they'd be shouting at each other over some obscure political difference. "I'll find my *own* cute fellows," she said, "if it's all the same to you."

Yetta yawned elaborately and got up from the card table they used for eating. "All right, have it your way," she said, which immediately made Dorothy suspicious. Yetta never gave up so easily. "But I just thought you might liked to meet my latest, Dan Rozinsky. Wait, wait, don't say it! I know I change boyfriends too often to suit you, but I think this time it's the real thing."

Like ice, Dorothy thought. Yetta treated them all the same: fell madly in love, slept with them, got bored, dropped them. Often, the young men would pine for months, writing letters, making drunken phone calls in the middle of the night, pounding on the door at all hours, don't ask! And guess who held their hands and made them hot tea and consoled them in their misery? She might as well meet this one, so she'd recognize him when he appeared at two in the morning, sometime next month.

So here she was, in Rock Creek Park with twenty-two people she didn't really know, and she was having fun. She really should have expected to have fun. Wherever Yetta was, there were lively, interesting people; she seemed to create excitement wherever she went. Either that or she just knew how to find it.

Of course, she also tended to push people around a little, especially her twin sister, who was considered The Quiet One. Well, at this moment, Dot was feeling very kindly toward The

Lively One—so much so, that she was almost ready to forgive Yetta for teasing her in front of everybody about what she was wearing.

"Just because we all work for Russia, that didn't mean you had to dress like a Ukrainian peasant!" Well, Dorothy was darn glad she had chosen the full print skirt and the peasant blouse with the big eyelet ruffle. It was cool, and, with her round breasts and hips and tiny waist, it was very becoming. It was certainly prettier and more feminine than Yetta's bare-midriff playsuit!

The dance was over. Thank God! She was beginning to sweat. Fanning herself with a newspaper, she collapsed onto their blanket, spreading her skirt so it wouldn't get too wrinkled. Her dancing partner, she realized, wanted to sit with her, but when he asked if she'd like him to bring her something cool to drink, she said no in a voice that told him Go Away. He was nice but somewhat boring.

Now Yetta's boyfriend, Dan, strummed loudly on his uke and began to sing something in Spanish, a Carmen Miranda number from one of her movies. Everyone laughed and joined in, Dot included.

Yetta, of course, wasn't content just to sing along with the rest of them. No, she was up on her feet, doing a Carmen Miranda imitation, holding a can of Dole's sliced pineapple on top of her head instead of a real one.

Dot watched her twin with admiration. Yetta could care less what anyone thought of her. If she felt like dancing, she danced. If she wanted a cigarette, she just lit up—even walking in the street! And when Dot said, "Yetta, smoking in the street makes you look cheap," her sister only laughed at her and said, "*I* should care what people think?" And blew smoke at her. That Yetta! One of a kind. And to be truthful, she *was* always looking out for her "little sister"—that was because Yetta was two minutes older—and inviting her along on all kinds of expeditions.

So here she was, as ordered, and she'd met the latest heartthrob, as ordered. Dan Rozinsky was like all of Yetta's boyfriends. He talked a mile a minute and laughed a lot, and was very good-looking. Dorothy couldn't see anything about him that might make him The Real Thing. But then . . . Yetta really didn't care *what* Dot thought about him.

Now he gave Yetta a kiss that lasted so long, all the others began to hoot and whistle. Dot felt embarrassed. Good Lord, it announced to the world that they were sleeping together! Not that any of them cared, probably. Yetta was considered a free spirit; and everyone, especially her, seemed to think it was wonderful. Well, maybe it was. And then again, maybe it wasn't. One of these days, Yetta was going to run out of luck, and this was a constant worry to Dot, who knew from her own bitter experience what it was like to run out of luck.

She sat on the edge of her bed that hot summer's day in 1936, staring at the faded flowers in the wallpaper, her arms wrapped tightly around herself, rocking back and forth, back and forth, moaning. But moaning softly; if Ma ever heard her, it would be all over. What was she thinking? It *was* all over. Everything they'd been told about how boys were only out for one thing, about how they should be careful, about how bad girls always got into trouble . . .

Oh, God, oh, God! She was pregnant! Pregnant: the ugliest word, the word that meant the end of her life. Sixteen years old and *pregnant*. Oh, God, what was she going to *do*? How could she face Ma? And Pa! Pa would beat her with his belt and throw her into the street. She had stopped crying, but just thinking about Pa and how furious he'd get . . . she began again, the tears pouring down her cheeks, swallowing hard so as not to make a sound.

How had this happened to her? It wasn't fair! She'd always been a good girl. She did her homework and she got good marks, she helped her mother—and she'd never let the boys take advantage of her, not like some girls in the neighborhood. She hugged herself fiercely, thinking, Maybe if I close my eyes and count to a hundred it'll all be a dream, thinking, What a stupid idea. But what was she going to do? *What was she going to do?* She was really in Dutch! And all she'd done was take a job for the summer on Pitkin Avenue at the Sunshine Laundry.

She stood behind the wooden counter at Sunshine and took in people's laundry stuffed into a pillowcase or wrapped in a man's shirt with the arms tied in a knot. There was a fan on the counter blowing all the time and the door was propped open, and she got to talk to people all day long and they listened to her. She, Dot, the shy one, told them when they could expect their laundry to be ready, explained how the shirts were done. Dolores, the owner's daughter, breezed in from time to time and she filled Dot in on all the guys who worked there . . . how much money they made, what their prospects were, which ones were fresh, which ones you could trust. She encouraged Dorothy to giggle and flirt and so she did. She giggled a lot and flirted with Bernie and Joe and Albert. And Murray.

That Murray! They didn't meet until the middle of July and, right from the beginning, she was drawn to him. He was little and dark and quick-witted, an assistant manager they'd just sent in from the Canarsie store. Pitkin Avenue was the mecca for all the young assistants because it had all the operations in back, and Murray was full of his future. "You wait. In ten years, I'll be making, oh, five, six thousand dollars, easy. And spending all of it on beautiful women like Dotty here." And he'd laugh and pinch her cheek or pat her arm and make her blush.

The night he offered her a ride home in one of the company trucks, she could hardly breathe. She was a little nervous from all the stories about fast men, and Murray certainly *looked* fast, with his slicked-back hair and deep-set black eyes. But he just drove her home, and let her out, leaping out of the driver's seat to open her door for her. "Dotty, if I were a little younger, believe me, I'd snap you right up." And he squeezed her hand! And that was all! He winked and he turned and he walked away. She couldn't even remember getting into the creaky old elevator. She was in love.

The next day when he sauntered up front from his desk in the back office, she could feel her face go hot and she couldn't look at him. He laughed at her and asked her if she'd already seen the movie at Loew's Pitkin. Of course, she hadn't. It was very expensive. She handed her paycheck over every week and anyway, Pa didn't believe in movies. "How about going with me, then?" Murray said, leaning on the counter, grinning the way he did, crinkling up his eyes.

Of course, she went. Who wouldn't? Murray Nathan was the handsomest, most sophisticated man in Brooklyn. And he was a comer; he said so, all the time. Soon he would be first assistant manager. He was already making twenty dollars a week! And he was asking her out: her, little Dot Strauss from New Lots Avenue, quiet and shy and not terribly pretty—even though Mama always said, "Don't worry, your day will come," and "Never mind them, they don't know what they're missing," and stuff like that which anyway she didn't believe because it was her mother.

Murray explained to her how they had to be very careful because of all the big mouths around this place. She wasn't about to argue with him because if Pa ever found out, he'd kill her and Murray, together! They met in the lobby and he told her to choose anything she wanted to eat or drink. Popcorn? Candy? Soda pop? But she was too excited to eat anything.

Loew's Pitkin was like a palace with its soaring gilded ceilings and the carved Cupids in the corners, the sparkling chandeliers, the dark red velvety seats. They went up to the mezzanine—no cheap balcony seats for Murray Nathan!—and when they sat down, he put his arm across the back of her seat and she felt her heart stop for an instant. She was so aware of his arm and his hand, not quite touching her. She couldn't believe she was really here, really sitting next to this handsome older man who *liked* her, who had come after her, given her a ride home, been a gentleman, asked her to the movies, offered her anything she wanted at the candy counter. She was so filled with happiness, she thought she might float away. This was it: true love. It must be, it felt exactly the way it was always described in books. She couldn't believe it. And then his hand dropped down, cupped itself around her shoulder, pulled her gently closer until her head was resting on his shoulder. Heaven!

Murray Nathan kissed her twice that first time. Between that first time, on June 28, and the middle of August, he drove her home in the company truck twelve times, took her to see three movies, and five times made love to her in the back of the store on a pile of clean sheets on Sunday afternoon.

Just thinking about it again made her moan. Oh, what a fool she had been, falling in love with him, letting him sweet-talk her into Doing It! By the time she missed her period twice and was sure, he had already stopped hanging around the counter to schmooze with her. No more rides, no more movies. It was so humiliating. And then, to find out she was *pregnant*! It was just too horrible.

She was embarrassed to push herself at him, but she had to tell him. It took her a whole week to get up her nerve and then, he snapped at her: "For God's sake, not here!" and made her meet him after work around the corner. He was ten minutes late; she was sure he wasn't coming and, oh, God, now what? But he came, very grim, very solemn. He said they should walk, and while they walked, he talked. He was engaged to Dolores, the owner's daughter . . . "I thought you knew; everyone knows. We were having some fun, you and I, you knew that. And anyway," he said, "how do I know it's mine?" When he said that, she felt about as low as a worm . . . lower. He meant that she—she couldn't even think it, it was so awful.

And so she came home and here she was, feeling like she

wanted to vomit. Feeling like she wanted to *die*. Another moan escaped her. And the door opened and there was Jack, home from work, loosening his tie as he stood there. "Ma says you came home sick today. What's wrong?"

She couldn't help it; she burst into tears, crying so loudly he closed the door and sat on the bed next to her, patting her hand and shushing her. "God, don't let them hear you. Tell *me*," he said.

"I—I . . . oh, God, Jack, I'm pregnant!"

"You're . . . p—! No! No, not you!" He jumped to his feet. "You damn idiot, how could you be so stupid? Who is he? How could you get mixed up with a *no-goodnik* like that? Dammit, didn't you ever hear anything I ever said? Didn't I tell you to watch out for boys, they're animals, they're pigs? Didn't I warn you? Christ! From Yetta I might expect something like this. But—*you* Dorothy?"

She tried to answer him, to explain, but he shushed her, leaning close to her, his face flushed with anger, and said, in a hoarse whisper, "Dammit, Dorothy, you're a beautiful girl. Every boy in this neighborhood is dying just for a smile from you. *Nice* boys, *good* boys, who'd respect you, who'd never touch you . . . Just let one of them and he'll have to answer to *me*! Christ, Dorothy, what were you *thinking*? Never mind, you weren't thinking at all. Christ! I can't believe you really did this!"

He was scaring her; he loomed over her like he wanted to hit her. And there was Mama at the door, banging on it, yelling, demanding to know, "What's going on in there? Jack, Jack, leave your sister alone, do you hear? She doesn't feel so good!" And she was crying again, unable to stop herself, biting her fist to keep from sobbing aloud. Mama mustn't hear, mustn't know.

Abruptly, Jack stopped, and in an entirely different tone, called out: "It's okay, Ma. We're just kidding around, honest." And they both waited until they heard her shuffling away, back to the kitchen. "Okay, Dorothy, wipe your eyes and listen. Here's what we're going to do," Jack said, suddenly very calm. "First, you'll tell me who it is and I'll get him and I'll kill him. And then, I'll make him marry you." She couldn't believe she was laughing, actually laughing in the midst of her despair. But that was her brother, Jack.

"He . . . he's engaged to someone else. And don't try to find out his name because I don't want you to know. I'm so ashamed! Please, Jack."

"You really picked a winner, didn't you? Okay," he said.

"Even if this schnook—and if I ever get a clue who he is, I'll give him a few broken legs to remember me by—even if he wanted to marry you, forget it. You're too young; it'll ruin your life. So. Here's my plan. I'll make a few phone calls and I'll take you to Jersey City and we'll get this taken care of."

"No, Jack. Please. Girls die from abortions."

"No, no, this is a real doctor. He does it because he thinks the law is crazy. It's clean and it's safe. Would I take you to a butcher, to an old woman with a coat hanger? No, no, I'll protect you, don't you worry. I'll take care of it and you'll be fine."

Ever since then, needless to say, she had been very careful with boys, very cautious, very slow. Yetta always said, "You're so inhibited." She wasn't, of course, that wasn't it. But the abortion wasn't something she could talk about with her sister, she just couldn't. If you ever got into trouble, Yetta was not the person to go to. She'd just shrug it off. Or tell you how dumb you were. You could never even say to her that you didn't know what to do about something. Yetta *always* knew what to do; she was incapable of understanding that anyone was any different. Whenever Dot hesitated, Yetta would yell at her. "What's the big deal, Dot? Do something . . . do *anything*! Just stop talking about it!"

So, Jack was the only person who knew. He did go with her, too, all the way out to Jersey City. Lied to Ma and Pa for her; paid for it; sat with her for hours before they went back to Brooklyn, making sure she was all right, that the worst of the bleeding had stopped. He was an angel; he never said another word about it.

She managed to put it all behind her, not to think about it or dwell on it. It had happened and she had learned her lesson and that was the end of it. Except that she became extra picky about the boys she went out with. She always knew right away when she met a young man whether he was a *Yes* or a *No*. When it was *No*, Yetta was always after her. "Give a guy a chance! One date wouldn't kill you!" But they didn't get even one date with Dorothy Strauss, not if they were a *No*.

On the other hand, every once in a while, a *Yes* came along. And there was one here today, not two feet away from her. He was roasting hot dogs at the fireplace but looking up every couple of minutes to give her that cute smile. And every time he did, her heart began to pound. She knew his name—Jonah Golodny—and she knew his eyes were green, and she knew that

when he took her hand when they were introduced, she was
hoping he would never let it go.

He was a definite *Yes*. Oh, how she hoped she was a definite
Yes for him! She didn't really mean that. Yes, she did. So why
was she sitting here on the blanket, looking at him and hoping?
She could get up and start a conversation. She wasn't that shy,
not anymore. They had fallen into the habit that Yetta made all
the friends for both of them. Yetta took it for granted that Dorothy couldn't do it without her. But Yetta was wrong. Where
was it written that Dot Strauss couldn't attract someone on her
own?

So this time, when Jonah Golodny looked her way, she smiled
back, the way Yetta would, tipping her head a little to one side
and letting her eyes go wide. Without missing a beat, he handed
over the stick with the frankfurters to someone else and came
over to her. He was so attractive, so different from the young
men she usually met. There was something about him, something that appealed to her. The beret he wore at a jaunty angle,
tipped over one eyebrow? That little limp that said he'd done
exciting things? Someone had whispered to her, before, that he
had been with the Lincoln Brigade in Spain and had been
wounded in the fighting. She wasn't sure what that was all about,
why American boys had thought it necessary to join in a Spanish
war, only that it had something to do with Franco and fascism.
But it was courageous, that she knew, courageous and daring
and admirable.

"May I?" Oh, and he had a trace of an accent. How sophisticated! She nodded and he eased himself down on the blanket
next to her. His shirtsleeves were rolled up to his elbows; the
golden hair on his arms glinted in the sun. His hands looked
strong and sinewy.

Dan was still strumming on the ukelele, switching from one
song to another, and Jonah Golodny sang along, smiling and
looking right into her eyes.

> *The girl with the gypsy eyes*
> *Has taken away my heart*
> *And now I am her captive*
> *And we shall never part.*

The nerve! Singing a love song right to her! She loved it.

"So. You're the little sister."

"Not so little. Shall I stand up and prove it?"

"Excuse me, Dorothy . . . that's right, I remember your name. Do you remember mine?"

"First *and* last. Jonah Golodny."

He grinned at her, pleased. "Oh, I know your last name. Strauss. Of course it is, same as Yetta. You see how brilliant I am? I can figure out that two sisters will have the same last name!" He tapped his head with his finger and laughed. He had a wonderful laugh, artless and full-hearted, like he didn't have a care in the world. It was hard to picture him carrying a gun, fighting in a war.

"Did you really fight in Spain?"

The big smile disappeared instantly. "Yes. One of the ill-fated Lincoln Brigade. One of the few lucky ones who managed to come back home again." He patted his leg. "With a few scratches, but at least alive."

"You must be very brave."

Now he smiled again. "You want to know something, Dorothy Strauss? I think I must be. Foolhardy, yes, but brave, also. We were all brave, we didn't even know *how* brave until we got there. We were so outnumbered . . . unbelievable . . . one time, we had three rifles for two hundred men. Sounds like I'm making it up, but it was true. Three rifles . . ."

"But how could you fight?"

He gazed at her for a moment, thoughtfully, and then said, "We couldn't. We were killed. Hundreds, in just one night. Agh, I'm sorry. War makes gloomy conversation on a beautiful summer's day, with a beautiful young lady by my side."

"No, no," Dot insisted. "I don't mind. I feel so ignorant, though. I don't quite understand . . . about the Spanish Civil War. I know it was important."

"I'm going to tell you something, Dorothy Strauss. It's the most important thing I've ever done, fighting fascism." His voice became vibrant with emotion. "If only America would have sent help! We could have beat them. We held them off for so long, with nothing, with *nothing*, I tell you, but our guts and our brains and our belief in a better world. But no help ever came! It was like shouting into the wind. Well, now the whole world will have to pay. Yes, the whole world! Hitler becomes stronger and stronger; this week, his army has surrounded Odessa. My city, my . . . hometown. Soon he will crush all of Russia, all of *Europe* under his boots!"

One of the other fellows interrupted him, angrily. "This war is an imperialist war! Bosses fighting other bosses! It has nothing to do with the working class, Golodny.''

''I could care less that Stalin signed a pact with Hitler! Stalin doesn't tell me how to think! I know what's what! Fascism is still fascism and it's everyone's duty to fight it!''

''The Party says—''

Jonah's voice was heavy with sarcasm. ''The Party says! My advice to you, my dear Optakeroff, is that you stop following the Party line and use your brain—if, of course, you have one.''

Optakeroff, much taller and bigger than Jonah, balled his fists. ''Where do you get off, telling me I don't have a brain?''

''Listen. If you have a brain, which I still doubt, why don't you go away and use it? Oh, stop with the fists, will you? I'm sitting here, talking to a good-looking girl, and you're spoiling it! Go lay an egg!''

''Agh, dry up and blow away!'' But he left, much to Dot's relief.

''Oh, I'm so glad you two aren't going to fight.''

''You mean—'' He held up his fists, and she nodded. ''No, no. We argue all the time. Doesn't mean anything. Look, in Moscow, they made friends with Hitler. So naturally, now this isn't a war against fascism anymore; suddenly, it's an imperialistic war. And whatever they say in Moscow comes right out of his mouth.'' He laughed. ''You know how often the Party line changes? It's ridiculous to change your mind every time someone tells you to. A man has to decide for himself what's right and what's wrong—and stick to it—or he's no man at all.''

She didn't understand half of what he was talking about, but she wasn't going to let *him* know. He was interested in her and she wasn't going to let him know what a dummy she was.

''I admire a man who's willing to fight for his ideals.'' She was surprised to discover that she meant it. And he'd been shot at, he could have been killed because he believed in something bigger than himself. She'd never in her life met anyone like this. The boys in her neighborhood were out for a good time and a decent job, that's all *they* thought about. Even her brother, Jack, who was more ambitious than any of them. As far as she knew, Jack had no ideals, no beliefs; why, he didn't even vote in the last election.

She gazed at Jonah Golodny, a feeling of excitement climbing in her chest. She had a feeling about him. She couldn't put it into words, not yet, but she had a definite feeling.

''The Fascists were doing such ugly, horrible things . . . in

Germany, in Spain, everywhere. Windows smashed! People arrested for nothing! I saw those thugs dragging a Jewish woman naked across the street! I couldn't just sit back and watch it happen. We're supposed to be making a better life for people! And the United States government, that big believer in freedom, wouldn't let us go to Spain. I had to go to Spain by way of Sweden, did you ever hear such a thing? It wasn't our fight, they said. How stupid can you get? To fight fascism, that's everyone's fight!''

From above them, Yetta's voice: "Yeah, that's right, Jo, everybody's fight. Too bad everybody couldn't come back."

He shook his head, looking pensive. "I agree."

"No, you don't. I say it was a lost cause from the very beginning, that you guys let your ideals blind you to the realities and that the brigades were just cannon fodder. Everyone's fight! So many dead: what good does that do any of us?"

Darn that Yetta. She was going to go on and on and chase him away. And Dorothy now knew she did not want this Jonah Golodny to go away, to disappear from her life.

"Some people believe in more important things than just having a good time, Yetta," she said, "and are willing to put themselves on the line for them." And she was rewarded by his clapping and laughing and saying, "Hear! Hear!"

Her sister laughed. "What can I tell you? He's a Communist, I'm a hedonist!"

"And what am I?" Dot said. "Chopped liver?"

She was delighted to see her sister's look of surprise. The little sister wasn't supposed to talk back. Well, maybe little sister didn't have a lot of pizzazz, and maybe she wore a dirndl skirt instead of a bare-midriff playsuit, and maybe she wore Ma's little pearls in her ears instead of those gypsy hoops . . . but she wasn't meek and mild, not on your life, not this time! This was too important.

"I think I like this girl," Jonah Golodny said, and he put an arm around her shoulders, giving her a friendly squeeze.

"If you like her so much," Yetta responded, "I can tell you her phone number."

Dorothy glared up at her sister. Was she determined to scare this guy off? Let her go do a dance for Dan Rozinsky, let her make a speech or sing a song or kiss him again. Anything, but let her go away before she ruined everything.

"Don't worry, I was already planning to ask for it. If it's all right with Dorothy." He hadn't moved his hand from her shoulder. It just stayed there, as if they belonged together. He was so cute!

Dot looked right into his eyes. She felt so bold. But so good. "Don't worry," she said. "It's plenty okay with me."

❦❦❦❦❦❦❦❦❦❦❦❦❦❦❦❦❦❦❦❦❦❦❦❦❦❦❦❦❦❦❦❦❦

Chapter Five

Friday, August 17, 1945   The train was jammed, the aisles filled with passengers standing so packed together that when the car jolted sideways, everyone swayed in unison, first to one side and then the other. And then everyone would laugh.

The long trip—six hours from Union Station in D.C. to Penn Station in N.Y.—was heady with laughter and high spirits. The crowded car felt like a furnace, the fans just pushed hot air sluggishly from one place to another, it was nearly impossible to move through the aisles. Still, nobody complained. Everybody was euphoric. The war was over! The Japanese had surrendered, just three days ago! Total capitulation. At last, our boys could come home. The train was full of them: soldiers in light khaki, sailors in their middy blouses and little white hats, belted Marines, all with their duffel bags, their dog tags. And two WACs and a group of WAVEs standing in the vestibule, smoking and laughing. Happy. Everyone so happy.

Dorothy sat squeezed up against the window, trying to feel the same. There were three people crowding into seats meant for two, and Jonah had given up his space to a young soldier on crutches and his buddy. So how could she complain? Because the sweat was rolling down her back and itching fiercely and she couldn't even move enough to scratch it? Because she had a headache from all the smoke, not to mention Irwin had kept her up all last night with his crying? Because Karla, just past two and sitting on her lap, was not only heavy but couldn't settle down?

"For God's sake, Karla, sit still!" Dot snapped, and immediately felt guilty. Karla was such a good girl; it was just that she couldn't get over the novelty of being in this large, noisy

place that whizzed through the world so that New Jersey went
hurtling by in a blur. She was only a baby. Who could blame
her if she kept turning to look around—to see what else she
could see—her eyes wide with interest at everything: the people,
the voices, the swirl of smoke in the sunlight coming through
the window.

As for Dorothy, she was hot, she was sweaty, and she was
being squooshed into a pancake. She'd be so happy to see Penn
Station and Jack! And Sylvia and the little girls. It'd been almost
a year since they made the trip up to New York. Jack was going
to meet them and take them downtown in a taxicab. Luxury!

She was so tired, so terribly tired. It was a fiendishly hot
August and with two babies to schlepp around and tend to . . .
well, don't ask! And Irwin was a *kvetchy* baby, crying all the
time, colicky, not a good eater.

The doctor told her she had to relax and let her milk come.
Let the doctor stay up half the night, every night, with a screaming baby and a husband who managed to not hear it, and *then*
let the doctor tell her to relax! Well, when they got back home
from this weekend, she was going to put him on a bottle, doctor
or no doctor. Anyway, that's what she said *now*. Let's see how
brave she could be, facing Dr. Weinstein and telling him she'd
gone against his orders.

Karla squirmed around, wanting to stand up on her lap.
"Karla, baby, not on Mama's nice new dress," Dorothy said.
But when she looked down, the skirt was already totally wrinkled—what difference could it make? And with a couple of gray
smudges, too, she saw. What a picture she'd present to her
brother in Penn Station, her hair slipping out of the pompadour,
her dress crumpled, her legs bare because where could you get
silk stockings, didn't you know there was a war on?

She hoisted the plump baby so she could look over the back
of the seat and immediately, Karla cried: "Papa!" as she spotted him, standing nearby, bouncing baby Irwin in one arm while
he gesticulated with the other.

Karla was surprised to see her papa. Not Dorothy; she had
been only too aware of him—of his voice, really, going on and
on and on behind them. He was trading war stories with a bunch
of servicemen; the one with the crutches had half turned in his
seat to join in. They were having such a good time, talking about
bombs and mortar, buddies and mud, using all those combat
words, the words that set them apart from ordinary mortals.
Foxholes . . . C rations . . . strafing . . . hand grenades . . .

tommy guns. It gave Dot the willies. The way they were talking, full of excitement, interrupting one another with yet another gruesome detail—it made war sound like a game. Some game! When what you lost could be your legs or your life!

Even Jonah, who still limped sometimes; who still complained of aching whenever the weather changed; who just the other night, as a matter of fact, woke up sweating from a nightmare about Spain. And yet, listen to him, just listen to the man:

". . . twenty of us against their tanks and planes. But we fought, God, yes, and we pointed empty rifles when we ran out of ammunition—"

One of the soldiers burst in with, "In Italy . . . in Italy, we didn't *need* ammunition. We could have walked around with water pistols. They came up to us with their hands in the air . . ."

Then Jonah: "For two years, we fought them—in the rain, in the mud, in the cold, in the ice, in the heat . . . God, the mosquitoes . . ."

And a soldier: "Yeah, worse than bullets. I was eaten alive. And in Guam, believe me, the mosquitoes were *bigger* than bullets."

They all laughed. Little Karla laughed with them. "Papa!" she called. But he didn't hear her. He was too busy reliving the days of adventure and glory. Men! Dot had heard his stories, all of them, a hundred times, no, make that a thousand. Whenever Jo got together with his comrades, it was the same thing, the same replay of the same incidents, in the same words, over and over. The thing that got her was that all the stories, no matter how dreadful, were cleansed of all their horror. They were told as if they were tales of ancient times, nothing to do with real life. The terror and the fright, they were saved for the middle of the night! She was sick and tired of it. Enough of these stories, already! Time to put it behind him, to forget all of it.

She shook her head, impatient with her own impatience. When she first met Jonah, these same stories had moved her. It wasn't fair that they irritated her so much now. She hadn't gone to Spain; he had. She hadn't seen friends die in front of her eyes; he had. She had to try harder to understand.

Then, behind her, Jonah let out a *geschrai*. She knew exactly what had happened. "You little devil!" he shouted, and in the same breath called, "Dorothy! Your son! Who would think such a little baby could make such a big stink!"

One of the soldiers laughed and said, "He could've been our

secret weapon.'' And another one: ''The war would've been over last year!''

Dorothy bit her lip in vexation. It wasn't funny. It especially wasn't funny because Jo was automatically going to deliver the messy baby to her to clean up. And sure enough, his next words were: ''Take the baby; I'll take Karla.'' Sure, he'll take Karla. He'll take Karla because she's clean and dry and well behaved. And why? Because I trained her. But again, here she was, carping and complaining and about what? A man who wouldn't change the baby? What man would?

So when she turned to take Irwin, she was smiling and able to say to him, ''I don't understand it. A man who is brave enough to face bullets can't face a dirty diaper?''

''So sue me,'' he said, and he was smiling, too.

By four o'clock in the afternoon, they had all finally settled into Jack and Sylvia's apartment in Peter Cooper Village. What a nice place to live! Like a real village, all enclosed and fenced in, with lawns and playgrounds, with its own guards and a buzzer system with a telephone attached so nobody could get into the building if they had no business being there. The apartment was beautiful, with a great big living room, which is where they all were.

Karla was already happily playing with her two cousins, Elaine and Deena. The three little girls were on their stomachs on the carpet with coloring books and crayons—brand-new Crayolas. Where Jack had found them she didn't know. Deena and Karla were so adorable together; as soon as they saw each other, they held hands, and they hadn't allowed themselves to be separated since.

Dot sat back in the rocker—the place of honor, hers because she was the one with the baby—and smiled at the sight of the three little curly heads together: two black as ravens' wings and Karla's copper and gold. Even Irwin was behaving, for a change. He lay in her arms, fast asleep, his mouth slightly open. She gazed down at him. Why didn't she feel more love for this baby?

He'd come too soon, that was the trouble. Karla had still been nursing. You weren't supposed to be able to get pregnant when you were nursing: that's what everybody said and that's what she had believed. When she began to feel sick in the morning, she thought it was the grippe. But then she started feeling so sleepy all the time and she knew, she knew it before she saw the doctor. It was impossible, but it had happened.

She was sick the whole nine months with him, and then when he was born and she thought it was going to be all right now, he had colic. She felt as if she hadn't slept in ten years. At least right now, she was being left in peace, rocking gently in the chair, letting the voices wash over her.

Jack was talking about business, as always. Something about buying land while it was cheap, something about the need for housing. She agreed with *that* one. They were still living on Q Street in the little one-bedroom apartment she'd shared with Yetta. The children had the bedroom. She and Jo slept in a hideaway bed in the living room, which had to be unfolded every night and folded back up every morning, and she was thoroughly sick of it. But try to find a place in Washington! Impossible! Maybe now that the war was over. But here was Jack saying it was going to be years, two years anyway, before any new housing was ready to live in.

She was drifting off, their voices fading into the distance, mixing with the sounds from the kitchen where Sylvia was preparing supper, mixing and fading, mixing and fading . . .

And she was jolted awake, suddenly, by a sudden loud yelling. Irwin. Of course. He always woke up grouchy, even before he opened his eyes. And hungry. She sighed. So much for her little nap. She put him over her shoulder, shushing him, and pushed herself up. "If you'll excuse me, people, this child needs to be fed."

"Where did you put his bottle?" Jack said. "I'll get it for you. Sit."

Dot laughed a little. "*I'm* his bottle, Jack."

To her surprise, he made a face. "You? Nursing? Like a peasant?"

"Like a woman," she said acidly. "That's what they're for, you know."

He looked around quickly. "Dorothy! The children!"

"Oh, Jack! You can't mean it!"

Karla had been listening to this exchange with great attention, and now she got to her feet yelling, "Mama! Me, Mama!"

Dorothy knew what the child wanted and she wasn't about to give in to her. "No, Karla, *bubeleh*. For you, I have a nice bottle. You're a big girl."

"Not big! Not big!"

"What's this about?" Jack said, sweeping Karla up into his arms and throwing her in the air, making her shriek, half with delight, half with fear. Not so high, Jack, Dot wanted to say.

But the child seemed to be enjoying it, and she wanted her children to feel close to their relatives. Better not spoil the moment.

Jonah explained, "She wants to nurse, too. She remembers and she's jealous of the baby."

"A big grown-up girl like you?" Jack demanded, grinning at the little girl he held out at arm's length. "Deena drinks from a cup. You'd like to drink from a cup, like Deena, wouldn't you?"

"Cup! Cup!" Karla repeated, and Jack laughed with delight.

"That's my girl. You see how easy it is?" he said to Dorothy who had four or five answers, quickly censored. Was there a man alive in this world who knew *anything* about what really happened all day with children?

"You're a cute little gingersnap, that's what you are, and I'm going to find a cup for you and a cookie to go with it!"

"Cookie! Me Cookie!"

"Did you hear that? She said, 'Me Cookie.' She likes that name. Cookie. Okay, sweetie-*piele*, from now on, I'm calling you Cookie! Because you're good enough to eat!" He swung her in the air again, laughing at her high-pitched laughter.

"Her name is Karla," Jonah said, an edge to his voice.

"Karla's a mouthful! She's Cookie, that's who she is!"

"You want to know something, Strauss?" Jonah said. "You're a typical Capitalist, thinking you can boss the whole world and everyone in it."

Jack put the little girl down, his full attention on Jonah. "Oh, yeah? Well, you're a typical Red, full of big talk and not much more. You and your Russia! Russia finally declares war on Japan—five minutes before they surrender! After *we* beat them! You call that an ally? I call that phoney baloney!"

"What do you mean, my Russia? Just because I was born there, doesn't mean I agree with everything they do. For your information, I'm a citizen of this country. It happens that I'm a workingman who is willing to fight for the rights of the downtrodden working class all over the world."

"Downtrodden! I pay my men good wages and I treat them right and furthermore—"

"Jo!" Dot pleaded. "Jack! Please! Don't get started!" She was totally ignored, as her husband's voice rode right over hers.

"Ha! You *have* to treat your men right and you know why? Because the progressives in this country have taught the workingman that unity brings power! You're only good to your workers because they're unionized!"

"Unions! The unions are going to ruin this country, you mark my words. Back in May, didn't the United Mine Workers take a 'holiday' when we needed that coal so badly for the war effort? And the War Labor Board had to *order* them back to work! Is that what you taught them?"

"Listen to me, Strauss. Without the unions, the workers of America would be no better than slaves, at the mercy of their master, be he good or bad. Like the serfs in Russia. Like the Negroes in the South.

"When I first came to this country, ten years old, just a child, I didn't live in New York, like most immigrants. I went to Atlanta, Georgia, because I had family there. I'll never forget it, never! I had just gotten off the train and I was walking down the street a little behind my cousins and my uncle—you know, looking around—and coming toward me was a man, a Negro, a grown man. And that man stepped into the gutter—automatically, he stepped into the gutter—to make way for me. For *me*, a little *pisher* not even in long pants yet! How many times I saw that—and worse!—and it made me sick to my stomach. It still does.

"You know what's going to happen down South? Somebody's going to get smart and organize the colored, teach them about collective bargaining, show them how to fight for their rights!"

Jack laughed briefly. "It'll never happen, Golodny. They're just . . . different from us. Don't give me that look. I know what I'm talking about. I have three colored guys working for me and all they care about is Friday when they get their pay envelopes so they go get booze and women . . . excuse me, Dorothy."

"Listening to your bigotry," Jonah said, his voice shaking a little, "makes me more than ever determined. Now that this war is over, I'm going to go to work as a union organizer and I'm going back to Georgia for starters."

"Jonah!" Dorothy cried. "What are you talking about? You have a wife and two children. You don't just pick up and go down South to organize the Negroes, just like that!"

"That's right," Jack said. "Don't you think your family should come first?"

"Jo?" Dot tried in vain to get him to look directly at her. "Jonah? You're not going!"

"We'll see."

We'll see didn't mean *we'll see*; it meant *End of Discussion*—

and it was something she didn't like about him. But now was not the time. She was actually happy when Karla began to whimper about something or other and they all turned to see what was the matter.

"Here, Cookie," Jack called. Her brother really was like a Sherman tank. Once he got started on something, there was no stopping him. Personally, she didn't mind the name Cookie; it was kind of cute. "Here, Cookie," he said expansively. "Never mind the broken crayon. Look what Cousin Lainie is giving you: this little lamb." He reached down next to his chair and picked up a little pink fuzzy lamb. "Do you like this little lamb?"

As Karla's hand went out for the toy animal, Elaine set up a howl you could hear all the way into Brooklyn. "My lambie! Mine, Daddy, mine!"

Jack held the toy well above her reach. "Shame on you, Elaine Madeleine, you have a thousand toys. You can't give one to your cousin who came all the way from Washington, D.C., just to see you?"

"No!" she bellowed. "Mine! Mine!"

Elaine began to wail, soon joined by Karla. Let Jack work this one out, Dorothy thought. He deserves whatever he gets. And then Deena picked up a plastic teapot and toddled over to Karla, holding it out, her big green eyes wide. Karla ceased midyell—she loved playing with dishes—and reached out for the teapot, the lamb forgotten.

"Look at that," Jonah said. "What a sweet child."

"That's my Deena, my good, generous girl," Jack said, smiling down proudly on the little girl. "Give your cousin Cookie a hug and a kiss, sweetie-*piele*." The two children obediently embraced, making kissing noises in the air.

"Look at that," Jonah said. "They're friends already."

And Jack nodded. "They love each other. Well, and why not? They're cousins, aren't they? Blood is thicker than water!"

And then the baby really started to fuss. "Nudnik," Dot murmured. "You just ate an hour ago." But she was glad to get out of there, away from those men with their political arguments, to the calm of the kitchen. "Don't *hok*, *tateleh*," she said to the baby. "Dinner is about to be served."

She settled herself in one of the kitchen chairs and put the baby to her breast. "Now, *eat*, my darling," she ordered. "He's a nibbler, this one," she said to Sylvia. "Karla, you gave the breast and she sucked and *fartig*, finished. But Irwin . . . he takes a little, he looks around, he *kvetches*, he fusses, he takes a little more . . . I tell you, Sylvia, the first four months, he took so long, by the time he was finished, it was time for the next feeding already.''

Sylvia, busy with pots and pans at the stove, turned. "Give me a bottle any day . . . that, at least, you can hand over to your husband." They both laughed. "Well, look what the wind blew in," she added.

Dot looked. There, charging in with determination, came the three girls, led by Elaine. "We wanna watch," Elaine said.

"What's to watch? This is the way a baby eats."

"Oh, no!" Elaine said, shaking her head solemnly. "A baby eats from a bottle."

"In New York, maybe, but in Washington, D.C., this is how we do it."

"Dot!" Sylvia laughed. "She'll grow up with some strange ideas!"

The three little girls crowded closely around Dorothy, leaning against her, staring. "If he eats you all up," Elaine said after a few moments of deep thought, "then there won't be any left for next time."

Dot began to laugh so hard that Irwin dropped the nipple to howl in protest. Elaine's lower lip began to tremble. "Nothing to cry about!" Dot said. "It's just that . . . well, he's not eating *me*, *bubeleh*. Mommies have milk in there for their babies."

Elaine giggled, reaching out to touch Dot's breast. Sylvia said sharply, "Enough of that, Elaine! Leave Aunt Dorothy alone!"

"It's all right, Sylvia. She's not bothering me. She's just curious."

"She's bothering *me*. Do as I say, Elaine." Quickly, she came over, saying, "I know what. You girls sit down here—Elaine here, Deena, with Cousin Karla right next to you—and I'll give you all some Jell-O."

"Daddy says Cousin Karla's name is Cookie. Daddy says she's good enough to eat. Can I have a cookie with my Jell-O?"

"One dessert at a time, Elaine. This kid has such a sweet tooth, Dot, she'd eat the sugar out of the bowl if there wasn't anything else. Wouldn't you, sweetie-pie?"

"Why, Syl?" Dorothy asked.

Bustling about with dishes and spoons, Sylvia didn't look up. "Why what?"

"Why did it bother you, that she wanted to touch? Children are very curious and I'm not so modest. You can't be, and nurse."

"Well, maybe I'm modest, I don't know. Of course, I didn't nurse. I thought about it, but it's not for me." She laughed, but Dot thought there was an uneasy edge to the sound. "What if she wanted to eat when it was time for my mah-jongg?"

Irwin stopped sucking, the baby mouth dropping open as the eyelids drooped a little. Dot tapped his cheek to remind him this was not the time to sleep. She thought of several different ways she could answer Sylvia's last statement, but, before she could open her mouth, Sylvia added, "Agh! That's not what it was. My doctor and Jack, they both feel the same: breast-feeding is for the peasants. And I was just as glad. I give you credit, Dot, I really do. But I have to admit, it would embarrass me."

"I'm sorry. I came in here to nurse him without even thinking. Would you prefer—"

"Absolutely not! Okay, kids, time to get out of here. Go take out the blocks, Lainie, for the little ones." She shooed them out the door and then sat down, saying, "Now we can have a nice talk."

"Mmm. You smell so good."

"That's stuffed cabbage for you. Gets 'em every time."

"No, silly, your perfume. What is it?"

"It's new, something called Breathless. I got it at Bonwit's the other day. It *is* nice, isn't it?"

"But expensive, I'll bet."

"Thirteen dollars a bottle."

Dorothy whistled appreciatively, then sighed. "Too much for the likes of me!"

"Dot! What's that supposed to mean—the likes of you? The likes of you is pretty darn nice, if you ask me."

"We can't afford thirteen dollars for a bottle of perfume. Jo only makes—you know what Jo makes! He's a government employee. Oh, the money's not terrible, but there's never quite enough. And anyway, he'd never let me spend all that money on perfume."

Sylvia laughed and said, "Against his principles? Yeah, well here's what you do: you save from your household money and get it yourself."

"The thing that worries me, Syl, is I don't think he's ever going to make much more."

"Of course, he will. He'll work his way up. America's the land of opportunity. Look at Jack, what he's done with my father's little carpenter shop!"

"That's Jack, Sylvia. Jack's a go-getter. Jack's a charmer. No matter where he is, he does well. Jonah . . . well, I love the man dearly and I admire what he stands for. But he does get people's backs up.''

''What do you mean?''

''Jonah believes in speaking his mind. Now, so do I—I mean, it's a free country, isn't it? But sometimes, you have to be careful about what you're saying, you have to think about how other people might take it. Jo . . . he just doesn't. He knows he's right, see? He's so sure he's right, all the time. And when he's right, he feels he has the right to say so.

''For instance, when Truman used the atom bomb on Hiroshima, Jonah got so angry, I thought he'd have a heart attack. 'They could have dropped the bomb on an uninhabited island or something,' he kept saying. 'They didn't have to kill so many people . . . women, babies, old folks!' 'Look,' I told him, 'just be grateful this horrible war is over at last. And please, Jo,' I told him, 'don't start in with Chapman at the office.' Chapman is his boss, Bill Chapman, and he's very patriotic, very pro-Truman, and very gung ho about our war effort. The best idea, with Bill Chapman, is not to say anything he might think is criticism of his country. And believe me, Bill Chapman thinks it's *his* country. 'And, after all, he's the boss,' I told Jo.''

She paused, putting the baby on her shoulder to burp him. ''You know how much good that did. When he went into the office and the other men began to talk about the atom bomb, he said exactly what he thought. He says, in this country, a man is allowed to speak his mind. He says that's why he came here from Europe. He says he has a right to be heard. And maybe he has.

''But that doesn't get you ahead in this world. No, let me tell you what it does. It gets your boss mad. It gets *everybody* mad.'' She stopped, glancing at the baby. He was fast asleep. Good. ''That's why I say I don't think Jo will ever earn a lot more. I don't think he'll get ahead and I don't think he cares.

''I'll tell you something: I don't know *what* he cares about anymore, except, of course, his *ideals*, his *principles*, his *politics*. Those things, they're important, much more important than the little picky details like money, like his family, like . . . *me*.''

Sylvia opened her mouth as if she wanted to speak, but Dorothy went on. ''I know how important it is to think about the poor people of the world, the downtrodden, the disenfranchised, the underclass. God knows I've learned that! But, Sylvia, just

because a man is committed to a cause, does that mean his wife's
. . . satisfaction counts for *nischt*, for nothing?''

"Dorothy! You can't mean—''

"Oh, but I *can*. That's exactly what I mean. The man comes
to me once a week . . . maybe . . . and he's very passionate.
But between times . . . I don't know, he's just not interested.
No, it's worse than that. It's like I don't exist for him, not as a
woman.''

"Dorothy, listen. Don't—''

"I know. I know. I'm being selfish. But . . . I *like* sex. There,
I said it. But it's true. I like it, I enjoy it. And why shouldn't I?
It's a natural thing between a man and a woman. I even tried
talking to him about it. And he more or less told me I'm strange.
'It's not normal,' he told me, 'for a woman to be so eager,
especially a woman your age with two children already.' I don't
feel abnormal! You want to know what I feel? I feel frustrated!
Frustrated!''

"Dorothy, Dorothy, they'll hear you in the other room. Look,
that's how it is with men. The first couple of years, they can't
get enough. But then . . . well, things calm down. That's married life. If you want my advice, you'll be patient, you'll ride it
out.'' She paused, and then, with a slight hesitation, asked:
"You don't think it's . . . another woman?''

"Jo? Jo? The last man on earth who would think of such a
thing. God, Sylvia, I think you're going to make me laugh!''

"Just asking. Well, if it's not that, maybe a sexy nightgown?
Couldn't hurt!''

The two women looked at each other and burst out laughing.
"Men!'' they said together and laughed even harder, waking the
baby and making him cry.

❦❦❦❦❦❦❦❦❦❦❦❦❦❦❦❦❦❦❦❦❦❦❦❦❦❦❦❦❦❦❦❦❦

Chapter Six

Wednesday, July 14, 1948   Talk about hot! This was a day
to take the prize! It felt like a hundred degrees Fahrenheit on
Allerton Avenue, especially under the thin soles of her cheap

sandals. Not another soul in sight. Of course not: everyone else in the world knew better than to go out in the middle of the day in a heat wave. Dorothy leaned on the handle of Paul's stroller, wishing she'd been smarter.

Well, smart, dumb, whatever, here she was, with three little kids, two of them walking—if you could call it that. Cookie was dragging her feet and Irwin, as usual, kept wandering off. Thanks to him, she had to stop every few feet, and what should have been a ten-minute errand for milk and butter had turned into an endless schlepp. Here it was, already noon, no lunch prepared and, even worse, her milk had let down and she was beginning to leak. Damn!

Of course, she was a fool to still be nursing Paul; after being so tied down with Irwin, she'd promised herself she'd wean this one at seven months. That was long enough. But when the time came, she couldn't do it. This baby was such a doll! When she sat in the rocker, cradling him in her arms, and looked down at him, and he looked back at her with his big, round, thickly lashed eyes, she was filled with wonder that she had somehow produced this beautiful infant. And he was good-natured, happy, and intelligent. Even when he sucked, he was studying her face intently, his little hand kneading at her breast. Every time she nursed him, she was filled with joy. She just couldn't give it up.

But at this moment, she regretted her sentimental impulse. At this moment, her nipples were rubbing against the damp bra and already they were sore. At this moment, two patches of wet were spreading on the front of her housedress. Lucky it was a busy floral print and didn't really show, not too much.

Turning, she shouted, "Irwin! If you don't keep up with us, I'm going to leave you here, right in the middle of the sidewalk."

As usual, he paid her no mind and she had to stop, leave the baby with Cookie, and go get him. This time, she grabbed him harder than usual and he began to cry.

"Oh, be quiet! You're a big boy now!"

When she got back to the stroller, two men were standing there, smiling down at Cookie and Paul. Oh, God! The FBI! She'd been warned about this, coached very carefully by Jonah and their next-door neighbors, the Daubers. Don't look scared, don't act nervous, they can't do anything to you. They know everyone up here is on the Left, so they come up here to bother us. They're a nuisance more than anything else, a pain in the ass. But they can't do anything but ask questions and you don't have to answer.

And then Anna Dauber, who was a bit of a Bohemian, had to add: "You don't have to answer questions, but you could flirt a little!"

The men didn't think that was one bit funny, but *she* did. She liked Anna, who reminded her a lot of Yetta: a free spirit, as the saying goes. It was Anna who, a couple of weeks ago, pointed these very same guys out to her. Dot *thought* they were the same men, although it was hard to tell. All of them always dressed the same, in sharkskin suits, panama hats, white shirts, and striped ties. Nobody else in the Coops dressed that way!

But prepared or not, her heart immediately began hammering wildly in her chest. Without knowing it, she clutched Irwin's hand tighter, and he yelled, "Mama, ow, you're hurting me!"

"*Shah*, Irwin. Be a good boy, all right?" But she loosened her grip and stood as straight as she could.

They tipped their hats to her. "FBI . . . Mrs. Golodny?"

"No." Surely they could look right into her head and see that she was lying. But their expressionless faces didn't change.

"May we ask you a few questions, ma'am?"

Her heartbeat quickened even more. What if Jonah was wrong? What if they decided to arrest her, take her away? What about her babies? What if—? Bravely she said, "No. You may not. I have three little children, as you can see, and I have to get them home." And waited to see if lightning was going to strike.

"Do you mind if we walk along with you?"

Oh, God, what was she supposed to say? Her mind was dithering. Somehow she found the words: "I've nothing to say to you. And I don't let strange men walk with me. Good-bye."

She marched away, head up, and by some miracle, Irwin and Cookie sensed that this was serious. They just came along with her, without asking a lot of questions and without *kvetching*, either, for a change. She glanced down at them, so proud of them. They were smart kids.

She kept on going, never looking back, but wishing she had eyes in the back of her head. She was dying to know if they were right behind or just standing there, watching her walk away. She couldn't hear any footsteps behind her. And Irwin, bless him, just had to take a peek—he was a curious little monkey—and so Cookie turned around, too, and Dot was able to ask, "Are those men still there by the fence?"

"They're walking away, Mama."

"Good."

"Who are they, Mama? Why did you say no?"

"We don't talk to strangers on the street. Do you hear me? Never. Remember what Papa told you? You don't give your name, not to anybody. And that goes for you, too, Irwin. You understand?"

"**Yes**, Mama."

At last, home. The Coops . . . well, the United Workers Cooperative Colony, really, but everyone called it the Coops. They were so lucky to get an apartment here; nobody ever moved out. But somebody had, and here they were, living in the second house with its U-shaped courtyard facing Bronx Park. Every time she walked into the court, past the neat hedges, under the trees, she thanked God for this place. She'd said that to Jonah the other night and he laughed and said, "Never mind thanking God; thank the immigrant workers who thought up the idea of a cooperative apartment house—and then did it!"

And there was Anna in the courtyard, leaning against a tree, smoking a cigarette. Anna was small and slight, with tiny breasts and the face of a clever child under thick, dark, bobbed hair. She was quick to laugh, even at herself, and, though not pretty, Dot could see why men found her so attractive.

"Anna! Thank God you're here!"

"Which one you want me to carry? I'll—Dot! What's wrong? Are you all right?" Quickly, she stamped out her cigarette and came over.

"Those two FBI men just stopped me. Right in the middle of Allerton Avenue. It never happened to me before. My heart is still going a mile a minute."

"Is that all! From the look of you, I thought . . . I don't know what. Well, so all right. You're no longer a virgin." Anna laughed.

"How can you make a joke?"

"Dot, let me ask *you*: how can we *not* make a joke? The FBI is a joke! Hanging around, day after day, pestering everybody, hoping to catch a Commie red-handed—pardon the pun!"

"Well, they make *me* nervous. Jo already ran once from these guys. You know. Executive Order Number 9835. The Federal Employee Loyalty Program. Because of Executive Order Number 9835, he got fired!"

"Well, but he was working for the *government*. Now he isn't, and now it'll be different. Which reminds me, has he had any luck?"

"There's supposed to be a job soon at a private school, where supposedly they don't insist on you signing a loyalty oath. In the meantime, it's part-time this and part-time that." She sighed. "He says stop nagging, he'll find something soon. You know how it is . . ."

As they talked, Dot pulled the baby out of the stroller and, without asking or being asked, Anna took it to pull up the stairs. The kids were already halfway up, hollering and yodeling to hear the echo in the stairwell. They knew they weren't supposed to do that; she'd told them a million times. But right now, she just didn't have the *koyach* to go after them. If the noise bothered the neighbors that much, let *them* handle it.

When they were on their landing, huffing and puffing, Dot said, "You'll come in and have a little lunch with us? It's only salami sandwiches and pickles."

"I'll take salami and pickles, with pleasure."

Dot couldn't help but notice that Anna often happened to turn up when it was time for lunch. But, look, a sandwich was small payment for a little adult company. Not to mention that she usually kept the kids entertained while Dot fed the baby.

They went in, Anna shepherding Irwin and Cookie into the kitchen, getting them settled at the table, singing, "Barney Google with the Goo-Goo-Googly Eyes," and "A Peanut Sat on a Railroad Track," two numbers guaranteed to keep them absolutely enthralled, no matter how many times repeated. While she sang, she went into the fridge, got out the food, slapped together four sandwiches, and somehow managed to light another cigarette while doing it.

Meanwhile, Dot sat down and put the baby to her breast. The minute he got ahold of the nipple, he began to suck greedily. It was such a relief. Paul was a good eater. Five minutes the left side, five minutes the right, and *fartig*, finished. And then she'd go right into her room and change out of this stained dress. Feh!

"You never told me that whole story," Anna said, the cigarette drooping in the corner of her mouth.

"What whole story?"

"About Jo getting fired."

"You shouldn't know from it, Anna. While he finished college at night, so he could teach, Jonah worked for the Department of Agriculture. I know, it's funny; nobody could be further from a farmer. But he's a Russian and Russians are crazy about land. And anyway, he was writing instruction booklets about how to plant and what to plant, he wasn't *doing* it." Both women laughed briefly.

"He wasn't making a million dollars, but we were doing all right, he liked it, and it was secure. You had a job with the government, you were set. Ha-ha, until Executive Order 9835, that is! Now, suddenly, you had to be quote loyal unquote to work for the government . . ."

"Jo's a loyal American!"

"Don't tell *me*: tell the United States government." Dot sighed. "To them, he was a bad security risk. Look, in a way, he was asking for trouble. You know he fought in Spain, so, of course, he was friendly with a lot of Communists and sympathizers. And every Monday and Tuesday, he was signing another petition against this, for that . . . you know how it is. Nothing terrible—or so we thought.

"But what really got him into hot water was his mouth. Jo believes a man should stand up for what he believes in and speak out, no matter what the consequences."

"Good for Jo."

"That's right, good for Jo. I think so, too. But he didn't have to say that the House Un-American Activities Committee was stupid and meaningless and the work of small minds. Well . . . don't ask. He got a full field investigation."

"*Oy,*" Anna said.

"That's right. Well, you know what happened. They stopped talking to him at work; the neighbors cut me dead . . . even the kids, even innocent little children! And then the pink slip and with it, a form letter. A form letter!"

"What did you expect—an engraved invitation to kindly leave his job?"

Paul was finished at the breast. She smiled at him and pulled her dress closed, sitting him up on her lap, patting his back to bring up a bubble. Without a word, Anna pushed a jar of baby vegetables over. Automatically, Dot spooned the food into his mouth as she spoke.

"You know what his great crime was? And I quote: 'You made statements to the effect that you believed that the House Un-American Activities Committee is a greater threat to civil liberties than the Communist party. The foregoing information indicates that you are a member, close affiliate, or sympathetic associate of the Communist party. You are dismissed.'

"My first thought was, 'How did the FBI hear him say that?' And he told me I was naïve, of course the FBI didn't *hear* him; a fink reported him. Well, he *was* a sympathizer, absolutely! But not a member. Not until that day . . ." She paused, looking at the two little ones across the table as if she had forgotten they were there—which in fact, she had. "Okay, you two. If you're finished, go play. And no fighting! Yes, you could take a cookie. Only one!"

She turned back and continued: "Anyway, Jonah marched right out of his plant and right down to Party headquarters and joined—of all the crazy things!"

"What do you mean, crazy?" Anna demanded. "*Mazel tov* to him. Why shouldn't he be hung for a sheep as well as a lamb?"

"All well and good for *you* to say, Anna. But, if they'll fire him for being only a sympathizer, what would they do now that he's a member? That's what I asked *him*. And I got the regular answer: 'A man must do what a man must do.' And how about the women and children, that's what I want to know!"

"As usual, we get to fend for ourselves. Hey! Dot, listen. It's the same old story. Every family in the Coops has a story like that. In this day and age, in this country, if you're a progressive, you're persecuted, period. What can I tell you?" She threw up her hands.

Paul was finished eating, squirming to get down. Dot felt his diaper—damp but not too bad, it could wait a few minutes—and put him down, watching as he toddled off to bother his brother and sister. Not that they ever minded his being around. There was something lovable about Paul; everyone loved having him around. Even Irwin. Well, Paul was a baby who was born with a smile on his face. Even the doctor said he'd never seen anything like it.

"But wait, Anna. That's not the end of it. Jonah's such a mule, he was ready to stay in Washington and starve if necessary, while he fought the good fight against HUAC. But then . . ." She took a big bite of her sandwich, chewed, and went on:

"Not a week later, I'm folding my laundry and listening to the radio, minding my own business, the children behaving, peace and quiet for once and, suddenly, there's a banging on the door. And when I open it, there's a woman from the third floor, a woman I know only well enough to say hello to. Mamie Cooper, her name is. And she's like a crazy person.

"She's red in the face, waving a piece of paper under my nose, crying and yelling all at the same time. 'My poor Albert, all he ever did in this world was be nice to other people, now he should be punished? You tell that husband of yours, he's ruined my life. You tell him he should be ashamed of himself. How could an immigrant be disloyal to the country that took him in? He should be *arrested*, that's what! He should be punished, not my Al, an ordinary mail carrier, never hurt anyone in his life . . . !'

"She went on and on and on and I couldn't figure out what she was talking about. Finally, I managed to pry that piece of paper from her, to read it. And as soon as I had it in my hand, she quieted down. No wonder she was so hysterical. It was one of those wonderful letters, like the one Jo got.

"Only this one said, 'You've been a close associate of Jonah Golodny since 1942'—that's when they moved in, Anna—'of Jonah Golodny, an individual who, evidence in our files indicates, has displayed an active sympathetic interest in the principles and policies of the Communist party.'

"The only connection between her husband and Jo was that every once in a while they'd bump into each other at the bar and grill on the corner—that's right, bump into each other, each coming in separately for a beer after work. So they'd sit next to each other on the stools and chew the fat for an hour! I ask you! That makes a close associate?''

Anna lit another cigarette and shook her head. "Take it from me, Dot. There's a movement to destroy the left wing in this country. And it's going to get worse before it gets better.''

"Well, that was it for Jonah. When he got home and I told him what happened, he said, 'That does it. We're leaving this town. Too much Federal government around here.' And he told me about the Coops, about how nice it was, what a good place for a progressive to live . . .'' She waved a hand at the small sunny apartment. "And so, we left. Without a word to anyone. Nobody knows where we are.'' She laughed a little. "Except, it seems, the FBI. How do they manage to find out?''

Anna threw her head back and laughed. "The FBI! They always manage! Let me tell you a story: When I was a union organizer, I got sent here, sent there, all over the country. And every time I arrived in a new place, within a day, there they'd be: two schleppers in suits. Trying to blend in, if you can imagine! And then, they never did anything, never said anything. Just followed me around.'' She waved a hand in dismissal. "Useless to try to figure them out! So now you're here in the beautiful Bronx for a little while, tell me, do we live up to Jonah's advertising?''

"It's certainly pretty here.'' Dot said. "Of course, I'm not particularly political, but I agree with what everyone here believes in. And it's so nice, everyone working together, everyone cooperating—'' She broke off as Anna began to laugh. "What is it?"

"Nothing, nothing. I'm glad that's how you see it, Dot. But the truth is, the Party has always been full of factions, and everyone moved in here with all their old ideas intact. So there's always been infighting. Listen. In the twenties, when the first house went up, they refused to let businessmen live here. So guess why all the businesses they tried to run, failed?"

She stubbed her cigarette into the pleated cap from the milk bottle. "It's not all sweetness and light, Dot, believe me!"

Now Dorothy laughed. "Don't let Jo hear you say that. According to him, we are now in the promised land, a land where the Left rules and the Right is wrong!" She paused, got up, and turned on the gas under a teakettle. Without turning around, she added, "He's never home. He's always at some meeting, or rally, or at Wallace headquarters—unless, of course, he's out looking for work. My brother, Jack, already told him there's a job for him in his construction business. But, you have to realize that in the same breath, my brother, Jack, said Henry Wallace has about as much chance of getting elected as Howdy Doody. So you can imagine how Jo feels about working for him!

"I said to him, 'What choice do you have, Jo? You can't give any references. You can't get the kind of money he's offering, not anywhere else. And you know it,' I told him. Meanwhile, I never see him, he's never here, and I'm left alone to take care of three little children all by myself."

"That's life, Dorothy. That's what women do. Speaking of which, mine will be back from day camp any minute now. I'd better go get the Kool-Aid ready. Well, speak of the devil. Hi, Jo. I'm just leaving."

Jonah greeted her and sat himself down at the table, fully expecting, Dot realized, a glass of iced tea to materialize in front of him. She pushed down the little nudge of resentment. Poor Jo. He took off his jacket and she could see the shirt sticking to his back. It wasn't easy for him, she must remember that.

"So? What happened? Were there jobs or was it just another rumor?"

He took in a breath, his lips twitching. Finally, he said, "I'll tell you the truth, Dot. I stopped off at headquarters and they needed some stuff taken downtown. So I . . . well, I did it."

"Jo! I don't believe this! You couldn't! Not when you're supposed to be looking for work!"

Stubbornly, he said, "It had to be done and I was there to do it."

"You can't afford to run errands for the Party! They don't pay you!" Dot wiped her hands on a towel and prepared to have this out with him, once and for all. But as she opened her mouth, he pushed back from the table, announcing, "Well, so much for that. I'm late."

"Late! You just got here! Late for *what*?"

"I have to go down to Wallace headquarters. Big mailing."

"What! Again, you're working for free! You're never home. Your children haven't seen you for weeks! They're in the other room. Can't you just sit down and play with them, read them a story? Or, God forbid, you and I might even try to work out our problems. There'll be plenty of others at Progressive party headquarters. They could do without you this time!"

"Dorothy, don't nag me."

"Why do you call it nagging? What am I asking for, that's so unusual, so difficult, so terrible? You're not working; I could use your help around here!"

"Since we got here, you're constantly on my back about not having a job! Why can't you have a little faith in me? I know what *you're* after! You're determined to have me working for that tyrant brother of yours!"

"Calling my brother, Jack, names doesn't change the fact that he has a job for you—a job that pays very well, may I add—and you're too stubborn to take it. Too stubborn or too proud or maybe too jealous."

"Jealous! Me, jealous! Of what? His big car, his money, his fancy apartment on Central Park West? Peter Cooper Village wasn't good enough for him, oh, no! Dorothy, listen to me and listen good. I am not jealous of your greedy brother Jack."

"Then take his job and prove it!"

"You take his job and shove it!"

"*Jonah!*"

He made a small apologetic gesture. "All right. But it's your fault. It was *you* wouldn't let me take the job with the Party, organizing the mill workers—"

"In Georgia, where they kill people for even *thinking* union? Don't be ridiculous! You're the father of three children. You can't go running off, hundreds of miles away, not even for your beloved working class!"

"And I didn't, did I? I'm here, aren't I? But I still need to do something significant with my life, poor as it is, and that's where I'm going now!''

Dot sat at her place at the porcelain-top table without moving, watching the door slam, watching the calendar on the wall next to it shake from the reverberation. Where, she wondered, was the brave new world they were going to help create together? Where was the fine new-style marriage they were going to share, with everything equal? Where, in fact, was the man she had fallen for?

Here she sat, like her mother before her, her head down on the table, crying alone in the kitchen, nothing to look forward to, feeling old before her time, allowing an angry man to order her around, blame her for all his troubles, and beat her down.

Something made her look up. There they all were, the three of them, six round troubled eyes staring at her, frightened. Oh, God, what had she done with her life?

€€€

Chapter Seven

Sunday, September 4, 1949   The bus turned off the highway onto a quieter road and, suddenly, they were out of the Bronx. No more tall buildings. No more railroad tracks. Dorothy pressed closer to the half-open window, enjoying the view: all the shades of green of all the different trees, billowing up, up into the hills. She took in a breath. It was so nice to smell grass and hay. Not to mention bus exhaust, but never mind. The late summer light was rich and mellow, and even though the skies were clouded over, it was warm and pleasant. A perfect day for an open-air concert.

Too bad she couldn't really enjoy this. Even though the chartered bus was filled with families and picnic hampers, this wasn't a carefree outing. Far from it. She only hoped the concert wouldn't have to be canceled again, like last weekend. How could people be so full of hate toward a great singer like Paul Robeson? And he was more than just a singer. A genius, a Phi

Beta Kappa, the valedictorian of his class at Rutgers University. Why, they said the man spoke and wrote more than twenty languages! Not to mention he was an all-round athlete, an all-American. And a wonderful actor, too. So why call him a traitor to his country? Just because he spoke out against the oppression of his people? Couldn't they imagine what it must be like, to be a Negro in this country? Couldn't they have a little *rachmones*, a little pity and understanding? You would *expect* people to be prejudiced down South, but up here, in Peekskill, New York? She just couldn't understand it.

Jonah got impatient with her when she said things like that. "What do you mean, you can't understand? You lived in Washington. You saw Jim Crow. And don't tell me Washington's the South. It's also the capital of the United States. The point is, Dorothy, this so-called 'free' country, cradle of liberty, is run by greedy bosses exploiting the oppressed. Divide and conquer, Dot, that's what they're after. Get the white working class to hate the black working class! Then you can take advantage of both of them!"

That's what they were talking about now, the men sitting all together, up front. Shouting about. Jonah, sitting in the seat in front of her, with Cookie next to him, was even now leaning out into the aisle, his arms raised up, giving a speech. ". . . a man of Robeson's stature, it's a goddamn *shandah*, denying him his right to what? Make a political speech? Put together an army?" And he went on, answering his own rhetorical questions: "The man wanted to sing. To *sing*! I ask you, is that considered an act of aggression these days?" There was a great deal of loud agreement from the others.

The new comrade, Frank Green his name was, nodded and smiled and called out: "Golodny, face facts. When Robeson sings, it doesn't matter what the words are, it's a political statement."

"When Robeson only stands up, these days," Jonah agreed, "it's a political statement!" Again, laughter and yeses. Jo and Frank grinned at each other. They had fought together in Spain. Frank was the fellow who dragged Jo to safety the day he was wounded. And now he had appeared at the Coops and was an immediate hit. Particularly with the women. Well, there was no denying he was an extraordinarily good-looking man.

"Well, they aren't going to keep him from doing anything, not today, not if I have anything to say about it!" he shouted out now, and everyone near him gave a cheer.

From way in the back, a voice shouted, "Last week, they drove in a truck and trapped us there. Believe me, I was plenty scared. And when they started burning programs and books, let me tell you, I wondered for a minute what country I'm in!"

"Don't forget the chairs, Lou!" someone agreed. "They broke up folding chairs and threw them on the fire. Just like Nazi Germany! It sent chills down my spine. I wondered if maybe I'd be next."

"Well, they won't be able to get anywhere near us today," Jonah said. "The *Worker* printed the call-up and there'll be thousands of vets on our side, friends, on *our* side, protecting Paul Robeson and protecting us. They're forming a cordon of human bodies and just let those animals try to get by! I want to tell you something, friends! If anyone makes a move today, I'm ready to fight—yes, to the death if necessary!"

Dorothy detected a note of suppressed excitement in her husband's voice. She lifted herself up, peeking at Cookie, who was snuggled next to her papa, gazing up at him in obvious awe and admiration, drinking in every word. Of course, she was much too little to understand any of it.

To the woman in the seat next to her, Dot remarked: "You hear that, Leah? The anticipation? They secretly *hope* there's trouble."

"Dorothy Golodny! What a thing to say! Robeson could've been killed last week. Ever since he started speaking out in Europe about racial injustice, they've been dying to get him. They could try again today. Nobody wants that."

"All I know is that Jonah constantly says that going to fight in Spain with the Lincoln Brigade was the best thing he ever did." She shrugged. "Don't worry. *I* understand it's important to go to Peekskill today and stand up and be counted against those hicks who have nothing better to do than threaten innocent people . . . Look, Leah, didn't I allow Jonah to bring our six-year-old Cookie because I want her always to remember that her family stood up for what they believed in? All I'm saying is, my heart is palpitating; I can't even enjoy the scenery; and you'll notice the men feel just fine, thank you. They're raising clenched fists and laughing. Men! Always spoiling for a fight."

Leah mumbled something and went back to gossiping with the woman across the aisle. Two *yentas*: why did she waste her breath? She wished Anna and her husband, Ben, had come with them on the bus, but they were traveling by car, with a cousin of Ben's. Again, Dorothy looked out the window, trying not to worry about the angry people in Peekskill—the anti-Robeson group, the *New York Times* called them. It suddenly struck her: there was something ridiculous about all of this. Why should people become so enraged about a man who had no power whatsoever—except to open his mouth to speak or sing? If he wasn't telling the truth, it would soon come out, right? And if he *was* telling the truth . . . didn't they want to know?

Just then, the new fellow, Frank, jumped to his feet and called out: "Comrades! Let us promise one another not to give an inch, no matter what they do! When we were organizing the migrant workers down in Greensboro in '38, we set up tents right by the side of the road and nobody could tell us to move! We were strong because we knew we were right! Not a man, woman, or child gave them one inch!"

There was wild applause at this and several of the men shouted, "Comes the revolution—" and were interrupted by the husky voice of Bella Rosenzweig, an old maid, one of the so-called Nuns of Section K, in the Coops: "I've been promised the revolution my whole life and I'm getting old already! When it comes, *then* I'll believe! Meanwhile, how about a salami sandwich or maybe a deviled egg, handsome?"

The last was directed at Frank Green, who good-naturedly came down the aisle while everyone laughed, saying, "I happen to be one hungry fella." He looked around with a crooked grin, and all the women near him giggled.

Leah poked Dorothy with her elbow. "That one's a devil. Believe me, I could tell you stories."

Dorothy had to admit that he was just about the handsomest man she'd ever seen in her life. He looked like a movie star. "Leah, he just moved in a month ago!"

"But I hear he's a real hot number. Already he's been with Bryna, you know her, from C Section, the one with the much older husband; and now he's taken up with Harris's daughter. At least she's single, but it's a *shandah*—she's only nineteen and he's got to be thirty-five if he's a day. Shhh . . ."

Frank came up the aisle again, chewing with relish, and sat back down, right in front of Jonah, turning and holding out two sandwiches wrapped in wax paper. "Golodny? Salami on rye, not too much mustard?" And when Jonah shook his head, he leaned past Jonah, offering it to Dorothy. He was smiling broadly, very pleased with himself, she thought, showing off his even white teeth, tossing his head a little to get the thick, wavy, dark hair out of his eyes. "How about the pretty lady with the gypsy eyes? A bite?"

The nerve of him, flirting like that, and in front of her husband! He must think women were just ready to fall at his feet, or something. "No, thank you. We brought our own food."

Did his eyes linger on hers a moment more than absolutely necessary? She felt terribly flustered and turned to Leah again, talking a mile a minute. Later, she knew, she wouldn't remember one single word she said to the woman.

"We should be there within half an hour," Leah said, consulting her big round wristwatch. "You know," she added in a lower voice, "they say he only joined the Party because he heard we believe in free love."

Dumb face. "Who?"

"Him. The gorgeous one. Green."

"Agh!" She didn't want to talk about him anymore. The way he looked at her made her feel strange and she didn't like it. He had no business looking at her that way! She was a married woman with three little children. Gypsy eyes! And yet, she couldn't help giving herself a swift look in the bus window, widening her eyes just a little.

Suddenly, there was a ruckus out on the road ahead. The bus slowed down and the driver called out, "Everyone stay seated. There's some kind of commotion at Mohegan Lake. Keep calm."

"Oh, it's their stupid march . . . the crazies, all the reactionaries."

Dorothy gazed out the window, frightened and fascinated at the same time. They were lining the road, so many of them, men, women, children even, waving little American flags, shrieking and shouting, carrying signs that said: WAKE UP AMERICA! PEEKSKILL DID! In front of them stood state troopers in their gray uniforms and thick leather gun belts. Dorothy's first thought, as they came closer, was that there were so many young women, mothers, standing there on top of the stone walls that lined Hillside Avenue. They were all wearing the same kind of cotton print dress she was; they all had their hair parted on the side and tied with ribbon, like hers. They looked like she did, but their faces were contorted and ugly with rage—with *rage*!— and with hatred. They screamed at her, as the bus lumbered by. "Go back to Russia!" "Moscow, straight ahead!" "Dirty Commies!"

Her next thought was that Cookie shouldn't hear this, that

someone should take the child away from the window. Six years old was too little to see and hear this ugliness. But when she leaned forward and whispered to Jonah, he shook his head. "Let her see, Dot. Let her learn. We're never too young to learn."

There was too much happening for her to argue with him. It had gotten much noisier outside, more crowded. Someone in the bus said, "Down there, at the bottom of the hill. See? Where the other buses are parked." And she looked down and saw a big, empty, grassy field and a kind of fence or something that curled snakelike through the grass. That was the concert grounds, the deserted golf course.

As the bus inched down the narrow road, more people were lined up at the sides of the road, hollering and shaking their fists and waving their signs. As they passed a bungalow colony up off the road, she saw a family standing: a mother, a father, a pretty little girl about Cookie's age, standing way back, not part of the angry crowd, not part of *them*, either.

"Papa, Papa, why are they so mad?" Dorothy heard her child's voice and she longed to be with her. What would Jonah tell her? Men sometimes brushed away children's fears.

"They're mad because we're going to hear Paul Robeson sing," Jonah said; and the little girl answered, "Oh, because they want to go?" and he laughed and said, "No, *bubeleh*, because they don't want *us* to go."

"But, why?"

"*Shah*, Cookie, enough questions, all right?"

"Wait!" Frank Green got up, a frown on his handsome face. "Don't put her off that way, Golodny. Even a child needs to know what the world is all about." Bending toward her, he went on: "I'll tell you why, little girl. Because a few months ago, Paul Robeson made a speech in Paris, France, and he said what we all here know to be the truth. He said that black men fought and died in the war—for a country that has oppressed them and continues to oppress them. And then he said that the white bigots in America are far more dangerous to American Negroes than the Soviet Union. Do you understand?"

Dorothy lifted herself up to see Cookie, who was staring, mesmerized, at this man who spoke so eloquently. She probably couldn't understand one word in ten, but she nodded yes.

"He made the government very angry because they don't want anyone to say what's bad in this country. They don't want anyone to spoil their story that America is a free country, the leader of the free world—"

From the rear of the bus, Bella yelled out, "They hate him because he exposed the hypocrisy in this country!"

Someone else cried, "And they call him a traitor!"

And another voice: "Look at them out there, waving their flags, like only they have the right!"

"Can I have a flag to wave?" Cookie asked Jonah.

"No! Don't be a *noodge*."

Cookie began to cry and Jonah turned to give Dorothy that look, the look he always got when his children behaved like children. "Dorothy, take her. Here, *shayfele*, go to your mother."

Dorothy lifted the little girl over the back of the seat and into her lap, wiping her tears as automatically as she spoke. "When we get back to the Bronx, then I'll get you a flag. Tomorrow. At Woolworth's."

She settled the child into her lap, facing her away from the window. She herself looked out, feeling more and more unreal. So many people, so full of hate. And pressing in, leaning out over the road, trying to get their angry faces as close as they could. Why? She couldn't figure it out, not really. Sometimes she felt as young as little Cookie, asking Why and Why and Why, again. Jo always had his answers, from the Party, from his leaders. But she was different. She couldn't help but wonder, when crazy things happened, how the world had come to this: today, how people could act so crazy, screaming at a busload of working people just like themselves! On May Day, too, when the unions marched, some working people threw eggs and tomatoes at them and yelled and screamed. Why? Why? It just didn't make sense!

The bus slowed down to make the turn into the big open field. Dorothy held her child against her breast, her hand over Cookie's ear, looking out at the distorted, twisted faces. Here, they were almost all women, cupping their hands like megaphones to make sure everyone could hear their filth. And in front of them, an older man, a state trooper, arms out to the side, his hat pushed back casually on his head, his enormous beer belly thrust out in front of him, grinning as the women taunted: "You'll get in! You won't get out! We'll kill you!"

And then they were on a road cutting through the grassy field. They were in. Inside the bus, there were cheers. But Dorothy did not feel like cheering. What was there to cheer about—that there were people in this world who wanted to kill you, for *nothing*?

She shuddered a little, wishing she weren't here. She hadn't planned to come. Paul was still a toddler and she hated leaving him all day. But Jonah insisted she be with him.

"Don't you understand, Dorothy? We have to outnumber the animals. We have to show them how strong we are. We have to show the *world*," he said.

And she was just carried along by his conviction. She was often carried along by his convictions. This time, she was sorry. And particularly, she was sorry she had let him talk her into bringing Cookie. She had said no, she had insisted. Especially since they planned to leave Irwin, too. Irwin, you couldn't trust in a crowd. He'd be sure to get lost, and there wasn't going to be any time to go looking for lost boys, Jo said. But Cookie was such a well-behaved child. And she *was* their eldest. And at least one of their children should be at this historic occasion. And that's how he talked her into it. And now she was regretting it.

The bus had parked and people were already getting off. Dot climbed down the steps, still holding the child, and looked where Jo was pointing. A thrill traveled down her spine. The curving "fence" she'd seen earlier was really a line of men as far as the eye could see, most of them wearing overseas caps, armed with sticks and pop bottles, standing guard shoulder to shoulder.

"Look at them!" Jonah marveled. "I should be there with them! They're all around the field," he said. "All around. No one will get in this time, believe me." He put an arm around her shoulder and gave it a squeeze. "You see how you worried . . . and look: it's like a picnic. So they yell and they call us names, so what? They can't stop us from coming, and they can't stop him from singing—any more than they can stop the world from changing!" And again, she felt that tingle in her backbone.

There were so many people, all here for the same reason, with the same purpose in their lives. It was exciting, to be part of something so important. To be a part of history! How many people got that chance? She and Jonah and Cookie found a place as close as possible to the big truck that was the stage, with all its electrical cables and the big grand piano and the two huge American flags and the line of veterans sitting on the edge looking grim and determined. Now Dorothy allowed herself to relax. Here they were, safe, among thousands of comrades, protected by brave men, waiting to hear the voice of America's greatest singer. She'd heard him on the radio and they had all his records, but Dorothy had never seen Paul Robeson in person.

At last, he stood up to sing. God, he was so much bigger than she had imagined! He was very tall and very broad and very strong and commanding. He was surrounded by a ring of men, who stood very close to him, looking out. There had been rumors of snipers stationed in the hills above, and she marveled that Paul Robeson was able to stand tall, smiling and easy, as if his life weren't in danger. What courage! And yet, what if—?

Everyone rose from where they had been sitting in the knee-high grass, applauding madly. Dot stood on tiptoe, trying to get a better look at him, with Jonah at her side, holding Cookie way up high, so she wouldn't miss a minute.

Suddenly there was a hand on her shoulder. Startled, she looked over to find Frank Green's face very close to hers. He had come up behind them, putting a hand on her shoulder and the other on Jonah's. "A moment to remember for the rest of our lives," he said quietly. Dorothy stood very still, very aware of his hand on her, very aware of the warmth of his body, wishing he would go away, wishing he wouldn't.

And then Paul Robeson spoke, his rich voice amplified by the loudspeakers, echoing: "I am here to applaud *you*." And the crowd went crazy. Dorothy found herself jumping up and down, Frank forgotten, Jonah and yes, even her own child, forgotten, yelling wordlessly. What a man! What a hero! And then he started to sing.

> When Israel was in Egypt's land . . .
> Let my people go . . .
> Oppressed so hard, they could not stand . . .
> Let my people go . . .

And the tears streamed out of her eyes. The voice was deep and rich and full of feeling. She felt somehow strengthened by the strength of this magnificent voice which seemed to be singing straight to her. How could she be so fearful, when she was on the same side as this giant of a man?

How long did he sing? She could not have said. She felt hypnotized by everything. The crowd all around her; the smell of drying grass, that end-of-summer aroma; the rich rolling baritone; the overcast sky, as smooth and white as an egg. Everything. It was splendid; it was glorious. She was in the presence of greatness, someone larger than life, and she wished that *she* could sing. Everything they had said about him being an inspiration to the working class was true.

The concert ended with "Ol' Man River." Jonah leaned over to her and said, "Listen to the words. He's changed the words to tell the story of oppression."

Cookie had fallen asleep on the grass with her head in her papa's lap. Jonah had to pick her up and carry her back to the bus. Hundreds and hundreds of people poured from the field toward the parking area, all together, many of them singing whatever they knew of "Go Down, Moses" and "Ol' Man River." It was thrilling. Dorothy kept telling herself to remember this, to savor all these little details, so that one day she would have it all intact, in her memory.

Just as they were climbing back on the bus, Dot heard, dimly, in the distance, a kind of high-pitched roar, and she stopped, holding up her hand. "Shh . . . listen. Jonah, what's that? Do you hear it?"

He laughed briefly. "The animals are howling. Pay no attention. They've lost."

But when the bus drove slowly out to make its turn into Hillside Avenue, suddenly there was the most horrible noise, like bombs falling, and the bus shook. Cookie, curled in Dorothy's lap, woke up and began to cry, and Dot held her tightly. If they dared to hurt her little girl—! They were throwing rocks at the bus, and every time one hit the metal side, it clanged and reverberated. Then there was a crashing sound and a hole appeared in the big front windshield. The bus driver yelled, "Everybody down!" and leaned on the horn while he reversed back into the parking area.

They sat, then, tense and fearful, unwilling to leave the bus, afraid to raise the windows, sitting and sweating and telling one another This is the United States of America, nothing terrible is really going to happen. Cookie, the youngest child there, huddled against her mother, whimpering a little, too overwhelmed to ask her usual "Why?" The driver went running out, then came back and said, "There's a police line on either side of the road, holding them back. We have to detour to Oregon Corners and go back to the city the long way."

So once more, they tried leaving. It was only four-thirty in the afternoon, Dorothy was surprised to realize. It seemed to her they had been here forever. At the same time, it felt very unreal, as if it were all happening to somebody else, or in a dream. She would not have been surprised to feel someone shaking her, to awaken safe in her bed. Because this couldn't be happening. Looking out the window as the bus made its careful way toward Oregon Corners and safety, she watched, frozen in horror, as a scrawny old woman, her face twisted with rage, looked her right in the eye and threw a Coke bottle at her. Before Dot ducked below the window, she saw that same beer-bellied trooper watching the woman and laughing. This happened to other people, in other countries, not here, not to her!

At Oregon Corners, instead of peace and quiet, there were several deputies and a crowd of people, mostly young men wearing T-shirts with VET chalked on them, holding huge rocks—boulders, really. As the bus rumbled off the little bridge and made the turn onto Peekskill Hollow Road, the crowd began to scream for blood. Again, a barrage of huge rocks hit the bus, making it quiver. Off the side of the road was a car, turned on its side, smashed and wrecked. Where were the people from the car? Dorothy's heart began to beat very fast. What was going to happen to them?

This time, when the driver turned and yelled for everyone to get down, she was already on the floor. She placed her body protectively over her child, hearing herself murmur over and over, "Don't worry, don't worry, don't worry. Mama's here."

From somewhere above her head, she heard Frank Green shout, "For God's sake, man, get down!"

"These wild animals are not going to put *me* on my knees, dammit!" Jonah answered him. "I'll die first, before I'll let them—" And then he let out a cry that brought Dot's head up in panic.

"Oh, God!" she cried. Jonah was standing in the aisle, slumped over, his hand to his temple; between his fingers, blood oozed. "He's bleeding! Somebody help! Jonah's bleeding!"

Frank Green was there in an instant, tying his handkerchief around Jonah's head, forcing Jonah to lie down on the floor, clearing a space, and somehow in the middle of everything, telling Dorothy that it was just a flesh wound, not very deep, and it would stop bleeding in a minute.

Dorothy sat on the dirty floor holding Cookie with one arm, saying, "Papa will be fine, darling. Look, look, he's smiling at you, don't be afraid." And her other hand she put on Jonah's shoulder, to show him she was there.

The bus picked up speed. "It's okay, folks, we're safe now," the driver called out.

The worst was over! Dorothy looked down at her child's filthy, tear-streaked face. The big solemn eyes were pink with all the crying, and her beautiful copper curls were tangled and dusty. And her new dress, her favorite Raggedy Ann dress, was torn. That torn sleeve and the tender little arm showing through the tear . . . that was the last straw. The last straw!

Not two hours ago, Dorothy thought, listening to Robeson sing, she had been filled with the certainty of the nobility and dignity of their cause, the cause of the Left to bring freedom and equality to all people, everywhere. It *was* all going to happen. They were the wave of the future. Paul Robeson, in his hugeness and his grandeur, had seemed to her the perfect personification of all that was magnificent in human beings.

Magnificent! Inspiring! But those twisted, furious, unthinking rednecks out there—magnificent? No! Horrible! And worst of all, they were *not* animals, as Jonah liked to think. No, they were human beings, too, just people. If you met them on the street, you wouldn't run and hide. They looked so ordinary; they *were* ordinary. And, God help us all, Dorothy thought, holding her firstborn to her breast, they are the majority. And we have already lost.

〜〜〜〜〜〜〜〜〜〜〜〜〜〜〜〜〜〜〜〜〜〜〜〜〜

Chapter Eight

Friday, December 28, 1951   The children were all busy, making paper chains, building with blocks, fingerpainting, squabbling with each other. Over in the corner, Adele Lowenstein was teaching a group to sing a Hanukkah song that was so simple and repetitious that Dot's head was beginning to hurt almost as much as her feet. She really had to get herself a better pair of shoes for working in the nursery. She wiped off a table where they had been working with clay and then a little movement caught her attention, something just out of her vision.

She turned. He was in the doorway, very casual, as always just strolling by, just happening to be down here in the basement. Her heart began to pound in her chest and she turned quickly away, scrubbing with the rag without looking or seeing.

All she could see was the image of Frank, in his chinos and plaid shirt, the collar open, no T-shirt underneath—he said undershirts were for sissies—and a little bit of the thick, black, curly hair that grew on his chest. She really didn't want to think about the hair on his chest; it made her feel faint. Her, a married woman with three small children! She was in love. It was unthinkable. It was ridiculous. My God, she was thirty-two years old, no longer a spring chicken. She had some gray hair! But he was so beautiful. When he touched her, she was on fire. It was so exciting—it made her feel like a girl again.

She went to the sink with her rag and rinsed it, glancing into the little mirror. Her hair could use a comb, but it was naturally wavy . . . and considering it was two o'clock in the afternoon and she'd been here since seven in the morning, she didn't look too awful. She needed lipstick. But he'd only kiss it off. Again, she felt that breathless sensation.

In a minute, she'd yell over to Adele or Harriet, tell them she needed to go to the bathroom.

She'd walk out into the hallway, turn the corner, and there in a deserted place near the furnace room, he'd be waiting, leaning against the wall, arms folded across his chest. As soon as he saw her, he'd smile. His smile! He had such white teeth. He was dark-skinned, and such black, thick hair! All the women in the Coops thought he was a dreamboat. He'd had lots of girlfriends—women were always after him—but he'd never chosen one to be Mrs. Frank Green.

Every once in a while, Dot had the chilling thought that maybe she was nothing more than the latest conquest, that he was playing her for a fool. When she was feeling that way, suspicious, she'd promise herself to stop seeing him, stop thinking about him. She'd cut him dead the next time she saw him. She'd ignore him when he drifted by the open door of the nursery.

And then, the minute she spotted him, she wanted only to be near him, to feel his arms around her, to smell his scent, to hear him tell her how much he loved her and longed for her. Like right now. And when that happened, nothing in this world was important enough to keep her away from him.

It was wicked, she knew it was wicked. Maybe *she* was wicked. After all, hadn't she snuck under the stairs of their building in Brooklyn with Leon Feld, all of thirteen years old the pair of them, dizzy with her excitement? And hadn't she done worse, later on? And she still had liked it, even afterward, even after all the trouble and all her promises to God. It was shameful. Maybe she had a terrible weakness, something in her that kept leading her astray.

She had to stop this thing with Frank. One day, Jonah was sure to find out. Someone, sooner or later, would see them together. In any normal building of this size, you could get lost, easily. But here, everyone knew everyone else. It was really like living in a small town—an unusual small town where everyone was progressive. A woman super down the block once said she'd never live in the Coops. Why? "Because there, if someone loses his job, they make you feed his children." It made everyone laugh. They were all so close, and it was a good feeling.

But on the other hand, everyone knew your business, too. If you got fired, they knew. If you had a fight with your husband, they knew. If you didn't like your mother-in-law; if you hit your kids; if you were having a love affair. Sooner or later, whatever it was, they knew. But she couldn't help it. She hadn't asked to fall in love at this late date, with another man. It had just happened. So, as she always did in the end, she called out to the others and went running down the hall and around the corner to find him.

He was there. Of course, he was there. And suddenly she was wrapped tightly in his embrace, she was on tiptoe, clinging to him, desperate for the touch of his mouth. They were kissing, their mouths grinding against each other, both of them making whimpering sounds. She could not get close enough to him. She pressed against him, she pushed her hips into his, she rubbed her cheek against his jaw, loving the roughness because it would leave his mark on her, if only for a moment. But nothing felt close enough. She hadn't seen him since the day before yesterday and then only for a minute or two, like this time. They hadn't been to bed together in twelve days. She was starving for him, starving!

He kissed her and kissed her and kissed her, until they were both breathless. And then, he held her away from him, holding her face tenderly in his two hands. "Dorothy, Dorothy, this is craziness. Come to me, leave your husband, tell him the truth and leave him and come to me."

"Oh, Frank, you know I can't."

"You don't love him anymore; you've said so a hundred times. There's no point in living with a man you no longer love."

"The children—"

"There's no point in them being with parents who don't love each other."

She was beginning to laugh. He was so serious, so intent, so naïve. "Frankele, it's obvious you've never been married. Things are not so simple. There are other things that bind two married people together: their shared life, their children, what they've gone through together. You make it sound like life has to be a love feast. That's not how it is."

He kissed her again. "That's how it could be with us."

"Frank—"

"Dorothy, I'm crazy about you. I want only to spend the rest of my life with you—"

"Please, no more of that talk. You know it's impossible. Nobody in the Coops would ever talk to either of us again."

"We'll go away, far away. We'll make a new life."

"And what happens to my three little children?"

"I'll take them, too! Dot, I mean it. I love them, I love you. We can't go on this way. Come away with me. And bring the kids, too."

"Even Irwin?"

He gazed at her, exasperated, and then he smiled. "Always with a joke, Dorothy. What am I going to do with you?"

"Make love to me, I hope, very soon."

"I want to make love to you forever."

"Don't put me through this again. You know how unhappy this kind of talk makes me feel. Please, Frank. Don't make it any worse than it is."

"What do you mean 'worse'?"

"You know what we're doing is wrong."

Stubbornly, he said, as he always did, "It's not wrong to love. Oh, Christ, I do love you, Dorothy. Promise me you'll never stop loving me."

"Of course, I'll always love you."

He held her close for a moment and then released her, saying, "Maybe not, maybe not." He looked so sad, all of a sudden. Or worried. But she didn't have time now to make him feel better; she'd already been gone longer than was smart. Hastily, she kissed him good-bye and half ran back to the nursery. She could feel his eyes on her until she rounded the corner.

As soon as she came through the door, Adele came marching toward her, shaking her head. "That was the longest pee in the history of the world, Dot. Of course, the minute you left, your baby put down the truck, looked around, and demanded Mommy." She laughed. "So where were you?"

Dorothy felt sure her face got hot, but she kept her voice very natural. "Do I ask you your bathroom habits, Adele?" And here came Paul, blubbering a little, rubbing his fist into his eyes and saying that plaintive, "Mama!" he did so well. He was such a doll, her baby, so beautiful, so charming, so smart. But he did get tired around this time of day and she should know better than to leave without telling him. Next time, she'd remember.

She had to carry Paul home—all the way up the stairs, too, because he fell asleep in her arms. He was really too big to carry anymore, four years old, almost old enough for kindergarten. But when he held his arms out to her and said, "Mama, I'm too tired to walk," she couldn't say no. She was going to spoil this one rotten!

She put him down on the sofa and began to make supper. There was leftover pot roast. She'd peel some more potatoes and carrots and boil them up and there you go: a meal. What she'd really like was a nice juicy tomato and corn on the cob, maybe a peach all warm from sitting in the sun on the window-sill. But of course, that was a dream. She'd have to wait until summer.

What a joke, pretending to herself that she was really thinking about food when it was just a way not to allow herself to think about Frank. What she really was longing to do was to stare out the window at the sky and relive today's meeting with Frank, to recall their passion, their hunger for each other. She'd never known a feeling like this before in her life, something that swept over you, left you weak, helpless, breathless with desire. Even as she thought about it, she became excited, and she tried to shake the memory.

Just then, the door burst open and in came Cookie and Irwin, home from their club meetings. Noisy, as usual. Scrapping, as usual. Cookie was saying, "Irwin, cut it out I said! That's mean! Mom! Make him stop." Stop what, she didn't say; it didn't matter. Irwin was a tease.

"Irwin! How many times do you have to be told!"

But he was too busy jumping around, opening and closing a folded piece of paper, cackling and calling out, "Cookie's got cooties! Cookie's got cooties!" And every time Cookie would swing at him, he'd dodge and circle around her and do it again. "Cooties, cooties. My cootie catcher caught Cookie's cooties!" And Cookie, her face scarlet with fury, just couldn't seem to get to him.

"*Irwin! Genug!* Enough already! You're making everyone crazy!"

"Crazy cooties, crazy cooties!"

Addressing the ceiling, Dorothy said, "This boy will drive me out of my mind." Then, in a completely different tone, she said, "Irwin. Out of here. And hang your jacket up on a hook."

"What about Cookie? Cookie has to put her jacket on a hook, too! But she better not put it next to mine, because it's full of cooties!"

One day, she was going to lose her temper with him. Just the sound of his voice, whiny, nasal, was enough to grate on her nerves. And he never let go, never. Where he got it from, she didn't know. So, of course, now Cookie was in tears. In a way, Dot didn't blame her, but she wished her daughter would toughen up a little. Learn to ignore him. "Don't pay attention to him and he'll stop," she said, for the hundredth time.

"No, he won't."

From the living room came Paul's sleepy voice, crying for her. "Now look what you've done, you two, you woke Paul. Go take him to the bathroom, Cookie, and then keep him out of my hair, will you? Read him a story."

When they were all in the other room, she continued with their supper. *Oy*, what a life. When she told Frank, "I have three little children" this wasn't what she was thinking of. If he should walk in the door right now and ask her again, she'd go in a minute.

The door did open, startling her; but, of course, it wasn't Frank, it was Jonah, and he was already complaining about her brother, Jack, as he shrugged off his jacket.

"Can you beat it? He thinks workers are stupid, I guess. Here's his latest . . ." And he began a whole song and dance about unions and double time and pay envelopes and God knows what else. She never listened anymore; it was always the same. The boss was the devil, and all the workers, angels from heaven. Well, at least he was in a good mood tonight. Much better than one of his silent times.

"Jack," she agreed, "will try to get away with whatever he can! And why not? Don't we all try to do the best for ourselves, for our families?"

"It's not the same. He squeezes his workers. Don't you see? He makes his profits on their sweat. And if he makes a bigger profit, do you think he's going to share it with his workers? Are you kidding? Those three little princesses will have fur coats, that's what'll happen." He laughed.

Dot stopped peeling her potatoes and turned to him. "I

hope," she said earnestly, "that you won't talk like that when we're there for Hanukkah next week. Let's have peace and quiet for a change . . . how about it?"

"Why do we have to go there? What's so wonderful? All that happens is that he lords it over us, shows off all his possessions, and makes us feel like poor relations!"

"Maybe that's how *you* feel, Jo. Me and the kids enjoy it. I like Sylvia, I like her a lot. And he may be a Capitalist, an exploiter of the workers . . . but he's still my big brother and I love him. And, look, if you're really unhappy working for him, why don't you quit? Nobody's forcing you to work for him."

"I know, I know. You don't have to keep reminding me. I'm being paid very well. It's keeping a roof over our heads. But dammit, Dot, it's so frustrating. He treats his men as if we were idiot children. His word is law, and the other men have been so enslaved by the Capitalist system, they don't even see what's happening. I keep telling them there's a better way, but I have to fight through a lot of resistance."

"Jo. Do me a favor. Please. Don't try to teach Jack's workers. I know it's your duty. I know they'd be better off if they were better organized. But you know it infuriates him. And we don't want to make trouble in the family."

"So you keep telling me!"

"Jo, please. Let's have a good time at Hanukkah, with the *latkes* and the candles and the presents. For the children's sake."

"You know I'll behave . . . as long as he doesn't start up with me! I'll even stay in the room when they're chanting the blessings. Blessings! As if anyone is listening!" Again he laughed and came over to her, giving her a kiss on the back of her neck. "I'll go wash up for supper. It smells good. Familiar, but good." And he walked away laughing.

Well, so what if it was the third pot roast dinner in a row. She wasn't a great cook. And anyway, to hear Jo tell it, her major concern should be to make a better world for her children, not necessarily a better dinner.

She finished the potatoes and put them into the pot with the meat. Done. It did smell good, even though she hated cooking. She looked around the apartment with satisfaction. It was clean, it was neat, it was a good place to live. Cross-ventilation, plenty of windows to let in the sunshine and fresh air—when available. The smell of dinner cooking, a man washing up in the bathroom, the children's heads together over a storybook. This . . . *this* was her life. This was reality.

What was she thinking of, sneaking off to hug and kiss another man? What was in her head, that she wanted to think she was in love? What was "in love," anyway? She was a fool to take chances with her entire family, and over what? Over a man who happened to be born with a handsome face and a way with women. Well, that was easy enough to end!

Later, when the children were all in bed and all asleep for a change, she decided to give herself the luxury of a long, hot bath. She put the bath salts Sylvia had given her for her birthday into the steaming water and breathed in the flowery scent with pleasure. How often was she really alone and free to do nothing but indulge herself?

She was glad, now, that Jonah had yet another meeting tonight. When he told her at dinner that something big was in the air and a special meeting had been called, she had been very annoyed. Here she was, feeling very satisfied with her life, very warm toward him, very comfortable. On this night of all nights, he had to have a meeting? And it sounded like a long one, too. He probably wouldn't be back until midnight. Well, now that suited her just fine. She sat back in the tub, luxuriating in her own pleasure.

And, just like that, Frank's face popped into her head. And all her good intentions disappeared. She closed her eyes, remembering the last time they'd made love, how sweet it had been, how satisfying, how different from anything she had ever known. Jonah was a good man and she admired him. But when he put his hand on her flank or on her breast, it was a hand on her body, it was not a bar of searing heat—it was not heart-stopping excitement—it was just a familiar hand on her.

And when he entered her, it was all right, it was good, it was comfortable. But that's all it was. That's all it had been for a long, long time. With Frank, she could hardly think, her senses were so overwhelmed. Even after he had climaxed, he still pushed into her, wanting to get still closer . . . and she put her hands on his tight buttocks and pulled as hard as she could because she wanted him completely inside her, completely, totally. And after he had left her, often she couldn't recall exactly what they had done together, only the mindless, wild ecstasy.

And now, thinking about it, soaking in the hot scented water, she wanted him. She wanted him, she ached for him. She began to cry. It was all so complicated and hopeless. And she was so terribly in love!

She pushed herself out of the tub, dripping, weeping, hating this feeling. She grabbed a towel, dried herself, dressed herself. Gazing at herself in the mirror over the bureau in their bedroom, she studied her face. Yes, she was a pretty woman. And she had become much livelier in her old age. Once Yetta left and she was forced to be on her own, she found she loved not being one of the twinnies, she loved being her own person. So why, she asked herself, had she been in such a hurry to tie herself down to Jo and to children, where she could no longer be her own person?

She knew the answer to that. When you got married, that was the sign you were an adult woman. Everything else was play. In a marriage, the wisdom went, you could begin to be your own person. What nonsense! You were more than ever absorbed into someone else's ego. You even lost your name. Mrs. His Name.

"And I thought he was special," she said to her reflection. "And he is, but not the way I thought he was." Jonah the war hero, Jonah the man of ideals, Jonah the man of principle: she had admired him so extravagantly. He was so different from Pa. But was he? She was no longer so sure. He was quieter, he was reasonable, you could talk to him. But he was set in his ways, stubborn, angry at the world. She made a face at herself in the mirror. They were all bullies, every last one of them!

It was a quarter to one when Jonah quietly let himself into their room. She was still wide awake and she could tell he was agitated. Instead of easing himself under the covers as he normally would have done, he paced. Up and down, up and down. "What's wrong?" she said.

"Oh, you're awake." He didn't even ask why. "I've quit, Dot." His voice sounded drained and empty.

"Quit what, for God's sake?"

"The Party! The Party! What else?"

Now she sat up and switched on the bedside lamp. What now? They were always disagreeing about political issues, here in the Coops. For a place where everyone supposedly believed in the same things, there were certainly an awful lot of factions. "What happened?" she asked.

"They're saying Frank Green's an informer."

She thought her heart had stopped beating. She had to stay very, very calm. "Why do they say that?"

"Oh, I know you could care less about Frank Green."

In spite of the pulses beating in her temples, in spite of the nausea that rose in her throat, Dorothy felt exultation. It had worked! In public, she pointedly ignored Frank. She had tried very hard to give Jo the impression that she didn't quite approve of Frank and his women. And it had worked!

"Is it true?" she said. "Is he an informer?" It flashed into her head, how this afternoon, Frank had asked for her promise to love him, *no matter what.* Is *this* what he meant? Is this why he had clung to her so tightly? Oh, God!

"It can't be true!" Jonah burst out, clenching his fists. "The man's my friend, for Christ's sake! We met—you know how we met! On the battlefield. He saved my life. He's eaten at my table. I can't believe he's a traitor!"

Dorothy could not answer him; her mind was whirling with questions.

"Dammit," Jo went on. "I can't believe it. But some members have already been arrested! All naturalized citizens. They could be deported! *I* could be deported!"

"Oh, God, Jonah! No!"

"Yes, yes."

"But that means—"

"Dammit, don't you think I know what that means? It means you'll be left alone without a man to take care of you. You think I like that thought? But it can't be Frank! He's always worked hard for the Party. He got beat up plenty, in the old days. No, no, they've made a mistake. Someone who doesn't like him is out to get him, that's what it's all about!"

"Can't you convince them of that?"

Jonah laughed bitterly. "Ha! They say they have proof. They say he's gone."

"Gone!" She felt hollow inside. "What do you mean?"

"Gone. Disappeared."

"But . . ." Carefully, carefully. "How can they be sure?"

"I don't know. All I know is, they told us tonight to turn him in if we ever see or hear from him again. They ordered us. They insisted."

"And what did you say?"

He grimaced. He kept striding around the room, small as it was, restless. "What did I say? I said, 'Fuck you, I quit!' "

"Oh, Jo!"

"I should blindly obey? I should turn against a man who's been my friend for years? Never!" He pounded a fist on the dresser. "Dammit, Dorothy, that's what I've always hated about some of these people in the Party—that they change their principles on demand! I can't do it! But . . . Listen, you think I *wanted* to quit? I didn't! I hate this! I hate being forced to choose!''

"I think you should go back and tell them you've changed your mind, that you still want to be a member!"

"Are you kidding, Dot? You think they'll trust me now?"

"You know what I can't stand about this place? On the surface, everyone's together, it's one big happy family. You get fooled. While all the time, underneath, there's anger and jealousy and hard feelings. There are too many secrets here, too many suspicions, too much backbiting! Trotskyites! Leninites! Agh! Who cares? If they don't stop, we'll *all* be in *drerd*! Tell me, has anyone faced Frank with these charges?"

"They tried all day to get him. He wasn't at work, he wasn't home. Didn't answer his door, didn't answer his phone."

Dorothy closed her eyes briefly. In her heart, the fear was growing—that he had really left. Please no! she thought fiercely. Please, please, no.

She took in a deep breath. "So what?" she said bravely. "You know Frank. He could be anywhere, in anyone's bed." It hurt to say it, but she must. "He could be home by now. It's late and he's a workingman. I think you should go, right this minute, and see if he's there, tell him straight out what's going on."

For once, he listened to her and went; and now, she got out of bed to pace the room, her mouth dry. She kept telling herself, Don't worry, don't be silly, he didn't leave, it's not true, he's just out tomcatting. In a few minutes, Jo will come back and he'll be smiling and he'll curse those dummkopfs who leap to conclusions. We'll say how that SOB McCarthy has turned friend against friend and comrade against comrade, and this nightmare will be over.

She sat down on the bed, wringing her hands, feeling the sweat gather in her armpits, cold and dank. It had to be all right, it just had to be. If it wasn't, how would she be able to bear it? When she heard the apartment door open, her heart began to thump painfully. Her eyes met his and she knew.

"Gone." Jonah covered his eyes with one hand. "The door's open, the closets are empty. No papers around. Nothing. I've been a damn fool! A damned fool!"

"What are you going to do?"

"Do? What *can* I do? I'm going to wait and see if he gets in touch. Then I'll talk to him and then I'll see. Dammit, I came to this country to be free, and here I am, waiting for Herbert

Brownell's cossacks to take me away! Well, they're not going to deport me so easily! From now on, don't answer the door, not for nothing. Do you hear me? Not for nothing, not for nobody. And tomorrow make sure you tell the kids, too. *Somebody's* talking, and that means nobody's safe anymore.''

He had been taking his clothes off as he spoke, letting them just drop to the floor. Now he lay down heavily next to her, grunted, turned away from her, and instantly fell asleep.

She was not so lucky. She lay awake a long time, listening to the slow, sad thudding of her heartbeat, letting the slow, sad tears run across her face and slide silently into her pillow. Was he really gone? Without a word to her? Without saying good-bye? Just those meager hints this afternoon? Maybe Jonah wasn't the only damn fool. Frank was gone and it was over.

€€

Chapter Nine

Sunday, December 30, 1951   ''Men!'' Dorothy said, her tone sardonic. She was doing her best to smile as she said it. She couldn't let her sister-in-law know that inside she was aching with anxiety—after all, this was a holiday—so she raised her teacup in a mock toast, when Sylvia agreed, ''Overgrown babies, all of them.'' They both took a careful sip—the tea was steaming hot—and gave each other an appraising look. There had been a very uncomfortable scene earlier, and they were both always very careful when it came to their husbands.

Outside the heavily draped windows it was snowing, and a high wind blew gusts of white swirls against the steamy panes. Inside, though, all was warmth and light. Sylvia's dining room was lavish, with Oriental carpets, mahogany, crystal. The guttering Hanukkah candles were not in an ordinary menorah, no, but in an ornate outsized silver antique one. Everything was rich and comfortable—a bit overdone, Dorothy had always thought, but somehow *haimish*.

The two women were sitting, leaning toward each other with their arms on the table, nibbling at the remnants of *ruggaleh* on a china plate, sipping at their Sweetouchnee tea. Their husbands were in Jack's den, watching *Toast of the Town* on television and carefully ignoring each other. They had cooled down since their argument, but they weren't yet on speaking terms. The children were all in the kitchen, watching Earline load the dishwasher, spinning their *dreidels*, and bickering. Faintly, from beyond the pantry, the children's shrill voices could be heard, although not the words.

Sylvia sighed, sipped, sighed again. Finally she said, "Look. Dot. I'm really sorry Jack wasn't more diplomatic, but you know Jack . . ."

"Didn't I grow up with him? I know Jack. He loves to be generous. He loves having it to give, I understand that. But *he* has to understand that we're in a difficult position. He knows exactly how much Jo makes. When we're going to exchange Hanukkah gifts, they have to be on an equal par."

Sylvia held up a hand. "I know, Dot. Twenty dollars for each child is too much. I told him so. I *tried* to tell him, I should say. But you know Jack . . ."

"It's okay, Sylvia. It's not your fault. He just has a tendency to go overboard."

Sylvia got up abruptly and went to the window, staring out at the swirling, twisting snow. "Overboard. You said it. But what about Jo? I know he has his principles. Let him be angry, let him fight it out with Jack. But not in front of the children, am I right?" She turned to face Dorothy. "Why should the children suffer? *He* goes overboard, too."

"It's not right that my children's uncle gives them and their father can't," Dot said stubbornly.

After a moment, Sylvia sighed again. "Jack overdoes it with money. Don't I know it! That's his answer to everything. He spoils the girls rotten, and when I talk to him about it, he won't hear me. 'I never had a damn thing when I was a kid,' he tells me. 'My kids are going to have everything money can buy.' And they will, too!" She sighed noisily and refilled the teacups. "Especially lately. Every night it's another present. The more he works late, the more presents he buys."

"He has to work late so much—in the middle of winter? I thought in the construction business they slowed down in the cold weather." Dorothy was suddenly alert. It had struck her, during dinner, how often Jack mentioned his new secretary . . . what was her name again? Linda. It had been Linda this and

Linda that, until Elaine said something smart-alecky about it.
Could it be—?

Now Sylvia looked directly at her. "There are . . . *things*
. . . he has to attend to, and he can only do them after regular
office hours." There was a bitter edge to her voice. "He *says*
he needs the quiet, to concentrate."

Dorothy shifted uneasily in her chair, searching for the words
that might give comfort. "Sylvia, Sylvia, remember, he's running the company all by himself. When you're in business for
yourself, your day isn't over when the whistle blows."

"I know that. But I want him home for dinner with me and
the children. I want us to be a family. My father was always
home for dinner, come hell or high water."

There was something in the air, Dot thought, an unspoken
knowledge, a half-revealed secret, and both of them knew it.
But there was no way either of them could speak. It wasn't done.
There wasn't ever supposed to be trouble in paradise. And if
there was, you were expected to lie, to pretend, to cover up, to
put on an act so it shouldn't be a *shandah* for the neighbors, a
scandal.

Dorothy took in a deep breath, leaned forward, reaching a
hand to her sister-in-law. "Sylvia—" she began, her voice lowered to intimacy. "There's something I—" And then there was
a commotion out in the pantry and a moment later, the swinging
door flew open and what sounded like three *dozen* children came
charging in, all talking at once, even Sylvia's Marilyn in her
sister Elaine's arms. The rare moment for honesty passed.

"Children, children, hold your horses!" Sylvia was laughing.
"One at a time!"

Eight-year-old Deena pushed herself forward. "Elaine says
the Russians are going to bomb us! With H-bombs! And I said
Daddy wouldn't let them. And she laughed at me and called me
a baby!"

"Well, you are! Daddy can't do anything about H-bombs!
Daddy isn't President Truman!"

"Sylvia! Make her take it back. They're *not* going to bomb
us, are they?"

Cookie ran to Dorothy. "Mama, tell Elaine! The Soviet Union
is our friend!"

Now the two women exchanged meaning-laden looks, and
Dorothy murmured, "Even with kids, it's got to be politics?"
She hugged her daughter and said, "Look. Nobody's bombing

anybody. Period. The people who are making a *tsimmes* about bombs are stupid reactionaries.''

''What's that?''

Cookie looked at Deena with surprise and disdain. ''Everyone knows what a reactionary is! They don't want anything to change. And you know what else? They're afraid of the working class because the working class is going to change the world!'' she finished triumphantly.

Elaine put the wriggling baby down onto the floor. ''Oh, who cares, anyway? I only said it to make Deena squeal. Now can we have candy, Syl? You said after we digested our dinner!''

''Good idea. Stop fighting and come with me.'' Sylvia opened a drawer in the sideboard and brought out half a dozen little mesh bags, filled with gold-wrapped chocolate coins. The children all jumped up and down, holding their hands out, all but the baby, Marilyn, who happily sat under the table sucking her thumb.

Sylvia handed out the bags. ''Now go!'' Then she noticed the baby. ''You, too!'' She lifted Marilyn up, gave her a quick kiss on one chubby cheek, and handed her over to Elaine. ''Lainie is her second mother,'' she said with some pride.

''You should try to start a nursery,'' Dorothy said. ''Like we have in the Coops. It's wonderful for the little ones *and* for the women, too. You have a big building. You could do it. All you have to do is organize the mothers. There must be plenty of women who'd like to get out for a few hours every day.''

Sylvia grimaced. ''You don't know this neighborhood, Dorothy. The women who like to get out have nursemaids for their children.''

''How can I keep forgetting? No, no, don't look like that. I don't resent you. I'm not complaining. It's just . . . well, this is no picnic for Jonah, working for his brother-in-law. Jo's a proud man. He's an intellectual, a teacher, a writer. I know he misses it terribly . . .''

''Maybe that's why he gives speeches to the other men on the job,'' Sylvia said dryly. ''You know, Jack isn't going to put up with that much longer.''

''What, Jo's not an American? He's not allowed to talk about what he believes?''

''Not to Jack's men and not on company time. The worst thing you can do is come between the boss and his men. They have a special relationship . . .''

''Excuse me, Sylvia, but that's a fairy tale bosses like to tell.

You want to know what that famous relationship really is? The boss says jump, and the men say how high. That's how it's always been with Capitalism. That's why we're the wave of the future. The workingman is not stupid, you know. It's Jack and the other bosses in this world who are wrong-headed. And they won't change until they're forced to!''

"Jack's not stupid!"

"Sylvia, I didn't say he is. I'm only saying that sooner or later, he's going to have to realize that it's the workers' sweat that makes the profit and the workers must have a share in that profit. Jonah's only trying to educate the men to understand their rights. He's not telling them to riot; he's asking them to think for themselves.''

Sylvia took another sip of tea, visibly calming herself. "Funny," she said after a moment. "I seem to remember you, not too many years ago, telling *me* that Jonah's speaking out got him into trouble all the time. But forget it. I don't want to fight with you. But, tell me—and this is an honest question, from my heart—do you think it's worth it, to be Comm—to believe the way you do, if it means you're forced out of your profession, forced to leave town? Is it worth it, to live in fear, to have the FBI hanging around, stopping you in the street and harassing you all the time, for an *idea*?''

"Them! Who pays attention to them? We all ignore them. And we don't live in fear, in the Coops.'' Under the table, she crossed her fingers. "We're all in the same boat, all on the same side. No matter where you turn, you have a friend.''

"You never hear that kind of thing about Comm—about the Left. It's always The Red Menace.''

"I know. People make us sound like monsters. Listen. I didn't know what to expect when we moved in. Tell you the truth, I was a little bit nervous. Jonah's ideas were so different from the way I was brought up. They made sense to me, but living with them? That was not so simple.

"But now? You want to know what I really like about living in the Coops? Women are equal. Oh, don't look so doubting. If a woman wants to do something, she goes and does it, Sylvia. We don't have to ask permission of our husbands. They expect us to participate, in everything. We march, we demonstrate, we lead tenant strikes, we run nurseries and *shuls* and work and handle money and have a say.

"Look at me," she went on. "When I was a kid, my father said my sister and I were 'only girls.' We weren't worth edu-

cating, and we certainly weren't capable of making decisions.
We only got a lot of attention on account of being twins. I grew
up not knowing *what* I could do.

"But now." She ticked off on her fingers. "I run the nursery;
I led a tenant strike; I'm in every demonstration; I make
speeches." She paused and then laughed. "Like right now, in
your kitchen. But that's what happens to you in the Coops. No
more hanging back! No more thinking men are kings of the
world!"

"Now *that*, I'll buy," Sylvia said. They smiled at each other
tentatively. "And if that makes me a Red . . ."

With a sly smile, Dorothy asked, "Tell me something, Sylvia. Before, you asked me, now I'm asking you . . . Is it worth
it, living a life where your husband has all the money and all
the power?"

"I love him," Sylvia said. "I have three small children. Do
I have any choice? And if that makes me a reactionary . . . what
can I tell you?"

Dorothy laughed and reached over to pat her sister-in-law's
hand. "Listen, it's not all perfect in the Coops, believe me. Yes,
the women are expected to do their bit in changing the world,
but they're also expected to keep on changing the diapers, too!"
Swiftly, she added: "Don't ever tell Jonah I said that! Please!"
And they both laughed.

Once again, the door swung open. It was Dorothy's Irwin,
not Sylvia's favorite, a skinny seven-year-old with a mop of
black hair and already a nose that dominated his pinched face.
Not a good-looking boy, poor kid.

"Mama," he whined, "I want—"

Rather sharply, his mother interrupted him. "Always you
come to tell me you want something. One day, I'd like to hear
something else from you." As soon as the words were out of
her mouth, she reached for him and pulled him into her embrace, talking over the top of his head. "Irwin, *bubeleh*, you
better watch out or you'll grow up to be a *kvetch*."

"But it's not fair, Mama! They all hid my bag of candy coins
and they won't tell me where it is!" The little boy struggled to
be released, but she held him close.

"See what I mean? *Kvetch, kvetch*. You're always going to
get picked on because you won't fight back. He just stands there
and whines, Sylvia. Go back and tell them to give you your
Hanukkah gelt."

"I can't! They won't do it!"

Dorothy pulled in an exasperated breath. "Tell them Mama said."

Now she loosened her hold and he scampered out, already shouting, "Mama says you have to give me my candy!" as he went out the door.

His mother shook her head sadly. "He asks for it. I hate to say it, but he does. I don't know *what* to do about him. He just doesn't seem to know how to make friends. Paul, at four years of age, has more playmates." She smiled. "That Paul. A living doll. So sweet, so good, so . . . charming. You know, he reminds me of Jack."

Dryly, Sylvia said, "You remember Jack at the age of four, Dot? You were not quite two."

"Well, no, but they're a lot alike, *I* think. Paul has a way with him. Like Jack."

"That's funny. Deena's my charmer, but I think of Elaine as being just like Jack. Smart, and good-looking, but with a will of iron. Once she sets her mind on something, it would take that H-bomb of hers to shake her loose."

"Deena's quick-witted," Dot said. "Like Cookie. Always a smart answer."

"I hope that's meant as a compliment."

"I'm telling you what I see, that's all. I pride myself on calling a spade a spade. A smart-mouth kid is nice sometimes, and sometimes a pain in the neck."

"I've never considered Deena—or any of my children—a pain in the neck."

"Oh, Sylvia, I didn't mean it that way. I'm crazy about your kids. I only wish I could have been a smart mouth. For years, Jo was after me to speak up—you know Pa, Sylvia, you can imagine how much we were allowed to have opinions, Yetta and me!—and now that I've learned how to speak up, he tells me I talk too much!"

"Men! What do they know? You don't talk too much . . . that's what they tell you when they don't like what you're saying!" Sylvia's cheeks were pink with indignation. "You want to know what I've always noticed about you? You're honest. You're straight. Nine out of ten women, they'll lie. Their husbands are like honeymooners. Their children are angels and geniuses. They get along with their in-laws. They make me laugh; they make me sick; they bore me to tears.

"But you, you're different. You've always been different. You call a spade a spade? That's fine. That's why I like you. With you, I can let down my hair. That's quite a luxury, believe me.''

Dorothy colored with pleasure. "I'm glad you said that to me, Sylvia. I always feel like I'm in Jonah's shadow." There was a pause, and then she looked up, almost shyly, and said, "Well, I wasn't going to say this—I thought it was disloyal—but let me tell you something: it's terrible having those FBI men around all the time. Oh, I act brave. If they stop me on the street and ask if they might have a word with me, I say No, they may not and walk on. But inside, I'm shaking. I'm afraid. And, not only that—''

"Poor Dorothy. I don't blame you. My God, it must be horrible. That McCarthy is a menace. He's wrecking lives right and left! He's poisoned the whole country! We're all afraid!'' She made a face of disgust. "But you were saying—?''

"Jonah could be deported. Something happened last week . . . I really can't go into detail, but—''

"Oh, no! They wouldn't dare! Jack would never allow it! He knows a very big immigration lawyer . . . lives right in this building, on the tenth floor.''

Dot stood up. "Oh, Sylvia, I only wish it was that easy. You've heard of the McCarren Act; it's the law. And they're using it against the entire Left. They'd send him back to Russia, they'd do it in a minute. Never mind. I don't want to talk about it. It depresses me." She tried for a smile. "You don't need to hear all my sad stories, believe me, you don't. Anyway, it's time for us to go. We have a long trip up to the Bronx, especially this time of night.''

"Oh, no. You can't. Don't you want to watch some television?''

Dorothy smiled. "I have to be up at seven, Sylvia. Ed Sullivan will have to wait.''

"All right, if you say so. But, before you go . . ." Sylvia reached deep into a shelf above the sink. She pulled out a sugar bowl that had one mended handle and pulled a wad of bills out of it. "Please, Dot. Let the men be principled and stubborn, but we don't have to be. Here. No, no, it's from me to you. It's Hanukkah, remember? Take it, please. For the children.''

Dorothy's lips were set in a firm negative line. But just then a voice hollered down the hallway, "Girls! Girls! Ed Sullivan is almost over. Enough in the kitchen, already!''

Sylvia said, "Come on, Dot. And stay awhile. How often do

the kids get the chance to see television?" She was still holding out the money. "For the children."

"For the children," Dorothy repeated, and took the roll of bills. "Okay. And, Sylvia, thanks. For the children, I'll do it. For the children."

€€€

Chapter Ten

Friday, February 15, 1952   Jonah bent his head against the bitter wind that blew off the Hudson and hunched himself into his pea jacket. Damn Jack! Ordering him to come in all the way from Long Island at the end of the day! He was bone-tired and ready for the weekend, but forget it. The master calls and the slave schlepps himself into Manhattan instead of being able to go home to his family. It was cold, it was dark, and it was a long, long trip on the subway to Allerton Avenue. But what did Jack Strauss care? He would ride home in a Cadillac.

As he took the elevator up to the office, Jonah wondered briefly what was so important that Jack couldn't give him hell over the phone, like he usually did. Jonah was sure that's what was planned; another one of Jack's long-winded lectures on loyalty. So what had he done lately, to get his brother-in-law going? He'd given a couple of guys some pamphlets and handed out copies of the *Worker*, but he'd done that before—and anyway, they'd asked him, and this was a free country, wasn't it? Even Jack's men had a right to read what they pleased; they had a right to see there was a better way.

Of course, in a way, he had *asked* for trouble. Maybe. Most of the men were superpatriots, and maybe he hadn't been careful enough. Yeah, they were already unionized, but that wasn't enough. He just couldn't stand listening to them talk about politics; they were so ignorant! The Capitalist system—the American Way, they called it!—they talked about it like it had come straight from God on Mount Sinai. Yeah, sure, the Eleventh Commandment: Thou shalt honor thy Capitalism for it will make you rich. Make you a slave was more like it! But these guys didn't seem to realize they were part of the future of the world, the working class.

He knew his brother-in-law would threaten him. He knew Jack's line by heart: If he didn't keep his mouth shut, he'd be out of a job. Like hell! Jack loved Dot too much to let her and her children go hungry. Hell, why did he give Jonah a job in the *first* place—a man with no experience in construction? And, as it turned out, he wasn't very good at it, either. The only reason he was working there was Dorothy, so if there was one thing he was sure of in this world, it was that Jack would never fire him!

There was no one else in the office when he got there. Of course not; on Friday, everyone left very fast for their weekend. It was empty and eerie, with no sound but the buzz of the fluorescent lights.

"That you, Jo?" Jack called out from his office. The door was open, so Jonah just walked in.

"It's me. Who else would you call in at the end of a working day, at the end of a working week?"

"Never mind that! You've *really* done it this time!"

Now Jonah was puzzled. Jack didn't look angry—which is how he usually looked whenever he called Jonah in—he looked worried. Something was different this time. It wasn't just a few issues of the *Daily Worker*, not this time. These days, with McCarthy on the rampage and nobody with guts to stop him, it could be anything. It could be *nothing*. There was a sinking feeling in the pit of his stomach.

"What's the problem?" He kept his voice even.

"What's the problem? The FBI, that's what! Thanks to you, I now have the FBI nosing around! Two of them came in this morning, looking for *you*, Golodny. Wanting to know was it true that my sister, Dorothy Strauss, had married 'one Jonah Golodny of Washington, D.C.' "

"So what did you tell them?" Is that all? he was thinking. Thank God. Having a couple of FBI men nosing around was no novelty.

"I told them yes, what else?"

Jonah just raised an eyebrow.

"Don't give me that look, Golodny. I said yes, but I did save your worthless hide. They asked me did I know where you were? And I lied for you. I said I had no idea. They gave me a very hard time, but I stuck to the story. Believe me, I choked on it. But I did it, anyway. Since you left D.C., I told them, I hadn't heard a single word. For the sake of my sister and her children, I lied to the United States government.''

Jonah allowed himself a little smile. ''Was it the same two that hang around the Coops? They look like they could be twins? Both in dark blue suits, both in red striped ties?'' He could tell by the surprised look on Jack's face that he'd hit the nail on the head. ''We call them the Katzenjammer Kids. They've been assigned to watch the neighborhood, on and off, for the past couple of years. Well, if *that's* all it was . . .''

Jack flushed and he pounded one meaty fist on his desk, making piles of paper jump and slide onto the floor. ''Dammit, don't be so goddamn nonchalant! We're not talking just about *you*, Golodny. We're not even talking about my sister this time. We're talking about my business, my life, my livelihood, here! I could lose it all, you lousy Red! They'll never leave me alone now!''

''Don't be a jackass, Jack. They're not after you; they're after me.''

''But you're here, working for me!''

''They don't know that. I'm not on the books; you pay me in cash. They don't know anything. They're just fishing. That's how they do it, you know. They hang around and hang around and nag you to death.''

Jack scowled. ''I got the feeling they *knew* you're working for me. They way they asked . . .''

''They always do that. Don't worry about it.''

''Don't worry about it, the man says! What are you—meshuggah? The FBI chased you from Washington . . . because of them, you can't get a job! And you tell me, don't worry! Mr. Big Shot!''

''I could have found work. That's not why I left D.C. I left D.C. because they started going after innocent people. My neighbor, a nice guy, a nebbish, a mailman, every once in a while we had a beer or two together. And you know what they did to him? They took away his job! He was fired for being a quote close associate of Jonah Golodny unquote. A guy I drank beer with once in a while, for God's sake!''

''My point exactly. You're a dangerous man to have around, Golodny, a dangerous man! I went out on a limb for you. But dammit, you won't keep your mouth shut. That's the trouble with you. The word's getting around I have a crazy Red working for me. Soon I'll be blacklisted from every government job in this city! This is getting serious, FBI men in my office! Enough already! That's why I had you come in tonight. I want your promise to shut up from now on—and I want it now! If you want to work for me, let me tell you something—I get your loyalty, period, *fartig*, finished.''

"Nuts to that! My loyalty belongs to the working class. It's not for sale to the likes of you!"

Jack pounded his desk again and came to his feet in a fury. "The likes of me? *The likes of me?* Just what in hell is *that* supposed to mean? How about the likes of *you*? I know you think you're a cut above me because you fought in Spain and read a few books and think you've got all the answers!

"*I've* been working my whole life to get where I am. I'm a rich man today, yes, but I did it on my own, with my own sweat. You can't stand that, can you? You're out to ruin me. Don't think I don't know that!"

"You know what? You're full of crap!" Jonah laughed. "I could care less about your money! All your money doesn't make you less of a ganef!"

Jack's face became even redder. He stood up, pushing his chair so hard it rolled back and slammed against the wall. "Ganef!" He stormed over to Jonah, his fists clenched by his sides, his jaw jutted out. "Where do you get off calling me a thief, you dirty Commie!"

Jonah allowed himself a sneer. "You think you're so clever. But anyone with a brain in his head sees what's going on."

"You ingrate! You're nothing but a fucking traitor!"

"You'll pay for that!"

"Fuck off!" Jack reached out and shoved him. "What can *you* do to me? You should go back to Russia, you love it so much! I hope you do, goddammit. I hope you do. In the meantime, you'll do me a favor and get out of my sight!" He reached out a meaty hand and gave him another shove. "Better yet, do my little sister an even bigger favor and get out of her life!"

"Keep your hands off me, you *momzer*!" Jonah felt the rage rising in him. He pushed at Jack, surprised at the solid bulk of the man. "I'm proud of being a Communist, and Dorothy's proud of *me*! At least I'm working toward a better world; I'm not out to steal other people's money! You talk about loyalty? You have only one loyalty and that's to Jack Strauss, period. At least my loyalty is to the working class, which believe me, will triumph in the end!"

Jack laughed, a nasty bark of a sound. "Your loyalty is to the working class? Does the working class pay your wages?" His

face was suffused with blood and he spit his words out like
bullets. He advanced another step, his fists raised now. Jonah
felt a little twinge of real fear. If Jack took it into his head to hit
him . . . He was a strong SOB. But he wasn't going to back
down! Never!

"Always it comes down to the almighty dollar! A man pays
wages and right away he thinks he owns you!" Well, in fact, in
a way he *did* own you, Jonah suddenly realized. He could tell
you what to say; he could demand your silence; he could command your obedience. Well, Jonah Golodny was no man's serf—
especially not Jack Strauss's! Jonah gave his brother-in-law a
jaunty little smile.

"You can take your wages and shove them! You can't buy
me. My principles are worth more than *all* your money!"

"So go pay the rent with your fucking principles! I'm done
arguing with you, I'm done lying for you. I'm done with you,
period, *fartig*, finished, the end! You're fired!"

"Like hell I am. I quit!"

He saw a little smile tug at the corner of Jack's mouth. "You
rotten bastard. You're happy, aren't you? You *wanted* to push
me to quit. You think if you get rid of me, you're safe from my
ideas. But you're wrong. What I believe in is too powerful to be
defeated by a big ape like you! There are millions of people all
over the world who are working toward the revolution. It's *inevitable*!"

With those words, he turned and barreled out, slamming
Jack's door as hard as he could. As he marched toward the
elevator, he heard something crash against the closed door and
now it was *his* turn to smile. He'd gotten the last word and, in
the years to come, he'd have the last laugh, too. Because what
was happening in this country now, the blacklists, and all the
Party leaders on trial, and the deportations, and the hearings
. . . pfui! The American people wouldn't stand for that kind of
crap much longer.

Out in the street, he stopped and took in a deep breath. His
head was pounding. He felt like he'd gone fifteen rounds . . .
punchy. But triumphant. He'd won, by God. He'd left that jackass without a word to say. All he could do was throw something,
break something. The man was pitiful, pitiful.

The subway was noisy and crowded and the fat woman next
to him, who bumped into him with every lurch of the train as it
sped around the curves, was wearing a coat that smelled very
strongly of moth balls. As usual, people sat or stood without

expression, their faces set, looking numbed. Jonah squeezed himself into a tiny space where he could lean against the door and closed his eyes, thinking.

Thinking about his life. He had come from Spain, limping and beaten, but with a sense of being part of history. He and his comrades had been the first to try to beat off Hitler. The next heroes of that war in Europe were the Russians at Stalingrad. He could still remember how everyone here cheered the starving but indomitable Russians who would not give in, who would not give up. You heard "Green Eyes" everywhere you went; the stores featured *mamuschkas*, the doll within a doll within a doll within a doll that was so typical of the land of his birth. Russian War Relief: that's how he and Dorothy met, at one of their picnics. Everyone was so proud of working for the RWR. So how did the brave people of Stalingrad, our allies through the entire war, suddenly turn into The Enemy? That's what he'd like to know.

Well, that wasn't quite true. He did understand. Communism, just by being, was a threat to bloated capitalism. Capitalism had had its day and now there was a new day dawning and it was Socialist. But this McCarthy business—this was crazy! Blacklists, guilt by association, lies and then more lies . . . and everybody too scared to move! Not even the president of the United States would take a stand! He had been reading the other day, an article by a lawyer who said the Loyalty Program made a mockery of due process. Jonah liked that phrase . . . *made a mockery*. This country was making a mockery of all its constitutional guarantees. But when he spoke this way to his fellow workers, they hooted at him, they called him a traitor. What had happened to the promise that the working class would rise up in this country? Where was the revolution? This country needed it worse than ever.

But instead of being part of the future, he found himself shunted off to the sidelines, working for a man he despised, captive to the hysteria of a whole nation!

Halfway home, it suddenly struck him. He had really done it. He'd quit his job. He was out of work! In just a little while, he was going to have to explain to Dorothy. She was going to be so angry! He knew right now exactly what she was going to say to him. That he was lost in a dreamworld, that he was living in the past, that they had three little children, had he forgotten? And she was sure to bring up that they owed Jack a debt of gratitude.

A debt of gratitude! He had worked for every cent Jack paid him. Jack had made a profit from his sweat. He owed Jack nothing! But try to tell that to a woman who thought Jack Strauss was some kind of saint. She should only know! He could tell her a thing or two about Saint Jack! He could tell her plenty.

Oy, it was his stop and the doors were almost closing! He pushed himself off, just in time. Still lost in his thoughts, he trudged up the stairs and out into the cold. *Schmuck!* So why didn't you say something to Jack when you had the chance? He's not the only one who could threaten!

He walked slowly, even though his fingers were frozen. Never mind what he might have said to Jack . . . what the hell was he going to say to *her*? She was such a worrier, even though she shouldn't be. They had a little put aside. He was young and strong and willing, he could always find work. He'd dig ditches, he'd wash dishes. He was ready to do anything . . . except give up his principles! But would he ever find wages that good anywhere else? Not likely. Jack had been paying him more than the going rate, as Dot was sure to remind him.

If he explained to her how important it was that he had walked out rather than act like a serf, she would give him that look. ''Sometimes I think you are not of this world,'' she would say. Dorothy was just not political, that's all.

He let himself into the apartment, into the warmth and the smell of pot roast and the news on the radio and from the bathroom, water splashing. Ah, Cookie must be giving Paul his bath. He didn't call out, just walked into the kitchen and waited for Dot to turn from the stove. She must have been lost in her own thoughts, because when she turned and saw him standing there, she gave a start and a little scream. ''God, you scared me. Couldn't you say hello or something?''

''Sorry.''

''What happened? You don't look so hot. And you're very late.''

''So I won't be late anymore because tonight, I quit!''

''Excuse me?'' Dorothy said, her mouth dropping open, the wooden spoon dripping gravy onto the floor.

''You heard right! He pushed me too hard this time. I had to!''

''I don't believe what I'm hearing. In the middle of winter, with the children needing new coats and outgrowing their galoshes every five minutes, *now* you pick to quit your job?''

"Actually, for your information, he fired me. And I said, 'Like hell, I quit.' "

"Jonah!" she said, her lip quivering a little, the tears already beginning to slip down her cheeks. How he hated it when a woman cried . . . he never knew *what* to do. So he just kept talking.

"It was a matter of principle. He demanded that I shut my mouth . . . in America, yet. He had the nerve to command me to keep quiet—out of loyalty, he said! I'll tell you exactly what I said to him: my loyalty cannot be bought with money, not even by my wife's rich brother."

"You couldn't have been a little more tactful . . . for the sake of the children, if not for me? You know Jack."

"You know *me*, Dorothy. No one's going to censor me! Shut me up! Make me behave in a particular way! The United States government told me I couldn't fight in Spain, so I went to Sweden and from *there* to Spain! Nobody could keep me out. Nobody could stop *me* from doing what was right!"

"I'm tired of hearing the same old story! Spain was a long time ago. Now is now and we have three small children to clothe and feed. How about doing what's right by *us*? What makes you think you can sacrifice your family for your principles?"

Jonah stared at his wife. Going to Spain to fight for freedom wasn't just a story, it was the essence of what he believed in. And she found it *boring*?

He closed his eyes, fought against the hurt, took a deep breath, and said quietly, "I always thought you admired me for my principles."

Whenever she went to meetings with him, she hung on his every word; and when anyone asked her, "Dot, what do you think?" she always said, "I'm behind Jonah, one hundred percent."

He turned away. Let him go be with his children who loved him, and wait for her to cool down.

"Don't you *dare* leave this room!"

"How do you talk to me like that? I don't need this aggravation, Dorothy. I need a little understanding. I need for you to stand behind me and not always take your brother's side."

"I don't always take my brother's side. And you want to talk about understanding? Okay. How about trying to understand *me* for a change? The way I feel about Jack is not the usual thing. How many times do I have to tell you? Jack protected me and my sister. My father was a brute. He wouldn't let us do anything or go anywhere . . . he wouldn't even let us think! Jack's always taken care of me!''

"You see? That's what I'm talking about! Your brother, Jack, can do no wrong!''

"Don't do this, Jo. Don't make me choose. It's two different things, my feelings for you and my feelings for Jack."

"I don't think you have feelings for me anymore, Dorothy. If you did, you'd be on my side, no question.''

Dorothy squared off, hands on hips, her eyes narrowed, facing him, angry. "Never! You'll never find me going blindly on anyone's side, no questions asked! That's not the way I am. And if you wanted someone like that, why did you marry me?''

He was bound to lose. Her tongue was faster than his. She had an answer for everything, and when it came to changing the subject, she was the world champion. Like now.

"We're not talking why I married you, Dorothy,'' he said, keeping himself calm. One meshuggener at a time was enough. "We're talking why I had to quit my job. I quit my job because your brother is an arrogant, selfish son of a bitch who's lorded it over me ever since I took his job; who's never let me forget for one minute that I'm only there by the good grace of the Lord God Jack Strauss; and above all, that I'm not allowed to stand up like any man and speak my mind!''

There was a moment of silence. Then Dorothy took in a deep breath and expelled it noisily. "I understand why you thought you had to quit. I'm only saying, how are we going to live? Can you answer me that? Can you?''

Her very quiet voice and the little lift of her chin and the condescending way she looked down her nose at him reminded him so much of Jack, he wanted to smack her.

"You think so highly of your brother Jack. Well, I could tell you a thing or two about your wonderful brother that would change your mind, all right!'' He gave a little laugh.

Dorothy made a disgusted face and turned her head from him. "You're just saying that! You don't know anything!''

"Oh, yeah? Well, it just so happens, you're wrong. I know plenty!''

They stood, glaring at each other, both of them breathing hard, as if they had been wrestling.

"Dammit, Jo, you'd better not be making this up just to turn me against him!''

"I don't make things up. I'm telling you, he's not the man you think he is . . . No, no, don't start up again. A sister could be mistaken about her brother—especially if he protected her when she was young and helpless. I'm not stupid, Dorothy. I have a little imagination. Give me a little credit. But, he does things in business . . . things that are not on the up-and-up.

"Believe me, Dorothy, I could get even. I could tell the building inspectors enough to get him into hot water. I'm telling you! The things that go on at that job, you shouldn't know from it! Substandard materials. Shoddy workmanship. Payoffs galore! It's unbelievable, what he gets away with! He's typical of what's wrong with this system—he doesn't give a damn about anyone or anything except his profit margin!"

Stubbornly, her face flushing, Dorothy said, "He doesn't know about it. That I know. He would never allow it." Jonah's answer was a laugh. "Dammit, Jo, you should tell him! He'd thank you! He doesn't want dangerous buildings. No? Of course, you'd think no. You just don't want to believe anything good about Jack! And don't keep shaking your head at me. If I'm wrong, prove it. Tell him."

"*You* tell him," he told her. "Go ahead, call him up. You think he'll tell you the truth? Okay, call him and ask. Ask him about the concrete. Yeah, that's right. Just say, 'Hello, Jack? I hear you buy concrete from DeLaurio Brothers that isn't up to code.' Go on, I dare you. See what he says."

That got her. He watched the question come into her eyes, watched the question change to doubt. "It can't be true," she said, almost to herself. "It can't be."

He couldn't resist. "Well, it is. Oh, hell, I know you'd rather believe him than me, any day! If it's a choice between me and your brother, it's always him. Well, this time I've got the goods on him . . . and what do you think about that?"

"I think you don't know what you're talking about! You're jealous . . . of our closeness and of his success. You can't stand that he has everything. You always try to belittle him. Well, I'm sick of it! I've had it!"

Before he could utter a single word, she had thrown the cooking spoon halfway across the kitchen, and went running out. A minute later, as he was thinking maybe he'd said a little too much and ought to go after her, make up with her, the front door slammed so hard it shook the walls.

He ran out to the stairwell, calling her name, but it was too late. She was gone.

* * *

As soon as she slammed the door behind her, she was sorry she'd run out so fast. There was an icy draft blowing through the stairwell and she remembered the sidewalks were deep in slush and she hadn't stopped to put on boots.

By the time she took six steps, she could feel the icy wet seeping in through the thin soles of her shoes. The courtyard was deserted—of course, it was—only an idiot or an angry wife would come out on a bitter night like this. She hurried along the pathway, huddling into her coat. Out on the street, it was pitch-dark except for the pools of light from the streetlamps.

Damn him and his principles! What were they going to do now? Where was he going to find work? Every place nowadays, they insisted you sign a loyalty oath. He'd never stand still for it! He was so stubborn; he wouldn't bend for anything. The children! How would they live now? Her job didn't pay enough to keep them in food and pay the rent.

Why in God's name had she stuck by Jo through all his *narrishkeit*? What good had it done? She'd been taught that a good woman sticks by her man through thick and thin. But nobody ever told her her man might be so narrow and stubborn. Marriage was supposed to mean security; why didn't they warn her it could turn into a trap? And she could never complain to anyone. How could you find fault with a man who held such lofty ideals? He was ready to take care of all humanity but never mind his wife. No wonder she had fallen for Frank! She was a neglected wife!

She slopped through the slush, sick at heart, hardly noticing which way she went. But Frank was gone; it was two weeks and not a word. Every time she thought about it, she felt a constriction in her chest. It was over. It must be. And that meant she no longer had a way out. She was going to have to deal with what she had, and what she had was a husband with unpopular politics, no job, and a talent for getting himself into hot water.

She'd call Jack. She'd get him to take Jonah back. She'd explain how Jonah was under a lot of pressure and he didn't really mean what he said. But no. She'd already done that, twice. This time, no chance. Jack always said, "Three strikes and you're out." And Jack was as straight as they come. He might not always be completely diplomatic, but you always knew exactly where he stood.

So, how could it be true? How could her brother, whom she trusted with her life, really be a heartless bastard who would build something that might collapse? He would never cheat on something so important. He would never buy bad concrete just to save a few lousy dollars!

Let her try to be fair. Her husband wasn't a heartless bastard, either. Nor was he a liar. It must be he was blinded by his rage. Or wait a minute. Maybe he just didn't understand something he saw or heard. Or maybe he was exaggerating. But that wasn't like Jo; stubborn, yes, stupid, no.

But Jack couldn't! He couldn't do such a horrible thing. He had principles, too, even though he didn't sound off about them all the time, like Jo. But he was a decent human being. So he didn't think too much about the underclass; he gave to charity. Not only that, but he was always the one who saved her so many times—from fresh boys, from neighborhood bullies, from their father.

Home should have been a safe haven, but it wasn't, not with Pa! He was always in a rage. It could be anything, anything at all, that set him off. The one day she was remembering, they weren't doing anything wrong, they were studying together at the kitchen table, and he hollered, "Stop making so much noise! The way you keep pushing those chairs around, you could drive a person crazy."

And Yetta, always fearless, tossed her head and said, "You *are* crazy."

He jumped to his feet, his face purple, and began to whip off his belt. Dot was crying, "No, Pa, no. She didn't mean it," but naturally he wasn't paying any attention to anything *she* said. He just kept closing in on Yetta, like doom.

And suddenly there was Jack, standing right in front of Pa, nose to nose. Pa gave him a shove, and growled, "Out of my way." His usual way. But this time, Jack shoved him back so hard that Pa tripped backward and fell to the floor. Jack had knocked him down! She'd never forget it. Pa looked stunned. She and her sister clung to each other, terrified. How old could they have been? Twelve? Jack wasn't more than sixteen, if that. He'd taken an awful chance.

But their father did not leap to his feet and go after Jack. He didn't move! And Jack, his adolescent voice cracking, looked down, his hands clenched into fists, and said, "There'll be no more whippings of girls in *this* house. Not as long as I live. Period. *Fartig*. Finished." Pa muttered something or other, but he didn't argue, he just picked himself up and went back to his chair and his newspaper, as if nothing had ever happened. And that was the last time he had so much as threatened to raise a hand to either of them.

So it was hard for her to believe Jack would be so callous about people's lives. She turned the corner and stepped right into a puddle. Ow! Now that whole foot was soaking wet. And the bitter wind kept blowing right into her face.

Her thoughts kept skittering around, like her feet on the icy sidewalk. It wasn't that she thought Jack was perfect, like Jonah was always saying. Nobody was perfect. Take Jo himself. If you butted up against one of his certainties, you could talk yourself blue in the face, he wouldn't budge. He built himself a wall of principles and sat behind it, certain of his rightness. To him, it was truth. To her, it was a barricade, shutting out anything that might make him change his mind.

She wasn't being fair. He was the one under the gun. She knew that. But how could she be fair when he was treating her so badly, when he was just going his own way with no thought to anyone else? How could she be fair, when they had so little between them anymore? If only . . . but forget it. Sex was the furthest thing from his mind. As for her, she wasn't supposed to want it or need it. But she did. She missed it, oh, God, how she missed it. But what could she do? What could she do about anything?

Maybe she should leave him, make a new start. But if she hadn't been ready to leave him all the times Frank begged her to, she was never going to. The children were still so little . . . she just had to try harder.

She had to make herself think straight. She had to figure this out! If she let Jonah report Jack to the authorities, Jack might be ruined. He could lose the business, he could land in jail. My God, he could go to prison! He had three little daughters to take care of. And Sylvia! Sylvia could never go out to work! What could she do? What would become of them all?

If she called Jack now from the candy store on the next corner, she could warn him. She could tell him that Jo was going to report him. Oh, God, he'd be furious. But what could he *do* to Jo? Fire him? Get angry? Hate him? So what else was new? He'd never do anything *really* bad to Jo because if he did, it would affect her, too.

So, really, if she called him, it wouldn't change anything.

"But what if he's guilty?" she said out loud. She stopped. What was she thinking? This was her brother, Jack, she was talking about. She did remember that Jack was constantly complaining about unnecessary regulations, *kvetching* that a man couldn't make a decent profit, the way things were going. But did that prove anything? No. Yes. Maybe. Oh, God! No matter what she did, she was going to be disloyal to one of them.

There, right in front of her, was the candy store, still lighted, and inside, a telephone. She had a nickle in her pocket. She knew his phone number. What she didn't know was what she should do.

€€

Chapter Eleven

Wednesday, March 12, 1952 Dorothy's little kitchen was filled with cigarette smoke, and when Anna began to cough, Dot ran to open the window. "Lean out," she said. "Try a little *fresh* air in your lungs, for a change!"

Anna laughed, still coughing, and laughing and coughing together, shook her head no. "It isn't the cigarettes! I'm allergic to the Supreme Court, that's all. Do you believe it?" She made a face. "We've lived peacefully, concerned only for the rights of the underclass, raising our children to also work for the equality of every man, loving this country—and now, we don't have rights! Just because we didn't take out citizenship papers, now we can be deported!"

"Only Communists," Lillian Lubliner put in. "Remember that. It's okay if you're Ku Klux Klan; it's okay if you're a Nazi. But Reds are *dangerous*. Only we 'advocate the violent overthrow of the government of the United States of America.' " Her voice mocked all the radio commentators they'd been listening to for the past two days.

"Aaron says he's in *big* trouble. He's a member, he's head of a few committees, he's signed a dozen petitions. And Aaron's not a citizen. He came here at age ten! Who knew you had to go make yourself a citizen to be treated like a human being in this country? And they can hold any Communist without bail, how about *that* one? Land of the free, huh? Sure! Tell me another!"

Dot said, "Come on. We all know why the judges upheld that stupid decision. They want to get rid of all progressives. And then they can do as they damn please without anybody criticizing! You think we're not worried? You think Jo's not in danger?"

"But Jo left the Party," Lil said, helping herself to another glass of red wine. "They can't get him now."

"Oh, yes, they can!" Dot said. She put the window back down. It was chilly out there, with a high wind whistling through the courtyard. Where was spring? "It was right in the *Times*, the front page. 'Aliens can be deported if they've *ever* been a member of the Communist party,' " she said in a tone that announced she was quoting. "And, in case you've forgotten, up until a month ago, Jo Golodny was a card-carrying member. Oh, they can get him if they want to."

"The question is: do they want to?"

"All I know is, suddenly the Katzenjammer Kids are up here every hour on the hour, knocking on my door. Those mean little goyish eyes!" She laughed. " 'Good morning, Mrs. Golodny. Is your husband at home?' " she mimicked. "Do they think they're going to catch me off-guard, I'm going to go get him and bring him to them?"

Anna laughed and said, "They think we're as stupid as they are!"

"I tell them my husband's not home, he's out at work. And all the time, they're trying to see around me, maybe Jo's hiding behind a chair! Then I say, 'You have no business here!' and I slam the door right in their faces!"

"Good for you, Dot!"

"You have to stand up to those schlemiels!"

Dot smiled, then frowned. "Well, it frightens the children. I try to make light of it, but you know kids, they have a sixth sense about these things. They've been so quiet lately—and you *know* something's wrong when my Irwin is quiet! And the baby's started wetting the bed again!" She threw up her hands. "Thank God for Cookie. It's like having another woman in the house!" Her friends murmured their assent and nodded. "Can you believe, she gets up every night to pick up Paul and take him to the potty."

"Everyone in the Coops," Anna said, "knows how responsible Cookie is. You're so lucky."

"Don't I know it!" Dorothy turned away, ducking into the fridge. "You boys need ice?" she yelled, and from the living room came a bellow: "Yes!" At which, Dorothy struck a pose, tossing her head, and yelled back, "Then come on in and get it!"

This made both Lil and Anna laugh, but a moment later, Anna said, "It's all right, I'll take it to them."

Typical, Dorothy thought with some asperity. "If there's a man around," she said to Lil as soon as Anna left the kitchen, "she's fetching and bringing and doing and carrying: a regular little handmaiden."

"She must feel she has to, for Ben's sake. *You* know . . ." And Lil rolled her large dark eyes meaningfully.

"No, I *don't* know. What?"

"She had something going with Frank."

Dorothy was busy laying out cold cuts on a platter. For a split second, she stood so still she might have stopped breathing. And then, she continued putting down the neat slices, very carefully fanning them out in an even pattern. "Frank who?" she said.

"Frank who! Come off it, Dot! What Frank lived here and had every woman in the place panting after him. But Anna did something about it. Bold as brass, I hear. Just walked up to him and said, 'How about it?' Well, no big surprise. She had a rep from *before* she married Ben, you know."

"No, I didn't know." The salami was down, now the corned beef, slice by slice. Very, very carefully.

"Well, she's always been known as a hot num— And Aaron says if they raise the phone bills much higher, none of the working class will be able to afford to have one! An increase of less than one cent a day, my foot!"

Startled at the sudden change of topic, Dot looked up. Oh. Of course. Anna had just come back into the kitchen. She let out a little silent sigh.

"The president of the phone company says telephone service is a bargain," she answered. "And he wouldn't *lie* to us, would he?" They all laughed.

"Say, Dot," Anna said, snitching a slice of tongue from the platter, "what does Jo think about Frank Green flying the Coop?" She laughed at her own pun.

"Oh, Jonah!" Dot said. "He and Frank were good friends. He quit the Party over it. They said, 'Don't talk to Frank Green,' and he said, 'Like fun, I quit!'"

"I didn't exactly say, 'like fun.'" Jonah came into the kitchen, bearing an empty wine bottle. "But I can't repeat what

I did say, not in front of ladies. Dot, where's the other bottle of wine?''

"Right where you put it, not half an hour ago."

"So you don't think he was turning people in?" That was Lillian.

"No, I don't. Now wait a minute, Dorothy. I know how you feel about that." He addressed the other two women. "Dot thinks he's guilty as sin. She says she never trusted him, not from the first day she met him."

"That's right. He was just a little too slick for me, a little too cocky."

Lillian laughed. "Yeah, that's what I heard . . . he was more than a little . . . *cocky*, if you get my meaning."

Dorothy waved off her words. "He was always too ready with exactly the right speech . . . I don't know. Superficial, that's how he struck me. It doesn't surprise me a bit to find out he was informing on us."

"Wait a minute, Dot," Jonah said, scowling a little. "I know a phoney when I meet one, and Frank was no phoney, believe me."

Dorothy rearranged the platter of cold cuts with nervous fingers. "Jonah's determined to blame my brother, Jack, for our FBI visitors. But if you listen to Jo, my brother, Jack, put Batista back in power, started the Second World War, *and* raised the telephone rates!''

She waited while her friends laughed, and then said to her husband, "Jo, be reasonable. Jack talks big. He might give you a hard time—well he did, didn't he?—but he'd never, never, never do anything that would bring harm to me and the children."

"Don't make me laugh, Dorothy. Jack Strauss would walk over his grandmother to protect himself!"

Dorothy lifted the heavy tray of meats and smiled, although her voice was a bit tight. "You know what Jonah tells me? Jonah tells me I'm not allowed to talk to my own brother. Or his wife. Or his children, my nieces. The kids can't talk to their cousins, or their aunt and uncle. He forbids it . . . *forbids*. Can you beat that?''

Jonah turned to the other two women. "I ask you, ladies, when a man calls you a traitor and all of a sudden the FBI is upstairs instead of staying down in the street, and they're coming after you five times a day . . . my wife and children should give him hugs and kisses? Come on!"

Dorothy said, "But these two FBI schnooks know more about you than Jack could have told them. You go to the library every Thursday. And this last Thursday, they're there, waiting for you. Jack Strauss knows your library habits?"

"Enough, Dot," Jonah said. "I'm looking at that plate of food and it's making me hungry." From the living room came a male voice: "Did I hear the word *food*? I hope?"

"I can take a hint," Dorothy said, and laughed gaily, pushing by her husband.

Not another word was said about it until shortly after eleven o'clock, when their guests left. Dorothy shut the door, locked it, and leaned back against it.

"All right, Jonah," she said, "let's just quit saying bad things about my brother."

His face was grim. "On my mother's grave, Dorothy, I believe Jack Strauss sicced the FBI on me. And, the way things are these days, it could mean . . . *jail*. You know that." He tried a smile and held out his arms. "Please. I don't say it to hurt you. But Jack never liked me, *or* my politics. On the other hand, Frank was always my friend."

Dorothy regarded her husband. "Don't be so sure," she murmured, and then shook her head. "Isn't it possible Frank was an infiltrator, here to spy on us? It wouldn't be the first time that's happened."

Stubbornly, Jonah shook his head. "Not Frank. I just can't believe it."

Dorothy laughed a little and went to him, putting her arms around him. He was so down; it was the least she could do. "It's hard, I know. But the fact remains, he left . . . and without a word to anyone." Under her hands, she felt his whole body sag a little. "Jo? What's wrong?"

He hugged her briefly, bent and placed a kiss on her cheek. "I have something to tell you and it's very hard."

"Jo?" There was a note of alarm now. "What's wrong?" She pulled back so she could look into his eyes.

"I'm about to do the same thing Frank did. Leave, without a word to anyone."

"What are you talking about?"

"Disappearing from sight."

"Don't be ridiculous! There's no need for that."

"It'll be all right. There's a job waiting for me, and I'll send for you and the children as soon as I can."

"What are you saying: *send for*! Where do you think you're going?"

"I *know* where I'm going. No, I can't tell you. I don't want you to have to lie. When they come around again, you only have to tell them the truth. You don't know where I am. Period." He reached out for her. "Don't look like that, Dorothy!" He put an arm around her waist and gave her another kiss. "I'm telling you, I'll be fine. I've been through worse. It'll only be for a little while and then we'll all be together again."

"You really *mean* it, then? You really intend to leave me here, alone, with three little kids to take care of, not even knowing where you are, if you're alive or dead or what?"

"This is the only way right now," he said. "Hey, don't worry. You know the Coops; everyone will look out for you. I'll send money. But I have to do it. Here, I'm not safe. Sooner or later, Dot, they'll stop playing games with me and just arrest me. And then it'll be too late! There's no justice in this country anymore, not for anyone on the Left. I don't want to argue with you, not my last night home."

"Last night? What are you saying? You mean . . . *now*? To-night?"

"Six o'clock in the morning, someone's coming to take me to the train."

"Dammit, Jo! Why didn't you tell me? Why did you wait till the last minute? What am I supposed to *do*?"

"Do? What do you mean? I already told you. When the FBI comes the next time, you'll tell them I'm gone, you don't know where I am. And then, when I can, you'll get word from me and you'll pack up and bring the children. In the meantime, you'll stay here and live a normal life."

"Live a normal life! What are you, crazy? What's *normal* about any of this—" She had to stop talking as tears filled her eyes and began to roll down her cheeks. "You know what you're doing, Jo? You're running away." She did not add "again," although she wanted to. "You used to be a fighter. What's happened to you?"

His eyes clouded with anger. "I'm *not* running away. Don't ever tell me I'm running away! I'm not like that. We spent my whole childhood chasing after my father. His answer to every problem was to get out of town! It could be anything. A business failure—and there were a lot of those—he had no head for business. An argument . . . could be over politics, could be with my mother about how they should spend money, could be *any-*

thing. Once, he was running from a girlfriend who stood outside our house for weeks, just standing there, her hands folded in front of her, looking and looking. It must have been Greensboro, North Carolina, because it was after Philadelphia and before Atlanta.''

His voice became more and more agitated and he began to pace in front of her. "Run. Run. That's all he knew how to do, my father! I swore I'd never do this to my wife and children, swore a solemn oath! How could you say such a thing to me? You know my background! You know I'd never do this if I didn't have to!'' He stopped in front of her, thrusting his face close to hers.

But you've already done it, Dorothy thought. We've already run from Washington. But she held her tongue. When Jo started talking about his childhood, she knew he was already too emotional to listen to reason. He was going to do it—it didn't matter how it affected them—he was going to leave and she was trapped. A feeling of futility bore down on her and she bent her head, sobbing.

Jonah wrapped his arms more tightly around her and held her. "Come, sweetheart, come to bed.''

She couldn't remember the last time they had made love. And it was sweet. He was tender, so slow with his loving. For a moment, after he had climaxed and still held on to her, saying, "I don't want to leave you, Dot. I love you and the children more than anything,'' she had such a feeling of shame for cheating with Frank. No, wait, worse than that—for having gone to Frank so eagerly. All that year and a half. Yes, Dorothy, she told herself, face it. You've been unfaithful to your husband without a smidgin of remorse.

And here, Jo was going away, and Frank was already gone, and God only knew when she would see either of them again! And for shame, that she should be in her marriage bed with her husband thinking of another man! Hadn't she read somewhere that infidelity in the heart was worse than the act itself?

She was beginning to sweat. She longed to free herself from Jonah's tight, clinging embrace. But she couldn't! It would be a terrible thing to do to him, the night he was leaving. So she lay there in the bed for what felt like hours, watching the shadows on the walls, waiting until his body relaxed totally and he began to snore and she knew he was fast asleep.

He was wrapped all around her, his legs tangled in hers. Gently, she extricated herself, hoping she wouldn't wake him.

He'd be sure to insist that she stay with him, this night above all others. But sleep would not come to her.

She crept out of the bed, reaching over to the chair where she always left her warm robe. Belting it around her waist, she stood for a moment, gazing down at her sleeping husband. Look at him! So peaceful. It never occurred to him that he might be putting a hardship on them. In just a few hours, he would be gone to who knew where. And he hadn't even discussed it with her. Who did he think she was, anyway? Mrs. Nobody? What was she, his slave, that he could leave and send for her when he felt like it and expect her to jump at his command? Goddamn him and his politics! His precious principles! They took first place over everything and everybody else in the world!

She turned away, unwilling to give full vent to this burst of rage. Not on his last night. She wished she could wake him and tell him what she was thinking and feeling. But what good would it do? If Jonah Golodny decided that the thing he had to do was to go underground and leave them behind, there was no way on this earth to change his mind. It didn't matter who suffered.

Listening again, to make sure he was really asleep, Dot tiptoed across the room to the big bureau. Very quietly, she slid open her underwear drawer and, very quietly, eased her hand in under the slips and the panties, under the drawer lining, until her fingers touched the now dog-eared envelope. She pulled it out and put it into the big pocket of the robe, still holding on to it, in case it crinkled.

She went first to the kitchen and lit the fire under the kettle. A nice cup of tea, that's what she needed. A nice cup of tea and, if life was fair, her sister, Yetta. Yetta would know what to do. Yetta always knew what to think and feel; and even if she didn't, she'd make up her mind, anyway. Yetta always used to say, "I don't care *what* happens, good or bad; I just can't stand the suspense." But Yetta was in Yugoslavia; at least, that's where her last letter had come from.

When the tea was ready, she took it and stood, looking out the window into the darkness. God, look at the stars. Where else in this city could you look outside at night and see stars? Even a small slice of moon, sitting there above the rooftops.

She shivered suddenly. It was the middle of the night, cold and dark. What was she doing, admiring the night sky? She had things to think about. Where was Jo going? Chicago, maybe, or Los Angeles. She wouldn't mind Los Angeles; think of the sunshine and the palm trees! It could be a good life, in California.

Even Chicago . . . not so bad. Windy, cold, but they said it was an exciting city. And come to think of it, she loved city life. Give her the lights and the traffic and all the people and the tumult! Too many palm trees and no close neighbors and she'd go bananas! She'd never been anywhere, not really, except for D.C.—and that was Yetta's idea. It might be nice, settling into a new city.

She took her tea and settled into a corner of the sofa, sipping at it, holding the cup with both hands, enjoying the warmth. The letter in her robe pocket, she knew by heart. She had read it over and over again, since it arrived weeks ago, alternating between elation and a cold despair.

It was dated January 6, from Sheboygan, Wisconsin; but she'd lived in the Coops long enough to know any postmark was meaningless. It could have passed through a dozen different hands before it was actually mailed. The envelope was printed in block letters, but the minute she saw it, she knew. She *knew*.

"My darling," the letter said. "My heart has been longing for you, especially since I was forced to leave without saying anything to you. Have you missed me? I cannot describe how many times a day—how many times a night—I think of you and I feel so lonely and miserable . . ."

She closed her eyes in pain, letting the tears roll out and down her face and letting a little whimper escape her lips. Why did she torture herself, remembering it, repeating it to herself so many times? She took a gulp of the lukewarm tea and forced herself not to think about the letter and the emotion it brought out. The first time she read it, she had wanted only to pack a bag and go to him. He still loved her!

But she knew better. He could be lying. These days, *anyone* could turn out to be your enemy. Didn't she just find out tonight he'd been carrying on with Anna Dauber, too? Maybe even at the same time! She'd have to be some kind of idiot to trust anything he said, particularly at such a distance.

But even that thought made her heart lift. What if they landed in the same city with him? What if she somehow let him know? It was no use pretending. The letter haunted her, other women or no . . . traitor or no. And the last words on the page were exactly the same as Jonah's, this evening. That's what got her— exactly the same words, from both of them. "When it's safe, I'll send for you and the children."

Both leaving, both wanting to send for her. Dear God, what was she going to do?

For a brief moment, she had a picture in her head, of her and Frank, hand in hand, walking down a street in Sheboygan, Wisconsin, laughing, talking, happy. Of course, she'd never been in Wisconsin, but she imagined the streets in Sheboygan must be lined with big old trees and Victorian houses set back from the sidewalk by large lawns like squares of green velvet. She and Frank, just the two of them, in love.

What a foolish dream! She wasn't twenty years old anymore. She was a married woman with three little kids. And in her world, when you got married, you stayed married, especially if your husband was a good man. She could just imagine Ma's reaction if she left Jonah for another man. "Did he hit you?" Ma would demand. "Did he get drunk? Did he gamble? Did he stay out late with his friends? Did he, God forbid, have other women?" And the answer would be no, no, no, no. And no.

Her one complaint, that he was no longer so romantic . . . so, what else was new in this world? What did she think she was doing, anyway, behaving like a giddy girl instead of a middle-aged matron? No, she had promised her loyalty to Jonah and with Jonah she would stay. *Fartig*, finished, the end. The end.

❧❧

Chapter Twelve

Monday, August 18, 1952   Sylvia paused at the last landing, out of breath. She didn't want to go into Dorothy's apartment, panting like an old dog. God knows she was feeling like one! How in the world did they do it, the women who lived here in the Coops? To do this every day, maybe ten times a day! Four flights times ten, schlepping groceries, carrying a baby, dragging a cranky child by the hand . . . Oy! She didn't even want to think about it.

Okay, time to get moving. Up she went, and there was Dot, standing by her open door, waiting for her. "I know, I know," Dot said, smiling, "if these people are smart enough to plan a revolution, how come they forgot to put in elevators?" She laughed.

"When I get my breath back, I'll laugh, also." When she reached the top and had followed her sister-in-law into the apartment, she said, "So. Let me look at you. Because of those two nudniks, I haven't seen you in ages. You look good. But thin. I guess climbing these stairs keeps the weight off."

"If it was only the stairs! Never mind, I'll tell you over a glass of iced tea. Come."

Sylvia was curious. She'd been calling Dot at least once a week since the big blowup, making sure everything was all right, financially speaking, and just keeping in touch. But the last time they spoke, Dot had insisted they get together.

So here she was, without a word to Jack. Those two idiots, Jack and Jonah both, forbidding their families to speak to each other! Stupid! If they thought for one minute that she and Dot were going to pay any attention to such *narrishkeit*, well, obviously they didn't know who they were dealing with!

Of course, it was impossible to be openly defiant; that would get them nowhere and it might make it worse. But they could still talk to each other. And one of these days, she'd get Jack in the right mood and it would all be over and the kids could play together again.

They gave each other a nice big hug, and when they let go, Sylvia saw Dot brush away a tear.

"Men!" she said, and Dorothy said, "I second the motion!" What more was there to say? They sat down at the round table, where they could schmooze over tea and cake in comfort.

"I hate having to sneak around this way. It's ridiculous."

"So what else is new when you're dealing with men? You can't reason with them."

"You're telling me! Jack told my girls that Jonah was a traitor. 'We're never going to have anything to do with them again,' he told them."

"Same here. Almost the same words." They looked at each other in complete understanding.

"And it only gets worse," Sylvia said. She felt a little guilty, telling a tale on her husband. But never mind, he was also Dot's brother. "I said to Jack the other night, 'Dorothy called. Cookie cries all the time. She misses her cousin Deena.' I thought maybe he'd have a little *rachmones*, a little pity for the child. After all, Deena's his darling and he has a soft spot for Cookie. And you know what he said? He said, 'You mean you *talked* to Dorothy? You didn't hang up on her?'

"I said, 'Jack, Jack, your own sister!' And then he said,

'Okay, Sylvia, tell you what. When my own sister wises up and leaves that Commie, *then* we'll be on speaking terms.' I'm sorry, Dot, but that's what he said.''

"He always *was* stubborn, like a mule. Like my father." Dot laughed a little. "Would he hate to hear me say he's like Pa! But it's the children I feel awful about. Somehow we're going to handle this in our own way. But the kids . . . what do they understand about men's principles? I have two little ones asking me why, and all I can say is, 'Because your father said so.' Is that an answer?"

"What can I tell you?" Sylvia said, throwing out her hands. "Jack's adamant. If Jonah would only apologize . . ."

"Apologize!"

"Just a thought. Look, Dot. Whatever really happened, this isn't the way to fix it, by pretending you've all sunk to the bottom of the sea. I don't really understand how he can do this. My God, you're his sister. This is *family* we're talking about. Our *loved ones* he's ready to discard like an old pair of shoes!"

"It's not only Jack. The whole country's gone crazy. All I know is, my husband's been forced to go into hiding. A man who never did a bad thing to anyone in his whole life!"

"Hiding! Who from?"

"Remember, at Hanukkah, I told you about the McCarren Act?"

Sylvia stared at her sister-in-law. "I remember. But I can't imagine Jo, of all people, being considered such a danger that they have to throw him out of the country!"

"They don't care. All it takes is someone accuses him, somebody makes up a story about him, and boom! He's a spy. You know how it is these days! None of it makes sense. People's lives are ruined on the basis of a rumor!" She stopped, took in a deep breath. "So now he's gone. He's even changed his name. I don't even know where he is!"

"Poor Dot! What a terrible world we're living in!" Sylvia reached out and took the other's hand.

Dorothy's eyes misted over. "You said it. I'll never forget it. Jo left just at dawn—just like in the movies. I'm telling you, sometimes I can't believe this is really happening—and he went in to the children and kissed each one good-bye. It was so sweet, the way he did it. They were so sound asleep, they didn't even stir. They never even knew he was gone until the next morning when they woke up."

"When did this all happen?"

"Five months ago."

"Five months! And you never said a word until now! I wish—never mind. What made him think he had to hide, all of a sudden?"

There was a strange little moment of total silence. And then Dorothy stood up, saying she'd make some more coffee, and walked over to the stove. With her back to Sylvia, she said, "Right after he and Jack had their big fight, suddenly the FBI was coming to the door, five times a day, every day, asking for him . . ." And then she turned. "I won't bore you with the details."

"But Dorothy, you can't think it was Jack!"

"Of course not! Of course not!" There was a small pause. "You didn't repeat our conversation to Jack, did you? No, no, what am I saying? Of course you didn't."

"Oh, Dot! I'm positive I didn't! We didn't talk about you at all, after you left that night. He had something else on his mind. But, let me think, did I say *anything* that might have set him off? No, no, I didn't! I swear to you, Dot! Oh, Lord, I'm going to feel guilty every minute of my life until I recall every word I said that night!"

"No, no, don't do that. That's silly. And anyway, he's gone already, so what's the use?"

There was an awkward silence, which Sylvia felt she must break. "So," she said, "how are you managing, all alone with three little ones? Do you need anything?"

"Don't worry. I have my job at the nursery and we have plenty of friends. I keep telling you, we all take care of one another. That's the best thing about living here . . . even without elevators!"

"Best! Some best, with the FBI after you and people forced to disappear and change their names! I can't think of any political idea worth all this suffering! This country has been very good to immigrants, especially the Jews, Dorothy—and you people want to destroy it!"

"Don't say that to me, Sylvia Strauss! Nobody wants to destroy the country; we just want it good for *everyone*, not only the rich and powerful! Who do you think dreamed up Social Security? Where do you think all the ideas in the New Deal came from? The Communists!"

"Never mind the fancy talk, Dorothy Golodny! The Communist party advocates the violent overthrow of the United States government. Everybody knows that!"

"Oh, Sylvia, shame on you, repeating what you've heard, by rote. Look at me: am I violent?"

"Of course not. I'm sorry, Dot. I'm talking like a fool. For this, I schlepped myself all the way up to the Bronx on the subway?" She allowed herself to laugh a little, to show Dot she hadn't lost her sense of humor. "Look. What do you need? Tell me. Food? Money? A job? What? Tell me."

"No, nothing. Thank you, Sylvia. You've always been a good friend to me. No . . ." She stopped, drew in breath, let it out in a long drawn-out sigh. "Oh, God, Sylvia, I'm so mixed up. Look." She reached into her apron pocket and pulled out a crumpled envelope. "From Jo. It came yesterday. He's working on a dairy farm. He's okay, he's working hard, he'll be sending for us in a couple of months or so.

"Here's what he says . . ." She scanned the pages filled with cramped handwriting and then read: " 'Right now, I'm living in an attic room in the farmhouse. Attic room sounds terrible, no? But it's not. It's a large room with big dormer windows and when I wake in the morning, I see the sun rising behind the mountains . . . Pepe is still a great guy, but he's changed since Spain. He was skinny then; now he's got a big belly and he's very proud of it, pats it all the time and says, "This is a great country, Jo. Back in my father's village, no man could ever get fat. Life was too hard." '

" 'Believe me,' he goes on, 'life is not too hard for Pepe Ronda these days. He has the largest dairy farm in this part of the country. I'm sorry I can't tell you exactly where I am. But you'll see it soon . . .' " She made a little face.

"What?" Sylvia asked.

"Nothing . . . He goes on a bit about how many cows, how much fancy milking equipment, how many acres. You'd be bored, Sylvia."

Here, Dorothy looked up. "I get the feeling Jo's disappointed. He doesn't come right out and say so, but I can tell. See, he and Pepe met during the Spanish Civil War. Pepe's American, but he was visiting his home village in Spain when the war exploded around him and decided to stay on and fight against the Fascists. He couldn't get over the Lincoln Brigade. He couldn't get over Jo, born in Russia, living in America, coming to fight for Spaniards' freedom. He always told Jo, anytime he needed anything, he had only to call on Pepe Ronda and name it.

"So, Jo called him and said he needed a job and Pepe said

sure thing, come right away. I guess Jo had in his head that they'd just pick up where they left off in 1938. I guess he thought Pepe was a regular farmer and they'd work together, side by side, the way they fought together. Instead, he finds a rich man, a boss, running a big business that happens to be a dairy farm. And Jo is his hired hand, that's what it amounts to.

"Look, Jo has never run away from hard work; I don't think that's what bothers him. But he says here: 'Pepe's wife, you wouldn't believe. It's like she's out of the last century. His word is law, to her and to their four little boys. And to all of us farmhands, too. I call him Tzar Pepe the Terrible.'

"You see what I'm talking about, Syl? But then he goes on to say how beautiful the countryside is, how green, with apple trees and pear trees, the best loam, the big river running nearby. 'You can fish, you can swim, the kids will have fresh air and we'll have peace and quiet and—' "

She stopped reading and, suddenly, her face crumpled and she began to cry without sound. "I can't . . ." she managed, after a few moments. "I can't go there, Sylvia! I'd die!"

"Why?" Sylvia said. "It sounds wonderful."

"Wonderful? It sounds horrible to me! Sylvia, I *hate* the country. I hate the bugs and I hate the quiet—and who will I talk to? And how will I get to the grocery? And where will the children find friends? He never asked me where I'd like to go. He just decided on his own and to hell with me and the kids! Oh, Sylvia, don't look at me like that. I can say 'hell' and the lightning bolt isn't going to come and strike me."

"It's not your language, Dot. But I'm very surprised at your attitude. A woman goes where her husband goes."

"Oh, really? Even if he wants to schlepp you to *Yehupets*? Come on, Sylvia, where is it written that men get to go and women get to follow? I defy you to tell me, and you know why? Because it's not written *anywhere*. One day men said, 'We get to say what's what,' and stupid women didn't argue. There's no law in this universe that says I'm required to go to the ends of the earth just because Jonah chooses to!"

"Dorothy Golodny!"

"Yes, Sylvia, shame on me! But I'm not ashamed of thinking for myself a little. I'm mad! How come he couldn't talk it over with me so I could say I don't want to go to a farm to live? I'll die on a farm . . ." She stopped.

Another silence, another sigh. She started to speak, she stopped, she started again, she stopped again. Then she blurted:

"Look! You're the only person in the whole world I can really talk to, Sylvia. And I've got to talk to *someone* before I go crazy!"

Sylvia took her hand. "You know you can tell me anything. So . . . tell."

"There's someone else."

"Poor Dot! Five months, he couldn't wait for you?"

Dorothy flushed. She pulled her hand away. "Oh, God. No, I mean me. It's me and . . . another man. Please. Don't look at me like that, Sylvia. I didn't want it to happen, I didn't mean for it to happen! I fought it like crazy! But he's wonderful. He's everything I ever wanted: alive and funny and romantic and passionate and sensitive. I've never felt like this before in my life, never. And now, you see, he also wants me to come to him."

Sylvia stared at her sister-in-law. "You've been cheating on your husband," she said, keeping her voice even with great effort. "I see. Jonah has to leave, and the minute he's gone, you're out there acting like a whore."

Dot drew back as if she'd been slapped. "No! No! It's not like that at all! It's love! You've got to believe me! It didn't happen just because Jo went away. I've known this man for years!"

"For years, you've been unfaithful to Jonah? I don't think I want to hear anymore, Dorothy." Sylvia's heart was hammering in her chest. What was it with the three of them? Jack and Yetta and Dorothy, all cut from the same cloth, thinking of nothing but sex, sex, sex. Three selfish pigs. Who were they to demand loyalty from everyone else, all the time? Poor Jonah.

"Does Jo know?" she demanded, and Dot shook her head. Let her feel a little shame! She ought to!

Sylvia knew well what it felt like to be betrayed, too damn well. It felt like a thousand knives cutting into your soul, that's what it felt like! It felt like slow, painful death! It felt like there was nothing and no one in this world you could trust. When a man and woman got married, they made certain promises . . .

"Sylvia, our marriage hasn't been good for years now. I'm not even sure anymore *what* I felt when I married him."

"You loved him. Or you certainly gave a good imitation of it at the time. I seem to recall that your brother tried to talk you out of it but no, you were set on Jonah Golodny!"

"I know. I was young, I was inexperienced. I thought Jo was

so brave and mature. Afterwards, I discovered . . . Well, I don't know how to explain it . . .''

"How could you, Dorothy? You're not a kid anymore! You have a family, three children who need their mother *and* their father!''

"I'm not leaving Jonah! I never said anything about leaving him!''

"Mazel tov!''

Dot's eyes filled. "Sylvia, why are you so angry? I only told you because . . . you're a woman. I thought you'd understand.''

Sylvia pushed her chair back very carefully and stood. What she had to say could only be said on her feet. "I understand only too well, Dorothy. A man smiles at you when your husband's back is turned and all of a sudden, you're in love!''

"Sylvia, didn't you hear a word I said? I told you my marriage isn't good. My husband isn't interested in me anymore. What would you like me to do? Become a nun?''

"That's disgusting! At this moment, I'm *glad* Jack isn't talking to you. At least this, he doesn't have to know.''

Dorothy's eyes widened, filled, overflowed. "I thought you were my friend.''

"And I,'' Sylvia said, somewhat loftily, "thought *you* were something better than what you seem to be.''

"That's so unfair, Sylvia. Don't you see that I'm struggling with this? I'm tormented. I want my marriage to be good. But I'm not getting any help from Jonah, to make it good. You don't know what it's like, struggling all alone.''

Sylvia hardened her heart, kept her face still. Oh, she knew what it was like, to be alone with your heartache. Each time she came across yet another souvenir of Jack's extracurricular love life—a matchbook, a receipt, a phone number—it burned and hurt. The nights he had to "work late''! She knew the empty pit that opened up in the bottom of her belly as she realized it was still going on. That it would never stop! And the proof, the visible proof, there in front of her—! No, she could find no pity for a woman who would cheat on her husband.

Dorothy was pleading, the tears streaming down her face. "I didn't ask for this to happen! It just happened, that's all. It happens to people all the time!''

Sylvia grabbed her purse from the table. "Yes, and all the time people resist temptation and do the right thing. They don't kick a decent man in the heart when he's already in trouble!''

Good, Sylvia thought, watching Dot wince. Let her feel a little pain.

"I don't deserve that from you, Sylvia. I haven't hurt anyone. Jo doesn't know. My only crime is that I've fallen in love. I'm not a monster."

"As far as I'm concerned," Sylvia said, turning and walking out the door, not even bothering to slam it, "you are."

Chapter Thirteen

Monday, July 13, 1987   Cookie came into the restaurant, grateful for the air-conditioning, and asked for a glass of white wine even before she took her seat. She needed it. The waitress scampered off, her bearing and attitude saying she had nothing else on her agenda but to bring Cookie Adler her glass of chilled chardonnay at three dollars and fifty cents a throw. As soon as it came, Cookie told herself, she'd be able to relax. She was quite early, which was just fine with her. This way, she'd get to see Deena before Deena was able to see her.

She looked around. Two Oriental men, seated nearby at a small table, their heads close together, were talking very quietly and intently; other than them and three or four people at the bar, the restaurant was empty. It would soon fill up, as she knew from experience. Five-thirty to seven-thirty was Early Bird Special time, and for a lot of working people from the neighborhood, it was the only time Hisae's was affordable. Especially for the working *women*.

A lot of women, all in dress-for-success outfits, regularly appeared for the Early Bird dinner. It made her laugh; most of them were secretaries and file clerks, she'd make odds on it. But now every working woman wanted to look like a yuppie executive, in overpriced man-tailored suits, overpriced running shoes, overpriced leather attaché cases—and those damn bow ties! Idly, she wondered what genius had dreamed up the idea that a floppy bow was what everyone needed at the office, to tell a woman from a man.

She, thank God, never had to dress for success. Social workers didn't, at least not at Haven House, drop-in center for troubled, homeless, aimless, desperate, and usually runaway
teenagers. At Haven House, the counselors dressed the way they
wanted to, some like gypsies; some like college kids; and some
like the people they worked with. All except Sam, of course.
Sam came in every day looking like every kid's idea of a class
act: suit, vest, impeccably clean shirt, neatly knotted tie, everything coordinated beautifully. Naturally, in the course of the day,
the jacket came off, the sleeves got rolled up—neatly—the vest
unbuttoned, and the tie loosened. But he never seemed to sweat,
like ordinary mortals.

She herself usually opted for comfortable pants with an elastic
waist and a nice loose top. When she looked at herself, very
quickly, each morning on her way out, she was generally satisfied. Neat, clean, and no safety pins in her underwear, in case
of being hit by a truck. When you were chasing after teenagers
all day long, often ending up God knows where on the Lower
East Side—excuse her, the East Village—five flights up in a
tenement, comfort was the ticket, not high fashion.

Today, in honor of her reunion with Deena, she'd decided to
wear a skirt. And that meant she was forced into panty hose,
which in turn demanded pumps. Once finished, she felt the
outfit really called for the string of amber beads that she saved
for special occasions. So today, the kids at Haven House kept
saying, "Yo, Cookie! Fresh gear!" She kinda liked it.

The wine, in a nice big glass, was set down in front of her.
Gratefully, she took a long swallow, and as soon as it hit her
stomach, she could feel a lot of the day's tension dissolving.
Even for a Monday, today had been a doozy. She had awakened
this morning to find her period—something of a miracle nowadays, when she only got it a couple of times a year—and it was
a bad one. So she'd been dosing herself with painkillers all day.

When she got to work, there was already a new kid waiting
for her, a heartbreaker, a skinny little teenaged girl with bruises
all over her body and a shiner you could hardly believe. This
child had finally run away from her pimp—her *pimp*, for God's
sake, and she was barely past puberty! This was the sort of thing
that made you weep inside, that wrung you out, no matter how
many times you saw it, or for how many years. Well, at least
now, Carlotta—who knew if it was her real name or not—was
safe for the moment from that creep with his patent leather hair.
Cookie had seen him often enough, cruising Avenue B in his

pink pimpmobile. He had Carlotta on coke, just like he always did with his girls, so their first move after giving her a bath and some clothes to wear, was to take her to the detox unit at Beth Israel.

She'd fight like hell, of course, to save this kid, but the odds were against the girl, who would probably land back on the street as soon as she had a problem she couldn't handle. The victories in this job were so ephemeral! For every plus, there was always a minus—and maybe two or three or a hundred.

Today, for instance, Clyde Washington showed up, eyes downcast, feet doing a slow shuffle on the floor. She knew Clyde should be on the job right now, at McDonald's—it was the first paying job he'd ever had in his life and he was so proud of himself! She had a feeling she knew why he was refusing to look directly at her. She marched over to him and held his chin, looked into his eyes, and knew. Goddammit. Stoned! He'd talked back to the boss, got fired, and immediately went out looking to get high. Damnation! It had taken a long time to get him off crack. One of these days, Cookie kept promising herself, she was going to take a gun and shoot every crack dealer in the city of New York dead.

She dealt with Clyde and his multitudinous problems, starting with sending him upstairs to bed, and then did what she'd been doing all day long: dug into her purse for more aspirin. A typical, usual, impossible day at Haven House.

Thinking about it now, she didn't feel the usual stabbing pain in her temples. The wine was really doing a nice thing to her poor abused emotions. And the restaurant, with its old-fashioned plush dining chairs and dim lighting and thick carpeting, was doing the rest. She was beginning to feel real mellow.

There was Deena, coming in the door. Oh, my God, quick, another glass of wine. Another glass of wine *and* a face-lift, please. Because Deena looked gorgeous, Deena looked vibrant and glamorous and young, young, *young*! Ten years younger than me, Cookie thought, with some anguish. No, *more*! Not fair . . . they were almost exactly the same age, just a month or so apart. Yet, here was Deena, still unlined, ungray, unspread, wearing a print dress that actually clung to an actual waist! And those cheekbones!

What would she do, Cookie thought, if Deena looked right through her? What if she was totally unrecognizable, with her gray hair and her potbelly! And then Deena's eyes lit on her and she ran over, grinning from ear to ear.

"I'd know you anywhere," she said, leaning to give Cookie a kiss and a squeeze, smelling wonderful. Cookie wished she could check herself out. On the other hand, she really didn't need to. She knew what she looked like, and she wasn't in Deena's league.

"You look super," she said, as Deena settled herself in the chair opposite. "I'm jealous. You look young and sexy, whereas I look my age. *Our* age." She laughed.

"Oh, Cookie!" Deena motioned to the waitress, pointing at Cookie's wineglass. "You look swell, and unless my eyes have gone bad, you aren't wearing any makeup at all. Whereas, *I* am forced to apply makeup liberally, being once again on the loose and single and eligible and on my own and all that stuff. I'm glad you think I look young and sexy because believe me, it takes work. A *lot* of work. In fact, more work every day." She laughed and rolled her eyes in a way Cookie immediately recalled. "If I dared to go out of the house without makeup, small children would scream and every dog in the neighborhood would flee to Canarsie."

"Deena, don't try to kid a kidder, know what I mean?" But she had to laugh. Deena had always been able to make her laugh. "I never pay attention to the way I look. Maybe I should start," she added.

Deena eyed her carefully. "If you really think you ought to do something, you might start with a little mascara. I promise you one thing: your eyes will look twice as big. Ah, my wine. I really need it today. School's already out—you know how private schools are: pay more, get less. Alas, now we have summer school, which means all the kids with problems have come home to roost. And, let me tell you, most of them roost right on my desk." She raised her glass and said, "Anyway, here's to reunion," and they both took a sip.

After a moment, Deena said, "I'm *so* glad to see you, Cookie," and her eyes filled. "Dammit, Deena, stop that! I promised myself I wasn't going to cry and, dammit, I'm not going to."

"Me, neither," Cookie said, as her eyes filled and one or two tears slid down her cheeks. "Here's to reunion," she said, and raised her glass again, sniffling a little.

"If we toast everyone in the family, one by one, we should be nicely sloshed by the time we eat. Here's to our fathers."

"To our fathers."

"And to your husband . . . Yes, I tuned into Channel Two

and I caught him being articulate and passionate and terribly impressive. I'm doubly sorry now that we never met. Before now, that is. I mean . . . we all *are* going to meet, aren't we?'' she said hopefully.

"Oh, yes," Cookie said. "It's a wonderful idea. Pop is raring to go. How about *your* father?"

Deena emptied her glass and signaled for a refill. "If it's such a wonderful idea, how come I haven't gotten up the nerve to talk to Daddy about it, huh?" She laughed, but Cookie got the feeling it wasn't entirely a joke. "Honestly, you'd think a great big grown-up girl like myself could face an elderly man who's already had at least one stroke . . ."

"Stroke!"

"It wasn't a bad one, Cookie. It slowed him down some, but he can still make me do that little tap dance around the throne, hoping His Majesty will grant me my favor!" She made a face and lifted her glass. "Enough of fathers, for the moment. Here's to us!"

They started to talk. Before she knew it, they had talked their way through four glasses of wine. Then, feeling a bit dizzy, Cookie suggested they eat before the Early Bird Special had flown the coop, pardon the pun. She was amazed to find that it was already a quarter past seven. But it had not been time wasted. She now knew that her Aunt Sylvia was the same, feisty and cute . . . that Deena's older sister Elaine was still big and beautiful, still married, and had taken over Uncle Jack's construction company, fast becoming a major real estate developer.

"When I was little," Cookie offered, "I thought Elaine was going to grow up to be Queen of the World."

"That's next!"

And baby Marilyn was a doctor up in the wilds of Vermont, married to the owner of a ski resort—"In answer to your question, Cookie, no, he's not Jewish"—and had a new baby boy.

"I should care if Marilyn's husband is Jewish?" Cookie laughed. "My son's posselque is black."

"Does it matter to you?"

"Not a bit. Remember my background."

"How could I forget it, with Daddy threatening mayhem if he caught any of us looking at or talking to any of you pinko Commie Reds."

Cookie paused. They were both laughing, but that didn't change what had happened, did it? The stupidity of it! The outrage was still there, as far as she was concerned. But now wasn't the time to confront the painful past. It was time to change the subject.

"So, Deena, you've talked a lot, but you haven't told me a damn thing about yourself."

"Let's see . . . myself. What about myself? Well, here I am: living proof that there *is* life after divorce."

"Do you . . . date?"

"Of course, I date. That's what we older single ladies do, you know. We do like the teenagers. We wait by the telephone. We giggle together about the cute boy over there. We get all excited when the captain of the football team asks us out and when he comes to get us, our heart pounds. Like that."

"You're making a joke of it, Deena, but it still sounds like fun to an old married lady."

"Most of the time, we sit at home, Cookie, and clean closets. Because, as you may have heard, there aren't that many good men out there. And there *is* AIDS. But seriously, folks, at the moment, there's a man who wants to get serious and I don't, so I think I'm going to have to tell him to go away"—and she went on about this man who apparently was a business tycoon, widowed, a proud Yale graduate, very, very eager to be married, very, very nice—"and very, very boring," Deena finished with a laugh.

Cookie felt a twinge. She examined the feeling and she decided yes, it was jealousy. How easily Deena talked about her men, how lightly she was able to write off her husband—no, her "ex" . . . what a horrid word, Cookie thought. *X*: a great big black *X*, crossing someone right out of your life. Or she referred to him as "Michael J. Berman, Esquire," as if he were someone she'd never even known. If you lived with a man for so long and had children with him, how could he suddenly be a stranger?

She asked Deena that. "I mean, it seems so harsh, after so many years of intimacy . . ."

Deena gave her a funny look. "Michael and I," she said after a minute, "were always strangers to each other. We just skated around on the surface of a relationship." And then she blithely went on, talking about her tenant, a young man, a "funny guy, not at all handsome but super charming; not my type at all, but he's got a certain something . . . When I rented, he was half of a couple, only now the missus has split and there's Jake, right downstairs, making eyes at me at every opportunity, trying to make his way upstairs, into my bed if not my heart."

Cookie wasn't quite sure if she liked this trivialization of marriage. But maybe that was something else that happened when you got divorced. Trying not to sound too dopey, she said, "What are you going to do?"

"I don't know. It's a temptation, but I don't think so. Maybe. But . . . I don't know."

"I wouldn't have to think about it for more than ten seconds!" Oh, my God, what a thing to say. She didn't mean that! Deena gave her a keen look. "And then I would finish cleaning the kitchen before I went to my tryst," Cookie finished, copying Deena's lighthearted laugh.

She wished she really felt that way. Deena was free in a way she never could be. Free to talk any old way she wanted about her husband, free of all those enforced loyalties and the loyal lies you got to tell yourself all the time when you were a Good Girl. It would be nice, wouldn't it, to have that kind of freedom. And what would she do with it, if she got it? She only knew she was filled with a kind of longing . . . for what, she wasn't sure— wasn't even sure she *wanted* to know.

Deena sounded and looked like a woman who knew what she wanted and went after it. She said so, and Deena just threw her head back and laughed. "I'm telling you, Cookie, it's all in the eyeliner!"

And then, to Cookie's relief, their food came, and after they had eaten and were sipping at their tea, Deena said, "Supposedly, we were supposed to talk about a reunion. So let's talk reunion."

Maybe now was the time to start. "That means, let's talk separation," Cookie said carefully. "Do *you* know what happened?"

"You mean, between our fathers? What happened to cause the big breakup? No, Cookie, I don't. I only know what he told us: that your father was stirring the men up, trying to get them to strike, after he gave him a job out of the kindness of his heart, etcetera, etcetera. His big gripe against Uncle Jo was family disloyalty."

"Well, what *I* always heard was that the FBI came around and your father informed on Pop, and then fired him, just to prove that he was a loyal American. No moral principles, that's what *we* heard. Not to mention 'a lackey of the Capitalist system,' and 'a leech on the sweat and blood of honest workingmen.' " She gave Deena a sly look and was rewarded with a smile.

"So we both got cliches. And is that all we know?" Deena

asked, and answered herself, "Yes. That's all we know. I never asked my mother a thing, I never dared. Did you?"

"Are you kidding? There were things I could talk about and there were things I'd better not try . . . and for sure, I knew which was which."

"Funny, isn't it? I mean, both of us were known for our big mouths and for always asking questions about every damn thing. And yet, we both wimped out."

"It wasn't being wimpy, Deena, it was knowing damn well you weren't going to get a real answer. And in fact, you might get such a hit, you would never forget it! I don't know about you, but I pretty quickly accepted it as the way things were. Now it's bothering me. I don't really know anything about it, not anything at all."

They stared at each other. Then Deena said, "And it's too bad, because we had such good times together, remember?"

"Yeah, but I also remember, now that I think about it, that my father and your father were always tangling over some damn thing or other. I remember one Hanukkah, when we first were living in the Bronx, we came to your house. Oh, God, it was like a palace to me. All those rooms and the rugs and the lovely colors and the silver menorah and, especially, the crystal chandelier over your dining room table. I was mesmerized by it."

"It was only a regular ten-room apartment on Central Park West," Deena said wryly.

"I remember what it 'only was,' Deena, believe me. If you remember, our whole apartment would have fit in your foyer."

"Cookie. Please tell me. Did that bother you?"

"Not to say *bother*. Did I want it for myself? Hell, yes. But that was not something you could admit, in my house. We weren't supposed to covet mere material possessions. In fact, wealth was considered the Ninth Deadly Sin."

"What's the Eighth?"

"Wanting anything for yourself," Cookie said. "And that reminds me of that Hanukkah. We must have been about eight . . . maybe nine. And Uncle Jack gave us each a sack of silver dollars."

Deena sipped at her tea. "I remember."

"How many dollars do you think it was? Ten, maybe? No, twenty. Twenty dollars. And Pop wouldn't let us keep even one."

"I remember." Deena's voice was grim.

Cookie found herself feeling defensive. "Well, come on, Deena. We agreed to give each other small presents; and we came with three little plush animals! Imagine how Pop and Mom felt. Twenty bucks was a lot of dough, back then. Never mind twenty . . . make that sixty! Sixty dollars, Deena! I'll bet our rent wasn't much more!''

"I always was taught that it was the thought that counted. Daddy meant well. All right, so it was excessive. That was his way. He only wanted to be kind and generous.''

"Kind and generous . . . and make my father feel like a pauper? Be real, Deena.''

"Well I remember *other* things, too, Cookie. Like the way Uncle Jo muttered under his breath when we did the blessings over the Hanukkah candles. That was pretty insensitive . . . and embarrassing, too. It was pretty clear he didn't approve of us or anything in our house . . . and he was our guest!''

"Your father knew damn well how my father felt about religion!''

"Well, your father knew damn well how Daddy felt about being generous.''

"Generous? Is that what you think it was?'' Cookie's heart was beginning to pound with anger. "Generous? It was a put-down of the worst kind because, dammit, Pop was forced to be Uncle Jack's employee. He was really a teacher.''

"Well, if he wanted to teach, why didn't he sign the loyalty oath?''

"You know damn well why! Because he was a Communist and it was McCarthy time. Anyway, it was bullshit! Nobody with conscience signed that loyalty oath!''

"If it meant feeding their family, they did!''

Cookie pushed her chair back. She was furious. "I can't believe you're saying these things, a woman of your intelligence!''

"And *I* can't believe that, after all these years, you haven't been able to forg—'' Deena stopped midword, and shook her head. "Sit down, Cookie. Sit back down, for God's sake. This is ridiculous.''

Cookie sat, taking in air, willing herself to calm down. Deena was absolutely right. It *was* ridiculous. "Hoo boy!'' she said, after a moment. "And we think it's going to be a piece of cake when our *fathers* get together?'' They both laughed.

"Seriously, maybe it's not such a hot idea, after all, this re-union? Maybe you should tell your father that Daddy wouldn't go for it.''

In a flash, Cookie saw an aspect of Deena she had forgotten—the conciliatory denying part. Stubbornly, she shook her head.

"Pop's a dying man, Deena. It's his wish and, difficult or not, I think we all ought to give it a shot."

"Of course, you're right. I don't think I really meant it. But I wish we didn't have to dread what might happen."

Cookie waved the thought away. "Agh! We keep forgetting. Nearly forty years have passed. These aren't two young fighting cocks anymore. And I don't want to sound melodramatic, but . . . I mean, Pop's good now, but . . . we don't know the time-table."

"Of course, of course. What a jerk I am. You know what, Cookie? Let me go right now. I'll beard the lion in Elaine's den. He and Sylvia are having dinner there tonight and what the hell, it's not far from you. I'll drop you off, how about it? And then, later tonight, we'll talk and set a date and start making plans."

Cookie marveled as Deena deftly maneuvered her car up Third Avenue, between a double-parked moving van and a mail truck. They talked job for a while, and found it mystifying and also somewhat satisfying that they both worked with kids, even though Cookie did it by choice and Deena had kind of fallen into it by accident. Well, and after thirty-seven years, why not try to find something in common? It was better than doing battle over old grievances.

God, thinking about it, she couldn't believe what had just happened. How they both had so easily taken up their fathers' old battle. Cookie remembered that holiday very well indeed; she recalled being embarrassed when the gifts were exchanged. She remembered looking at Uncle Jack, who was beaming and preening, waiting for his niece and nephews to fall upon him with cries of joy and delight, and, in her nine-year-old way, being aware that this was unfair and not very nice.

On the other hand, she also remembered how magical the moment was when she opened her gift and saw the glitter of all those silver dollars. She'd confided in Deena earlier, about how she was longing for a two-wheeler, a bright red Schwinn she'd seen in Macy's. As soon as she had seen her gift, she had looked up, straight at Deena, and Deena had mouthed at her: "Now you can have that bike."

But then, like a bad dream, Papa shook his head, vehement, and she knew he was going to make her give it back. She re-membered looking at him imploringly, and she remembered how he reached over and patted her head as he said, "No, it's too much. We can't accept it." How valiantly she fought her tears of disappointment, but they came from her eyes in spite of everything she did. She knew then she would never have a bike, never.

Thinking about it now, she had a flash of awareness—of how those two men had used their children for a battleground! It was so mean! And yet, all these years later, both she and Deena so quickly, so *automatically*, jumped to their fathers' defense! It was pathetic. Two Daddy's girls.

They talked about this and that. It was nice; it was cozy. Even though she hadn't been in touch with her cousin, there was an easy intimacy. And Deena was divorced and Out There. And she didn't know Dave. She was the ideal person to talk to about . . . her secret.

She couldn't. It was too silly. But she wanted to. And they were already on Central Park West, approaching her block. It was now or never.

"What would you say," she said, halting a little, "if I told you there's . . . a man . . . and—well . . . I'm, er, um, attracted to him?" The minute the words were out of her mouth, she was sorry. If Deena gave her a wiseass answer, she'd never forgive her.

But she didn't. She said, "What do you mean—'attracted'? You like his looks? You think you'd like to get to know him?"

There was silence for a block and a half. Then: "I mean, I've been to bed with him. Once. Just once. Dave's been so involved in his own problems and—"

"You don't have to explain, Cookie. Really you don't. Plenty of people do it, you know. It needn't threaten your marriage, if that's what's worrying you."

"That's not what's worrying me."

More silence. "Then what?"

"I don't know. All of a sudden I needed to tell someone. I needed to see if I could tell you . . . and if you'd be shocked. I mean, we don't really know each other."

"Who, me? Shocked? Listen, Cookie . . . I had a lover while I was still married. But that's not what caused my divorce. It just clarified my feelings. There *is* such a thing as therapeutic sex."

Funny. Now that she'd opened the subject, she discovered she didn't want to tell Deena anymore. So she laughed and said, "My mother would kill me! My mother would say I take after Aunt Yetta!"

"Aunt Yetta!" Deena laughed, too. "The Bohemian. The one they used to switch into Yiddish to talk about! 'Three—

count 'em—three children, and not only that, but three different fathers . . . and two of them from the nobility! And not only *that*, no—count 'em—*no* marriages!' ''

"Hey! This is my corner!"

Deena burned a turn from Columbus Avenue into Ninety-fourth Street that would have had Mario Andretti falling all over himself, pulled to a screeching halt in front of a fire hydrant, and killed the engine. They looked at each other for a moment.

"Listen. Not a word of this to anyone, okay, Deena? What I just told you."

"Of course not."

"Not even Elaine?"

"We're close, but not *that* close, Cookie. I never told her about *mine*."

They smiled at each other. It was time to say good-bye. "I'm on my way to *hondle* with Daddy," Deena said. "Don't worry, Cookie. It may take more negotiation than SALT Two, but this reunion is going to happen."

&&&&&&&&&&&&&&&&&&&&&&&&&&&&&&&&&&&&&&&&&&&&&&&&&

Chapter Fourteen

Monday, July 13, 1987   Deena sat in the car and watched her cousin run up the steps and disappear into her lobby. Ten blocks to Elaine's. It would be past eight o'clock by the time she found a parking space. She hoped she would find Daddy and Sylvia still there. Probably. As they got older, they tended to hang out at Elaine's more and more.

It only took six minutes to find a space, but that was long enough for her to decide how she was going to broach the subject to Daddy. Head-on, that's how. It was the only way. If you tried subtle hints, he'd get annoyed. And if he got annoyed, he'd pretend he didn't understand. He'd done it to her often enough, when she was saying something he didn't want to hear.

She knew the scenario: he'd appeal to the world at large, his arms thrown wide, to demonstrate exactly how huge was his perplexity. "Does anyone understand what my daughter is talking about?" he'd demand. Even if they were alone. If there were a way to tell him without going through that routine, she was all for it. She'd end up having to tell him outright, anyway. Having thus convinced herself that what she wanted to do was the right thing, she got out of the car and made her way to Elaine's building, a block and a half away.

Her brother-in-law Howard let her in. She gave him a warm kiss. She really liked Howard, who was not only a nice guy but the only middle-aged college boy she knew.

"Are the folks still here?"

"Just finishing supper," he said. "I cooked Chinese tonight. In little white boxes." They laughed. Howard was the take-out champ of the Upper West Side since he'd started on his MSW at Columbia. He could do half a dozen different ethnic meals using nothing more than his dialing finger.

They were all sitting around the oak kitchen table, schmoozing, the dregs of their meal still scattered around. "No, no, don't anybody get up," Deena said, already a little nervous about the confrontation to come.

She went around the table giving kisses, first to her sister Elaine, then Daddy, and then her mother, who put a hand up to Deena's head and instantly said, "Deena, darling, do you really like your hair shaved up the back that way?"

Deena straightened and exchanged a swift look with her sister. "I hate it." She waited a beat and then added, "But Albert Ciccarelli, my hairdresser, chained me to the chair and had his way with my hair."

Elaine and Daddy both laughed, but Sylvia only gave her a wry look. "Very funny, Deena, very funny. Don't worry. I'll never say another word about your hair as long as I live—"

In unison, Deena and Elaine said, "That'll be the day!"

Unperturbed and undisturbed, Sylvia went right on talking. "But if your mother doesn't tell you, who's going to tell you?"

When they were able to stop laughing, Elaine said, "Can I nuke you something? Moo shu pork? Shrimp lo mein? Beef and broccoli? Whatever your heart desires, Deena, providing Howard ordered it."

Now or never, Deena thought. "No, no, nothing for me. I already ate. And you'll never guess with who?"

"I hope he was Jewish," Howard muttered. Sylvia turned quickly, saying, "I heard that, Howard!"

Deena waved their words away. "Not a man, not a date. No,

it was"—she threw her arms out—"Da-dah! Cousin Cookie! Cookie Adler of West Ninety-fourth Street!"

Her father's face was a study in stone. He sat so still that, for a moment, she was filled with apprehension. Maybe it wasn't such a wonderful idea to surprise him? After all, he had had a stroke.

But then the hard look changed to a full-blown sneer. "I thought I made it clear in 1952 that I never wanted to hear about that family again! And I *meant* never."

"Well, Daddy, darling, I hate to tell you this, but *never* ended this evening. The situation has changed."

"The situation, as you call it, couldn't change enough to change my mind. Once a traitor, always a traitor!"

"Daddy!" Again, the two sisters spoke together.

And then Sylvia spoke up. "Jack, just listen a minute, for a change, will you? So many years! And Cookie was always your favorite."

"I gave her that nickname. Karla! That's a name for a sweet little red-haired doll? That's a name for a prison guard! Karla!"

Deena tried hard not to laugh. "What's wrong with Karla? It's a perfectly nice name."

"After Karl Marx? That's nice, by you?"

"Oh, Daddy, you don't know that!"

Sylvia laid her hand on Deena's arm and said, "Jack. She was named after Tante Kaila, remember?"

"That's what they'd like you to believe! That's what they said for publication. But, believe me, I know. They named her after that maniac. All those Reds did that!"

"Did what?" Elaine said. "Named their children after Karl Marx?"

"You know what I mean, Elaine. Don't be fresh. She was named after Karl Marx. Listen. Her name is Karla Maxine. I rest my case."

Sylvia said, "You're wrong, Jack."

"If I bust a blood vessel right here in Elaine's kitchen, Sylvia, *then* will you be satisfied?"

"Daddy! Sylvia, tell him not to talk like that."

"Tell him yourself. I can't tell him anything anymore."

To Elaine and Howard, Deena said, "They don't have a marriage, they have a vaudeville routine."

Her father leaned across the table, tapping her hand. "So tell me," he said in an entirely different tone, "how is she?"

"Who?"

"Who, she asks. Who are we talking about? Your cousin Cookie. How is she? She had twins, didn't she?"

"You knew she had twins, Daddy?"

"My sister wrote me a letter every once in a while."

"And you never *told* us?"

"What's to tell?" A massive shrug.

Deena opened her mouth and immediately closed it again. What was he saying? That the rule of total separation he had imposed was for everybody but him? Yes, that's exactly what he was saying. The cheat! She couldn't look at him. She sat at Elaine's table and stared intently at the noodles in cold sesame sauce, concentrating on it, its color, its texture. If she raised her eyes or said one word, she was going to lose her temper.

Finally she was able to say, very calmly, "Cookie's incredible. Her job sounds like you have to be a saint. I don't know how she does it."

"What does she do, for God's sake?" Elaine looked amused. "Wash the feet of the poor?"

"Just about. How about counseling runaway kids in a drop-in center in the middle of the East Village?"

"Sorry. Sainthood isn't good enough for her."

"Never mind Cookie's job," Sylvia said impatiently. "Deena, darling, why don't you tell us all why you and Cookie got together after all these years?"

Deena ducked her head to hide the smile. "Okay, Syl. Everybody: Cousin Cookie and I got together, after all these years, because we got sick and tired of this childish quarrel." Here, she shot a look at her father who was ready with his protest. "That's right, Daddy. Childish. Unnecessary. Dumb. And it's been going on too long, *much* too long." She ignored his muttering. "You're the only one who's objecting, Daddy. Does that tell you something? Anyway, if everything goes as Cookie and I would like . . . soon we'll *all* get together. We're going to have a family reunion!"

"Over my dead body!"

"Bite your tongue, Daddy! For your information, Uncle Jonah *is* dying." Sylvia gasped and quickly put a hand to her mouth. Even her father looked grave. "He has cancer. So let's quit quibbling, okay? Let's not dwell on the past. Uncle Jo only wanted to see *you*, Daddy, before he . . . And Cookie and I decided, why not have *everyone*?"

"I'm sorry the man's sick, but it doesn't change anything."

"I'm sorry, Jack, but *I* think it changes everything."

"Whose side are you on, Sylvia?"

"I never did think it was right, what you did—don't give me that look, Jack Strauss, the children are adults now. They can hear the truth. I only went along because you were my husband and in those days, we did as our husbands told us."

"Hoo-*hoo!*" Jack drew back in mock surprise. "And what do we do *these* days?"

"These days, we do what we know is right."

"Excuse me for living, *Ms.* Liberated Woman. *You* go see that bunch of ingrates. I bent over backwards for him, and what did he do in return? Incited my men! Told them they should strike, that I was taking advantage of them! Didn't I always treat my men fair and square? They always got bonuses for a job that came in on time. They always got a turkey at Thanksgiving. When a baby was born, there was extra money in the pay envelope. I needed that rotten Commie to turn my men against me?"

"Daddy, for God's sake! You're talking about more than thirty years ago!"

"Never mind! Some things, you never forget! Like being stabbed in the back! That, you *never* forget, believe me!"

Very, very slowly and calmly, Deena said, "Daddy. Listen. What happened, happened. We can't change that, but what *has* changed is that Uncle Jo has cancer and wants to see you and make up with you before he dies. If you want to know what I think—and even if you don't—*I* think you have no choice. You can't—"

He waved her down. "Deena, Deena, enough already. Of course, I'll see him. I don't have to like it but yes, I'll see him. Considering the circumstances. You know me: would I say no to a dying man? I understand the right thing to do—no matter *who's* right and who's wrong."

Deena said not a word. There was only one way to do things, and that was Jack Strauss's way. She'd lived by his rules her whole life. She shouldn't have to always dance around, convincing him.

She looked over at her mother. Now it came back to her—the many times she'd found her mother and Aunt Dot sitting in the kitchen, heads together, their cups of tea growing cold as they talked. The long separation had never been discussed. Now that she thought about it, that was damned strange. Daddy had ordered them all to forget that whole family, and they had just all mindlessly obeyed.

She had a lot of questions, a *lot* of questions. But not tonight. She was so damn tired. I did it, she thought. I told him, he gave me a hard time, I stood my ground, and now it's over.

He was going to see Uncle Jo, and what else did she want from him? It was, anyway, enough for now. Considering who she was dealing with, it was more than enough, it was a bloody miracle. All the rules about who you could and couldn't speak to were rescinded. They were all free to see one another again. She could hardly wait to call Cookie and tell her the good news!

❮❮

Chapter Fifteen

Saturday, July 18, 1987   Cookie came sailing out of the revolving door of Bloomingdale's into a half-empty Third Avenue. A man walked by, gave her a glance, then turned and gave her another. Cookie ducked her head so he wouldn't see her smile. Yes, it was true, it was really true. He wasn't the first, since she'd climbed down from Nelda's stool in front of the Shiseido counter. Several guys had given her the eye, and it felt wonderful. Even if one was someone she'd never look at, and two of them were her father's age. So what? It had been a long, long time since she'd felt so . . . pretty. And she looked younger, too. Imagine that: three or four little pots of powder and you could take ten years off your age. All right, five years. Five for the makeup and another five for the haircut and the Golden Glow rinse.

She stood a little taller than usual and started for her bus stop. It was hot, but she felt like walking. Actually, if she told the whole truth, she felt like having more people look at her and approve. Unfortunately, there weren't a helluva lot of them around. As soon as it got really hot in New York, people disappeared on the weekends. It wasn't chic to stay in the city in the summertime—you were supposed to join the throngs in the traffic jams and escape to a lake or a beach or a mountain. Personally, she loved New York in the summer; it was nice when it was deserted. It was quiet. More on a human scale. More *hers*. And anyway, she wasn't from the chic.

She sucked in a deep breath of damp, warm air, slid a look at herself in one of the big store windows and, once again, got that little shock of pleasure. She looked so different! Her eyes seemed to slant a bit, she had cheekbones, her chin looked half its usual size. She loved it. The miracles of modern makeup!

She'd gone to Nelda about forty-five minutes ago and said, "Do your best."

Nelda raised one eyebrow delicately. "You want to tell me what brought this on?" She smiled a little. "Maybe you're going to be in the next big TV appearance with Dave?"

"Nothing like that." Cookie paused, feeling a flash of irritation. What was she—just an extension of her husband? "If I told you I saw my long-lost cousin the other night and we're the same age only she looks ten years younger, would that give you an idea?"

Nelda widened her big brown eyes and laughed. "Gotcha. Sit right down here at my counter." And she patted the stool, waiting for Cookie to climb on.

It was embarrassing as hell to perch there in front of the whole world as it strolled by and stopped to gawk. But Nelda, totally unperturbed, studied her captive with an appraising eye, then went to work with her potions and powders, smoothing and patting and penciling Cookie's face.

Cookie longed to cry out to the passersby, "Hey, listen. I'm Cookie Adler and I don't shop here! I was just on my way to Alexander's to buy a sensible raincoat on sale and I bumped into my friend Nelda on Lexington Avenue and she *made* me!"

Then Nelda pronounced her done and triumphantly handed her a mirror. Cookie nervously drew in a breath. And then let it out with astonishment. The face staring back at her had high cheekbones, a bit flushed; smoky dramatic eyes; a lush pink mouth. It was pretty. It was sexy. But it wasn't her; it couldn't be! "Oh, my God!" she said.

"Isn't it wonderful?" Nelda was so pleased. "Aren't you just thrilled? Aren't you excited? You look beautiful!"

Cookie sat there like a dummy, trying to figure out what she could say without saying what she was thinking, which was, Help! I'm a prisoner in a department store, wearing a face that isn't mine! The glamorous girl in the mirror wasn't Cookie Gordon Adler, married lady, mother of twins, sister, daughter, social worker, registered Democrat, marcher for causes, regular, ordinary West Side person, whose most daring foray into the world of fashion—up to this very moment—had been to get her ears pierced.

"You know Dave hates makeup . . . and so does my father."

"You look like you were born that way."

That wasn't exactly true, Cookie thought. Nobody that she knew of was born with jade green eyelids. Even so, she kept peeking at herself—in store windows as she walked, and then in her compact mirror while she waited for her bus. Yes, she loved it. It felt strange, and she still wasn't used to the idea that she was really looking at herself, but she had eighty-five dollars' worth of cosmetics in a *very* small bag and, by God, she was not going to wash it off.

Seated on the bus, she kept seeing herself reflected in the window. Couldn't help looking and admiring. She really had to stop this. Once upon a time, when she was young, she had been considered quite cute—hell, back then, she'd considered *herself* good-looking . . . when she thought about it, which was practically never. The way you looked just wasn't a top priority. The way you thought was. The state of the *world* was number one topic of discussion at her family's dinner table, not the state of anyone's wardrobe or popularity. You didn't want to stop clocks, but that was the extent of it. And she had never really changed her attitude . . . not until just now.

What was so different now, all of a sudden? Why, suddenly, was she looking in mirrors all the time, studying herself, turning this way and that way, sucking in her gut, throwing her shoulders back, lifting her chin, getting good shadows onto her face? What was her *problem*, for Christ's sake? She'd told Nelda it was because of Deena. But Deena had *always* been a beauty; what, she was going to go into a tizzy because Deena was still a looker? Well, yeah, maybe. Because if that's what single women of a certain age, roaming the streets of Manhattan, looked like these days, she was going to have to take another look in the mirror and make an executive decision.

Well, she'd looked in her mirror that night and asked her mirror that time-honored question: "If you were a construction worker, would you whistle at me?" And her mirror sadly shook its head no. "That's what I thought you'd say."

She had an agenda. The worst was over. If she still wanted to, she could leave Dave now without feeling so guilty. But she didn't know what she wanted anymore. She was three years older and five pounds heavier and a lot more insecure. Oh, hell, the M96 bus was no place to make life decisions. So she planned their dinner instead. She had made a big bowl of chef salad, it only needed dressing, and there was a fresh loaf of rye bread and a pitcher of iced tea in the fridge . . . nothing to it. She'd get home and pull it all out of the refrigerator. Da-*dah*! Dinner! Cookie Adler does it again!

Was she ever wrong! Even before she opened the apartment door, she heard them—all of Dave's cronies. Again! It made her feel utterly weary. They had been hanging out here almost every single night since last Sunday, playing the tape of Dave's interviews, listening while he read his fan mail, leaving their beer cans and their cigarette butts and their candy wrappers all over her living room.

The air was thick with smoke and heat. Shit, couldn't anyone turn on the fans? No, of course not! They were too busy to notice, all sitting around in their shorts, playing with the VCR, stopping the tape, making lewd comments, reversing, replaying favorite parts. She was getting so goddamn sick of the entire thing, she wished *City Sounds* and all its staff twenty feet underground.

They didn't hear her come in; they didn't see her come in. Even after she slammed the door behind her. To hell with them. She stomped through the kitchen into the dining area and snapped on the big window fan. They still didn't notice. She gazed at them, exasperated. Look at them: five, no six, grown men, all in shorts and T-shirts, nobody shaved because it was a weekend and you didn't have to, right? And they were absolutely intent on the television set, fighting a little over who gets the remote control, laughing, swigging beer out of the can, eating . . . *eating*! Eating, goddammit! Eating what she'd planned for her dinner!

The living room was littered with bowls and cutlery and crumpled-up napkins, and, sure enough, all over the dining table, the remains of her beautiful chef salad, what was left of the rye bread, and, goddammit, everything *else* edible that might have been in the refrigerator! The jar of pickles, the container of cold lo mein from last Wednesday . . . and then she got furious, because there was the jar of salmon caviar, empty but for half a dozen little golden-red glistening bits. That was nearly eight bucks of caviar—and she'd bought it to make an egg-and-caviar pie for Pop. It was a favorite of his, and she thought she'd take it over when she went to visit them on Sunday. And these overgrown babies, intent on themselves and nothing else, had just ravaged her refrigerator without a thought. Tears stung at her eyes. She knew if she said one single word, she'd begin to cry.

So instead of saying anything—very unusual for her; she was usually not afraid to speak her mind, and certainly not afraid to tell these guys just what she thought of them eating up her supper—instead of giving them a piece of her mind, she just marched herself down the hall. To hell with them!

She went to the bathroom, thinking she'd just shut herself in there, turn on the water, and have a good cry. But then she caught sight of herself in the mirror and realized she couldn't do that. What, and ruin her newly gorgeous face? Not on your life! And she began to laugh.

She was still smiling when she reemerged a moment later, and now Dave looked up and spotted her. "Hey! Hi, honey! I didn't hear you come in."

"How could you?"

They all greeted her and she waited, smiling, patient, for someone to say, "Hey, Cookie, what'd you do to yourself?" Or at least, "Isn't there something different about you?" Even a negative comment would do, at this point. Was she invisible? Nobody said a word. Dave smiled at her and looked right at her and *bopkes*, nothing. Was the man blind? For over twenty years, he'd been carrying on about how she shouldn't wear makeup, he hated that greasy stuff, he didn't like kissing lipstick, and on and on and on and *on*. And here she was, standing before him, a painted woman, a *freshly* painted woman at that, and he was blind to it.

Oh, screw it! What did she want, after all these years? He never noticed what she was wearing or if she had put on a couple of pounds or if she had a bad haircut. And she'd always thought that was terrific. So now, she was going to carp? That wasn't fair. On the other hand, she'd given up her own needs ever since this whole whistle-blowing business started. She'd sat up nights listening to him; she'd held him in her arms and rocked him when he was in despair; she'd typed letters for him and placed calls for him and screened calls for him and taken calls for him. She'd defended him and supported him and stood by his side in spite of her own feelings. God, the least he could do, now that the worst was over, was open up his eyes and *see* her when he looked at her, for a change! Surely, it wasn't too much to ask, after all these years of marriage. But, apparently, it *was* too much to ask; apparently, anything was too much to ask.

Oh, hell. Let her go see if the sharks had left her anything to eat. As she turned away, Dave called out to her. Aha. She had misjudged him. Smiling, ready to defend her make-over—come to think of it, what *was* she going to tell him? "It's my face," that should do it: short, quick, neat, and no ambiguities—she turned. And he said, "Did you remember that Dick called me an authentic American hero? I didn't. Jesus! An authentic American hero."

An authentic American schmuck, Cookie thought but did not say. He was far too busy admiring himself to notice anything as subtle as jade green eyelids and smoke coming out of her ears. "Pop called you that, too," she said tightly, and was about to add, but you don't keep replaying *that*, but he had already turned away, saying something to Ron Schwartz that made Ron just roar with laughter. "Dick," she thought with asperity. Not even "Dick Wallach" anymore . . . Oh, no, not for your authentic American hero who was intimate with the great and near-great of authentic American television. She regarded him, thoroughly disgusted. This whole business of interviews and TV shows and articles and news programs was beginning to go to his head.

"I'm going for a walk," she said, suddenly making a decision. She was talking to the lamp, apparently, because no human being acknowledged her. So she patted the lamp on its shade and let herself out, slamming the door behind her.

All the way down on the elevator, she castigated herself. What was the matter with her? After all he'd been through, he had a right to be pleased with himself, to focus on himself, to enjoy his newfound fame. That was the rational way of looking at it. But she didn't feel like being rational; she felt like being appreciated, goddammit!

So thinking, she walked out through the stifling lobby, and into the warm, damp dusk. New York, New York. Here she was, all made up and no place to go. Might as well head for Central Park West, where there might be the possibility of a breeze. What time was it, anyway? Seven twenty-seven. What the hell, she could just sit here on the front steps for a few minutes and see if anyone interesting walked by.

At seven-thirty, as usual, he did. Phil Mitchell. Walking Rover—as she knew damn well he did every evening about this time. She heard him behind her, coming out the front door, telling the dog to "Take it easy, take it easy, we're neither of us so young any more, Central Park will still be there in five minutes," in that nice, deep, rich voice of his. And then, in that nice, deep, rich voice of his, he said, "Cookie! What a nice surprise!" He sounded so pleased to find her sitting there on the steps. And when she turned, trying very hard to look totally nonchalant and as if she hadn't known he'd probably be coming out now, he *looked* pleased, too. And then he did a double take. "Hey!" he said, grinning at her. "Look at the glamour girl!"

The dog strained at the leash. "Heel, Rover," Phil said, and then he laughed. "Who'm I fooling? Certainly not the dog. He knows who's boss and it ain't me. He's about to take me for my evening walk, Cookie. I'd ask you to join us but, looking so gorgeous, you must be on your way out to someplace special. Saturday night, and all . . ."

"Someplace special," Cookie echoed. "How about Central Park? I thought I'd take a walk and get some air so, yes, I'd love to come with you."

"We'd better get going. I think Rover's in a big hurry." Still laughing, he crooked an arm. "Hang on, this is the evening express."

They chatted about this and that—about nothing, really—all the way to the park. Cookie was on edge with a growing excitement and she could feel a kind of electricity from him. She *thought* she could. What did she know? She'd never really flirted with anyone in her adult life. With her and Dave, meeting for the first time, it had been instant communication and a meeting of the minds, not sexual tension and the exchange of lingering glances. Phil was a very open and friendly guy. How could she be sure he was still thinking about their little encounter? He was single, and she'd seen him with different women over the years. Maybe it was just another lay to him, no big deal. She was so goddamn ignorant about this stuff! The sexual revolution had arrived while she was out of town.

Did he tighten his grip on her arm or did she imagine it? Was he snuggling up to her just a little or did the dog pull him closer to her? She didn't know; she didn't know anything. But she was so elated being with him, feeling his pleasure in her company, seeing it clearly written on his face that he found her attractive. She felt beautiful, walking quickly to Rover's pace, along the walks in the park, watching the sky start to lighten.

"Oh, look, Phil. It's going to clear!"

"Tomorrow's supposed to be terrific. That'll be nice, for a change. Maybe I'll take myself out to Jones Beach, or something. Probably not."

"Why not? Other than the fact that it's terrible traffic and crowded on the beach and full of teenagers playing their radios loudly, it sounds terrific.''

"I don't like to do things alone. I'm a companionable kind of guy, you know what I mean? Not that I'd ever go back to my wife—sorry, my ex-wife—but I miss the comforts of being married.''

"Even after six years, Phil?''

"Even after six years. Oh, it's not *her*, not Susan. I've really been over her for a long time. But I like a lady around the house. I like stockings hanging in the bathroom and the smell of cooking when I get home at night. I'm just domestic, I guess.'' He laughed a little. "Rover's a pal, but a dog just doesn't do it for me!''

She waited a moment and then, hesitant, said, "You had a . . . girlfriend for quite a while.''

"Joan. Yeah. We lived together for three years. Three years! Unbelievable!''

"Three years is a long time. What happened?''

Now he laughed heartily. "You won't believe this. She didn't want to get married! And when I said that's the only way we could stay together, she left. She left! I thought all women wanted commitment. I thought it was in their hormones.''

"Hey, I don't think *I'd* ever get married again.''

He gave her a sharp look. "Is there something you haven't told me, Cookie? Like . . . you've split with your husband?''

"Oh, no! I meant . . . hypothetically. If I ever got divorced, I don't think I'd choose marriage again.''

"Well, speaking hypothetically,'' Phil said, sliding her an amused look, "it doesn't feel . . . *right* to me, being single. And if that sounds old-fashioned—well, I guess I'm just an old-fashioned guy.'' And he laughed.

Here she was, in romantic Central Park, with a man who was obviously interested in her, strolling under the trees as the sun sank in the west, and he was talking about *marriage*, of all the damn things. Didn't he want to take her to bed tonight? She was waiting for him . . . was he waiting for her?

She looked over at him. A big man, very tall, very broad, with thick muscular legs. A bit of a belly just beginning, but a fine figure of a man, as they used to say. Actually, a typical cop in looks. Well, he was a cop, a lieutenant in a precinct in the Bronx. He had a nice face; she didn't know how else to describe it. Not handsome, exactly, but not homely, either. Nice. Open. Shrewd eyes, deep set under heavy brows, a regular nose, a regular mouth, a broad jaw, a man her mother would describe as salt of the earth. Nice. Better than nice, actually. Masculine and strong. So what was he waiting for? For her, obviously. Did she have the guts to do it? She opened her mouth, she closed it, she thought yes, she thought no, she thought maybe—and then she thought, Enough already!

"Phil?"

"Yeah?"

"I was waiting for you."

There was a beat. Then he stopped walking, pulling hard on the dog's leash, and looked intently into her eyes. "You mean . . . tonight."

"Right. On the steps."

He grinned even more broadly. "You wanna know how good that makes me feel?"

"Frankly," Cookie said, amazed at her audacity, "yes. Yes, I do." Relief flooded her.

He dragged in a deep, audible breath, the grin fading, being replaced with something much more interesting. "That makes me feel . . . a lot like I felt the last time we took a walk."

Cookie felt suddenly breathless. "Yeah," she managed.

He didn't touch her, but she could feel the warmth of his body, which seemed to be reaching out to her. "So," he said. "How about an ice cream?"

That's how it had begun the last time. They had bumped into each other, walked and talked, eating ice-cream cones they got at Baskin Robbins, and ended up in his bed, making slow, sweet love. Nice Phil, sending her a message this way, so she could say no without hurting him and without embarrassing herself. Right up until this moment, she had been sure that's what she would say: no. She was not an unfaithful woman. She was loyal to family, colleagues, clients, and friends. Yes, she had slept with him once, but that was because—because that particular evening, she needed something more than anyone in her life was willing or able to give her. Even a faithful wife could falter, could slip, could fall. And after three years of marking time, of sticking around because it was the right thing to do . . . come on, she deserved one night of pure pleasure!

Still, tonight she had waited for him. She'd admitted it to him. What's more, before she went out, she'd made sure not to cry her new face off. So she really knew what she was hoping for, the minute she left the apartment. On the one hand, she hadn't exactly *planned* it. But, on the other hand, she hadn't exactly avoided it, either. But on the third hand, she hadn't called him up, had she? She knew his phone number; she could have picked up the phone anytime, and made a definite date. But she hadn't. So, she'd been able to tell herself that she only wanted to see what would happen if she happened to bump into him tonight. That was all she had wanted to know, sure! That was why she was saying "Yes, I'd love an ice cream"; that's why she was smiling back at him. And that's why she just got a little thrill of anticipation down her spine—and not for cherry vanilla with sprinkles, either!

They walked on together, arms barely brushing but very, very aware of each other. When they got upstairs to his place, would he do the same things he did the last time? Kiss her tenderly, wrap his hands in her hair, rub his big hands down her back? But this was crazy, walking across West Ninety-fifth Street with a man who was almost a stranger, thinking about sex!

Not so crazy. Understandable, for anyone who knew the whole story. Which meant her, period. She'd never told anyone how bad it had been for her the past three years, taking tender loving care of a man she didn't even love anymore. The total absence of any kind of feeling put a taint on everything. But it was the constant lying, the constant pretending: that's what finally got to her. And now, dammit, wasn't there to be any payoff for her, not even a friendly little *shtup* for the little lady? Not from Dave, there wasn't! But there were other men in this world, men who thought she was pretty, men who *wanted* her. Well . . . one man, anyway; and tonight, she wasn't going to say no. And if that was wrong, well, too goddamn bad!

"Cookie!" Phil was grinning down at her, very amused.

"What? What?" she said. "I'm sorry. I was daydreaming."

His grin broadened. "Me, too. But first things first, Cookie. The lady wants to know: which flavor?"

They had come inside Baskin Robbins, into the bright lights and the shiny floor, and she hadn't even noticed. She could feel the blush creep up her face. Cookie! A woman of your age. You should be ashamed of yourself!

Quickly, she said the first flavor her eyes lit on, on the big board: "Jamoca Almond Fudge." Oh, God, and she hated almonds. She had to laugh when he said, "And I'll have one scoop of Rocky Road and one scoop of vanilla and make sure the vanilla's on the top." The young black woman who was dipping the ice cream gave him that New York Look that says "I am in the company of yet another weirdo"; but she did it.

When she handed him the cones, Phil said, "I'm not crazy. It's my dog. He loves ice cream. I'll knock the vanilla onto the sidewalk, and while he's busy with it, I'll get a chance to eat mine in peace."

They took separate elevators up. Phil went first, and when she stepped into the other one, damn, it went down—to the basement, to the laundry room. Christ, what if someone she knew got in? No way she could get off at the twelfth floor. People in this building felt very free to comment, to say, "Hey, Cookie, this isn't your floor," or "Where you going?" She could go up, get off at her floor, the sixteenth, and then maybe take the next car down, but maybe it would be even better if she took the stairs. And then the door opened and a teenaged couple, looking slightly startled and very guilty, got in. She thought the boy was one of the Chans, but the Parks had boys, too, didn't they? She realized she was blithering. Thank God, the two kids in the corner were too intent upon each other to notice who she was—if they even knew. And there she went again. She felt strange and uncomfortable. Silly. Sneaky. Like a liar. Like a— come on, Cookie, say it, straight out of your childhood—like a *hoo*-a. Standing in the elevator, sweating, not looking at the two kids necking in the corner, she asked herself just what she thought she was doing. When it stopped at the twelfth floor, she paused. All she had to do was let the doors wheeze open and wheeze closed. And go home.

For perhaps ten seconds, she thought that's what she'd do; and then she had a flash—a memory of how he moaned deep in his throat last time, when he first entered her—and away went *that* plan in a hurry!

As soon as she was in his apartment and the door was firmly closed and locked, his arms were around her. She had forgotten how she had to stand on tiptoe to be kissed. She had forgotten how he had to half lift her from the floor to bring her closer against him. She had forgotten, but not forgotten, the smell of him, the bulky feel of his big, well-fleshed body, the catch of breath in the back of her throat when his lips moved from her mouth to the curve of her neck, to the place on her throat where her pulse pounded. She wanted her clothes off, she wanted *his* clothes off, she wanted to get on with it. But Phil Mitchell had all the time in the world . . . he was in no hurry whatsoever. When she started to unbutton his shirt, he gently took both her hands in one of his and moved them away. Then he wrapped his arms even more tightly around her and continued to kiss her, biting her ever so gently, sucking on her lips.

She knew he wanted her as badly as she wanted him; he was holding her tight up against him and there was no doubt about his erection. She may have forgotten what it was like to kiss and hug and feel that dizziness flow over you, but *this*, she hadn't forgotten. He was erect; yes, yes, he was, and it was hers and what in hell was he doing kissing her so leisurely, taking his own sweet time like this, making her crazy?

Finally, she squirmed enough so that he loosened his hold, just enough so she could tip her head up and meet his eyes. He was amused. The devil! "Something bothering you, Cookie?"

"You bastard! You know I don't have much time!"

"Then why are you wasting time talking?"

She never got a chance to answer him. He scooped her up— her, ten-pounds-overweight Cookie Adler—as if she were a young girl and not a middle-aged matron . . . and he gave her a look, right into her eyes, as if she were his dreamgirl and not the frustrated, horny married woman in 16G.

He carried her into his bedroom. There was no more waiting. He tore his clothes off, just throwing them behind him, and she did the same. For a split second, as, naked, they gazed at each other, she thought, How ludicrous we must look, two ordinary people no longer young, no longer firm. But yes, indeed, he was erect, triumphantly and ecstatically erect, and without thinking, she reached out for it and then all thought stopped.

It was so good to feel that hardness pushing into her, so good it was almost painful. It was silent lovemaking, serious and intent and wordless . . . only the little sounds they both made as they moved and shifted, clung and separated, turned and changed positions. She was breathing so hard, her mouth had gone dry. She wanted to stop, just for a moment, to get a drink, to catch her breath, but she couldn't, she just couldn't. She couldn't stop. She was so caught up in sensation, in feeling, and it was so good, so good, so good! And then it was finished and they lay on the rumpled sheets, still holding each other, giving each other tiny grateful kisses.

Now was she going to feel guilty? She prodded and poked at her conscience. *Nu?* Her conscience was either as exhausted as the rest of her or it just didn't give a damn. She felt nothing but release and blissful satisfaction.

"That was so good!" she said.

Phil shifted, still holding her, making them both more com-

fortable. "Always happy to please. It was good for me, too."
He laughed again. "I hate to admit it, but the last time I made
love was six weeks ago."

It took her a minute, and then she got it. "You mean, with
me?"

"That's right. It's almost getting to be a regular thing." He
squeezed her lightly. "Only kidding, only kidding. I know . . .
you're a married lady. I mustn't get used to it."

"Well, just for the record," Cookie said, "that was the last
time for me, too."

"You're kidding!"

Grimly: "Alas, Phil, I am not kidding. But you don't want
to hear my problems."

"I'm a cop, remember? I deal with people's problems all the
time. I know how to listen. So if you want an ear, here's mine."

It was dark in his bedroom, cooled by the air conditioner,
and she was so relaxed, feeling so at peace with her body, for a
change. She began to talk. She found herself telling him the
whole damn thing.

"For months now, we haven't made love," she finished.
"Somehow, lately, we never seem to be going to bed at the same
time." She took a breath. "Last week, after *City Sounds*, after
everyone had left except one or two old friends, he put his arm
around me and gave me a kiss and said, 'I know it's been tough,
kid, and you've been wonderful. But now the worst is over. Now
we can get back to normal.' God, I was so sure he meant *everything* could get back to normal. That night, I waited for him.
I was exhausted, really wiped out, so I went to bed even though
two of his old cronies were still there. But I figured . . . Well,
anyway, he never came to bed, not for hours. And it's been the
same all week. I mean, *nothing's* back to normal—especially
not our sex life." She paused and then laughed a little. "Not
that our sex life was ever spectacular . . . but at least it was
there."

Phil chuckled. "Not spectacular? With you there? I can't believe that! You're one helluva lady!"

"Dave's on the shy side, and when we got married was a
virgin. I began to notice after a while that I was the one who
usually made the first move, but what the hell, whenever I made
a move, he was always willing. What did I know? I thought we
had a complete and satisfying sex life. Hell, I thought it was
modern and egalitarian and superior! Is that a scream? And,

let's face it, I'm kind of a bossy lady. I guess I liked being in control. And then . . ."

And then, it began to nag at her. He *always* had to wait for her! Didn't he really want her? What did it mean? So she asked him about it. She said, "Dave, how come you never make the first move . . . in bed, in sex?"

He didn't even answer her question. He got all hurt, and he said if she didn't like the way he made love, well, he was sorry, but wasn't it a little late to bring it up, after thirteen years? He was who he was and as far as he was concerned, this was a helluva time for her to realize she preferred something else.

She couldn't believe her ears. She just sat there across the kitchen table from him with her mouth open, staring at him. And it ended that she had to apologize to him. She had to re-assure him over and over again that she *didn't* want anyone else, that isn't what she had said! It certainly wasn't what she had *meant*! But he sat there, shaking his head, lips pressed tightly together, frowning and looking hurt. She finally realized he wasn't really listening to her; or if he was listening he wasn't *hearing* her. He never answered her question. To him, it hadn't been a question at all, it had been an attack. She had to drop it. Finally, she said, "Just forget this conversation ever took place, all right, Dave?" and he said he'd be more than happy to do just that.

"You want to hear a shameful tale?" Cookie said, thinking, I've got to stop this blabbing, I've really got to stop it. But she didn't. "All this past week, I've been making moves on him. Sunday night, he was too drunk. Monday night, he was already asleep. Tuesday, I put a hand on him and he said, 'Not now, Cookie.' And so on and so forth."

"As far as I'm concerned, lady, any man who doesn't jump on you anytime he gets the chance, he's gotta be out of his mind. And any lady who puts up with that, well . . . she's out of *her* mind. If you don't mind my saying so."

Well, she did mind his saying so. She suddenly felt very uncomfortable. She'd talked too damn much; she'd told him more than he really needed to know. More than he *wanted* to know, probably. Dammit.

She said something, she wasn't even thinking about what she was saying, and got out of the bed and put on her clothes. She wanted to get out of there, go home, get back into her regular life.

And then when she got there and let herself in, fifteen minutes later, she wondered why she had been so eager. From the bed-room, she could hear the sounds of the television, and it made her so goddamn mad. She hadn't realized before how sick and tired she was of that damn TV being on all the time. And then, from the bedroom, Dave's voice: "Cookie? You back already?"

Back already! Was that all he could think of to say to her? She'd been gone almost two hours. As usual, he didn't notice, and couldn't care less. What fantasy had been in her head that made her think this was normal and regular and real and what she wanted? She felt like turning around and walking right back out, but that was stupid—because where did she have to go?

She checked herself out in the little round mirror above the phone before she went in to Dave. Her new face was nearly all gone, rubbed and kissed and stroked and fondled right off. Only, faintly, a gleam of jade green on the eyelids. She should feel relief that her husband wouldn't notice. But what the hell, he wouldn't notice if she walked in wrapped in Saran!

"That's right!" she called. "I'm back!" And then, as long as he couldn't be bothered to lift his arse and bring himself out here to speak to her face-to-face, she did what she was always yelling at her teenaged charges not to do: she gave him the finger. Next time, she'd do it to his face.

She really ought to sit down and think things through. God knows it was past time. Phil's words were echoing in her head. Any lady who took it was crazy. She agreed, and how she agreed. So why was she still here? Where was her courage? She didn't love him. There was nothing left of their old camaraderie, their old togetherness. He didn't even want to make love to her any-more. So why this terror? Why was she so afraid to tell Dave—who surely ought to be the first to know! Why? Why? So many questions, and no answers forthcoming. Not from her, anyway. Not now, not yet.

Oh, to hell with it, she thought and turned and headed down the hall for the bedroom.

Chapter Sixteen

Sunday, August 2, 1987   Paul Gordon, cursing, drove the car as fast as he thought it safe to do. They were going to be late to Pop's birthday party. He'd promised Steffie he'd be back home by eleven—the party was at noon in the city—and here it was, twelve-fifteen, and they were crawling along, just past the gas tanks on the L.I.E. It would be another half hour—at *least*—before they got to the Upper West Side, and then he'd be circling for fifteen minutes, looking for a parking place. Shit! Never again would he allow himself to be sidetracked that way!

"If we'd started on time," Laura griped, "we wouldn't be in this traffic jam."

"We never get anywhere on time," Deirdre said. A look in the rearview mirror showed three pretty but sullen faces.

"That's not true," he said. "Neither of those things. Don't you guys know this is called the Long Island Parking Lot?"

"Oh, very funny."

"Isn't that a brand-new joke?"

"I can't imagine where he got such an original idea!"

Wiseass kids! But now they were all smiling, at least. They were all pretty girls, although Laura was a bit chunky and Cara was going to be flat-chested. Deirdre was the real beauty. She was already five seven and only fourteen. Tall and slim and willowy; she could be a model. To tell the truth, she was his favorite. He wasn't sure why, she just was.

Now she said, "I wonder if Mickey will be there." She had a kind of crush on her big cousin.

"Probably," he said. Then he grinned at all of them in the mirror. "Mickey's a *good* girl. Not like some I could mention."

"Hey, Dad, is it true we're putting Mickey through school?"

"Who told you that?" Steffie demanded. "And I never want to hear you repeat that, do you understand? Especially not to Aunt Cookie or Uncle Dave!"

"I get it. It *is* true."

"Listen," Paul said. "Your uncle was out of work for three years—you know all about that—and, hey, a kid who can get

155

into Harvard should *go* to Harvard. I wouldn't mind," he added, "if one of you ladies got into Harvard."

Cara just laughed. "Oh, sure, Dad. Me with my B-minus average—it's a sure thing. And if not Harvard, how about Yale?"

And then Laura said, "That's what I'm going to do."

Laura would do anything to get attention from him; he realized it and he wished it didn't make him squirm, the way it did. Something about Laura made him uneasy, something begging. But, of course, he'd never let on. "Yeah, baby, I'm counting on you," he said.

Then something came on the radio that they all wanted to hear, so he concentrated on his driving. If you could call bumper-to-bumper, twenty-three-miles-per-hour creeping driving. He'd been feeling kind of blue today, kind of down. As soon as he woke up this morning, he felt that knot in his stomach, the knot that said something was wrong. What could it be? In not too many years, his kids would all be gone, away to college, or in their own homes. Maybe that was it, the end of his youth. Getting old was the pits!

He lay in bed this morning, staring at the pink ceiling and suddenly remembering Betty Field, the head cheerleader for Millville High the year he went into eighth grade. Big tits, tiny waist, great personality. Christ, Betty Field. He'd never forget her. She'd given him his first French kiss—a lot of them—behind the high school during a Sock Hop, and when he got hard, she'd laughed and put her hand on it, rubbing a little. He thought he'd jump out of his skin!

He wasn't even supposed to be at that dance. It was for high school kids only, and Cookie had warned him, "If you *dare* to show up there, Paul Gordon, I'll *kill* you. I'll die! Little kids aren't wanted!"

He knew why she didn't want him there. She didn't want him looking when she danced close to boys. She didn't want him seeing her leave in a car. He knew all about it. The big boys all whistled when they saw her. He heard them saying she was built like a brick shithouse.

But no sister was going to order him around. Betty had come up to him after school and told him she'd be looking for him at the Sock Hop. The most popular girl in school!

That was the night he knew for sure he had something special, that girls really liked him. She asked him to dance, she dragged him out back, she showed him how to kiss, where she liked him to put his hands. Jesus, she was hot! And she didn't care that he was only fourteen; she said so. "If you're big enough," she said huskily, pressing closer to him, "you're old enough!"

In his bed this morning, he found himself excited just remembering, and he had to laugh. God, where had that memory come from? He hadn't thought about Betty Field since they left Millville. And then he remembered. He had a date this morning for a quickie with Roz LeVine.

He told Steffie he had to meet a client and he'd be back in time to get to the party on time. Goddammit, he'd always kept his promises to Steffie; he prided himself on that. He'd been damn lucky to get her, he knew that. He made himself a promise, the night before they got married, that he'd always be good to her. And he always had been. Okay, there had been a few women here and there. What she didn't know wouldn't hurt her.

In every other way, he was the ideal husband, if he did say so himself. For instance, a couple of years ago, she and Shirley, her best friend, had gone into business. They opened a little boutique and, well, it didn't work out. People just weren't willing to spend that kind of money on handcrafted things. And Shirley's husband, Steve, hadn't let her forget it for a minute. He kept on and on about it, like they were dumb. But not Paul. "It's your money, sweetheart," he said. "You had to try it and it didn't work out. So? Nothing ventured," he said, "nothing gained. And now we have twenty of the greatest-looking baskets in Great Neck!" He remembered the look on her face, like she'd just been given the Nobel prize.

And anyway, his saying that, about the baskets, gave her an idea and now they lined one wall of the kitchen. And goddamn if everyone who saw them didn't want to buy them! Wanted to know where she found them, offered her twice what she'd paid! All it took was the right sales pitch—and that went for *anything*.

This morning, Roz had to go and get those warm oils out and begin rubbing his body, describing just how beautiful every part was. Talk about the right sales pitch! But he let it go on too long, like a dummy, and by the time she finished, he smelled like a whorehouse; so he lost fifteen minutes, scrubbing himself in the shower with Ivory soap so he could go home.

He gave Roz a nice kiss at the door, but she clung a little and said, "Let's not wait so long until next time." And he had to push her off and look her straight in the eye and tell her again how it was. He called the shots, and he decided how things were going to be, and women who couldn't follow his rules didn't see him anymore, okay? Got that? She got it. She didn't like it, but

she got it. And then he couldn't figure why he was even telling
her anything. If he was smart, he'd walk away and never see the
woman again. And then he felt bad because in the backs of her
eyes there was hurt. He hated hurting women. But Christ, they
did set themselves up for it. They thought, when the sexual
revolution came along, that they were going to be able to handle
it, same as men. No way! They needed men too much. They
needed too much, period. They always wanted to make a relationship out of a hard-on.

But women could always get to him. He couldn't just leave
her standing there, her hair all tousled and her makeup smeared,
feeling old and rejected. So he gave her a little soft soap, to
make her feel better, stuff like "I find you too attractive, I have
to keep a distance, I can't afford to be tempted the way you
tempt me." And he watched as she melted. Did he know how
to treat a woman, or what? He was going to have to be very,
very careful with this one—she really had the hots for him.
There was nothing more dangerous than a woman in love.

They were finally in the Midtown Tunnel. He checked himself out in the rearview mirror now, just a glance. He knew what
he looked like. Not bad, for a guy nearly forty years old. From
a distance, not a day over twenty-five. He kept himself in shape
playing squash three times a week and there was a sunlamp in
his office. Once or twice a day, he'd close his eyes, tilt his chair
back, and give himself some rays. So he always looked fit and
healthy, and they did say he was a good-looking man. Hell, he'd
known that since he was twelve or thirteen and girls first started
flirting with him. Ever since Betty Field, really.

He was going to have to be a lot more careful. He kept forgetting how big his girls were, how much free time Steffie had
nowadays. One of these times, he was going to get caught with
his pants down. Literally.

Here was Sixty-fifth Street, his turn. Soon, they'd be there.
He swerved abruptly, just missing a car that shot out of a parking
garage, leaning on the horn to show how he felt about *that*. He
hated this. Every time he knew he had to see his father, he got
this constriction in his chest. He was always afraid of spotting
deterioration. Even on the phone. Like the night Dave was on
City Sounds—He couldn't be at Cookie's for her party but he
called—of course, he called. And he found himself schmoozing
on and on and on, trying to put off the inevitable moment when
he'd have to talk to Pop. He couldn't even remember what he
said, only that when he kidded around about Dave becoming a

media celebrity, she said, "We're all entitled to our fifteen minutes of fame, Paul, sweetie."

"That's clever, Cook!"

"That was a quote, honey. From Andy Warhol. But, of
course, you know that."

He could never be quite sure when Cookie was making fun
of him and when she was being serious. He wished she wouldn't
do that. But whenever he tried to tell her, she just laughed and
said, "Go read a book, *bubeleh.*"

Then he talked to Dave and said all the right things and that
used up some more time. And then, finally, he had no choice.
It was time to talk to Pop. And God, it was even worse than he
had feared. He was very excited about Dave, of course, but his
voice! He sounded weak, tired . . . Christ, he sounded so *old*!
Dave was a hero, he said.

"The man deserves a medal, Paul. There aren't many left in
the world who care about the poor and oppressed. You know
what I mean, Paul."

"Yeah, Pop, I know what you mean." The same old Party
line! Paul had heard it his whole life; he didn't need any prompt-
ing at this point. And frankly, he found it boring, he always had.

Thank God he'd known enough to get off that left-wing tread-
mill. His whole childhood had been an endless sacrifice to the
working class. Before he knew he was Jewish, before he knew
he was handsome, he knew he was a member of the working
class. It was the one great, important thing in the world. He was
brought up thinking—hell, forget thinking, *knowing*—there
would be a revolution; and he was going to be a part of it. Christ,
by the time he was in first grade, he already knew it was baloney!
None of Pop's fancy ideas ever turned out to be real or true.
And that meant his exile in upstate New York was garbage.
Maybe it all was!

He'd never said any of this to Pop—hell, it wouldn't do any
good, would it? And at this stage, he certainly wasn't going to
start in. Christ, Pop was dying! And there went that clutch in
his chest again! Damn.

At last. He turned out from the transverse and onto West
Ninety-sixth Street. "Almost there," he announced, "And only
half an hour late, too. Hey, the old man hasn't lost his touch."

The three girls cheered, and when he looked in the rearview
mirror, he could see they weren't being sarcastic or anything,
And Steffie reached over to pat his thigh, "You'll never lose

your touch, darling,'' she said, and the girls all hooted and whistled and stamped their feet.

Goddamn. He had everything he'd ever dreamed of—*more*. A gorgeous house, a showplace. A beautiful wife, three terrific daughters. His own company—or it would be, one of these days. Plenty of money, well known in his community. Goddammit, he was a successful man!

So why should he be feeling letdown again? Every once in a while, it snuck up on him, this kind of blue feeling. Bullshit. He had everything a man could want. Everything.

<hr />

Chapter Seventeen

Sunday, August 2, 1987   Jonah came into the crowded living room from the back of the apartment, laughing.

"You wouldn't believe what's going on in our bedroom! All of them, all the kids, on the floor, lying all over one another, resting on one another, just like when they were little. Remember, Dot? They always used to disappear into another room and make like a pretzel factory!''

He shook his head, but he looked so pleased, Cookie thought. And she blessed the kids, all of them—hers *and* Paul's and Sonora, too—for doing something so simple that made Pop feel so good.

Pop *looked* good today. Yes, he was holding his own. In fact, he looked better than the day of Dave's party; in fact, he looked better than he had last Thursday when they went out for Chinese. There was a temptation to make believe that Dr. Goldberg had made a terrible mistake and Pop was getting better, wasn't really doomed. She fought that temptation. Enough that he was looking so well today, for his birthday party. It would have been nice if Paul could have arrived on time, for a change. But never mind. He was here; that's what mattered.

Sixty-eight years old! Not everyone got to have their sixty-eighth birthday celebration with all of their children and their children's children. She looked around the room, thinking, Well,

it's nice. It's been a long time since my brothers and I were all
together with Mom and Pop and it's nice. Of course, it would
have been a lot nicer if he didn't have a damned terminal disease.
It would be nicer to plan his sixty-ninth birthday, his seventieth,
hell, his eightieth! No. She had to make herself think about
something else.

Pop eased himself down into his favorite chair, motioned that
he wanted a refill on his drink, and when Cookie took his glass
said, "I wonder if when they're all middle-aged and married
and with children of their own, they're still all going to go lean
on one another like that?" Again, he smiled. "There's nothing
like family!"

"I'll drink to that," Cookie said. But as she headed for the
makeshift bar, she leaned over and murmured to her mother, "I
wish he'd felt that way when we were kids."

"*Shah*, Cookie. It's the man's birthday, and what's past is
past. So he's a little more sentimental lately. That's what happens—"

Quickly Cookie put in, "I know, I know. That's what happens
when you get older." Her mother was very big on facing the
awful truth. Sometimes it was a pain.

"Who will toast our big family reunion?" Cookie said.

"Some reunion!" Jonah griped. "We'll all be lucky if that
so-and-so ever agrees on a place."

"For so-and-so read Jack Strauss," Dave said, laughing.

"What *is* happening, anyway?" Paul said.

And Irwin, sitting on the floor, his long legs stretched out so
that nobody could walk without having to step over them, added,
"Yeah, somebody tell *me*. I'd like to know what's happening.
Nobody ever calls *me* to let me know what's going on."

"Irwin, Irwin, still *kvetching*," Dot said. "So pick up a
phone and call. Listen. I have plenty of friends whose children
call them regularly, every Sunday afternoon, like clockwork
and—"

She was drowned out by the hoots and catcalls of her three
children, all saying, *"Kvetch, kvetch,"* in unison.

Win was laughing with the rest, Cookie saw, but there was
no smile in his eyes. In fact, she could see the invisible pout.
God, look at him: forty-three years old, artistic, bright, talented
. . . and still the same whiny, dissatisfied, bewildered little boy
she remembered from Millville—hell, from always.

She knew damn well that people were capable of change; she
was sometimes at the fulcrum of that change. What was wrong

with him? Why couldn't he get his act together? He had always
gone from one dream to another, always expecting manna to
fall from heaven. He'd been Orthodox for a year; he'd been on
a kibbutz in Israel for a year; he'd gone to college for a year;
he'd even been married for a year. But nothing seemed to be the
magic answer. Once, he'd had a success, a book of photographs
of the civil rights movement. He'd been called, by one small
photography magazine, the Stieglitz of civil rights because "he
and his camera are willing to go anywhere." The reviews said
that he had created images that would never fade.

Well, maybe the images wouldn't, but he certainly had. That
had been his first and last successful venture. He was pathetic.
Tonight, for instance, he'd come in the door, late as usual,
breathless, having missed the shuttle he had planned on taking.
Typical. He never came on time, never. Come to think of it,
neither did Paul. Where in the world did they learn that from?

Win had breezed in, late, full of apologies. "I don't have
your present with me. I'll send it."

Cookie had to take him aside and remind him that the three
of them were giving Pop a VCR and a bunch of Hitchcock films.
"I signed your name on the card, Win," she said, exasperated.
"Don't you remember me telling you about it?"

It was always this way. He never remembered those meaningless details, like what was happening to other people. Sometimes she thought that other people hardly existed for him, that
he inhabited a world of half-real shadowy figures who existed
only when they drifted into his viewfinder.

"Oh, that's right. I forgot we were doing the VCR. I'll send
you a check, as soon as this guy calls me back."

"Oh, Win! I thought you were selling regularly to the *Globe*."

"It didn't work out. The guy kept making me promises and
not coming through. But now, Cookie, I've got something much
more exciting—"

He waited until she prompted him. "Yes?" And then he went
on and on, a very long and involved tale about a guy he met at
a party named Herb Cohen, a publisher, who thought they could
do a book about the Constitutional Bicentennial . . . something,
she didn't really bother to listen.

"Is this on spec, Irwin?"

"*Win*, please. God, Cookie, the least you could do is remember my name. It's only been twenty years!" As usual, he was
ducking the real question.

Cookie had looked deeply into her brother's eyes, trying to

divine what was going on in that brain. It was always this way, with him. Didn't he know the difference between somebody admiring his work and a contract with his name on it? She'd seen it happen over and over. The least flicker of interest, he immediately turned into a commitment. And then he'd tell you exactly how much this commitment was going to bring in and how much he'd have to be traveling—and the next thing you knew, he was out buying himself all kinds of stuff . . . and all on the basis of exactly nothing. And then he'd complain that you couldn't trust anybody anymore.

"Win," she said now, superpatient. It *was* Pop's party, and nothing must spoil it. "I've been calling you regularly, filling you in on the details. You know as much as the rest of us."

"And anyway, bro," Paul said lazily, sipping on his glass of wine, "we don't know anything about what *you're* doing. So . . . what're you doing these days?"

"How would you like to tell all your friends that your brother is the official photographer of the Constitutional Bicentennial?"

"Is he?"

"Well . . . close to it. I mean, nothing's been signed yet, but I'm on my way to Philadelphia to show my work to the committee. And my agent says if I don't get this job and make two hundred grand out of books and posters, then I'm not the photographer he thinks I am!"

Paul laughed. "Jesus, Win, that's just words! You're taking that as a promise?"

"Why would he say it if he didn't mean it?"

Paul leaned forward. "Don't you get it, Win? The guy says if you don't make it, it ain't *his* fault. That's all he's said. That's all. Think about it."

His eyes met Cookie's briefly; she mirrored his exasperation. Then he turned back to Win, waiting for a reply.

Paul regarded his brother. Win was so different from the rest of them. Not just in his vagueness but his looks, too. Craggy. A little shabby. Always needing a haircut. He was the only one in the family that looked really Jewish and, oh, God, had he suffered for that in Millville. Millville had been hell for poor Win . . . Irwin, back then, of course. Maybe that's why he'd never been able to get his act together.

Now Mom got up and began to bustle around, which is what she did anytime she didn't like the way the conversation was going. "*Genug*, enough already! What difference does it make what his agent says or doesn't say, or means or doesn't mean?

Win is a wonderful photographer. Anytime people come here and see his pictures, they have nothing but praise."

All beside the point, but Paul knew better than to say anything to her. "I'm sure," he murmured, wondering what she'd say if she knew how many times he *shtupped* Win with money. His brother was working up to it—Paul could smell it coming—but he knew Win. Win would wait until they were alone somewhere and then he'd ask for one of those famous "loans." It was all right. He had it to give, thank God.

"And anyway," Dorothy went on, as if the past ten minutes hadn't even happened, "it's not Jack."

"Huh? What's not Jack?"

"Changing where we're going to have the reunion. That's what we're talking about, isn't it?" And she put on an insulted look when her children hooted with laughter. "I'm sorry. Call me *pisher*, but I thought we were discussing the reunion."

"*Now* we are."

"Anyway, it wasn't my brother Jack. It was the children. Deena and Elaine . . . and Cookie, too. She's one of the guilty parties."

"You're right! You're right!"

"They kept changing their minds. First it was Jack and Sylvia's, and then they were afraid it'll be too much work for Sylvia, she'll overdo. Sylvia never overdid a day in her life. She always had plenty of help—"

"Mom!"

"*Shah*, Cookie." Mom was trying to keep a straight face, but it was obvious she was having the time of her life.

Not for the first time, Paul Gordon thought that his mother probably should have been an actress or something. She loved being the center of attention, just loved it.

"Next, a hotel," she continued. "But somebody said no, a hotel is too impersonal. Too impersonal? Too expensive, that's what *I* say! Then it was supposed to be at Deena's house, but what can I tell you, she lives in Brooklyn. Brooklyn, I ask you!"

Through her laughter, Cookie objected. "Mom, Mom, it's Brooklyn Heights. Not exactly Siberia."

"Heights, shmeits! It's across the river, that's all I know!"

By this time, they were all laughing so hard it brought the kids out of the bedroom. They clustered at the entrance to the living room, saying, "What? What's so funny?"

Jonah said, "Your grandmother, who else? She's telling us

the story of the reunion—which in my opinion will never happen."

"It'll happen," Dot said, giving him a hard look. "You and my brother, notwithstanding. Anyway, then it was going to be at Cookie and Dave's, but I told Cookie, 'Why should you do all the work? And anyway, your apartment's too small.' So this week it's going to be at Elaine's and . . . what's the name of her husband? I keep forgetting."

"Howard. Howard Barranger."

"Right. That's where it's going to be, and I hear they live in a very fancy apartment on Central Park West, only the one son and he lives in Battery Park City, so there's plenty of room, even for the proletariat!"

Dave got up, stretching, and said, "No wonder it took thirty-five years for these two families to get together!"

One of the kids said, "Anyway, what started this whole feud, Grandpa?"

There was a funny silence, like everyone was holding their breath, and then Mom said, "That's a story for another time. Now is a birthday and now we're going to have birthday cake."

Something struck Paul about her tone. Of course, when she came out of the kitchen, carrying a gigantic layer cake covered in what looked like three kinds of chocolate frosting, she was all smiles, and whatever he had thought he saw, before, was gone.

Everyone crowded into the small dining area and sang "Happy Birthday," and Pop made the grandchildren blow out the candles. "You could all have my wishes, all of you. I give you my sixty-eight wishes."

He walked around to give each of the kids a kiss and a silver dollar, including Jon's girlfriend. When he was smiling and talking and lively like this, it was easy to let yourself forget how sick he was. And Paul, for one, wanted to forget that. He couldn't imagine the world without his father in it. It gave him a very weird feeling.

Then Pop lifted his glass of champagne and made a little speech that was really very nice. About how he came to this country, already half grown, and what a wonderful country it had turned out to be, except for the Capitalists, and everybody laughed and dug into their cake. And then it was over and everyone kind of scattered, Cookie and Steff into the kitchen to clean up the dishes, and the kids right back to the VCR and *Rear Window*.

He poured himself a refill on the wine and went down the hall to the second bedroom, the room Mom called the TV room and Pop called the library. He wanted just to look at his daughters, to count them, kind of, to make sure they were still there. Of course, they were—and just the way Pop had described them, sprawled all over one another, using one another as pillows. It made a man feel good, seeing the cousins so friendly and easy with each other. What else did you have in life that really mattered, except your family?

He waved at the kids and went on down to Mom and Pop's bedroom. It was already five o'clock. He had thought they'd be out of here by four, but no way was he going to be the one to break up the party. Quickly, he punched out the familiar number and when she answered, spoke softly, directly into the mouthpiece. "Listen, I'm not going to see you again tonight. This is lasting a lot longer than I figured. I'm not going to make it."

"Not at all?"

"That's right. Don't fuss, okay?" He wasn't liking this, he wasn't liking it at all. There was something wrong with calling Roz from his parents' bedroom, and he found himself getting angry with her. He didn't owe her an explanation; he didn't owe her anything, in fact. She ought to know he couldn't chat with her from his parents' apartment. But along with his annoyance with her was his undeniable excitement. She did something to him that most other women didn't. He didn't know why, he didn't know how—it just was, that's all, and he wasn't about to give it up if he didn't have to. "Rozzie, baby, listen. I don't like it any better than you do," he murmured into the phone.

And then, right in the middle of the sentence, in comes Win. Without knocking, without warning. Schmuck! Putting on a bright, cheery business tone of voice, he said into the phone, "Well, that's swell. We'll have to discuss the details later this evening. Thanks a lot, Sid." And he hung up.

"So, Win, besides the constitution thing, what else is happening with you?"

"Well . . . in fact, I gotta get myself down to Philly and . . ."

"You broke?" Why go through this charade, every single time? Did Win really think he was fooling anyone? Paul wanted to laugh in his brother's face.

"A little. Just at the moment, you know. I'm waiting for a big check to clear . . ."

Bullshit, Paul thought, but he reached for his wallet. "How much do you need?"

"Just enough to tide me over . . ."

"Sure, sure. How much? Coupla hundred?"

"Could you make it three?"

Paul counted out the bills and handed them over.

"It's just a loan, Paul. I'll have a check to you . . . let's see, in a week or ten days." And he walked out.

"Sure, sure. Don't worry about it." He was just relieved Win hadn't heard any of the conversation with Roz . . . but, hell, when Win was intent on getting his money, he didn't notice anything else. Luckily.

He bent forward a little to check himself out in the dresser mirror. Women found him handsome. Did he think so? Well, he didn't look his age, and he had to admit he looked a helluva lot better than most of their friends. But Paul Newman, he wasn't—even though Roz said so.

"You're gorgeous."

He whirled around, startled. He'd really been lost in thought. It was Cookie. He grinned at her. He really loved his sister; he liked her, too. She was a good pal, Cookie. No phoniness, no bullshit.

"So're you."

"Liar!" She laughed. "But thanks, anyway. I saw that."

"What?" He became nervous.

"Money passing hands, *bubeleh*. Does he ever see you that he doesn't ask for money?"

"Never."

They both laughed, and she added, "I don't have to ask if he pays you back."

"That's right. You don't have to."

"Paul, you're not doing him any favors, you know. He'll never straighten up and fly right if you keep giving him dough every time he whines."

"Agh! I can afford it. Don't worry about it. He's an artist; you know how they are. Don't give me that look, Cookie. He's got a real talent. And anyway, I'm only doing what I learned at my daddy's knee . . . sharing the wealth."

"Oh, Paul! Come on. Give me a real answer, would you?"

"That's real. I like doing it. Okay? That's the real truth. I like having it to give."

"And maybe you like lording it over the big brother who always gave you such a hard time?"

Paul laughed. "Could be! So what? What does it matter? So I give him a couple hundred bucks and so he lies to himself about what he's doing. Are any of us any better? Do you know what the hell you're doing with your life?''

"I certainly hope so!''

"Well, I wish I could be so sure. I don't know, Cookie. Here I am, almost forty, right at the cusp, like they say . . . and what have I done? Made a lot of money. Built a fancy house. If you asked Pop, 'Is Paul a success?' you know what he'd say. He'd say it's too damn bad that Paul has no purpose to his life, that he only cares about a profit . . .''

"Do you *care* what Pop thinks?''

"Yes. No. I don't know. Agh, forget it. I'm feeling sentimental because it's my father's birthday and he's an old man and he's going to die." He smiled at her and lightly pinched her cheek. "And I feel guilty, I guess, because I never was the person he wanted me to be.''

"Paul, we have to be the person we are, not somebody else's idea of who we ought to be.''

"Cookie. Do me a favor. Tell me to read a book.''

"Read a book, Paul.''

He kissed her lightly on the forehead. Then he said, "Cookie, I love my wife, I love my daughters, I treasure them. Do you understand what I'm saying? Who I am is a guy, a married man with three little girls. That's who I am, that's Paul Gordon. I love them, I'd die for them . . .''

"Mmmmm . . . ?''

"Ah, shit. Cookie, I cheat. I cheat all the time. I sleep around. I fuck other women. I don't know why. I just seem to have to. Christ, it's a puzzle to me. Why do I do it?''

Dryly, Cookie said, "I don't know, Paul. Why *do* you do it?''

He pressed his fingers against his forehead. He could feel a headache coming on. "I wish I knew! Christ, you don't know the half of it! Lately, I've been . . . seeing someone and . . . Christ, Cookie, she's fat, she's sloppy, she's older than me. I don't even like her! But it's like I'm obsessed. I've always been so careful, before. You couldn't ask for a better wife, three better kids. I don't want to lose them! And yet, all this woman has to do is call me on the telephone and I'm gone. I'm getting so careless! It's so goddamn self-destructive. And it's not just my family life. I think I lost a very important sale Friday, screwing around and coming in late. What the hell am I doing? I'm risking *everything*!''

There was silence for a moment and then he laughed. "Don't

listen to me. Don't listen. Like I said, it's having an effect on me, this whole . . . business, with Pop. It's getting to me."

To his horror, he felt two tears ooze out of his eyes and, quickly, he turned away from his sister so she wouldn't see that he was crying, and damned if he didn't meet her eyes in the mirror.

ᕍᕍᕍᕍᕍᕍᕍᕍᕍᕍᕍᕍᕍᕍᕍᕍᕍᕍᕍᕍᕍᕍᕍᕍᕍᕍᕍᕍᕍᕍᕍᕍᕍᕍᕍᕍᕍ

Chapter Eighteen

Tuesday, August 11, 1987   It felt like love, lying here in the rumpled sheets, his head pillowed on her breast, her arm around him. Peaceful. Satisfied. Relaxed, actually. Comfortable. Then why, Cookie asked herself, was she searching so diligently for the exact description of how she felt after having made love with her husband? Could it be that she wasn't quite sure *how* she was feeling? Yes. She was definitely uncertain. Nevertheless, she was filled with tenderness. It had been a long wait for them, a long, long time. In fact, she was *still* surprised it had happened at all.

She'd come back from work today, totally wiped out. The kids were fussy and frustrated, not happy with anything; and frankly, she didn't blame them. She didn't feel much different. It was very difficult to be cool when it was nearly a hundred degrees Fahrenheit with a humidity to match. She had three shouting matches, two of them with colleagues, and when the day was finally over, she got a blister on her heel walking to the train. The subway didn't bear thinking about. She just stood there, jammed up against six other steaming, wretched people, and tried to blank out her mind until Ninety-sixth Street.

By the time she let herself in—to a stifling apartment, not a breath of air—she was ready to commit some kind of crime. She headed right for the bedroom, ready to strip down—and then she heard it. The television. The goddamn, heat-producing, mindless fucking television. Dave! What was *wrong* with the man, that he couldn't be alone for two and half minutes without the damn tube on? You'd think he didn't have a brain in his head,

And anyway, what would he be watching at this hour? *Mr. Rogers? Divorce Court?* Now *there*, she thought, was an idea!

And then when she flung the door open, she felt like a fool. The air-conditioning was on and it was blessedly cool. The boob tube was tuned into the news. Two tray tables had been set up and there were packages from Zabar's and a big sweating pitcher of something cold and ice-cubed. And there was her husband, in a pair of antique Bermuda shorts and not much else that she could see, and he was leaping, yes actually leaping, off the bed, grinning, yes actually grinning, at her. "Hey! I've been waiting for you!"

Speechless was putting it mildly. He'd actually schlepped himself into Zabar's so she wouldn't have to cook. It was a miracle. And she was so hungry. They fell upon the food like a pair of wolves and then, still greasy around the lips from Zabar's best pastrami, he fell upon her, avid and urgent, like he hadn't been for a long, long time.

So here she was, allowing herself to love him again, allowing herself to believe that maybe they had a chance. The lovemaking had been, as always, considerate and predictable. The earth didn't move, it didn't even quiver; but she felt good.

Good, but, she realized, air-conditioning or no, she wanted a shower, badly. Dave was dozing off, leaning heavily against her, beginning to snore. She shook him gently and said, "Move, sweetie. I'm going into the shower."

She took out perfume and dusting powder and a nice, clean, fluffy towel. She picked out a cotton voile nightgown she'd never worn—too fancy, too sheer. But now, in the afterglow, it seemed right.

She could just imagine the nice cool water sluicing over her overheated skin . . . it would be so nice. But when she turned on the shower, the bathroom began to fill with steam. She turned off the hot water tap and nothing was left but a little trickle of not-quite-cold.

Dammit, Dave had promised to put the water pressure problem on the building board's agenda! He kept forgetting. She'd written three very funny letters, hoping that humor would galvanize them into some kind of action. She'd complained and nagged and yelled. It had been going on for months. What was the matter with Dave? He lived here, too; he took showers!

She grabbed her old robe from the hook and wrapped it quickly around herself. Forget sexy nighties, dammit. She was hot and tired and sweaty and she deserved to have a shower.

"Dammit, Dave, the cold water still hasn't been fixed!"

He was still stretched out on the bed, his eyes closed, a little smile on his lips. He opened his eyes and looked at her quizzically. "Why are you bringing this up now?"

"Why? Because *now* is when I tried to take a shower and the water is boiling! Dammit, I thought you guys on the board were going to take care of it! I thought you were going to take care of it *last* month!"

"Cookie, Cookie. Does your yelling at me make the cold water pressure improve?"

"Don't do that to me, Dave Adler! Don't make my anger the issue. The issue is there still isn't any cold water in this apartment."

"I know there isn't. We've called the Water Department. We've had a plumber in, who said he fixed it. You know all this, Cookie. How come you're so mad all of a sudden?"

"All of a sudden! If one of your *clients* called from the South Bronx and said she was being boiled alive in her shower, you'd move heaven and earth, goddammit. You'd have cold water for her if you had to go fix it yourself!"

"Cookie—"

"Don't you dare deny it!"

"I'm not denying it, Cookie. You've got me pegged." He smiled at her. "That's who I am, that's who I've always been."

"The problem, Dave, is that you always think admitting your faults makes them all right."

"Hey. I happen to think that going with the flow is not a fault. It's sure better than railing and ranting and losing your temper all the time."

This, of course, was calculated to make her lose her temper. So she stood very still and drew in a deep breath. She wished he would get angry. The least he could do was tell her not to spoil the nice feeling they'd had. But, no, not Dave Adler. Dave Adler prided himself on saying, "Cookie and I never fight." He was absolutely right. Oh, yes, sometimes *she* tried to fight, but he just wouldn't. What was wrong with her, that she found it so difficult to live with?

She forced herself to smile back at him. "Sorry. It was a bad day at Black Rock."

"It's okay, Cookie. I know how that feels."

She was awful. It wasn't as if he didn't have problems of his own at the office. "Is it still bad?" she said.

He sat up in the bed, propping himself with all the pillows.

"I had high hopes when they put Rodriguez in there. But I had a meeting with him today, about the turnover rate. Christ, ten caseworkers quit last month alone! You want to talk about problems? When you can't hang on to your people for even a year . . . and then, they leave mad and don't bother to bring their files up to date and the next caseworker doesn't know what the hell's going on. We're always starting from square one. God, it's frustrating."

"Poor Dave," she murmured. She only half listened as he continued. Rodriguez did exactly the same as every other commissioner so far. Nothing ever changed in the HRA. The caseworkers burned out quickly from overwork and the bosses shrugged and said, "What can we do?" Here was Dave, complaining bitterly about that attitude; yet, he did exactly the same thing when it came to his family: shrugged his shoulders and accepted whatever came along.

She sat down on the edge of the bed, waiting until he was finished, and then she said carefully, "I know it's crazy down there and I don't know whether you've noticed or not. But Jon hasn't been home, not once, not since the *City Sounds* party."

"Oh, yeah? We saw him at Pop's birthday. And . . . gee, I thought he was over once or twice."

"No. Not once, Dave." She waited. Would he do anything different?

"He must be very busy. It happens. Especially when you're young."

"Dave, listen to me. I think he's deliberately staying away because of your attitude."

"I don't have an attitude. He doesn't mind honest criticism. Anyway, he'd better not mind, not if he wants to be an artist!" He laughed a little. "Cookie, stop fussing over Jon. He's twenty years old, he's got a live-in girlfriend, he's not your little boy anymore. You've got to face that. He needs his space."

Cookie looked at her husband's dark, open face, looked into those large, dark, heavy-lidded eyes. Why did he do this all the time? She couldn't understand it. "Dave," she said very patiently. "Listen to me, please. Jon calls me at the office regularly—are you listening to me? I don't ask him to, he calls me to chat. He asks me to lunch. But he won't come home. I don't think he's trying to escape his *mother*, do you?"

"So, maybe he's trying to escape his father. All the more reason I shouldn't chase after him."

"I think you two should talk."

"Whenever he wants to talk, I'm available. He knows that."

She was losing patience. "Dave, for God's sake!"

Again he gave that little laugh. He threw up his hands. "Okay, Cookie, I'll call him. I'll call him soon. How's that?"

"That's terrific." Nothing would come of it.

"Why the long face? I said I'd call him and I will. Come on, Cookie. If my son wants his privacy and distance, that doesn't mean it's a feud! In *my* family, we accept differences, we live and let live. Excuse me, Cookie, but in your family, there's an awful lot of wrangling. People stop talking to each other left and right!"

"No, we don't. Only two people have stopped talking to each other. The men. And that's about to end; that's the reason for the reunion, in case you'd forgotten."

Dave rolled himself out the other side of the bed, reaching for his shorts which he had actually flung across the room in his ardor earlier. Hard to believe, looking at him now—calm, distant, phlegmatic. He got dressed and stood up, picking at the remains of supper. "Who could forget that reunion? Sometimes I think that's all you have on your mind, these days."

She felt defensive. "Well, it's important! Pop—"

Dave waved her words away. "I know, I know. But, frankly, I don't see what the big deal is. Why your father couldn't pick up the phone and say to his brother-in-law, 'Enough already. Let's shake hands and let bygones be bygones.' " He pushed a piece of pickle into his mouth and spoke around it. "But, no, not in your family." He swallowed, turned the television back on, still talking but not looking at her. "No, in your family, nothing's ever simple. Everything has to be a big drama."

"That's a lousy thing to say—"

"There. See what I mean? You're mad as hell at me—and what about?" He looked amused; hell, he *was* amused. She knew him. He found all her quote emotional outbursts unquote very goddamn funny, always had. "And anyway," he finished, on a tone of sweet reasonableness, "what's so lousy about the truth? Let me remind you of the two years your mother wouldn't speak to her sister Yetta. Remember? After Yetta had her second out-of-wedlock child . . ."

"Well, Yetta was horribly rude—"

"And shall I remind you of the year you wouldn't have anything to do with Irwin? I know: he took advantage of you, he used you. But still . . . My brother Harold and I were very different from each other, but *we* never stopped talking."

"Your brother Harold," Cookie said acidly, "died thirty years ago."

Dave shrugged, sat down on the bed again, eased himself back against the pillows, his eyes fixed on the small screen. He was finished with the conversation, therefore the conversation was finished.

"You don't understand—" she started, and then stopped talking. First of all, he was totally engrossed in a rerun of *Moonlighting* so forget it. And besides, she'd already told him all about Millville and he didn't get it. A man who believed in accepting what came to you wasn't about to understand the anger and futility of that time. He'd never awakened one morning to find his father gone . . . gone where? Shhhh, we don't ask that question, we don't know where he's gone, one day he'll send for us. He had never had to leave home in the dead of night, tiptoeing and whispering. He'd never had the experience of getting off the train in the dark at a bleak, deserted station where stranded freight cars loomed like black shadows in the weak electric light. He hadn't found himself living in an ugly little town, and with a new name. His father hadn't changed from a man who gave all the speeches and led all the demonstrations to a sullen and frustrated stranger in overalls and railroad cap who rarely smiled and never laughed.

And her mother? Her mother seemed to get more and more vivid, as her father retreated into his apathy. When she thought of Mom in those days, she always saw her with her hat on, the red hat with the jaunty feather, always busy, brisk, businesslike, always on her way out. She realized, much later, that her mother was the one in charge when they lived in Millville, all those years.

But she must have stayed home sometimes because Pop worked nights and children were not left alone in a house at night in the fifties. It was certainly a rare night when her parents were home together. And it was on just such a night that she caught them in what looked to her like a fight to the death.

What time was it? Ten o'clock? She'd been asleep and then, suddenly, she was wide awake in her bed, staring up at the ceiling where the streetlight cast shadows through the big oak tree outside. There were loud voices; at first, she didn't know where they were coming from. Tancredi's Tavern was right down the street and sometimes men got drunk and fought outside the house.

But she knew, the minute she thought it, that this was not a fistfight on Cannon Street. It was her mother and father, in the living room, trying to keep their voices down but too angry to remember that her bedroom was right there, next to them.

With concentration, she could make out what they were saying; and after a few minutes, she couldn't stand it. She climbed out of her bed and crept to the door, opening it a crack. There was Pop, in his undershirt and pants, striding back and forth, back and forth, scowling, running his fingers through his hair the way he did when he was really upset.

"Don't you dare, do you hear me? If you so much as pick up that phone, I'll leave!"

Her mother, in her old pink chenille robe, her cheeks aflame, stood by the telephone table, defiant. "Don't threaten me, Jonah Gordon! The way we're living now, do you think I'd notice whether you stay or go?"

To Cookie's horror, her father lifted his arm, as if he would hit her mother, and she held her breath, biting her knuckles so she wouldn't make any noise.

"Go ahead. Big man. Hit me! Is that all you're good for anymore?"

Jonah ducked his head and turned from her. Was he crying? Cookie could no longer see his face. "Damn you," he whispered. "Damn you. What kind of wife do you call yourself?"

"What kind of wife do I call myself? I call myself a good wife. You quit the Party, you came up here, you never asked *me* what I thought! You left us alone—God knew when we'd hear from you again—and did I complain? Well? Did I?" Cookie saw her father shake his head slowly. "No. I waited, and then I schlepped up here with three little ones in the middle of the night . . . Agh! What's the use? What's done is done. Now we're here and I've made a life for us. I run the library, I bring in money, I keep the house, I take care of the children—and you, too. And you call me disloyal? You order me . . . you *order* me . . . not to make a phone call to a friend?"

"She's no friend to us and you know it, Dorothy!"

"Jonah, you don't talk to me from one week to the next. Who can I talk to? Who do I have? The kids? The neighbors? There's *no one* for me to talk to here." She made a face.

Cookie, crouching in the doorway, felt very uneasy at that face. They had been here in Millville long enough by this time for her to have almost forgotten the Coops. This was home. Why was Mom saying "the neighbors" in that ugly voice and making that ugly face?

"Her, I forbid you to talk to!"

"You forbid me nothing, do you hear me? Nothing!"

"Have you forgotten who turned me in and ruined our lives forever? Your loyalty is to your brother, not to your husband! You love him more than you love me, that's the trouble!"

"Stop with my brother, Jo! They *told* you it was Frank Green! Why do you keep insisting it was Jack?"

Cookie saw the blood rising in her mother's face, saw her literally begin to shake with anger. She wanted to run out and fling herself between them, stop them somehow from the horrible thing they were doing.

"You see! You'd rather stick up for your brother. Okay. Go to him. Go to him . . . if he'll have you. Let him take care of you and three children . . . if he'll have them!" He laughed a jeering laugh.

Dorothy's chin came up. "Maybe I will!" she said, hands on hips, small smile curling her lips.

Cookie, watching, held her breath again. She could not have moved if her life depended on it. It was just like being in the middle of a nightmare; and she began to cry.

They must have heard her. Both heads snapped around. She remembered seeing both scowling faces, both heated with anger, both totally startled.

"What are you doing out of bed?"

"I'm sorry, I—" She began to sob, unable to hold it in any longer.

Her mother came to her, put a hand on her back. "What's there to cry about, here? Your father and I are having a disagreement, and if you weren't such a busybody, you wouldn't be here, listening to us."

To this day, Cookie remembered how that hurt. It was so unfair! She tried to explain, but her mother was not listening to her. "Back to bed! Right this minute! Look at the time. You'll never be able to get up tomorrow morning." And Cookie was hustled back into her room.

Coming out of her memory now, she looked again at her husband, laughing at something on the screen. If *he* had witnessed a scene like that between his parents, wouldn't he have been terrified? Wouldn't he realize that no family was as simple as he liked to think? "My family just gets along," he loved to say.

Well, mine doesn't, she should have told him. My family has a history. We disappeared from the real world for seven years and were cut off from all the relatives we knew and loved. It's a terrible thing to go through, when you're a kid.

But to hell with it. He'd never understand. Dave was into denial. Except for his clients, of course. His clients, he knew he had to take care of, be careful with. Oh, but they were disadvantaged, disenfranchised, despised! That was *different*! His family needed no attention. His family, he thought, came with a guarantee—for better, for worse, forever.

Well, she knew there were no guarantees, not in this life. Sometimes, in spite of everyone's good intentions, things went bad. She longed to warn him: watch out for your wife. She still cares for you, but if you continue to ignore her feelings, she just might leave you. But to hell with it. He'd never understand.

€€

Chapter Nineteen

Monday, September 7, 1987   "On your left, Cookie," Deena declaimed, as they walked onto the Promenade from Pierrepont Street, "we have the harbor and the Statue of Liberty. On your right, the fabulous and fabled Brooklyn Bridge. And straight ahead, the tip of the Isle of Manhattan." She spread her arms wide and added, "Fellas, meet my cousin Cookie."

"Oh, my God!" Cookie said. "It is *fabulous*! What a view! Now I know why people live in Brooklyn . . . because they get to *see* Manhattan."

Deena laughed. "And it's free!" Together, they drifted over to the railing and leaned over, looking out at the ferryboat traffic. "I'm so glad you're taking time off today. Weekends get impossible. And this way, we have a whole day." She gave Cookie an affectionate smile.

"I thought I might be able to help with the reunion, but Elaine says she has it all under control. And when your sister Elaine says she has it all under control, I *believe* her."

"Wait'll you see her place! It's drop-dead, I assure you. Not exactly my style, but . . . if I tell you three huge leather sofas in a thirty-foot living room, with an original Frank Stella on the wall. An original *huge* Frank Stella. And these huge pillows on the floor covered in antique Oriental rugs.''

"My father will have an ideological fit, I'm sure. He's already fussing about it's 'too lavish and too much money is being spent . . . you could feed three thousand starving Africans on what it's costing for one family to have a little nosh!' ''

"Please, Cookie, let's not. I'm sorry Elaine has so much money." She laughed. "We had lunch the other day and . . . well, it surprised me that she doesn't remember the past the same way I do. The separation didn't bother her that much. As a matter of fact, she more or less told me I was being overly emotional and sentimental about it all. In fact, she was damned brutal . . .''

It had begun innocently enough, exchanging news about their kids. And then Elaine, in her best superior voice, had the nerve to pass a remark about Deena's youngest, Saul.

"He's constantly in trouble," she said.

Swift, sudden anger rose in Deena's throat. "Saul is not constantly in trouble. Saul got into trouble *once*."

"He's not going to college in the fall."

"Oh, excuse me. Is that punishable by death?"

"If you'll stop being defensive for a minute, Deena . . . You know as well as I do, if he doesn't go now, he'll never go."

"I don't know anything of the sort. And I find your attitude harsh, intrusive, judgmental, and a royal pain in the arse."

Elaine looked startled, and then she laughed. "That sounds like a perfect description of me! But I mean well, Deena. I love your kids, you know that. I'm looking forward to seeing them at this . . . rejoining of the far-flung branches of the Strauss clan.''

"You don't have to be so caustic."

"All I want to know is, is it still at my house? It's becoming harder to do this reunion than to cut an eight-million-dollar deal. God, the carrying on! If I weren't living through it, I wouldn't believe it. And just to get two families together! Well? Is it?"

"Is what what?"

"Still at my house."

"Of course, it is."

"Oh. *Of course?* The plans have only been changed seven times."

"Elaine, come on. It's a very emotionally-charged situation, for everyone."

"Excuse me, Deena, not for me."

"Oh, pardon me—the big real estate tycoon has no time for sentimentality."

"I'm as sentimental as the next guy," Elaine said, busily spearing her asparagus. "But this is phoney baloney! There was no love lost between those two guys from day one. And now you and Cookie are trying to turn it into an episode from *The Waltons*."

"No, we're not. But we both feel we were shut off from that warmth and closeness you only get with family. It's a lost and lonesome feeling when you're cut off from your roots."

"Bah, humbug!" Elaine said. "Forgive me, Deena, but that's a lot of romantic rot. Relatives can be a pain . . . in fact, Deena dear, most people groan and excuse themselves from the room if they're invited to a Cousins' Club meeting."

"Those people loved us, and we were denied that love!"

"*I* never felt so damn loved! And Marilyn doesn't even remember them! So that leaves *you*, Deena."

A bit coolly, Deena answered, "I don't expect you to understand. You're much too tough to feel lost and lonesome."

"I'm not so tough; I'm just realistic. So we may have missed a few family get-togethers, okay. But we also missed a helluva lot of yelling and screaming. Daddy and Uncle Jo were never together, that I can remember, when they weren't fighting over *something*. They're such hard-nosed bastards, those two. Once they decided they weren't talking to each other, there was no way they could ever back down. So now we have a situation where they're getting old and one of them is dying and, all of a sudden, it's love and kisses."

"Uncle Jo just wants to make peace."

"Uncle Jo wants to make peace, all right, but not with Daddy. With his own guilty conscience. That's what this is all about, Deena—not lost love and the healing of family wounds."

"You really are heartless, Elaine. I hate to say it, but you're sounding just like Daddy at his worst."

"Deena, darling, what do you want from me? Never mind, don't answer. I know what you want from me: family feeling. Look, you have the use of my house. Let that suffice, okay?"

". . . What I'm trying to say, Cookie—" Deena broke off her thoughts and turned to her cousin, "—is that maybe putting out a lot of dough is Elaine's way of being involved."

Dryly, Cookie said, "And it allows her to be the boss."

"Could be. But who cares? It's gonna be so nice! I feel it in my bones. Our kids are finally going to meet each other! I can hardly wait! Maybe they'll become friends like we were."

"That would be so nice . . ."

"We'll all have brunch, and then we'll sit around and schmooze and Daddy and Uncle Jo will reminisce—"

"And our mothers will sit at the kitchen table and drink tea—"

"You remember that, too? God, yes. That's how I remember them, always over cups of something, and talking."

"Remember, sometimes after we'd have a big meal but nobody wanted to leave, we'd have scrambled eggs in the kitchen, late? Let's do that. The kids'll probably want to go do their own things, but you and I and—" Cookie stopped speaking. Deena was all of a sudden looking past her, was smiling broadly, was in fact no longer listening to her.

"Norman! The world is suddenly a brighter place!"

Cookie snuck a look over her shoulder. A man was advancing upon them, grinning broadly, a very handsome man in his middle forties. She turned back to her cousin, noting with interest the subtle changes that had come over Deena: her head thrown back a little; her eyes a little wider; her posture just the tiniest bit provocative, leaning back a little, arching her back a little. Deena was putting on a bit of sparkle for the benefit of this man. Well, of course! she scolded herself. Deena is single, you jerk! This is called *flirting*. Remember? That thing you were never particularly good at?

"Deena! Now I have two magnificent views: one of Manhattan and the other of two lovely ladies."

"Norm is my favorite artist, Cookie. You've seen his cartoons in the *New Yorker*, the squiggly people who are always in a bar . . ."

The man named Norman laughed. "They're always in a bar because I'm always in a bar!"

"You're not in a bar now!"

"But when I offer myself to you once more—and once more you turn me down—I will surely need to find one!"

Cookie found herself turning her head, as if at a tennis match; this way then that way, back and forth. She felt absolutely leaden. Deena was so quick, so full of sunshine and laughter, whereas she felt turgid, dull, and terribly, horribly ordinary. He left a few minutes later, without ever having revealed his last name.

"How would you like to eat at a place where you can get a dessert called Chocolate Decadence?" Deena said.

"Are you kidding?"

"That's what I thought! Thank God we're still on the same wave length!"

Did she mean it? Cookie gave her cousin a quick look. Yes, she meant it. After spending all day together, surely she could see how different they were. But maybe she couldn't. Every once in a while, today, she had wondered if Deena really believed it had all been so perfectly wonderful, or whether she just *wanted* to believe it.

There was such a difference in their lives then . . . and their lives now. Money, for openers. Deena: always, Cookie: never. Politics. Cookie: always, Deena: never. Men, looks, and sex appeal. Deena: yes, yes, yes, Cookie: no, no, no.

She loved Deena—of course, she did. The feeling they had shared as children was still there. Well, that was probably all Deena meant.

As they headed for Henry Street, to a restaurant called Henry's End—"it's at the end of Henry, get it?" Deena said—Cookie said, very casually, "That artist. Norman."

"Yes? What about him? Nice-looking, isn't he? He's nearly sixty. Isn't that amazing?"

"Are you interested in him?"

"God, no! I've known him for years! Our kids played together in the olden days—you know, way back when I was married."

"You make it sound like a million years ago."

"You want to know something? That's how it feels sometimes. I think about Michael, I think about cooking dinner for him, or waiting up for him to come home at night, or about getting into bed with him and kissing him, and I can't believe I'm thinking about myself. I can't believe I put up with him all those years and thought myself happy!"

"Obviously you changed," said Cookie.

"Yeah, that's what I thought. But, you know, when he calls me, to complain about the kids or my attitude or my lawyer's attitude or any goddamn thing, my heart pounds like crazy. I still think I should be pleasing him. Isn't that loony?"

"You want a real answer? Then, yes. You might as well still be married."

"I'm working on it. I'm trying to find someone else."

"What does finding someone else have to do with the way you respond to your ex-husband?"

"When you put it that way . . . I like to have a man in my life!"

"I thought, these days, the idea was for women to make their *own* lives."

"Easy for you to say. You're married."

They were walking into the restaurant at that moment and Cookie was glad. She didn't have an answer. So there were still women in this world who needed a man to tell them they were okay. That was no surprise. The surprise was that her beautiful, witty, outgoing cousin was one of them.

As soon as they were seated, Deena began to talk very fast, very defensively. "I know what you're thinking. Well, I can't help it. I just like being with a man. I know it's against feminist philosophy, but that's the truth. I like men, period. I just feel better going out with a man rather than a girlfriend. I do go out with my friends and it's okay, but I have to admit I never feel completely comfortable."

"I remember that feeling. When I was first married, if Dave had to be out of town on a Saturday night, which he very often was in those days, and I went to the movies, say, with my friend Sandy, I felt terribly conspicuous and self-conscious. I remember wanting very much to wave my left hand around, to let everyone know—especially the couples—to see, that I was married and okay." She paused a moment and then very carefully added, "But I thought we all outgrew that, a long time ago."

"I did, I did! But then, I was safely married. It's different when you're single and you really *don't* have a man."

"Okay. Let me put this to you: you want a man. How about your ex? You say he's pushing for a reconciliation all the time. If having a man is so important, why not settle for him? Hey! Better the devil you know, right?"

The gaspacho arrived just then and Cookie dug right in. They had been walking all day long and she was starved. But Deena sat, holding her spoon, thoughtful. "No, I don't think so. I think Michael and I used up everything we had. But you know what I really want, Cookie? Lately, I've noticed, when I'm not busy doing something, I'm—*assailed*, that's the only word that fits— I'm assailed with a longing, a longing to be in love. I'll walk down the street, fantasizing that when I come to the next corner, a man will appear . . . and we'll look at each other and we'll both be struck dumb and that will be it."

"Excuse me. That will be *what*?"

"It, Cookie. *It*. Love. Romance. Passion. Whatever. That

overwhelming feeling of surrender to an emotion that's too big to fight. Two people, realizing instantly that they were meant for each other! God, sometimes I want it so badly, I could scream! God, I was married at nineteen. Nineteen! I never even gave myself a chance!''

Cookie couldn't help smiling. "The Sicilians call that kind of love The Thunderbolt. You don't really believe it happens outside of movies, do you?''

"I absolutely do. It happens. I only hope it happens to me before I'm an old lady and it's *really* too late.''

❦❦❦❦❦❦❦❦❦❦❦❦❦❦❦❦❦❦❦❦❦❦❦❦❦❦❦❦❦❦❦❦❦❦❦

Chapter Twenty

Thursday, September 10, 1987   The Orchard Street scene at noon could have been a hundred years ago. The owners of all the little shops on either side of the narrow street were taking advantage of the fine weather, putting most of their goods out on the sidewalk, forcing foot traffic out into a thoroughfare already filled with bikes, trucks, people, cars, and the impatient blare of lunch-hour traffic.

"This must be what it was like when my grandfather came over,'' Cookie remarked. "Except, of course, no cars.''

"And a lot of horseshit,'' Sam said with a laugh. "You really had to watch your feet in those days.''

"And all the signs were in Yiddish.'' She laughed. "If he were alive today, my *zayda* would have something to say about all the signs being in a *foreign language*! *'Feh,'* he would say.''

"*Zayda?*'' Sam said.

"Grandfather. In his day, the entire neighborhood was Jewish, even the cops and the mailmen. Everyone. It was a world unto itself.''

They walked on, carefully ducking as they passed a display of sheer baby-doll nightgowns in bright Day-Glo colors, hanging from an awning and swaying dangerously in the breeze.

"How about those?'' Sam said, grinning.

Cookie smiled. "Not while I'm in charge. Sheer nighties our

girls don't need!'' She sighed. "God, when I think of what they *do* need . . . Oh, look, Hester Street. My grandfather used to tell us stories about Hester Street. He was eleven or twelve when they got here, dirt-poor, and religion permeated every aspect of their lives. He told us about one Saturday, the Sabbath, when he and another boy discovered a nickle lying on the sidewalk. Well, you were not allowed to handle money on the Sabbath. Yet, here was a fortune, glittering at their feet. So my *zayda*—who to the end of his life would go to great lengths to get a nickle—got an idea.'' She laughed. "They carefully shoved the nickle with their feet until it was against a building, and then those two little boys took turns standing on it, guarding it all day long until sunset, when they were permitted to pick it up.''

"He sounds like quite a guy, your grandfather.''

"Actually, Sam, he was a very difficult man. There's a story that he threw pieces of leather—he was a shoemaker—at boys who dared come by to court his twin daughters: my mother and my aunt. They practically had to run away from home. Of course, he was much different with his grandchildren. He always had a shiny new quarter for me. Oh, hell, I don't know why I'm getting so carried away with nostalgia . . . trying to find my roots? I do feel rootless lately.''

"Rootless? What about?'' He took her arm and steered her across the street.

"I don't know, Sam. It's every damn thing . . . My father, for God's sake. My father is dying and I need my husband to be there for me and he isn't. For three years, I've been there for him, through all of his shit. Now *I* need some of that support and he's just not there.''

Sam opened the door of a dairy restaurant and gestured her in. "Come on, let me give you some blintzes with sour cream and you'll tell me all about it. What's the problem now? They're not still messing with him?''

"Oh, no. To the contrary, in fact.'' She sat herself in a booth, ignoring the huge plastic-coated menu that she knew listed seventy or eighty dairy dishes and which she knew by heart, and let Sam do the ordering. She felt like sitting back and being taken care of. "You'll read all about it in tomorrow's *Times*. Dave is to be vindicated—he'll get an apology from the city of New York—*and* he'll get all the money they owe him, retroactive to the very first day he was demoted. He's going to have his picture in the paper and he's going to be quoted and *everything*. He's in seventh heaven, but . . .''

Sam, intent on the plate of blintzes being put before him, ignored her hesitation. "But that's great! Now you'll see: things'll get back to normal."

Cookie looked at her blintzes, wondering why she had no appetite. " 'Normal' is this guy named Dave Adler who never tells me what's on his mind. Maybe I don't *want* to get back to that; maybe I want to surge ahead."

His eyes came up to meet hers. He was so big and so powerful-looking. When you first met him, you expected a real tough guy, but those big warm puppy eyes gave him away. They invited you to spill your guts and tell him everything, in spite of yourself.

In spite of herself, Cookie found herself babbling on. "The other night, I asked him how it was going at the office and he gave me his usual 'It hasn't been the best day I've ever had.' He calls that an answer, but I don't, and I said, 'Why don't you tell me how you really feel about the whole thing?' And he said, 'What whole thing?' Do you believe that? I gave him such a look! So he said, 'Cookie, how I feel about it is: I don't want to think about it. See, if I don't think about it, it can't bother me. Can't you understand that?' And, Sam, I had to say, 'No, Dave, I can't. Where I'm coming from, we talk things out—and *then* we feel better.' "

She paused to take a breath and Sam gestured with his head to her food. "Eat," he said, and without thinking, she obeyed. It was delicious.

"You know, Sam, he told Dick Wallach and the rest of America things he *never* told me!" To her consternation, her eyes filled and she blinked rapidly. "Dammit, I feel like an idiot, complaining he's more intimate with Dick Wallach than he is with his wife! It sounds so stupid! But that's exactly how I feel! And that makes me feel stupid! Who am I, with everything I have, to moan and *kvetch* because my husband doesn't tell me everything!"

"Have you spoken to Dave about this?"

"Of course." She sighed. "And he told me he was willing to reveal himself that way on television for the public good. He told me he'd say or do anything, on television or in Madison Square Garden, if it would keep one more child from being neglected or abused!

"And, God, Sam, how can I argue with that? Dave and I were raised the same way, by the same kind of progressives. My God, my father lived and nearly died by his principles. He fought in Spain; he went to Selma for the big march. He always gave money—to any liberal cause, to any person down on his luck—even if it meant we did without. He taught us that the only meaningful work was for the good of mankind. I was brought up believing there were only three jobs for me: social worker, teacher, nurse."

Sam gave her a look and she dug into her lunch once more. "Don't stop me, I'm on a roll. Do you see what I mean? Dave and I both grew up dedicated to doing good for the world, period. So for me to carp and criticize him for being who he is . . . I don't know, it's so mean."

She stopped talking for a few minutes and concentrated on the now-cold food, just stuffing it into her mouth without really tasting it. She felt . . . restless, uncomfortable. Not with Sam. No, no, never with Sam. With herself. So she put down her fork and said, "Can we go?"

They went back outside, into the bright warm autumn sunshine. "I'd better take myself back to my shrink, I'm so confused lately."

"Here I am."

"Oh, Sam, I do love you." She stopped and turned to him, her eyes filling again, damn them. Really, she didn't want to boo-hoo, not to her boss, and not in the middle of Essex Street. She started walking, looking straight ahead. "The thing is, I feel guilty."

"Guilty!"

"I know. Terribly old-fashioned of me. But that's what it is. I cavil and carp because my perfectly decent husband doesn't understand me, and here are the kids at the center, *really* in trouble. Girls barely out of childhood, pregnant, some of them by rape. Twelve-year-olds, turning tricks. Little kids shooting up. How long did I keep Carlotta off the streets? Four days? *Maybe* four days! Do I do any better with any of them? Oh, they'll learn to trust, a little, and to talk, a little, and to get their shit together, a little, and then, it's all for nothing! They slip away, they go right back! What good is it? What good am *I*?"

He put his hand on her shoulder and began to talk. His rumbling bass voice was soothing as he reeled off a list of their success stories: Angel, who got off drugs and was now a counselor at Haven House; Larry, who was now in a community college. Cookie stopped listening: she knew what his message was. She even believed it . . . sort of. Sometimes. Of course, some of the kids were really helped, of course, it wasn't totally hopeless.

"Sam, I hear you, I really do hear you. My problem, Doctor, is much worse than burnout. It's called Who Am I and What Am I Doing Here?"

"It's called Cookie's Midlife Crisis and Why Doesn't She Take a Vacation."

"Oh, Sam, it's so awful. I look at the kids we get and I feel how lucky I am. And then, half an hour later, I meet my cousin Deena—who's rich and slim and beautifully dressed and great-looking and sure of herself and has it all—and I'm consumed with envy."

"I can't believe I'm hearing you say this, Cookie Adler."

"Listen to me, Sam. This is my cousin. We used to be best friends when we were little girls. We're the same age, Sam. She looks ten years younger. She writes plays. She has a job for fun—for *fun*, Sam—being a guidance counselor for kids at a private school: clean, neat, polite, well-brought-up kids who call her ma'am and will certainly go to college."

"Listen to *me*, Cookie. When did you ever admire a woman like that: self-indulgent, spoiled, rich, with a make-believe job? What does *she* do to leave her mark on the world—stop some kid from smoking in the bathroom? Big fucking deal!"

"And when *her* marriage went sour, she had the guts to get out." Cookie went on as if he'd never interrupted her. "She has freedom, Sam, autonomy . . ." She stopped, looking at him for understanding. But he was only puzzled. "She has *lovers*, Sam! She's forty-five years old, just like me, and instead of having headaches, she has lovers!"

Sam put a hand on each of her shoulders and looked deep into her eyes. "Oh, yeah. Midlife crisis, for sure. Nobody can blame you, Cookie. You work hard at a thankless job. Well, let me thank you. Thank you, thank you, thank you. And now, do me a favor. Take the leave you have coming, take it next week. Take your husband and take a trip somewhere where they don't have telephones . . . and make up, make out, make love!"

"I wish it were that—Oh, Sam! What's happening?" There were loud screams from nearby, a woman's voice. They both looked around, trying to see where it was coming from. More screams, around the corner. Horrible high-pitched shrieks. Why wasn't someone doing something? This rotten, heartless city!

And then they came into view: three teenaged girls, one of

them carrying a large portable radio, playing rap. They were screaming—with delight.

"Oh, God," Cookie said, shaking her head. "I can't take it anymore."

"Just what I've been saying." Sam took her arm and they walked. "I mean it Cookie. Take some leave."

"Here's the thing of it, Sam: my marriage is in trouble. Oh, Christ, just listen to me! When my brother Paul fools around and tells me his marriage is in trouble, I always tell him, 'It's not your marriage that's in trouble, sweetie-pie, it's *you.*' "

"Are you telling me what I think you're telling me?"

"I'm telling you there's this guy named Phil, a real sweet man, a cop—"

"You have a lover!"

"Who'd believe it, right? But, yes, I have a lover. In a manner of speaking. Because love has nothing to do with it. He's lonely; his live-in lady left him and he likes having a woman around. I'm a fill-in, until the real thing comes along. I know . . . It's surprising a guy would hit on a middle-aged broad like me."

They were almost back at Haven House; two of the kids were hanging out in front. In a minute, they'd spot her, and any hope of private conversation would be finished. Thank goodness. Enough already, of her ambivalences! God, how boring! But Sam came to a halt and stood in front of her.

"I know what you think of yourself, Cookie. You think you're fat, you think you're plain, you think you're unexciting, uninteresting. Well . . . you're crazy and you're wrong. You're a damned attractive woman . . . Don't look at me like I'm telling you lies to make you feel good. I don't do that. You know how many times I've had to stop myself from thinking those thoughts? You know the kind I mean? As far as I'm concerned, you're sexy as hell!"

Cookie looked up at him, grateful. That was her overwhelming emotion at this moment: gratitude. She didn't even care if he *was* lying a little. "Sam," she said, and was able to smile with genuine amusement, "I wish I was married to *you.*"

He laughed, shaking his head. "Cookie, baby, take it from me—no, you don't."

Chapter Twenty-one

Friday, September 11, 1987   "Joyce," Paul said into the phone, "I hate to interrupt when we're talking about one of my favorite things—I mean money, of course—but the boss just walked in . . ." He was on the phone with their accountant, a damn smart woman, who liked his brand of humor. So did his father-in-law, for that matter. Sid Handleman gave him a wink. He knew Joyce, of course, they both worked with her. Paul motioned him to a chair, but the old man shook his head. Uh-oh. Something serious, if he wouldn't sit down. ". . . I'll get back to you," he said, and hung up. "So, Sid? You won't take a seat?"

Sid shook his head. Then he began to grin, like a kid who just won first prize. "I'm too excited to sit. Look at this!" He waved a fistful of computer printouts. "Like a rocket! Like a goddamm rocket!" In answer to an unspoken question, he said, "Custom Closets! Off the goddamm charts! You're a genius, Paul!"

Paul grinned. "Come on! It was the write-up in *New York* magazine that did it. When you're a 'Best Bet,' you can count on sales going up."

"Yeah, sure, but there's no getting away from the fact it was the right idea at the right time. A changing room in a closet! 'Make room for baby!' " Sid laughed out loud, waving the sheets of paper like a banner. "Right in time for the new baby boom! You're a genius. Don't argue with me if I say you're a genius—you're a genius!"

Paul laughed. His father-in-law was really a pussycat. Look at him: in his mid-sixties, almost totally bald now, but with a year-round tan that told you he could afford to follow the sun—which he did. Saint Martin in the winter, the Hamptons in the summer, and Vegas anytime he felt like it. Which was often. Sid loved gambling almost as much as he loved golf. And he loved golf almost as much as he loved money. Nothing could make him cheerful and content like an upward sales curve.

Everyone loved Sid Handleman. Not a mean bone in his body.

Paul always enjoyed watching the women at the country club making up to his father-in-law. Sid didn't look like God's gift to women, being a short tubby little guy with not much hair and jug-handle ears. No, he wasn't much to look at, maybe, but they loved him, anyway. He was always happy, always up. Paul had been working side by side with Sid for nearly twenty years now and he'd never seen the older man in a bad mood. Never. From the first, Paul had carefully watched how Sid handled people—always charming and reasonable—nothing like *his* old man, who frankly didn't care what anyone thought of him—and almost from the first, he'd decided *this* was the kind of man he wanted to be.

He remembered what happened when he brought Sid his first Great Idea: a travel hanger that folded so you could pack it. Sid smiled and encouraged him to work it out, patted his shoulder and told him he was a good boy to think about ways to expand business, that was the way to success, and he'd go far if he kept it up.

Paul recalled well walking out of Sid's office in a self-congratulatory glow. He was smart, he was good, he was a comer; he was doing well and going places. It took another week or so before he realized what was wrong with his marvelous folding travel hanger: the mechanism had a tendency to snap shut; it almost got his finger one time.

And when he came back to Sid, all down in the mouth, to tell him about it, Sid said, "Hey, don't be sorry, kid. If it does that, it could hurt someone, a little kid maybe. Be glad you discovered it in time. You wouldn't want to get us sued, would you? Hey, you'll have plenty other ideas!"

Paul was then twenty-three years old and certain he knew everything. Sid was an old fogey. So he fiddled with the design and finally came up with one that didn't shut itself with a snap—ninety-two percent of the time. That was good enough for *him*. Sid argued with him. "Do you want to take even an eight percent chance?" he asked. And when Paul said, rather belligerently, Yes, he did, that was that. "Do it your way, then," said Sid. Three shipments of Foldaway Travel Hangers went out and, within six months, the complaints were coming in. They had to pull them all off the market.

Paul felt like a shit, then. He waited for his father-in-law to read him the riot act. But it never happened. Never a word about all the wasted time, the money down the drain—never even a hint of I Told You So.

On the other hand, every time he came up with something halfway decent, he got the genius speech. And shortly thereafter would come the You're More of a Son Than My Own Son speech. Paul looked over at his father-in-law, grinning and waiting. He'd done the genius bit. Paul leaned back in his leather swivel chair and waited for the rest of it.

"Paul, you're more of a son to me than my own son. Not that Perry's a bad boy, but he never wanted the hanger business, what can I tell you? He's a chip off the old block, a gambler through and through. So I do it in Vegas and he does it on Wall Street. An arb! I ask you, is that a name for a profession that makes you a multimillionaire before you're forty? An arb! But there you go—and meanwhile, he's too busy to get married and have grandchildren for me. So thank God my daughter, Stefanie, was smart enough to go after *you*—"

"Excuse me, Sid, your daughter, Stefanie, didn't have to go after anyone. She was easily the most beautiful, most popular girl in A E Phi."

Sid charged on. "Look, Paul, I love my Perry. After all, he's my own flesh and blood. But . . . you ever hear Harry Chapin sing?"

Paul blinked. Harry Chapin? What was *this* about? But before he had a chance to say yes or no, Sid was continuing. "He used to write songs, back in the sixties, folk songs, sort of. I have his albums at home, that's how I remember. This particular song, it's called 'Cat's in the Cradle.' You must have heard it! No? Well, it's about a guy who's too busy making money to spend time with his son and now his son is grown up and *he's* too busy. Now, when his father wants to see him, *he's* the one saying, 'Maybe later.' Very true to life, very true to life. That's me and Perry to a *T*.

"Paul, let me tell you something: we sow and then we reap. You know what I'm saying, Paul? I can't blame Perry. That's how he grew up, with me always too busy to play ball with him or take him to a game or something. And now when I call him, he's always on his way somewhere. But, like the song says, 'It's so good talking to you, Dad, it's real nice talking to you.' "

There was a long pause after this recitation. Paul hesitated. This was the first time he could remember Sid sounding so—so regretful. It was poignant, dammit.

Sid turned, staring out the window; and when he spoke again, it was almost to himself. "I left them all alone too much. I left Essie alone too much."

And then, finally, he turned back with that familiar smile, that familiar shrug. "What can you do? What's done is done. That's life." This was more like it. "So, if I can't have my own son in the business, I could at least have the next best thing. You, Paul. And it's really turned out that you're not the next best, you're the best.

"You want to know how I feel?" Sid came over and put a hand on Paul's shoulder. He cleared his throat a little. "You're as much a son to me as Perry. I trusted my daughter's choice and I've never had reason to regret it. And you were no sure thing, a history major with a minor in football! Go know a jock is going to come up with three or four of the best ideas ever, in the hanger game! I lucked out, no two ways about it."

Paul was touched. Yes, Sid was a big talker—and he was known to get emotional more easily than most, the kind of man who openly wept at weddings and bar mitzvahs and even sad movies. But this was different, somehow. A cold fear clutched at his chest. Was Sid ill, maybe? Was this his way of letting Paul know he was dying? Oh, please God, not that.

"Essie *hoked* me for years. 'Take it slower. Take it easy. Take me to Israel.' Well, now, finally, I feel I have the time and . . ." He sighed. "And she's gone. Who would have thought my Essie, of *all* people, would go get a divorce—at her age!—and go off on her own! Let me tell you something, Paul. You can't be too smart, that's what I've learned. I thought I could have it all my way. Oh, well, live and learn. But it's never too late to go to Israel. And today, after I saw those orders, I said to myself, 'Sid,' I said, 'you don't have to be around here every minute, the boy can take care of it all by himself!' "

He thought he knew what was coming next and it made his heart beat very fast.

"To make a long story short," Sid said, "I'm retiring. Well, semiretiring. I'm kicking myself upstairs. By this time next week, you'll be legally the president of Handleman Hangers and Wire Products." He stopped, put his other hand on Paul's other shoulder, and beamed at him. "How about that?"

"Sid, Sid. What can I say? I'm overwhelmed. You don't know what this means to me . . ." Christ, president! His own business. Freedom. Now, he'd never have to worry about money, ever again. Now he'd be one of the important men in Great Neck—at the club, at his temple. Paul, the dummy of the family, president of a company! How about that? Never mind putting up with jokes about marrying the boss's daughter. He had worked damn hard for Sid and for Handleman Hangers, damn hard. He'd put in his time in every department, from shipping to sales. He'd proved himself, over and over. It was quite an accomplishment, if he said so himself, with his C average at Syracuse.

Too bad his own father couldn't be proud of him. He knew damn well what Jonah would say when he told him—and it wouldn't be, "Well done, my son." More like, "The accumulation of personal wealth is the greatest evil of the Capitalist system!" Pop would be sure to ask him, in his best caustic voice, if he was planning to use some of his wealth to help the oppressed. God, everybody in the fucking world knew Paul Gordon was generous—everyone but Pop. To Pop, he was just a wasted life, someone who wasn't political, someone who was a Capitalist pig.

It was different with Sid. His father-in-law respected him, admired him, even loved him. God, he was lucky. He reached up and took Sid's hand in a manly grip. "Dammit, Sid, I'll make you proud of me. I'll make you happy you put the business in my hands. I swear it. You've always done right by me, you've always been fair and let me tell you something, if anyone in this world is a role model to me, it's you. Now that my father's dying . . ." Dammit, he was going to cry! Quickly, mumbling something, he got to his feet, clearing his throat to cover up the emotion, walking to the window and gazing out at the parking lot, blinking. "Dammit, Sid, you're very important to me. I can't tell you how much this means to me."

Sid came over and they embraced, briefly and awkwardly, Paul being almost a foot taller than the older man. Then Sid stood back, clearing his throat, and said, "You've been a good boy, Paul. You've made my Stefanie happy. I can tell, believe me. And you and Steffie have given me three beautiful granddaughters . . . a man couldn't ask for better, not with those three. Beautiful, smart, athletic!

"These days, when men think nothing of running out on their wives and children, you've been the ideal husband and father, always saving time for them, always making sure you're home for dinner. Not like I was. I learned, but I learned the hard way. And I learned too late. I lost the best woman I've ever known . . ." His voice cracked a little, and he said, "Listen to me—an old man getting sentimental. So call me *pisher*, I'm a sentimental guy! And now I'm out of here! So long"—he paused dramatically at the door and then added, with a wink—"Mr. President."

Again, the mist in front of his eyes? Christ! Paul thought. What the hell is wrong with me? Lately, every time I turn around, my eyes are filling up. If this doesn't stop, I'll end up at Long Island Jewish Hospital in a rubber room. Why now? I should be ecstatic, he thought. I should be planning my wonderful future. But instead of that, why do I keep thinking about what Pop is going to say to put me down, to make me feel terrible, like my life isn't worth a damn thing? Why do I see that ugly flat in Millville, that horrible green living room suite, the tan linoleum on the kitchen floor, my mother's lousy cooking, always stew or pot roast, pot roast or stew? . . . God, the years he wore Irwin's hand-me-downs, never anything new, never anything that fit him right. If he hadn't been lucky enough to be good-looking—he shuddered a little—he might be like his brother, a nobody.

He focused deliberately on his car, parked almost directly outside the window. His brand-new white Mercedes convertible: Paul's new toy, Steffie called it. But she laughed and kissed him and said, "Nobody in this world deserves it more than my wonderful husband." Dammit, she was terrific, always behind him, always his biggest fan. He didn't deserve her! He stood, again blinking away incipient tears, and made himself a promise to be a better husband to her.

His private phone rang. Good. It was probably Steffie. Before she hung up, he was going to tell her how much he loved her. God, he was a lucky man. From nothing and from nowhere, he'd made himself a good life, a full and rewarding life. He ran to the desk and picked up the phone, already smiling.

"Hi, lover," said the familiar voice, "how's the best fuck in the Western world?"

Roz! What balls the woman had! He *told* her no more calls at the office. No more calls, period. He'd call *her*, that's what he told her. And now, just when he was feeling so on top of the world, when life was looking so beautiful, here she was talking dirty to him. In his office, his place of business! He felt sick.

Suddenly, in the space of a minute, he was totally turned off—the thing was over and he felt only disgust. How could he have gotten so involved with this woman who thought it was sexy to have a filthy mouth? She had no class, that's what it was. No class at all. He pictured her posing and prancing around her bedroom, swinging her hips and giving him that coy look. Christ! And he'd gone for it. The thought of her pale blubbery body made him nauseous.

"I told you never to call me here."

"I'm sorry, angel." Obviously she couldn't or wouldn't hear the ice in his voice. "But I started to think about tonight and I just couldn't wait."

"Don't think about tonight. Don't think about me, period. It's over."

She laughed. "You've said that before."

"This time I mean it." She laughed again and he longed to say, You're fat and ugly and repulsive and I'm finished with you. But, no, it never paid to make an enemy. He'd learned that from Sid Handleman. Why be cruel and set her against him? Maybe have her talk about them? Maybe—his blood ran cold at the thought—decide to go to Steffie?

So he softened his tone and said, "My wife's catching on. You . . . really made me forget how to be careful. Look, Rozzie, a hot number like you, you deserve better than once a week from a married man. And I won't be able to do even that, not for a long time. You know—"

"I know. I know. You've been so sweet." There was a pause. Had he done it? And then she said, "I'm going to miss you, lover. Terribly."

Crossing his fingers, Paul said, "Me, too."

When he heard the click of her hanging up, his knees went rubbery with relief. He'd done it and he was home free. Dammit, never again. Never, never. He had too much at stake now. He'd taken too many goddamn chances. He must have been crazy to risk losing everything for a fuck! Well, that was all in his past now, all in his past.

Chapter Twenty-two

Sunday, September 13, 1987   Dappled sunlight shimmered on the venerable buildings and the pathways that crisscrossed the broad grassy rectangle of Harvard Yard.

"It's like a different world," said Dorothy, looking around in obvious pleasure. "It even *feels* old—and very intelligent, too."

This brought laughter from Michelle, walking on her right, as well as Cookie on her other side.

"Now aren't you glad I made you come up with us?" Cookie asked. "Even *you* need a rest occasionally, you know."

"Your father—"

"You know what Grandma's going to say, don't you, Mickey? That she has to be with Grandpa. But he didn't seem to think so. He nearly pushed her out the door." Cookie smiled at her mother.

"Never mind talking about me as if I wasn't here," Dorothy said smartly. "I may be old, but I'm not deaf."

"You're not old at all, Grandma. You could be my roommate, the way you look!"

Dorothy smiled. "Oh, you like my new outfit." And she stopped walking to do a little pose, hand on hip. She was wearing a tiger-print cotton, the very latest style, with a shorter skirt, panty hose to match, and leather sandals. And huge earrings, of course. Cookie could not remember a day of her life when her mother was not wearing earrings. She could not remember a day of her life when her mother was not well turned out. Which, considering how poor they had been, was something of an accomplishment.

"You always look stylish," she said. "You really like clothes, don't you?"

"If you'd spent the first sixteen years of your life forced to dress exactly like your sister, you'd think clothes were important, too."

"Really, Grandma? Your mother *made* you dress alike?"

"Absolutely! We were her claim to fame, her twinnies. Are you kidding? And my sister, Yetta—it's a shame you were too young the last time she came over to visit, to remember her—my sister, Yetta, was bossy right from the word go. We'd go shopping on Pitkin Avenue for new dresses and Yetta would say, 'No pink, Ma. I hate pink. Get us purple.' Yetta always loved purple. Never mind I looked *schvach* in purple. What Yetta wanted, Yetta got. Lavender. Lilac. Violet. If it looked purple, we wore it!

"Believe me, when I got out on my own and earned a little money, I bought myself a new outfit! I'll never forget it—a broomstick skirt printed all over with little rosebuds, and a ruffled peasant blouse you could wear on or off your shoulders. Oh, did I love that outfit. Yetta couldn't stand it, it wasn't her type. And I said, 'Tough, *I* like it.' Believe me, Mickey, it sounds like a little thing, but that was freedom and it was sweet!''

"I never had that problem with *my* twin! Of course, there was that time when both Jon and I had ponytails, but Mom didn't make us wear matching hair ribbons!''

They all laughed at the memory and continued to the steps of Widener Library. They were due to meet Win there at three o'clock and it was now five after.

They seated themselves near the bottom, in a sunny spot. Dot ostentatiously looked at her wristwatch. "So? It's ten past three and, of course, he's not here. Never on time! He hasn't changed a bit, that Irwin—''

"Win,'' Michelle corrected.

"Win, Shmin. He can call himself whatever he likes. I named him Irwin after my uncle may he rest in peace, and to me, he's Irwin. And he's late. He's *always* late.''

"Hey, Mom, it's okay. I figured us to leave around three-thirty. That's why I told him three; I know him, from the last movie. Please take it easy, will you? I don't want you starting up with him when we're cooped up in the car together. Okay?''

Dorothy made a little face, and Michelle said, "Grandma! Why are you always picking on Uncle Win? He's a little eccentric, yeah, but come on, he's got a lot going for him. He's creative. He's a wonderful photographer. He's a true intellectual. And, incidentally,'' she said, her voice loaded with meaning, "he's the only person in this entire family capable of sustaining a political discussion without any mention of capitalism, oppression, or the working class!''

"Shame on you, Michelle. Your grandfather taught this family everything they know about politics and, all right, things didn't turn out exactly how he thought they would; but, as far as his ideas go, no one has proved him wrong yet. In fact, the U.S. government stole a lot of Communist ideas . . . as you well know!''

"Yeah, but what have you done for us lately?'' Mickey held her hands up in surrender. "Only kidding, only kidding. But come on, this is a new generation, with a new set of problems. How about racism? The homeless? Feminism?''

"A bunch of fancy names for the oppressed!''

"You want to talk women's liberation, Mickey?'' Cookie put in. "Forty years ago, in the Coops, women were already liberated. They worked, they participated in political activities, they were equal!''

"What: 'equal'!" Dorothy said. "Oh, I admit, it *looked* good, and I was fooled in the beginning. But when push came to shove, we worked, sure, and we handed out leaflets and we marched alongside our men and we went on the picket line. But *then* we were expected to go back home and cook and clean and take care of the children also!"

Mickey laughed, and then quickly said, "Grandma, I'm not laughing at you. Nothing's changed. That's the big complaint now, too, that women are expected to do it all!"

"Ma!" Cookie said, a bewildered frown on her face. "You let me grow up believing all that stuff about equality! And all the time, *you* didn't even—"

She visibly stopped herself from saying more and drew in a deep breath. "Never mind. It was a long time ago. You did your best. I know you did your best."

But Dorothy was not quite finished. "You're not being fair. I never lied to you. *I* didn't realize . . ."

"I said, forget it, Mom. Really, just forget I said anything, okay?"

Dorothy turned to Mickey and said, "Your uncle isn't the only creative one in this family. When your mother was a little girl, she thought she wanted to be a clothes designer."

"Really?"

"Oh, Ma, stop it. Mickey, I drew clothes for my Elizabeth Taylor paper dolls, that's all."

"Yes, and they were wonderful, very imaginative."

"Oh, you really liked them? Well, that's not how *I* remember it. As I recall, you always laughed."

"Oh, you mean like the famous off-the-shoulder ski outfit?"

They all laughed, and Cookie said, "I'd forgotten about that. No wonder you found it all so silly." To her daughter, she added, "And, of course, your grandfather gave me a hard time on the basis of ideology . . . You know, designing clothes for movie stars. Not allowed!"

"That's not fair, Cookie. Your father was never that harsh with you. From the day you were born, you could wind him around your little finger."

Stubbornly Cookie went on. "Mickey, believe me, when it had to do with your grandfather's political beliefs—and everything *did*—he was hard as nails."

"It wasn't like that at all."

"Oh, Ma! You don't remember the famous night I said I loved

writing and that my professor had said there were interesting jobs on Madison Avenue, in advertising?''

"You're complaining? Assistant director of Haven House with a secretary, your own office, and a mention in the *Village Voice* last year? That's not good enough for you?''

Cookie laughed briefly. "Translation, Mickey. Your grandmother remembers very well what happened that night at the dinner table. I was told in no uncertain terms that advertising is but a tool of the Capitalist system, put into place to spread lies and exaggeration and entice the workers to spend more than they should!''

Mickey laughed. "Well, it's true.''

"Yes, I know it's true. But it did sound like a lot of fun . . . Mad, mad Mad Ave, they used to call it.'' She sighed.

"If you wanted to be a copywriter so much,'' Mickey persisted, "why didn't you just go out and get a job? You're not a wimp.''

"She could have,'' Dorothy said. "I didn't object.'' She turned to her daughter. "Cookie, I swear this is the first I'm hearing from you that you felt pushed around. You were free to do anything you wanted.''

"Is that how you remember it? I was never free, not really. I was expected to be a little mother, I was expected to be a good responsible girl, to get good grades, to take care of my brothers . . .'' She began to choke a little and stopped, clearing her throat. "And when the kids in Millville turned on me, I wasn't given any comfort. I was just supposed to take it.''

She was fourteen, just going into ninth grade, in the big high school building this year instead of just the top floor of the elementary school down the street. It was always exciting, the first week of the new school year. New teachers, maybe a few new kids who'd moved in over the summer—this year, there would be a whole contingent from the rural school because it only went up to the eighth grade—new books, new classes, new shoes. The first day, she ran almost the whole way.

She hadn't seen her best friend, Angie, for the whole month of August. They'd have so much to talk about! Did Angie still have a crush on Johnny Ray? Cookie had just finished reading *Catcher in the Rye*. The head librarian, Miss Manerino, had given it to her a couple of weeks ago, when she was getting so bored, and it was such a wonderful book. She couldn't wait to tell Angie about J. D. Salinger. He was a genius!

And then, she just couldn't seem to get Angie's attention. Angie was busy in the middle of a group of the Italian kids, kids she had never been friendly with before. And she was especially tight with Mary Bocca, who lived next door to her, and who she always said she couldn't stand. Cookie just couldn't believe Angie was snubbing her. The second day, she was afraid she was; and the third day, her stomach tightened into a knot even before she got to school, in anticipation of Angie looking right through her, pretending Cookie wasn't there. She finally got up her nerve and, after dinner, she called Angie. But Angie's mother answered and all she said was, "She's very busy. She can't come to the phone." There was a tiny pause, and then she said quickly, "I'm sorry, Cookie." And then she hung up—without even saying good-bye.

In social studies the next day, while Prof Cummings droned on about the great rivers of China, Cookie made a list of all the things that might possibly have made Angie mad at her. Was it the time last April when she let Ronnie Graham walk her home? Was it about the fight they had over God? Or maybe Mary Jane Bascom's party? Cookie had been invited, Angie not. Mom said Cookie should go if she was invited.

"God knows you and Angie are together every moment, it wouldn't hurt for you to do something on your own." So she did. Was that it? But they had been friends right up to the last day of July! Angie even called her on the telephone as her mother was trying to get her out the door and into the car, saying, "Good-bye. Good-bye. I'll write and tell you everything." Two letters had come and then nothing. And now this! What could it be? What horrible, unforgivable thing had she done?

Today, Friday, she had finally got up the courage to march over to Angie and say, with her heart beating so hard she couldn't even hear her own voice, "Angie, you've been ignoring me all week. Aren't we going to be friends anymore?" Angie looked strange, uncomfortable. She mumbled something, and Cookie said, "What?" and, finally, Angie said in a very low voice, "No. No. I can't." And walked away, leaving Cookie standing there feeling as if the world had come crashing down on her, feeling empty and lonely and sick to her stomach.

Now, at three-thirty, she was sitting in her homeroom, stalling, unwilling to face any of the kids hanging around outside school. She wanted to cry, but didn't dare. What if someone walked in and saw her?

She could hear the *swish, swish* of Mr. Elfand's big mop as

he made his way up the hall. She was going to have to leave
before he got here and asked her why she was still in school.
She didn't want to go home. Irwin could always tell if something
was bothering her and he would tease her and make her cry—
and then she'd have to hit him and he'd scream and cry and tell
on her and get her into trouble. Oh, Lord, she was in enough
trouble as it was! She felt absolutely lost. What had she done to
deserve this? She wanted her mommy!

And, it occurred to her, Mom was doing story hour for the
six-to-eight-year-olds in the library right now. And she wouldn't
even have to go outside. The library was attached to the high
school and you could go right in from the main hall. It made
her feel better just thinking about telling Mom. She'd called
Cookie in the other night and had a very nice, serious discussion
about boys and babies and petting and all stuff like that. Cookie
had been able to ask her anything, and she answered without
laughing or getting impatient like she usually did. So maybe,
today, she'd listen about Angie.

She almost ran to the library, letting herself in very quietly.
There was Mom in the children's section, sitting on a tiny chair,
right in the middle of a circle of little kids, reading *Babar the
Elephant*. How pretty she was, with her pink and green flowered
dress, the one Cookie loved, with all the pleats and the little
lace collar. Mom hated that dress. She always laughed and said,
"Oh, this thing. It's my librarian uniform." One day Cookie
said, "It's not really a uniform, is it Mom?" And Mom said,
"Are you kidding? They wouldn't let me in the door if I wore
my New York clothes." Anyway, Cookie thought she was the
most beautiful mother in all of Millville. She wasn't fat, like
most of the mothers, and she looked young. She wore her thick
black hair in a French knot instead of perms like all the other
mothers. She used mascara. Cookie loved to watch her put it
on, first from underneath, then another coat on top to thicken
the lashes, then a second time underneath, pushing the lashes
up, to curl them.

The little kids all listened to her read like they were hypnotized. One little boy was flopped on his stomach, right over her
feet. Three or four of them had stood up and were leaning over
her shoulders. It looked so comfortable and comforting and cozy.
And then her mother looked up and saw her. Her lips thinned
and she shook her head just slightly, just enough to let Cookie
know she mustn't be disturbed. Well, she knew that! She gave
Mom a pleading look and then Mom smiled a little and held up

one finger to show she'd be finished in one hour and then looked back down at the book again. And Cookie knew she was expected to go home now and do her chores.

When she got home, the boys were playing ball out in the street. Good. She went upstairs and started right in! She peeled the potatoes and tossed the salad and waited and waited. But when Mom finally opened the door, she came in scolding.

"Cookie, you know darn well you shouldn't be hanging around school after hours. And especially, you shouldn't come in and interrupt me when I'm busy with the children! And"— she had been looking around as she talked—"what are those potato peels doing on the table? You know I count on you for these few little things. Why can't you just *do* them?" She didn't even give Cookie a chance to explain.

Cookie couldn't help it; she began to cry. Her mother gave a sigh, leaned on the kitchen table, and looked at her—not angry, but not loving, either. "Cookie, I'm so tired. It's the end of the week. Why do you choose this time to be so oversensitive? Just because I'm a little out of sorts? Good God, you ought to be used to that by now. I'm never any good on a Friday after work. Dry your eyes, please, and then let's sit down and you'll tell me what's on your mind." She glanced at her watch. "But we'll have to talk quick because I have to go out to a meeting after dinner."

Cookie sniffled, wiped her face with her hands, put the potato peelings into the garbage, and then sat down opposite her mother. It wasn't easy, but the story finally came out, the whole thing, including today's stomach-wrenching conversation. "What did I do, Mom? I don't get it!"

Her mother took in a deep breath and then let it out slowly. She reached over, putting her hand on Cookie's. "Listen. You didn't do anything. It's not your fault. I guess it's time you learned the facts of life in Millville. Angie is Italian, and the Italians in this town are very close-knit. They have reason to stick together. There's a lot of prejudice against them."

"Not from me!" Cookie objected. The tears began to leak from her eyes.

"Of course not from you. What's that to cry about? Now, how am I going to explain this to you?" She sat quietly, closing her eyes for a moment, and then went on. "Do you know what some of the Irish kids told me? That they're not supposed to sit next to Italians because they'll get all greasy. And when I asked them where in the world they got *that* idea, they said the nuns at the parochial school! You *do* know that the Irish Catholics have their church and the Italian Catholics have another one, don't you?''

In fact, Cookie was vaguely aware that the McGuires went to St. Peter's and Angie went to Our Lady of Lourdes; but she had never wondered why.

''Naturally, the Italians are very sensitive because of this prejudice,'' her mother continued. ''They're the oppressed minority here. Everyone else likes to blame everything on the Italians. Well, never mind. The point is that all Italian kids in Millville, when they go into high school, are told by their parents to be friends only with their own. For God's sake, will you stop with the waterworks?''

The tears just came pouring out of Cookie's eyes. ''But it's not fair!''

''Life isn't fair, Cookie. Haven't you learned that yet? Especially in this horrible little town where people have nothing better to do with their time than discriminate against anyone who's the least bit different. 'Greasy Italians.' 'Dumb Micks.' 'Christ killers.' The hell with them!''

''Mom!'' She didn't want to hear this from her mother. Her mother wasn't supposed to be unhappy. If adults could be pushed around, if her own mother couldn't make it come out right . . . It was just too scary! ''You don't mean that!''

''What? You think I love it here? Millville wasn't *my* idea! You think I would have picked a dirty, narrow-minded railroad town in the middle of nowhere to live in, if I had any choice?''

''Then why don't we move?''

''Why don't we move!'' Her mother's lips narrowed into a bitter line. ''Because your father refuses, that's why! Cookie, listen to me. Don't ever marry a man with principles. Even though it's admirable, God help you if you ever bang up against them.''

Cookie stared at her mother, afraid of her mother's words, wanting to blot them out.

''Your father's principles mean I'm not allowed to speak to my own brother, my only brother, my own flesh and blood . . . or to Sylvia, a woman who was always a good friend to me, who I loved like a sister! Don't look at me like that, Cookie. I'm not the one who made that rule. I'm not the one who keeps you from your cousin Deena! Don't blame *me!''*

''I hate you! You're always picking on him!'' Cookie pushed herself away from the table and ran for her room. Her mother called to her. Cookie slammed her door and sat on her bed fighting tears, waiting for her mother to come after her. But she never did.

Now, on this sunny September day, she found herself fighting tears all over again, as if Angie DeCrescente had just snubbed her this morning.

"I'm sorry you felt put upon, having to help," her mother was saying. "But you have to realize—we needed the money I earned in Millville. You think I wanted to be in the library all day long—and plenty of evenings, too? I had to work so we'd have enough to live on. Your father refused to leave that terrible job in the freight yards. In his mind, it was a symbol of commitment to his principles. And of his anger at Pepe Ronda. No, never mind, it's a long boring story."

"What do you mean, *his* principles, Mama? *You* believed!"

"Me? What do I know about political theories. I was married to your father, I liked living in the Coops where we all believed in a better world—and even tried to make it. I didn't have that feeling of solidarity when I was growing up; with my parents, you were on your own! I was happy to march on May Day and stand up for tenants' rights and help run the nursery. I belonged! And I thought their ideas were very good, very forward-looking. But I was never—I don't know—a real Believer, you know, with a capital *B*. For instance, I was never a Party member. Of course, not many women were, but some.

"And then, once the true story came out about Stalin—the purges and the Siberian exiles, the executions—that was it for me. I said to myself, 'Hey, the Soviet Union is such a workers' paradise? Like ice! It's just another heavy-fisted government.' But it wasn't so simple for Jo; his whole life had been devoted to socialistic ideas and now that dream was dead. He went into mourning and couldn't be comforted. His answer to the Khrushchev speech, to learning the truth, was to dig in even deeper, in Millville. He seemed to think that staying there meant he hadn't really been wrong."

"You never said a word."

"Of course not! You don't tell children how you really feel. They're too young to understand."

"Well, I wasn't too young to understand being cut by Angie DeCrescente. Remember that, Mama? God, I was so hurt, and you just told me it wasn't worth crying over. You didn't even come to my room, to try to make me feel better."

Dorothy rounded on her, getting to her feet in her consternation. "How can you say a thing like that, Cookie, and in front of Michelle? Of course, I came to your room and I tried to make you feel better. I stood outside your door, begging you to let me in. You wouldn't. I pleaded with you, I promised you a Good Humor . . . You don't remember that? Well, *I* do, I remember like yesterday . . ."

The door remained stubbornly closed. She heard the child crying in there. Dammit, she didn't want her daughter to suffer like this, but what could one woman do against a world full of narrow minds? "Cookie," she tried again. "Come out now and help with dinner. I'm sorry Angie hurt you. Come, unlock the door and after supper, we'll get Good Humors."

The muffled voice: "I hate you! Leave me alone!"

Enough already! She didn't have the strength to stand there forever, yelling to a locked door. She went back into the kitchen and began moodily to prepare the evening meal. She had a sick feeling that she had said too much. Cookie thought the world of her father. It wasn't fair to criticize him to his own daughter. And it wasn't fair to be so selfish. After all, it was Jonah who had to go every night to the railroad yards, tramping up and down with his lantern and his chalk, marking codes on the sides of the boxcars. But on the other hand, he didn't seem to care whether or not they had a social life or a cultural life here—or a sex life, for that matter!

Talk about fair! She was still young and pretty—men told her that all the time—and she was stuck in this hick town with a husband who worked nights and brooded the rest of the time. Oh, she had friends, women who would have a cup of coffee with her or even take in a movie on a Sunday afternoon. But never, never was she going to be invited to join the Thursday Club or the Literary Society. And every once in a while, she overheard snatches of conversation and she knew that people considered them weird, outlandish. People couldn't forget, in the end, that they were New York Jews. If anyone ever found out, if anyone ever got an inkling that they were—never mind Communist, just say left-wing—they'd be run out of town!

Come to think of it, maybe that was a good idea. What she'd love to do was untie her apron, put down the paring knife, pick up her pocketbook, and take the first train that came along. In this lousy town, with all its lousy filthy trains—another was coming through every three minutes—it would be easy enough,

God knows. She just wanted to go someplace where she could have peace and quiet. No. Not peace and quiet. Love, love and passion, that's what she hungered for.

Where was the promise life had held out, when she was twenty years old? Where had it all gone? Why hadn't she gone to Frank when he asked? She could be in his arms right now, feel his mouth moving over her body, lingering at all the soft places. She had a sudden, complete picture of him, over her during lovemaking, his eyes glazed with heat, a lock of his black hair falling across his forehead, and the memory pierced her like a knife.

She straightened up with an effort and took in a deep breath. How, how did I get into this life, where I'm so miserable and discontented? This cannot be why I fought to escape my father's tyranny—only to end up trapped in another man's stubbornness. But there was no way out, she could only grab at a few moments of happiness now and again. And in the meantime, there was dinner to be put on the table.

"Yes," Dorothy said now, "I remember very well. I tried very hard to make it better for you, Cookie. For all three of you. Of course, Irwin . . . well, he was a little nudnik, always a problem from the minute he was born. He was colicky, you and Paul were angels. He wouldn't be toilet trained. He wouldn't sit still! Not for nobody, not for nothing. I love all my children equally, of course, I do, but Irwin—"

"He *is* a nudnik." Cookie laughed.

Mickey sprang up, protesting. "You're always bad-mouthing Uncle Win. But every time I've needed someone to talk to, about anything, he's the one who always has time for me. I can't talk to *you* about a lot of stuff. I know you think you're a great mother, but you're not as good as you think you are."

"Michelle!" her grandmother said. "Shame on you! Apologize to your mother!"

"Whoa there, Mickey," Cookie said. "First of all, facts are facts, and the fact is, your uncle Irwin—all right, *Win*—has never really grown up. He can't hold a job, he can't make up his mind what he wants to do with his life. He owes all of us money . . . Okay Mom, never mind. We all know you slip him money, you who can't afford it. And come on, he's forty-three years old, not fourteen!

"Secondly, your grandmother was only able to be 'liberated'

because she had me. I took care of my brothers, and *I* went to the store, and I usually made dinner.''

"You should be grateful for that," Dorothy said with a smile. "I was a lousy cook."

"And, last but not least, Mickey," Cookie plunged on, "I was always there for you and Jon. As a matter of fact, I made myself a solemn vow that I wouldn't do unto my children, and I didn't. I worked only part-time for years, and if you'll think back, there was dinner on the table every single night and we sat down like a family."

Mickey started to laugh. "Yeah, and then? How about after dinner? First it was night school. Then consciousness-raising group. And exercise class. Then you *had* to get another degree. Then they needed a counselor one night a week for NOW." She ticked off this list on her fingers. "In fact, Mom, you were never home. Jon and I always say we brought each other up."

Cookie stared at her daughter for a long moment and then her face crumpled. "I'm going to try to forget you said that, Mickey," she said in a muffled voice that shook.

Just then, a cheery voice hailed them. "Hey, gang! Am I late?"

Cookie turned, saw her brother—looking like a college boy— and it was just too much. How come he was allowed to remain a child forever, while she had *never* been allowed to be one? She burst into tears, aware that three of her nearest and dearest, tense and embarrassed, were waiting for her to get her feelings under control and behave herself. Well, she didn't feel like it!

An awkward arm went around her and an awkward hand began to pat her shoulder awkwardly. Irwin. He had never in his life been comfortable with anyone else's discomfort. She recalled this same self-conscious affection from him a couple of times in the past. It had never felt real to her and it didn't feel real now. But it would be so mean not to allow him to try to comfort her. At least he *tried*.

"Don't cry, Cookie. It makes me feel terrible," he said.

Cookie lifted her head. "Well, it doesn't make me feel so hot, either," she said . . . and noting the look of hurt astonishment on his face, quickly added, "Just kidding, Win, just kidding."

Chapter Twenty-three

Saturday, June 20, 1953   It was so hot. Cookie was sorry now she'd taken out so many big thick books from the library. It was a long walk down Main Street to Halfmoon Avenue, and then she had that big hill up to her house. But two of the books were for Pop, and she'd been waiting for weeks for *Gone with the Wind* to be returned, and Paul had asked her to bring seven picture books—so there wasn't even one she could have left there. And anyway, she was almost home, and no matter what she did, someone would yell at her.

Everyone in her family was in such a bad mood because of the Rosenbergs. "First time ever! That damned law's been on the books since 1917 and never before has anyone been executed. It's only because they're Communists, that's the *only* reason. Damned reactionaries!" her father had fumed this morning, hardly looking at her, not touching the cup of coffee she poured for him.

"This has nothing to do with being spies or not being spies; this is about destroying the Left in America!" In the morning paper, there was a big picture of the rally in Union Square last night, everyone crying because Ethel and Julius Rosenberg were being executed. "I think that's Ben Dauber," he said, pointing to one of the tiny faces that looked to her like all the others. "I should have been there. Listen, listen to this: the cops turned off the loudspeaker, but they all went on singing anyway. 'Go Down, Moses.' " And he began to sing to himself:

> When Israel was in Egypt land
> Let my people go . . .

And *he* was crying a little. "I should have been there," he repeated, but he wasn't talking to her, he wasn't talking to anyone. "I should have been with my comrades."

Cookie trudged around the corner of Main and Halfmoon, thinking about the Rosenbergs and how sad it was; but at the same time, hoping there wouldn't be any boys in front of Sal's

Pizza Parlor, halfway up the block. She couldn't help thinking: Why *weren't* they back home, in the Coops, in the Bronx? If it was so important to him, why couldn't they leave Millville and just go somewhere else? It probably was because of hiding from the FBI and she knew better than to ask. It was one of those scary secrets grown-ups always had.

Like when Papa disappeared last year, when they were still in the Coops. Well, he didn't *really* disappear. Mom explained it over and over: He had to leave suddenly, because of McCarren and McCarthy and Herbert Brownell and the FBI. They'd be hearing from him any day now. But he left in the middle of the night without even saying good-bye! Mom kept saying, "He went in and kissed you, but you were fast asleep. How many times do I have to tell you?"

He wasn't working for Uncle Jack anymore, she told them. He was on a farm somewhere, and wouldn't that be fun? To live on a farm, all that fresh air, lots of animals. "You'll be able to feed the chickens and milk the cows," she said, her voice all excited, "and maybe there will be a horse to ride."

And then she took in a very deep breath and her face changed. "Listen, kids. This is important. Irwin, for once, don't be a nudnik. We—we aren't going to Uncle Jack's anymore. Cookie, I'm sorry—I don't like it, either—but you aren't allowed to call Deena anymore. Never again. I'm sorry."

Cookie cried and cried and cried. She couldn't stop. It was so unfair. So many terrible things were happening to her, she couldn't even figure out which one she was crying about. How could Papa suddenly leave without waking her up and saying good-bye? How could he make her leave the Coops and all her friends and the candy store on the corner? She didn't care what Mama said, she didn't want to leave! And no Deena? But she and Deena were blood sisters! They'd pricked their index fingers with a pin and pressed them together. They had a Secrets Book that they both wrote in. How could they stop talking! Forever! It was so mean!

And then, all of a sudden, after a long time of saying she didn't know *when* Papa would send for them, Mom announced, "We're moving. Tomorrow. Stop that crying, Cookie. It's hard enough without you making it worse."

Cookie felt terrible. She wanted to see her Papa, but why couldn't he come home? She'd like to kill Herbert Brownell, *and* J. Edgar Hoover, *and* Senator McCarthy, that's what *she'd* like to do! But dopey Irwin got all excited and kept jumping up and down and making animal noises. "Oh, boy! The farm! I get to ride a horse and you don't, Cookie!" He was such a pest.

But Mom got angry and grabbed him by the shoulder and forced him into a chair. "*Shah*, Irwin. There's no horse. No farm. Your father didn't see eye to eye with the farmer and had to quit."

"Quit?" Cookie cried. "Again? How many things is he going to quit, anyway?"

Mom got a very angry look on her face, but when she spoke, all she said was, "Your father is a man of principle."

So they ended up in horrible, terrible, ugly, smelly old Millville, the worst place in the whole world, where everything was covered with soot from the trains and everything stank from the paper mill. The first time she wrinkled up her nose and asked Pop what that horrible smell was, he said, "Hell." And when she said, "No, really, Papa," he laughed bitterly and said, "I'm not kidding. That's sulphur, and from everything I hear, that's what hell smells like. Well, why not? Millville's a hellhole."

The time they had that conversation, Cookie felt almost happy. This was almost like the old Papa—kidding a little but really talking to her. They always used to have such good conversations. But they didn't anymore. He worked nights on the railroad, marking boxcars. He told them, her and Irwin and Paul, that if it wasn't for him, a car full of lettuce meant for Maine might end up in Mississippi.

"And there'd be no salad in Maine that week!" Mom put in, and he gave her a dirty look.

"It's no joke," he said angrily. He was always angry lately. Or else sad and gloomy. But that wasn't the worst part of Millville. The worst part of Millville was how dumb everyone was. In Millville, they loved McCarthy. They said he was saving the country and getting rid of all the Commie traitors—she heard them say that, all the time—even the teachers! Her teachers yesterday were smiling and saying that the Rosenbergs were only getting what they deserved.

"They gave our atomic bomb to the Russians," Mrs. Casey said in current events. "In time of *war*. Now, children," Mrs. Casey said, lowering her voice and sitting on a corner of her desk, her hands clasped in front of her like she always did when she wanted to tell them something very important, "now, children, you may hear some people say we aren't at war with the Russians. But, you see, we really are, because *the Russians started the Korean war!"* And she smiled broadly. "And we all know we're at war with Korea, don't we?"

And everyone in the class nodded and smiled back at Mrs. Casey, even Cookie, although she knew that what Mrs. Casey was saying was all wrong, *all wrong*, every word of it. Cookie knew what was going on in the world. Of course, she never spoke her mind, she never said what she knew, she couldn't tell anybody *anything*. Not in Millville. It might get Papa into terrible trouble.

That first awful night here, they got off the train and they had to carry all the luggage up Vale Avenue Hill because there was no such thing as a taxi in Millville, or even a subway. It wasn't pretty, with gardens, like the Coops, or with big buildings with rooms for play or doing your laundry. When Pop said, "We're home," it was an ugly little house and they had to live upstairs.

The first thing he did when they first got into the flat was sit them all down and say, "Now listen to me and listen carefully. This isn't the Coops. This isn't The Bronx, New York City. This is a little railroad town in upstate New York and up here they're ignorant; and if they ever found out that we're progressives . . . I don't know what they'd do, but it wouldn't be nice. They love McCarthy up here!" That was shocking; in the Coops, everyone knew he was a liar and evil.

And then Pop said, "Listen to me, all of you. You're never to talk politics, *never*. Whatever they say to you, no matter how terrible it is, act dumb. Just smile and agree. Do you hear me? No matter what. You'll hear plenty about the dirty Reds up here, I can promise you that! You'll have to pretend it doesn't bother you. Remember what I said. Smile and agree. Smile and agree."

Cookie would never forget the look on her mother's face: bleak and drained, white as a papier-mâché mask. Her mother never turned to look at her or her brothers, just stared straight ahead. Then Pop said, "And our last name is Gordon now. Don't ever tell anyone Golodny. Forget Golodny. We're not Golodny anymore."

And when Paul, who was only five, began to cry, Pop fixed him with a glare and said, "Paul Gordon, enough! It's nothing to cry about. It's life, that's all, life. At your age, I was already working in my father's shop, like a man. I didn't cry about something as meaningless as a change of a name! Gordon, that's our name now and I want all of you to say it."

They all said "Gordon," kind of mumbling, all but Mom. It

was very frightening. Mom didn't look like her usual self and Papa—Papa had never yelled at Paul before, Papa never yelled at any of them. Papa was the one you went to if you got into trouble because he wouldn't start in on you right away. Papa always listened. Who was this stranger who barked out orders and looked mean and told you "not now," when you wanted to talk to him?

That was the worst day in her life, until yesterday. All day in school, it was so awful. Everyone, not just Mrs. Casey, everyone was saying horrible things about the Rosenbergs and about Communists; and they were so wrong. And she wasn't allowed to say anything. She couldn't argue with them, even when all the kids said the only good Commie was a dead Commie.

They talked that way in class and they were still talking about it at recess. Tommy Clancy said, "Send 'em all back to Russia!" Tommy said that. He was one of her best friends—or so she had thought—and the second smartest kid in her class. And then his big brother, Pat, laughed and said, "Hell, kill 'em all, that's what Da says." And the others all laughed and she had to turn away and pretend there was a stone in her shoe.

All day long, she was fighting tears. She couldn't believe that everyone, *everyone*, in Millville was against them. It gave her a queer feeling. She didn't have a real friend in all the world, not here. She thought of her friend Sonya back in the Coops and then she thought of Deena, and then she *really* wanted to cry.

She and Sonya had marched side by side in the last May Day parade and they had sung all the songs together, as loudly as they could. And they both stuck out their tongues at the people who lined the street and yelled, "Go back to Russia!" Who cared what those dumb people said? She and Sonya were marching with thousands of their own people. Just let one of those dumbbells try something! The entire parade would come to their rescue. But in Millville, she was utterly alone.

Her heart sank as she approached the pizza parlor. The boys were hanging around on the sidewalk in front and she saw one of them nudge his friend when they spotted her. Immediately, she crossed the street, looking straight ahead. She was telling herself, They aren't there. I can't hear them because they're not there. But really, she heard every whistle and every word. "Looky, looky, here comes Cookie!" "She doesn't look like a *cooky* anymore . . . cupcakes is more like it!" "Hey, cupcakes, don't be so shy! Come on over here and let me take a bite!"

Her face burned and she clutched the pile of books tightly to her chest. She hated them, *hated* them! Why did they always have to do that? It used to be her red hair. Now it was her chest . . . She had begun growing lately, all of a sudden. One day she was just regular, and the next day, her undershirt had bumps under it. And it hurt to sleep on her stomach. And all her dresses and blouses were too tight, and when she told her mother, she laughed and said, "You're going to be built just like me," and gave her one of her own blouses to wear. "We'll get you new clothes, Cookie, but let's wait until you stop growing." Cookie could never tell Mom about how the boys yelled. She wished they would stop, that's all, just stop.

At last she was far enough away so she couldn't hear them. She crossed the railroad tracks and made her turn to go up the hill. It looked so steep and dusty today. This was not a pretty part of Millville. There were no trees, like on the streets around the park. The sun blazed down on her. She could feel it burning through the cotton dress. She felt all sweaty and messy.

She let herself into the house, just as the paper mill whistle went off. Noon. Pop was still sitting at the kitchen table, his hands folded on top of the newspaper, staring off into space. He was listening to the radio, but he looked over when she came in and even gave her a tired smile.

"Mom home yet?"

"Not yet. But you know Doc O'Brien's office on a Saturday." Her mother had taken Paul to the doctor for his vaccination. "Oh, thanks," he added, picking up the books and examining each one. "You're a wonderful help, Cookie. A really good girl."

She glowed. It had been a long, long time since he'd said anything special to her. But his face was so sad and he hadn't slept yet. His eyes were all red and sore-looking. "Pop, why are you up? You should go get some sleep."

"Sleep! Who could sleep? All night long on the job, I kept thinking about them. Couldn't stop my mind from going over and over it. It's a terrible day for civilization, Cookie. Terrible. None of them up here has the slightest idea what's really going on in the world . . . in this country."

Troubled, she began to take out his favorite things for lunch. Pot cheese. Sour cream. Cucumbers to be cut up and put on top. Two cans of tuna fish and the jar of Hellmann's. She kept looking over at Pop, hoping he'd notice what she was doing and smile. But he didn't even look at her, not really.

"The Brotherhood of Railroad Workers," he said, talking to

himself the way he did a lot lately. "Brotherhood. What a ring that has, eh, Cookie? But the priest says Communists are god-less and evil and that's the end of it. Nobody questions, nobody thinks. They'd rather go to the tavern and drink beer. They don't even know they're oppressed! And they call that a union? That's no union!" He put his head in his hands and took in a deep, audible breath.

Cookie said nothing. She kept on making lunch. She hated it when he talked like this; it always made him feel so bad. And then he'd fall asleep, sitting up in his chair, reading, the book or newspaper still open on his lap. He'd started falling asleep like that since they came here.

In 1951, when they were still in the Coops and the Rosenbergs were convicted, how angry he was, how he talked a mile a minute. Right away he started planning a protest march, writing a petition, scribbling on the back of an envelope as he talked. There was no sadness in him then, not until they came to Mill-ville. He hated Millville. She knew it. Irwin knew it. Even the baby knew it. They hated it, too. Then why, she asked herself for the millionth time, why do we have to stay here? It must be a very good reason . . . a very *big* reason.

Pop left the kitchen without another word, and a minute later, she heard water running in the bathroom. He was washing up for lunch.

And then footsteps came pounding up the stairs. Irwin. For such a little boy, he made an awful lot of noise. He came in, already saying, "What's to eat? I'm hungry," before he even got into the kitchen. And then he put his filthy hand right into the tuna fish and took some. "Irwin! Stop it!"

"Make me!"

"I'll make you, all right, and you'll be sorry! You're filthy dirty. Go wash your hands."

He stuck his tongue out. "Make me! I dare you."

You couldn't talk to him, not about anything. He'd say "make me" or "shut up" or "drop dead." He was impossible! Angry, she came after him and he backed away from her, laughing that horrible, high-pitched cackle, and said, "Look how you jiggle when you run, Cookie. Why don't you get yourself a bra-*zeer*!"

"Why don't you go get yourself a coffin, Irwin!" Frantic with embarrassment and fury, she made a fist and hit whatever she could reach, which happened to be his shoulder.

Of course, he began to laugh. "Hit me again! Hit me again! Oh, ow, that really hurt!" She couldn't stand it. And then he gave her a big grin and reached into the tuna fish again, licking his fingers. "Can't hurt a fly—not with those big bazooms!"

That did it. To her horror, tears began to spill down her cheeks, and that only made him laugh. "Gotcha, gotcha!" he chanted, dancing around like a boxer, crowing. He knew damn well she was crying because she was mad.

"Damn you!" she yelled, and chased him around the table, pounding on him with her fists every time she caught up with him.

Suddenly, there was Mom, holding a large paper bag of groceries. And she was boiling mad. She thumped the bag down on the kitchen table and gave Cookie a hit across her back.

"What's going on here? Paul cries the whole way home from Doc's, and then I walk into the grocery store and Caldwell tells me no more credit until the bill's paid up . . . and I come home to *this*?"

She began to unpack the groceries, banging each thing down on the table. "You, Cookie! You're the oldest, I depend on you—and here you are, behaving like a *vilda chaya*!" It was so unfair: Irwin was the wild animal! "And the table's not even set!"

Cookie longed to talk back. How about the food I put out? How about the tuna salad I made? She said it silently. She stared at her mother—Irwin, at a safe distance, was making faces at her where Mom couldn't see—and then she couldn't help it, she just started to cry and she ran out of the room, bumping into Pop.

Behind her, her mother demanded in a loud voice, "What's the matter with that child? What's she crying about, anyway?"

Pop put a comforting hand on Cookie's head, absently massaging her scalp. "Dot, this is a sad and terrible time, even for a young girl."

"Sad? Oh. The Rosenbergs. Yes, yes. That's a great tragedy. But what does the execution of the Rosenbergs have to do with the fact that I came home to find these two fighting like they were brought up in a barn! *You* could have stopped it, but forget it! I might as well talk to the wall! And why is Cookie crying? The Rosenberg children, *they* have something to cry about! They don't have a mother and father to love them and take care of them, not anymore! Enough already! She cries over *everything*, these days!"

She rounded on Cookie, and those two angry lines deepened between her eyes. "Stop this nonsense, Cookie. Do you hear me? I count on you, you know that. You have to stop acting like a baby!''

"Listen to your mother," her father said in a gentle voice. "She only wants what's good for us. And you are a big girl now, practically an adult. You have to help. Do you understand?''

Cookie wiped her eyes obediently and managed to say, "Yes, Papa.'' But inside, she was still crying.

€€€

Chapter Twenty-four

Wednesday, March 10, 1954   Irwin shifted his books to his other arm, yawning hugely. Never had the walk down Half-moon Avenue seemed so endless; never had school felt so far away. He'd been up very late last night, for the Edward R. Murrow program, and he was very sleepy. This morning, Cookie had to pull off all the covers and tickle his feet to get him up. He hated being tickled and she knew it. He jumped right out of bed and chased her so he could pinch her, but she ran into the bathroom and locked the door, and then he had to pee so bad and she made him beg, she made him say "I'm a jerk," ten times before she let him in. But he got even. As they passed each other, he pinched her tush. And then Mama yelled at him.

"What's the matter with you?'' she said. "You *know* your papa needs his sleep!'' It wasn't fair. Cookie started it. But Mama *always* blamed him.

It was hard to follow the example of Edward R. Murrow and be a man of principle, like Papa said last night, when everyone treated you like a baby, even though you were already nine. He rounded the corner at North Main Street and ducked his head against the blast of cold air that always blew down Main Street. He should have taken his hat, like Mama said before she left for work. But he was too mad at her. Why did she always take Cookie's side? It wasn't fair!

He wished Papa was like he used to be, back in the Coops. *Then* they wouldn't get away with it! Back then, when he was a little kid, Papa used to take him to all the rallies and the marches.

He remembered going with Papa to Twenty-third Street with his own sign to carry. CIO HAS TO GO. He didn't know what it meant, but he remembered everyone cheering him and raising their fists. And then there were the times when Papa would put him up on a box and let him hand out leaflets and make a speech.

Irwin remembered when he was only five, Papa taught him a speech to give on a corner of Union Square. He remembered how all the people came up and smiled and listened to him, and how they clapped and laughed when he was finished, and all the ladies kissed him and the men shook his hand, and somebody even gave him a quarter! He didn't remember all of the speech anymore, just the part about "No welfare, no work!" It was something about the coal miners' strike. What he did remember was how everyone thought it was so great, how much he sounded like Papa, how they said "chip off the old block" and "Jonah to the life." He especially remembered the look on his father's face: so proud, so pleased with him.

He *was* good at imitating people, but Mama always said, "Enough, Irwin! Don't you realize people don't like to be mimicked?"

"Papa does!"

"Your papa lets you get away with murder!"

And Papa put down his newspaper and said, "Lay off, Dot! I'm telling you, the kid's a hit! You should hear him—he's a born speaker!"

Back in the Coops, it used to be so good. And then Paul had to become everyone's little pet, and then they had to move up here and Papa had to be tired all the time. It wasn't fair.

A lot of the kids were in front of school. Kids weren't allowed in the front door and they weren't supposed to be there; but there was a hard wind today and it was warm in the doorway. He knew a lot of the kids and they knew him. He was smart, the smartest kid in his class. Sometimes, he wished he wasn't—then maybe they'd like him. Then maybe they'd stop calling him names. The only time they were nice to him was when they needed him to help them with homework or they wanted to copy his test papers.

They never asked him to be in their dumb plays and he was better at acting than any of them. But Mama said, "Why do you want to be in their plays if they're dumb plays?" He couldn't explain; she wouldn't understand, anyway.

A lot of the kids had stayed up to see the TV last night because it was all about Senator McCarthy and Miss Carpenter had sent a note home to everyone's parents saying it was important for current events. They were all talking about it now, saying stupid, dumb things like how McCarthy was going to get back at Murrow, and how Edward R. Murrow was probably a Commie himself!

Irwin stood on the steps and said, "McCarthy's not so great!" And when they all said, "Get lost, you're crazy," and stuff like that, Irwin imitated him. He screwed up his face like McCarthy and said, " 'We've been kicked around, bullwhipped, and damned!' " and then he gave that crazy laugh. "He's a nut!" he said.

The kids just stared at him; and Sal Rizzo said, "You want a bloody nose?"

" 'Edward R. Murrow is a hero and a fighter. He's the only man in this country with the guts to talk back to McCarthy,' " Irwin quoted his father. And then he tipped his head down, the way Edward R. Murrow did, and raised one eyebrow, and in Murrow's deep, even voice, he said, " 'This is no time for men who oppose Senator McCarthy's methods to keep silent. We can deny our heritage and our history, but we cannot escape responsibility for the result.' "

Miss Carpenter's voice startled him. "Irwin Gordon! What are you doing? All you kids! You know you're not supposed to be here!"

Irwin's heart began to thump painfully. He hadn't even seen her approach; yet there she was, standing with two other teachers, frowning. "I'm only telling these kids that McCarthy is crazy!" he blurted. His heartbeat speeded up even more. What would she do to him? He knew he wasn't supposed to ever say anything about what they believed at home. Mama and Papa told them a million times that Millville was a hotbed of McCarthyism. He wasn't sure what a hotbed was, but it wasn't good, that was for sure.

But all Miss Carpenter said was, "Now, Irwin, I'm sure Senator McCarthy is only doing what he thinks is right for the country!"

"Well, but he accuses people! He puts them on a blacklist and they can't work! Edward R. Murrow says McCarthy tells only half the truth and—"

"If you're not a Communist, you have nothing to fear. Let's save this discussion for class. The bell is going to ring any minute now." And she made a shooing motion at all of them.

Sal Rizzo got next to him, too close, pushing him sideways,

and muttered, "Dirty Red!" And then he stuck his foot out and Irwin tripped and fell onto his knees, ripping his pants—and Sal ran off, laughing.

It was awful in school all day. Nobody would eat lunch with him. But he didn't care. He was above the behavior of ignoramuses . . . like Mama always told him. But it was hard to sit alone at a table and know they were all whispering about him.

When school let out, he walked very fast, to get ahead of everyone. His head was down, so he didn't see Paul until he heard him laughing. His brother was across the street with his two best friends, Georgie and Carmie. Everyone called them The Three Musketeers because you always saw them together. They had their arms across one anothers' shoulders and they were marching, doing cadence count. Carmie's brother Guido was a staff sergeant in the army and he had taught it to them. Irwin slowed down, watching the three boys, marching so close together in perfect step, their heads up, shouting in perfect unison. He wished he had two best friends. One, even. He walked along with them, from across the street, hoping Paul would look over and see him, hoping he wouldn't. Wouldn't it be nice if Paul yelled to him to come on over and march with them? But he wouldn't.

Irwin started to run. When he turned the corner into Halfmoon Avenue, he saw Cookie just ahead of him—and for once in his life, he was happy to see his sister. He called her name and ran to her, and for some reason found himself telling her the whole story. Not about Paul and his friends; about what happened in school.

"I hate it here!" he said at the end. "Why can't we go back to the Coops? Paul has friends! It isn't fair!" And he began to cry. He couldn't help it and he couldn't stop it. He just knew Cookie would laugh at him for being a crybaby, but she didn't.

She said, "I know what let's do . . . let's take the sleds and go to Vale Avenue Hill."

Irwin stared at her. He couldn't believe his ears. Cookie, offering to go sledding with him? Cookie, who called him Mr. Pest? Who told on him all the time? Who he was sure *hated* him? But yes, she meant it.

"I haven't gone down Vale Avenue Hill for a million years," she said. "And pretty soon the snow will *really* be gone for good." There had been a giant snowstorm the day before yesterday, after a big thaw that made everyone say it looked like winter was over. Now there were big, beautiful white drifts of snow everywhere . . . well, almost white. Nothing stayed white in Millville very long. It was wet snow, too, and that meant good packing and good sledding.

By the time they got their sleds from under the stairs, it was nearly dark. "Maybe we shouldn't go," Irwin said.

But Cookie gave him a look. "Scared? *I'm* not."

So he had to say he wasn't scared. But he didn't like the dark stretches between the little pools of light from the streetlamps. He didn't like the creepy shadows from the bare trees.

His hands were already frozen, even inside the mittens, as he and Cookie slogged toward the hill. Vale Avenue was the last street in Millville to be plowed, and it was thick with tramped-down snow.

Cookie walked too fast, and she kept turning around to complain. "Hurry up, Irwin. I'm supposed to be peeling the potatoes right now, not playing with you." He wanted badly to say, Then let's go home, but she'd really give it to him if he did that. So he hurried as best he could.

And then, when they got there, his heart sank. The big boys were there, the whole bunch of them: Joey Higgins, Sal Rizzo, Carmen Mangione, Lucky Knapp, Beans Carson, and his brother, Little Beans, the whole gang. Big boys, fifteen, sixteen, some of them, and two boys from his class. Without thinking, he reached out and grabbed Cookie's arm.

Cookie felt Irwin clutch at her and, irritated, turned to him. God, he looked like a twerp, with his runny nose and his big frightened eyes and that ugly green hat that was too big for him. Why, oh, why, did she have to have him for a brother? Right now, she was sorry she'd had that moment of pity for him. He looked like a scared rabbit. She knew why, and she didn't ex- actly love the idea of finding those awful boys here, either. But Irwin was a *boy*; he was supposed to be brave.

If they said one word—! She hated them. But they'd seen her, they were all looking at her and Irwin, and she wasn't going to let them think they could scare *her* away, especially not in front of her kid brother.

"Just ignore them," she told Irwin, and putting her nose in the air, marched the two of them past the knot of boys, pretend- ing she didn't even see them.

For a little while, it was okay. She and Irwin went down once, then again. She loved it: lying flat on the sled, feeling the ground rushing beneath her, the flying feeling, the feeling of being free of the earth.

It was getting darker and colder, and the more they went down, the slipperier the road became. It was only four-thirty, but it felt like the middle of the night. There were only three streetlights on the whole hill, widely spaced. But it was such a lovely feeling, sliding down so effortlessly, going faster and faster, riding in and out of the light and the dark. She forgot it was so late; she pretty nearly forgot she was there with Irwin, in fact.

And then, the second time she came up, she saw that he was crying. "What's the matter? Where's your sled?"

Blubbering, he told her, "They keep taking my sled. They bump me and then they send it down the hill. It's at the b-b-bottom!" He turned and yelled at Joey Higgins, "You dirty pig!"

Joey Higgins was thirteen, two years older than Cookie, but in the same grade, a tall, skinny boy with a reputation as a wise guy and a bully. She hated him. He was always looking at her funny and making comments under his breath. She glared at him now, and he grinned, saying, "It was an accident!"

"Oh, yeah?"

"Yeah!"

"Then, why don't you go down and get it?"

"Why don't *you*?"

"I didn't push it to the bottom."

Triumphantly, Joey said, "Me, neither!"

Filled with anger, Cookie turned to Irwin and said sharply, "Stop the crying, will you? I'll go get your sled." And she did, even though her toes were getting numb. She dragged it up the hill and handed it to him, saying, "Okay. Let's go down one more time and then get home. Mama will kill me if I haven't started supper when she gets home."

Still grinning at her, very pleased with himself, Joey bumped himself into Irwin, grabbing the sled's rope, and sent it whizzing down the hill.

"Dirty pig, rotten dirty pig!" Irwin shrieked, his nose dripping and his eyes filling.

Joey Higgins began to laugh. "Dirty little Red!" he taunted. "Dirty little Jew! You asked for it! You're a traitor! Sal told us!"

Irwin was sobbing now in frustration, and hot rage was rising behind Cookie's eyes, she could feel it. Words just exploded out of her. "This is a free country and you're a lousy bully! You're so stupid, you're still in the sixth grade! You should be in kindergarten, you're so stupid!" The words just kept pouring out of her. She was so furious; it was unfair. He was big and they were small, and hearing him say *Red* and *Jew* like that, so nasty, so evil, gave her a horrible sinking feeling in the pit of her stomach.

Joey Higgins just stood there, smiling and smiling, as if he didn't care. He was still smiling when he came over and said, "Stupid, am I? Here's how stupid I am." And he wrenched her sled away from her and kicked it so it went sliding backward down the hill.

Cookie stood there, wishing him dead. She hated him with a fury she had never before experienced. Her hands were freezing, she couldn't feel her feet, they were late already, it was so far down to the bottom of the hill—and then they had to come all the way back up to get home. Tears of rage began to slip from her eyes and she could feel her whole body shaking.

And then a new feeling flooded through her. She was going to get Joey Higgins. She took in a deep breath and yelled at him, "You'd better go down there and get those sleds or I'll make you sorry. I'll kill you. I swear I'll kill you!" She was surprised by the sound of her own voice, so calm, so sure of itself. She could hardly believe it was really her.

Suddenly Joey's big brother, Billy Higgins, appeared. He was really big, seventeen years old and already out of school and working at the lumberyard. "What's going on here?" he said. "What's all the noise about?"

Cookie marched right up to him, her fists clenched, her head tipped way back. He looked eight feet tall, his head far away, up in the sky. And he was the enemy. But she didn't care. She could hear Irwin's sobs and she was filled with outrage that these big boys should feel free to pick on a little kid this way.

She yelled at Billy Higgins. "You tell those boys to go get our sleds. They keep taking our sleds and throwing them down the hill and my mother is going to kill us if we aren't home. You tell them they're worse than Hitler, picking on kids smaller than they are!" She felt tall and strong, not afraid at all. Let him do his worst!

Billy Higgins leaned over from his great height and lifted her up until they were face-to-face. She was half expecting him to yell at her and then throw her away; and she flinched. "Whoa, there, little hothead. You've got a temper that matches your hair!" He began to laugh and Cookie found herself getting even madder.

"Put me down, dammit!" she yelled. "Don't you dare laugh at me!"

"Whoa! I'm not laughing at you. You're a gutsy little thing, aren't you?"

He put her back down gently, and at the same time, in a very different voice, turned and barked: "You! Joey! And the rest of you, too. Down there and get those sleds . . ." There was the beginning of a murmur of protest, which he chopped off with a swift gesture of one hand. "On . . . the . . . double," he said in a voice that meant business.

She had done it. She had stood up to Joey Higgins—to *all* of them—and she had won. She watched from the top of the hill with great pleasure as Joey and the others pulled the sleds back up, slipping and sliding on the icy road, silent and grim. And when Billy cuffed his brother on the shoulder and said, "What the hell's the matter with you, anyway?" she had to fight the urge to laugh out loud, right in his ugly face.

Loftily, she said, "Come on, Irwin, let's go home." She handed him the rope to his sled and began walking. Snuffling, her brother trotted alongside her.

"Please don't tell them *you* were the one who got the sleds back, okay, Cookie?"

She knew what that was all about. Boys were supposed to be brave and strong and protect their sisters, not the other way around . . . and he knew it. "Are you crazy? I'm not telling them *anything*! And you'd better stop crying right now, you dummy, or they'll know something happened."

They walked along in silence, and then she added, "And especially never say what they called you. Never." And she made him cross his heart and hope to die.

Mama was already home. As soon as they came in the front door, the door to their flat upstairs flew open and there she was, looming over them. "Where've you been? I've been worried sick! Get up here, both of you!"

"Remember, Irwin," Cookie muttered, "keep your trap shut."

Dorothy was all ready to give them hell for being out late and not telling her where they were going. And then she saw the sleds and she made herself calm down. They were two children, she reminded herself, trying to have a little fun in this lousy town with its lousy weather. How could she yell? But, dammit, they had to learn!

"Cookie! You couldn't leave me a note? I've been worried sick." Then quickly, she added, "Did you have fun?"

There was something a bit strange about the way they both said, "Oh, yes!" in bright little voices. But when they came up the stairs and she could see them, they were smiling and rosy cheeked. Irwin's nose was running, it always was . . . and try to get a small boy to carry a handkerchief! But it was a relief seeing them together without squabbling.

"Both of you, wash up. Then come right into the kitchen. Papa and I want to talk to you." Cookie gave her a sharp look. What was going on in that eleven-year-old head? It made her uneasy.

Everything was making her uneasy these days. She was a nervous wreck. Between that bastard McCarthy and Jo's depression—and this terrible place where everyone you met was either a bigot or a right-wing reactionary or a mindless bore—she was going out of her mind. She just couldn't stand having to hide every thought she had. And now, the high school bandleader, Bill Hightower, was after her. Oh, he was a nice guy, at least he had a little culture. He loved music, he read books, he came into the library all the time. The two of them had begun to talk together quite often and she liked having an intelligent person to talk to.

But with him, it was more. She wished he wouldn't, it was so embarrassing. He was a short fat man, rather nice-looking, and always neat as a pin. But he had a way of bouncing on his toes that was ludicrous and he tended to be pompous, and when he got excited about anything, his face turned bright red. Yesterday, when she was closing up, he'd actually tried to kiss her. It was so awkward. She pushed him away, feeling herself blush, and tried to act like he hadn't done it.

That wasn't the worst of it. The worst of it was that, oh, God, it had excited her. She wanted to die! Of course, it had been months since Jo had touched her; he seemed to have lost all interest. The sheer nightie she'd bought at the Boston Store had no effect and was now neatly folded and put away in the bottom drawer of the dresser. And she found her pulses racing when a man she didn't even care for came close to her, indicated that he wanted her! She was disgusting! How she hated her life! But she had no choice. She had three children; she must carry on. She was trapped here.

When she walked into the kitchen, Jo was sitting precisely as she had left him, hands folded on the table, his muscular shoulders slumped as they always were nowadays, his eyes fixed on the distance. Dammit, why he couldn't once straighten up and take some of the load. She was so damn tired.

So her voice was harsher than she wanted when the kids came in. "Sit down!" she said, hearing the edge in her tone, not liking it. "This is important," she explained.

"Miss Carpenter paid me a visit after school today, Irwin. Never mind looking at your sister, you can't blame it on her this time. So . . . you want to tell us why you had to imitate Mc-Carthy on the front steps of School One this morning, in front of the whole world?"

"But Mama, I didn't—"

"But Irwin, you *did*. Why didn't you go down to the *Gazette* office while you were at it, so the entire town could know about the enemy in their midst?"

"Oh, Mama," Cookie said, "Miss Carpenter didn't say *that*, did she?"

"No, no. But that's what she was thinking, believe me. Irwin, what in the world got into you?"

"Papa said a man of principle stands up for what he believes."

Now Jonah put his two cents in. "Dammit, that was just between you and me, Irwin. You're old enough to understand that in this town you have to keep your mouth *shut*. *Now* do you understand?" He pounded his fist on the table for emphasis.

In answer, Irwin began to cry. Well, he was only a little boy, a pest, but only nine, after all. What did Jo want from him, anyway?

So she interrupted. "Stop crying, Irwin. There's nothing to cry about. What's done is done. And anyway, I fixed it."

She fixed it, sure. But not without a lot of heart-thumping anxiety. When Claire Carpenter came striding into the library, a certain look on her face that said serious business, she had broken into a cold sweat. Had someone seen Bill Hightower with his arms around her? Was Irwin sick? Or had he done something?

But, of course, she had to put a smile on her face and act as if Claire came into the library after school hours every day of the week. "Miss Carpenter. How nice. Can I offer you a nice book?"

"Not now, thanks. There's something I need to talk to you about. Privately. Nobody's here, I hope." And she glanced around.

"No. Just me. In fact, you just caught me; I was on my way out."

"Well, then. There are very strong feelings in this town about the Communist threat . . ."

Worse than she had thought. Now her heart was going at such a rate, she was sure Claire Carpenter could see it throbbing under her sweater. "Yes," she murmured. "I know . . ."

"Of course, there's a good reason. Millville has the largest railroad freight yards east of the Mississippi and that makes us a prime target . . ." Why couldn't the woman get to the point? "The point is, folks tend to be nervous if someone seems too liberal. And, well, your boy Irwin this morning . . ." And she told her about Irwin imitating first McCarthy and then Murrow. "He's quite talented. But, you know, I'm afraid those kids are going to go home and repeat it all to their parents and, well, I thought you ought to know. Tell him to be more careful." She looked directly into Dot's eyes, very serious. Was she hinting? Did she know?

Dorothy swallowed, and then said in her lightest tone, "Oh, that boy! He does love to mimic. Well, we allowed him to stay up far too late last night. And, well . . . when Edward R. Murrow says this is no time to be silent, a nine-year-old boy believes him. That Irwin . . . he's a funny little thing. I'll certainly talk to him. But I doubt very much that he understood any of what he was saying." And may God forgive me for such big lies, she thought, her skin clammy under the wool sweater.

Claire Carpenter regarded her for a moment and Dorothy thought, Oh, God, what now? What if she asks me straight out, Are you a Communist? A fellow traveler? What if she accuses me? Her mind raced. They'd have to pack, they'd have to leave, and quickly. With three children. All that luggage. No, they'd have to leave things behind. The important thing was to get out of here and go . . . where? Where would they go? What if Jo got stubborn, like he always seemed to be these days? What if he refused? Well, if he refused, she'd just take the kids and go, herself.

Then Claire leaned forward, looking first left and right, and whispered, "You're not alone, Mrs. Gordon. I'm a secret Democrat, myself." And smiled.

Dorothy, sitting at her kitchen table, remembering, found herself smiling. And Jonah said, "What do you mean, you fixed it? And what's with the laughing? What's so funny about any of this?"

"Oh, Jo." She looked at him, so grim and humorless. Where was the sunny, laughing young man she had married, the hero, the impassioned talker? "Miss Carpenter and I had a nice little talk and she admitted that she, too, is a . . . liberal. That's what I was laughing at. She was acting as a friend, warning me."

Now she rounded on the children. "You hear that? Were you listening to me? She was warning me that, in Millville, talking against McCarthy will only get you into trouble. Get us *all* into trouble."

The silence in the kitchen was tense, and into it came little Paul, out of the kids' bedroom, wearing his cowboy hat, toy six-shooters strapped around his waist, pushing the swinging door to the kitchen open. "Howdy, strangers!" he drawled.

He was so adorable, her baby. Dorothy never tired of looking at him. He was beautiful, that's all there was to it. Never mind saying good-looking, saying cute, or trying to be modest. Paul Gordon was a gorgeous little boy. And a charmer. Always smiling, always sweet and good-natured. He was a perfect child. He made them all smile and laugh. He was a ray of sunshine.

Even Jo was smiling now. He loved the way Paul dressed for the part when he played. If he watched a baseball game, he had to have his mitt and his cap. If it was football, he wouldn't sit down until he had his little ball. And when it was cowboys he was playing, he put on the full regalia and the way of talking and even the cowboy swagger he saw on the TV.

"Howdy yourself," Jonah said. "Mosey on over here, pardner. What brings you to these here parts?"

She regarded her husband, complete with cowboy accent and cowboy grin. Only Paul had the power to break through his deep sadness. She only wished Jo would let the rest of them through. But, to be fair, Paul had a special gift with people. She knew, to her shame, that she was far gentler with him than she was with the other two . . . that truthfully, she favored him. She sent a glance at Irwin and Cookie, feeling a little twinge. Maybe they noticed and resented it. But they were both smiling, too, playing with Paul, so happy to see him.

The atmosphere in the kitchen had completely changed. Paul had made Jo laugh and, of course, as soon as she saw her father in a good mood, Cookie became a different person. "Let me start the potatoes," she said. Usually, she sulked the whole time. And Irwin didn't run up to untie her apron the minute she put it on. Instead, he began to set the table—without being asked.

As for the talk about McCarthy and his witch-hunts, even that was forgotten for now.

For the moment, they were a family. They even looked like a *happy* family. Was it enough? Not really. But for now, it had to be.

€€€

Chapter Twenty-five

Wednesday, August 16, 1961   They walked to the restaurant from their flat, side by side but not touching, not speaking, taking it slow because of the muggy July heat that lay over Millville like a heavy blanket.

What are we doing, going out for our anniversary? she thought. Just what is it we're supposed to be celebrating? Twenty years of . . . what? We don't talk together or sleep together, for that matter. Togetherness! What a joke!

And then she stopped. They had been heading for Santauzzi's Tavern. Not exactly The Stork Club but what the hell, it was a night out. But Santauzzi's Tavern was no more. Instead of the old hand-painted sign, there was a neon extravaganza, three colors, a gondola riding the waves, and even a new name: LITTLE NAPOLI. "Oh, typical!"

"What?"

"The sign, Jonah. The stupid sign!" She could see from the stubborn look on his face that he was ready to defend the entire Santauzzi family. He worked with two of the brothers-in-law in the railroad yard.

"Oh, Jonah, don't look like that. Don't you see? Little Napoli. With a gondola." She waited; he still didn't get it. "They have gondolas in *Venice*, Jo. Not Naples."

"Just don't say anything to them!"

He had become so argumentative about everything in this town. You couldn't say a single word about *anything*. So she agreed she wouldn't say anything to the Santauzzis. She wouldn't have, anyway.

They went in. Hoo-hoo! Air-conditioning! Nancy and Louie

must be doing real well. Dot and Jonah came in here for a meal maybe twice a year—on state occasions—and since the last time, what a transformation! Oh, the scarred wooden booths were still there, but now there was a red-checked tablecloth, a vase with a plastic rose, and a Chianti bottle with a candle stuck in it on each table. And Nancy Santauzzi greeted them at the door, wearing an Italian peasant costume, complete with little apron.

Dot put on a smile. "Very fancy, very nice," she said, and Nancy bridled and beamed with pleasure.

"Right this way," she said, and led them the two feet to a table overlooking the railroad crossing.

Jonah ordered a bottle of Chianti—a whole bottle!—and chatted with Nancy. When she left, Dorothy gestured at the twilit scene outside the restaurant: the lines of boxcars, waiting to be marked and shuttled and sent on their way; the few ailanthus trees, struggling to live; the neat, always freshly painted frame houses, each one with a square of carefully tended grass, each one with its collection of plastic lawn ornaments, cranes, flamingoes, elves and dwarves, even a Madonna or two in a little plastic shrine. "Scenic view, Millville-style," she commented acidly.

"Dot, it's our anniversary. Let it go, for a change, okay?"

Dom, the youngest Santauzzi son, brought their bottle, lit the candle, poured them each a glass and said, "What'll you have? Pop made clams marinara and there's a lasagna just out of the oven. It's great and I oughta know: I just had a big piece." And he blew a kiss into the air.

Expansive, Jonah said, "Bring both of them. It's our anniversary. Might as well live it up!" He gave Dom a big smile.

"Oh, Jonah—" Dot said, and then gave up. She wished he wouldn't do that. It would be different if they were a happy couple, wanting to make a genuine celebration of their years together. But all she could think was: Oh, my God, twenty years. It felt more like one hundred. She was in no mood to lift her glass and make believe she felt anything but tense.

And there he sat, with that phoney smile, playing the part of a happy man, out on the town with his wife, hail-fellow-well-met.

At home with them, he often sat silently for hours, sunk in gloom, either reading or pretending to read but, in any case, not interested in anything that was going on around him. Her heart ached for her children yes, for herself, too. Why not? Her heart was aching this very minute. She wanted to say to him, Jonah, please *see* me, please *hear* me!

But she had given up. She'd tried before to get through to him, to make him see what was happening to them, and he always silenced her with a wave of his hand and a muttered, "You think anyone has it any better?" Yes. That's what she thought. When would he admit the ugly reality of their life here?

She had it planned. If it took the last ounce of her strength, tonight she was going to *force* him to listen to her. And if he refused *this* time, well, she knew what she had to do. She was leaving this damn town! With him or without him!

Oh, hell. It was the first time in months they'd been out. She'd drink a lot of wine, wait until their spumoni and espresso, and then she'd tell him.

Jonah smiled at her and lifted his wineglass. He still looked much younger than his age—there wasn't a bit of gray in his red hair, although the color had faded some. And because he did physical labor, he was very muscular. You had to know him from years ago, like she did, to know what was missing . . . to know there had once been fire in those pale, dead eyes, that once he had burned with energy and commitment.

"A toast," he said, "to us. To our years together." She clinked glasses with him and then, instead of sipping at her Chianti, she took a hefty gulp. "What would you like for a present?" Jo said.

"Out of here!" she answered. The words just said themselves. Dammit, dammit, dammit! She'd meant to save it until later.

"Do me a favor. Just enjoy yourself tonight? Instead of bringing up the same old garbage?"

"If you'd *listen* to me, for once, I wouldn't have to keep saying the same things over and over."

Again, that dismissive wave. How she hated it. As if she were some kind of servant, instead of an equal breadwinner, a partner. How come all of the working class was so special, except for her? *She* worked, dammit!

But this time, she was smart. She held her tongue and thought about how to put it to him.

"I give you two words, Jo. Freedom . . . Riders. Civil . . . rights. Freedom . . . *now*."

"That's six words *I* count."

"Don't make a joke out of it, Jonah Gordon! It's too important! A couple of months ago, thirteen men, black and white, got on a bus in D.C., and you know as well as I do what happened! Beaten up in South Carolina! The bus burned in Alabama! Left to be torn apart by a mob in Birmingham! How can you stand it—to stay up here, nowhere, doing nothing, when the world is changing?

"Jo, if white ministers from elitist universities—Yale, Wesleyan!—if *they* can go put themselves on the line, if *they're* willing to sit at lunch counters with Negro students and be spat on, beat up . . . arrested! Jonah! What are we *doing* here?"

He averted his eyes, sipping at his wine. It made her so mad. Why couldn't he break out of his gloom and lethargy? She had been so sure he would respond to a call to arms, so sure he'd say Yes, let's go join the struggle down South. At least admit they should go back where they belonged—to New York! But there he sat, unmoved. She could cry!

"Jo, come on! We don't belong here, we never did! Let's go. Let's pack our bags and take the kids and get *out* of this hellhole!"

Alarmed, he looked around, shushing her. "Don't let them hear you."

"McCarthy's dead, dammit. We can say whatever we please. We can *live* however we want! Jonah, I'm begging you. Let's leave."

"You know why I'm here. And here I stay."

The familiar rage boiled up in her, so fierce, so hot, she thought she would explode with it. She began to shake, and when she spoke, her voice shook, too.

"In the first place, we didn't *have* to come here! Don't shake your head like I'm stupid. We could have gone anywhere, anywhere at all! Where was it written that we couldn't go to Chicago or Los Angeles, where we have comrades, once you left Pepe's place? We could have gone *somewhere* decent, someplace where your children could have had a life. Where *I* could have had a life!"

"How can you say you don't have a life here? You're very popular. Everyone knows you, everyone likes you. You can't walk down the street without someone calling hello to you . . ."

She bent her head and closed her eyes, drawing in a breath, trying to draw in some strength. How was it that he didn't understand one single thing she said to him? He couldn't see what was right in front of him!

"Popular!" she mimicked bitterly. "Is that what you think? I work in the library, Jo. That's why people say hello to me.

Popular? Hell, how can I be popular when I'm not even accepted?''

He mumbled something and looked uneasy. And suddenly it struck her. He didn't want to know from it. He never had. What was she doing with him? There was such emptiness inside her, such despair. How had she come to be here? Once she had been young and full of dreams. Full of *life*. And now her life was a waste. She reached out and poured herself more wine.

"Paul has so many friends, he's never home," Jonah said after a moment. "Cookie's doing well in school, she smiles all the time. And Irwin . . . so, he's a loner—but he's at the top of his class. What's so terrible?''

Dorothy took another gulp. She couldn't get him to look her in the eye. Dammit! "Are you deaf, dumb, and blind? Every week, every *day* it seems like, Irwin comes home with a bloody nose because he killed their Lord. I'm worried about Cookie, she's boy crazy! And Paul's never home because he's ashamed of us! Can't you see that?''

Stubbornly: "No. I can't see that.''

"We're Jews, Jo. We're aliens. And, even though we've kept our politics a deep, dark secret, they *know* . . . They know there's something different about us, something they fear like the plague.''

She looked at him, at his profile really, head bent, eyelids down, lips pressed firmly together, closed off and giving away nothing; and she realized she was going to do it. She was going to get out of here, with or without him. You would think he'd be eager to go back to the city, to work for progressive causes. You'd think he would jump at the chance. But no. He sat like a mute, unwilling to look at her, refusing.

Once again, she was struck with a sudden thought. He'd been away so long, he'd left the Party in a huff, he'd lost track of everyone back in New York. He didn't know what he'd find back there. He wasn't sure he'd be accepted. He was scared!

"Jo, it'll work out. You'll be accepted. Believe me. The way you left, it's all been forgotten.''

"How do you know?''

Ah. So her guess was right. He was afraid. "Jo. This is not a place for us. You know that. We don't have anyone here we can talk to. Nobody in this damn town reads a newspaper, for God's sake. Nobody cares what happens in the world. All they know is their church, their paycheck, their social hall, and the tavern on Friday night. This is no way for us to live. This is no way for us to teach our children what we believe in. By hiding and pretending to be something we're not.''

He didn't answer for a moment, and then Dom came over with their food. That took a few minutes, while he fussed with arranging platters and the bread basket. She waited patiently, her hands clasped together tightly in her lap. And then, after Dom left, Jo used it as an excuse not to answer her. He stuffed his mouth with bread.

Exasperated, Dorothy said, ''Jonah, if you don't answer me right this minute, I'm leaving.''

''This is supposed to be a little party, Dot. First let's eat. Then we'll talk.'' She shook her head and reached for her purse. ''All right, all right! How can you talk to me about going back to New York? They'll find me and they'll deport me! Is *that* what you want?''

She stared at him. She could hardly believe her ears. ''Are you crazy? Nobody's going to deport you! Nobody cares about you, Jonah! Who *are* you, anyway? Some *gontser macher*, some big shot, that they need to get rid of you? And it's so many years . . . they're not looking for you. In fact, Jo, I wonder if they ever really *were*. Oh, yes, I've thought about that plenty, stuck up here. I keep asking myself, 'Why did he have to go disappear? Why are we here? Who are we hiding from?' And I get no answers, Jo, no answers at all. So *you* tell me: *What are we doing here?*''

He had wound spaghetti around his fork and it was halfway to his mouth. He put the fork back onto his plate, untasted, not looking at her, not saying anything.

''You can't answer me because you don't even know anymore! Listen to me, Jo, and listen to me good. Maybe *you're* willing to stay up here and rot, but I'm not. It used to be that you went wherever you were needed. What's happened to you? *What's happened to you?*'' She wanted to scream, to grab him and shake him until he heard her.

Jonah put the fork in his mouth and chewed his food deliberately. And now, finally, he looked directly at her. ''I thought Spain bored you. Every time I bring it up, you tell me nobody wants to hear about it. Okay, and now, suddenly, when there's something you're after, it's okay to use it!''

In a low voice, she said, ''That's not fair.''

''Who's talking fair? You keep nagging me about leaving and I keep answering you. We're not leaving and that's that. I don't want to hear it anymore. You understand me? I don't want to hear it.''

"But I'm telling you—''

"Enough Dorothy! That's it. There can be only one boss in a marriage and I'm it.''

Dorothy sat very, very still. In fact, she felt frozen to the spot. *I'm it.* That said it. There were two people involved in this marriage but only one counted. She wanted to throw up. She wanted to sink into the earth and disappear. She was so tired, so weary of fighting this town and fighting Jo and fighting her own impulses. She had to leave, she had to get out of here!

For more than one reason. Jack Connery, Millville's most important lawyer and a notorious flirt, was after her. He had come into the library three times in the last two days and there was no doubt at all that he wasn't there for a book. He was there for Dorothy Gordon. She found him a bit ridiculous with his carefully trimmed white wavy hair and his fussy little mustache and the self-satisfied way he had of pulling his vest down over his belly. Nevertheless, she found herself watching the big double doors at the front of the library, waiting to see if it was him again. God, and she'd made herself a solemn promise—after it was over with Pete Marconi—never again, never, never, never.

Pete was the high school coach, a big dark man with dark-shadowed cheeks and black hair all over his body, a man who always smelled of Old Spice and tasted of peppermint chewing gum. He took her about once a week to the Tom Thumb Motel on Balltown Road. She stayed in the car while he registered, holding an empty suitcase . . . Well, not quite empty. It always contained a bottle of Seagram's Seven and several chilled bottles of 7-Up. He would gesture to her, sitting in the car, and she would get out and join him while he unlocked the door. And as soon as the door closed behind them, his arms were around her like a vise and his mouth was grinding on hers, the coarse stubble of his heavy beard scraping her skin. It was always the same. He undressed her eagerly, he carried her to the bed, pounded into her for five or ten minutes, sweating and grunting, and instantly fell asleep, sometimes still on top of her.

Not a great romance, but they were both hungry. He had a wife with an undefined ailment and an indefinite headache. Peggy Marconi apparently spent most of her days lying down in a darkened room with a cold compress on her forehead. And Jonah . . . well, Jonah had long ago lost interest in sex and she was too young to give it up forever. And anyway, she never saw him anymore. She worked days, he worked nights, and the hours when they might have spent time together, he buried himself in his books or sat silently, staring at the wall.

She and Pete had discovered each other at one of the Saturday night dances in the high school gym. All the staff and parents took turns acting as chaperones and it just happened they were on together. He invited her outside for a moment's escape from the din of rock'n'roll and she was more than happy to accept. They chatted a few moments and, when suddenly he reached out for her, she went into his embrace without a moment's hesitation and that was it. They never discussed it, they never analyzed it. Hell, they hardly ever talked. But in its own way, for a while, it satisfied her. They ended it because somebody saw his car outside Tom Thumb and told him, and he got an attack of conscience.

It had been awful, sneaking around that way, ducking down in the back of his car until they got well out of town, averting her face while he paid for the room. She'd had to lie to her colleagues, lie to her children, lie to Jonah. The meetings she invented! The extra work! And then at night, alone in her bed, she would squirm with her shame. She would pound the pillow and tell herself this was end. And the real shame was, it didn't end until *he* ended it.

He was only the first. There had been two others. Never did she feel any emotion, not really, just the desire, the overwhelming need, the burning in her body. Each time, she promised herself this was the end of it. She was not going to give in to her physical needs.

But in the end, she always did. She was cursed with her passionate nature. Yesterday, Jack Connery came softly into the library just before closing, looking around, making sure there was no one else there. Her heart began to pound. Yes, yes, he was after her. She kept moving, putting books away, tidying up, and he kept after her, talking about this and that, giving her little winks and sexy smiles. And then he got her into a corner and came very, very close, so close she could feel the heat from his body and her stomach began to churn. It had been months since she'd had sex and she was sick with wanting it.

He bent his head toward hers and, for a horrible moment, she thought she would melt into him, put her arms around his neck, and kiss him right here in broad daylight, in the library, where at any moment, someone would walk in. She shook her head

violently and said, "Jack, please move. I have work to do before
I can go home to my children."

He backed away, slightly, smiling a knowing smile. "I've
heard that sometimes you don't go straight home to your children."

Her heart almost stopped beating. The word was out. Jack
Connery was known to take any woman who was available—
everyone in town knew that. To be seen in one of the local bars
having a drink with Jack Connery was certain knowledge that
he was getting into your pants. Oh, God! She was getting a
reputation! They had to get out of here, they had to leave quickly,
before she became the town whore.

Now, in the restaurant, she looked at her plate of food. She
could not eat, she couldn't. She didn't even want to walk in the
streets of this horrible place. She didn't want to see Jack Connery again, see the knowing gleam in his eye, not ever. He knew
all about her! He must!

"You don't want to leave? Fine," she said to Jo, and her voice
was utterly calm. "Don't leave. But we're going to."

He laughed. "Oh, sure. And where do you think you're going
to go, without any money, with three half-grown children?"

"Don't worry about me. I've been thinking about this for a
long time."

"I know what's in your mind. You're thinking that rich brother
of yours will take pity on you. Well, fat chance. He won't give
you the time of day!"

She kept herself from smiling. What fools men were. Did he
really think she would cut herself off from her *brother*? They
had stayed in touch this whole time, the two of them, naturally.

She stood up, feeling just fine now that she'd made her decision; and she had, she had! She'd start making plans tomorrow, and by the end of the week, she and the kids would be back
in civilization. Just the thought of it lightened her heart.

"He'll give me, don't worry. We'll survive. I come from a
long line of survivors."

"Come on, Dot. Cut the dramatics. You're not going anywhere. You're just trying to browbeat me."

She could not bear that condescending tone. He didn't know
her at all, not anymore. He had relinquished the right to tell her
what she was about.

"You listen to me, Jonah Gordon, because I have something
to say to you. When the Party ordered you to stop talking to

Frank Green, what did you do? You said nobody could tell you who to talk to. You said, 'Fuck you, I quit!'

"And then, Jonah, you turned right around and ordered *me* to stop talking to my brother. Not just a comrade but my own blood! Okay, I did what you asked, I was a loyal wife.

"But things have changed, Jonah. Everything has changed. And here's my message. If you won't leave this horrible place, let me tell you something . . . you'll stay here alone.

"Because, Jonah, now *I'm* saying it. Fuck you, I quit!' "

<hr>

Chapter Twenty-six

Wednesday, August 28, 1963. The buses had to park blocks and blocks away from the assembly point, so everyone in their group from CCNY had to walk to the Washington Monument right through a poor Negro neighborhood. They weren't alone; everyone from out of town was walking the same way, it looked like.

Cookie couldn't believe how many had come: hundreds and hundreds of people on this block alone. Mostly Negroes, of course, but there were plenty of people like her who were white but still believed with all their hearts that colored people deserved exactly the same education and opportunites as whites. Well, a lot of them were here—marching for "jobs and freedom *now*," like it announced on so many of the placards that bobbed above their heads.

People from the neighborhood were lined up on the curbs, silently watching this endless stream of strangers, ordinary people making their ordinary way down the street. Yet, this was no ordinary occasion! This was history!

The papers in New York all said there might be trouble today. Never before had so many Negroes assembled, all at once, in the nation's capital, and it was an explosive situation—that's what they wrote. Everyone on her bus had noticed, when they drove into the city, how empty and quiet the streets were. Little traffic, few pedestrians. And now, walking to the monument, it was all so quiet, so peaceful. Nobody was talking very much. Why had everyone been so worried? Before they left, the group leaders had warned them to behave, to be orderly.

"Remember," they said. "Washington is a Southern city, with Southern attitudes. We just don't know what might happen when they see how many of us there are, ready to stand up and be counted."

Well, now she felt unafraid; but she had to admit, when the bus came to a halt right in the middle of a slum neighborhood, she had had one moment of fear. What if there was a riot? She wished she hadn't chosen to come down in the college bus. She could have taken one of the CORE buses, with her parents. Since they moved back to New York from Millville—a miracle she still couldn't quite believe in—both her parents had dedicated themselves to the civil rights movement, and even *they* had been concerned there might be trouble today.

But now, Cookie could see how silly that was. There were no violent people here. The scene was very peaceful. Well, why not? Everyone was here for the same reason, and everyone was determined to maintain dignity. It was going to be just fine.

She still didn't know why they had suddenly packed up and left Millville. It was a mystery. She'd asked how come, a couple of times, but all she had gotten from her mother was one of Dot Gordon's typical nonanswers: "What's the matter, Cookie, you're sorry we're leaving?"

She stumbled a little, she was so busy with her own thoughts. She concentrated on looking around, trying to see everything, trying to impress the sights and sounds onto her memory so she would never forget. Every few steps, someone watching them from the sidelines would call out encouragement, and when that happened, the marchers would yell, "Come on. Join us!"

Bernie Hoffman, walking along beside her, nudged her and said, "Isn't this great? It's really happening!" In his enthusiasm, when he spotted a young man standing on the corner holding a hand-lettered sign reading FREEDOM NOW, he called out, "Come on! March with us for freedom." And, to her delight, the boy stepped off the curb and began to march with them. Of course, *march* was not precisely the right word for the slow, almost ambling pace they kept. But *march* was the only word to describe the feeling of unity, of brotherhood, that she could feel, like a palpable presence, everywhere.

"My father calls me a crazy Red for doing this!" Bernie laughed.

Cookie laughed, too. "My father *is* a crazy Red!" she said, and immediately regretted it. The look on his face! It was dumb of her. Just because she liked him so much, she kept hoping . . . "What I mean is, he's marching here, too. Somewhere back there, along with my mother."

"Yeah, my father would include them in. He thinks anyone who believes in civil disobedience is— Hell, he thinks anyone who marches in the streets is a Communist!"

"So do George Wallace and Ross Barnet," Cookie retorted. "You mean your father is on the same side as two of the worst bigots in the South?" She quoted, her voice heavy with sarcasm, " 'All civil rights demonstrations are Communist-controlled.' "

"Aw, that's probably because Bayard Rustin used to be in the Communist Youth League, about a million years ago."

"Hey!" Cookie said, lightly, "you see any Commies here?"

And, thank goodness, he answered in the same tone. "Naw. D'*you* see any Commies, Cookie?"

"Not me! Why don't you set your father straight?"

Bernie laughed. "Him? He's a hopeless case! Hell, he voted for Nixon!" And he made an ugly face.

Not that Bernie Hoffman could ever look really ugly. He was so cute! She had such a crush on him! Every time she saw him in school or on the train—he lived four blocks away and they usually bumped into each other in the morning—her heart skipped a beat. He was dark and mysterious-looking, like she always pictured the heroes in books. He was a little skinny, but she didn't care; he was so adorable! Bernie was a good talker, very active in their meetings, smart, and a real live wire.

If only he'd get off the stick and ask her out! Why didn't he? He liked her; she knew he liked her. He even *said* so. He went out of his way all the time to save her a seat at lunch, he called her all the time to discuss their statistics class assignments. "I can't seem to get this stuff through my head," he'd complain. He was going to be a social worker, just like her. She had daydreams about the two of them, years from now, working together, discussing their cases, going home together to a house somewhere, where there were dimly imagined children patiently waiting for Mom and Dad.

But the magic words were never spoken. He never said, How about a movie? Or, Could I walk you home? Or *anything*! Maybe today, Cookie thought, marching together for a common cause, he'd realize how close they had become. Maybe today, he'd look at her and tell himself, "That's the girl for me."

But what chance did she have with him? She wasn't pretty. She remembered so clearly, her mother eyeing her—she must have been no more than four or five because the details were all blurry—just her mother's face with the narrowed, appraising eyes. And then her mother's voice: "Well, you're no raving beauty, but you'll do."

And Mother was right, Cookie thought. I'm cute, everyone says I'm cute. And I have a good figure, everyone says that, too. But no raving beauty, that was for sure. She searched the mirror from time to time, wondering if something had changed. Nothing ever did. It was always the same old face: regular features, nothing horrible but nothing spectacular, but at least her mouth was good, full-lipped like the mouths on drawings of pretty girls.

But if someone asked her to describe herself, she'd have to say "Ordinary." How dull, to be ordinary-looking. She'd almost rather look like her best friend, Lila Lustig, who had a big nose and small eyes but such style that she always looked glamorous. Lila had three thousand boyfriends. Her phone never stopped ringing!

They were getting close to the Washington Monument now, and now she could see streams of people, coming from all directions. Hundreds of people, *thousands* of people. And all walking quietly, just like them, all heading in the same direction, for the same purpose. God, it was exciting. It was incredible!

Bernie Hoffman turned to her, his face alight with fervor, and he took her hand. "Aren't you glad we're here and can be part of this?" she said—and he nodded, opened his mouth to say something, closed it, opened it again. She hardly dared hope, but . . .

Just then, their group leader came trotting alongside them. "Okay, everybody. Here's where we cross the street and go onto the Mall. We'll be on the right-hand side of the reflecting pool, right hand as you face the Washington Monument." There was a ripple of laughter. "In case we get separated, all our buses will be leaving at six P.M." And he ran on ahead.

Bernie looked very serious. "Cookie, in case we get separated in this crowd, there's something I've been wanting to talk to you about."

Her heart nearly stopped, and then it speeded up so fast, she had to pull in air. At last! She managed to keep her voice perfectly calm and steady. "Sure, Bernie. What is it?"

"Well . . . Oh, God, this is so embarrassing . . ."

"No, go ahead. Whatever it is, you know I'll understand."

"God, Cookie, you're such a great girl!" He'd better hurry, she thought, or she'd faint before he said what he wanted to say. "The thing is . . . Okay, let me just say it. I'm crazy about Lila . . ."

The rest of his speech was lost in the angry humming in her ears. He was crazy about her best friend? He had the goddamn nerve to play up to her, just to get to Lila, who had every boy in the world chasing after her?

". . . so do you think she'd go out with me?" he finished.

"I doubt it. She wouldn't go out with a dead man!" Cookie shot back. Where had she found the words? Where had she found the *nerve*?

The look of sudden realization that swept across his face, making him look stupid, gave her a feeling of triumph. She turned and scurried to catch up with some of the others, up ahead. She'd told him off, all right! She was mad as hell, but at the same time, she felt so good! It was peculiar, but wonderful.

She strode quickly up to the front of their group, where they were carrying the big placards, and offered her services. Her friend Barry gratefully handed his over, and in a minute, she could see why. It was heavy. And awkward. The day wasn't beastly hot, but the air was humid and sticky, and within two minutes, she was sweating, her arms aching with the effort to hold it straight.

With a laugh, Barry took it back. "That's a job for a man," he said. "And anyway, I want to be carrying it when we get to the monument." He gestured with his head to where the spire soared into the sky, not too far away now.

It was further away than it looked, and by the time they got there, along with hundreds and hundreds of other groups and *their* placards and *their* guitar players, they all sank to the grass with relief. Everywhere you looked, there were men and women—little children, too—neatly dressed, picnics spread out on blankets, talking and laughing. It was as calm as a Sunday in Central Park. And there was singing everywhere! One group had a leader who sang: "Freedom, freedom . . . Gonna take it to the President!" And his group sang out: "Yeah, man!" "Gonna take it to the Representatives!" "Yeah, man!" "Gonna take it to the press!" "Yeah, man!" "Gonna read it in the papers!" "Yeah, man!" "Are you satisfied?" "We're satisfied!" It was real catchy.

Then someone in her group began "We Shall Overcome,"

and she hummed along. They sang softly; they were all tired from the trip and the excitement.

And all the time, there were speeches and announcements and songs from the platform set up under the monument. A voice over the loudspeaker asked Roosevelt Johnson to come claim his son Lawrence. Then it asked for Miss Lena Horne. Over to their right, a group of people knelt on the grass while a preacher prayed in ringing tones. She couldn't hear all of it, but she did catch the words, "We know *truly* that we shall overcome . . ." and they all got up and began singing gospel songs, while the loudspeaker pleaded: "Lena, wherever you are . . . !" Much laughter.

Shortly after that, Cookie's eyes just closed. She must have dozed because, the next thing she knew, Barry was shaking her shoulder and saying, "Wake up."

Everyone had begun to move. Nobody told them to, everybody just began to walk toward the Lincoln Memorial, where all the star speakers were slated to appear. Cookie looked at Barry and Barry looked at Harold, one of the group leaders, and they all looked at each other and said, "Let's go," and they went. They strolled up Constitution Avenue, and as they walked, the crowd thickened and thickened. It looked, Cookie thought, as if the entire place had just silently decided to take a walk, all at once.

By the time they got near the Lincoln Memorial, there were people as far as the eye could see and a voice from the platform at the top of the long flight of steps was announcing a group, "straight from the prison of the South." And a choir, standing up there at the feet of Abraham Lincoln, began swaying and clapping as they sang lively emotional gospel songs, the rhythmic sounds floating out over the air.

"Who's that? They're great!"

"The Freedom Singers. From Mississippi."

While they listened and clapped along, there was the game of identifying all the notables sitting up there. Mahalia Jackson. Paul Newman. "And look! Marlon Brando! And Mayor Wagner! Harry Belafonte! Where's Martin Luther King, Jr. ? Where's the bathroom?" That brought laughter.

It was a very friendly mob. A group of colored people from Chicago, standing near them, pointed out the portable toilets and the first aid stations that dotted the lawns. Washington might be a city of the South, Cookie thought, but it had certainly prepared for this day.

"Hey, everyone. Listen to this," Barry called. "We missed the best."

"One of ours, from Chicago," one of the women announced proudly, shifting her pocketbook from one arm to the other. "He came all the way here on *roller skates*!" She paused and smiled as her audience oohed and aahed at this phenomenon. "They had him right up there with all the big men, right on the steps, so's he could speak."

"And did he?"

"In a manner of speaking, he did. He said, 'I'm tired.' And then he said, 'Let my legs speak for me.' I'm telling you, we like to clap our hands off. He got more applause than anyone so far!"

More famous people were spotted. Joan Baez. Dick Gregory. The group from Chicago offered to share their picnic lunch and Cookie traded half a bagel with cream cheese for half a ham sandwich. She was ravenous. They'd left before dawn and Cookie had eaten most of her lunch for breakfast, on the bus. It was a historic day for the nonviolent protest movement, as her father had said about three hundred times, a historic battle in the war for equal rights. But, historic or not, her stomach was rumbling and she was thirsty.

They were camped right next to the reflecting pool, and the water looked so cool and inviting. People were sitting on the edge with their shoes off, putting their feet in the water, and she wished she could do it, too. She checked her wristwatch. Twelve. She'd better not fall asleep again, the important part was coming.

She kept checking her watch, all day long. At one-thirty, Joan Baez was singing, "Hush little baby, don't you cry . . . All my trials, Lord, soon be over . . ." Ralph Bunche, one forty-five. Then Dick Gregory. It got to be interminable. People kept going up to the microphone to read statements. It wasn't until two o'clock in the afternoon that the important speakers began. And by that time, all around them, people were drifting off or falling asleep or talking among themselves.

Cookie moved around a little, talking to different people, trying to pass the time. And then she stopped dead in her tracks. Over there, under a tree, Bernie Hoffman was hovering over Lila, touching her shoulder, and then her hand, and then her back as he talked to her. Cookie closed her eyes in pain. It hadn't taken him long! The jerk!

Quickly, she turned and walked away. She didn't really care

where she was going, as long as it was in the opposite direction.
And then she saw the long snake of women waiting to get into
the portable toilets. Why not? She'd had to pee for an hour. So
she'd stand on line; so what?

As she got on the end of the line, she heard a strange voice
calling her name. "Cookie! Cookie! It *is* you, isn't it?"

She turned to see a beautiful young woman with dark hair,
obviously pregnant but beautifully groomed and dressed nonetheless. Not even sweating! It had to be—it couldn't be anyone
else but—her cousin Deena. Even if she hadn't recognized the
face—it hadn't really changed that much in ten years—she would
have known the air of certainty, anywhere.

"Deena, is it *you*?"

"Of course, it's me. Who else could it be?"

They both laughed and hugged each other, Cookie rather
gingerly, which amused Deena enormously. "Oh, don't worry
about him! He's well cushioned." She patted her belly with
satisfaction.

"Him? You're so sure?"

"If it isn't a boy, my husband will never forgive me. He's
counting on a son and heir."

"Well, let's hope he gets one then," Cookie said, thinking,
God, I'd never marry a man who demanded a *son and heir*.
What an outmoded medieval idea! But never mind that. Here
was her cousin Deena, standing right in front of her, with a big
belly, and at a civil rights rally, of all the places! "I can't believe
I'm really seeing you! God, it's wonderful. I really missed you."

"I missed you, too, Cookie. It really made me mad but—"

"So, Deena, what are you doing here? Are you a civil rights
activist?" She didn't want to discuss the past.

Deena laughed. "Am I a civil rights activist? I guess. Sort
of. Not really. But yes." She laughed again. "Of course, I believe in civil rights. Doesn't any decent person? But on the other
hand, I can't see how it really does any good to march around
and sing songs."

Something in Cookie's face must have warned her, because
she quickly added, "Not that I think it's dumb or anything, don't
get me wrong. I just don't see that it's going to change anything.
I wish it *would*, of course . . ." Her voice trailed off.

Oh, hell. She might as well rescue Deena, Cookie thought.
"I know what you're saying," she said. "I happen to think it
does help." Would it do any good if she filled Deena in on what
was going on in the movement? No. It wouldn't. "Very slowly,

but it does." Pause. "So why are you here? It's a terrible schlepp, and you must be uncomfortable . . ."

Deena patted her belly proudly and smiled. "Yes, I'm certainly being pregnant, aren't I? But I feel terrific. It's the last trimester and I feel wonderful. A bit awkward, but wonderful."

Cookie regarded her cousin. It was hard to believe they had once been best friends and blood sisters, telling each other all their favorite secrets. They were worlds apart. Deena's comfortable shoes alone probably cost more than Cookie's entire wardrobe. Deena's haircut was the very latest style. Even Deena's maternity clothes were nicer than anything Cookie had ever owned.

And she was talking cozily about her husband and baby and last trimester—things that never would enter Cookie's mind. *She* wasn't even sure she wanted to get married; there were so many important things to do in this world. But if she did, it wasn't going to be for a very long time. What a waste, to tie yourself yourself down to a life of domesticity, when you weren't even twenty years old!

"What about college?"

"What about it?"

"You couldn't have finished . . ."

Another laugh and a toss of the head. "As Daddy says, what do I need a degree for? My husband's going to be a great lawyer. And I'm going to be a great lawyer's wife."

How nice it must be, to be so sure of yourself, so sure of what you wanted—and to get it all. Not that she'd trade places with her gorgeous, wealthy, married cousin, no, no. But it would be nice to know there would be a man who loved her enough to want to marry her and have babies—instead of preferring her best friend. Nice, but not really important, she reminded herself. Not if you were committed to the cause.

The line moved up slowly toward the white booth and they inched their way with it. "The thing I don't quite understand, Deena, is, if you don't believe in the value of demonstrations, then what are you doing here?" She tried for a light laugh. "The whole purpose of being here is to influence legislation, you know."

The look on Deena's face told her that she did *not* know. "We're all here to convince Congress to pass the civil rights bill. That's what it says on all the placards, see? WE MARCH FOR INTEGRATED SCHOOLS *NOW.* WE DEMAND AN END TO BIAS *NOW.* ALL WE WANT IS THE RIGHT TO VOTE *NOW.* DECENT HOUSING

NOW. FREEDOM *NOW*." She didn't have to read the signs; she knew their messages by heart.

"That's why we're all here, Deena—to show with our numbers that we mean it, that we believe the time has come for change. All these people here''—she swept the scene with a gesture—''they've come from all over the country, from Los Angeles, even. From the Deep South. Why, there was a man before who roller skated from Chicago—"

She stopped and looked questioningly at her cousin. Deena shrugged. She looked a little uncomfortable. "Maybe this'll sound silly to you, Cookie, but . . . Well, there was a group coming down from our synagogue and, well, I thought I'd like to show I think Negroes are entitled to equal rights—and everyone said this would be historic and I thought I would like to come down and see what was happening for myself . . .

"Well, what happened was that I mentioned it to Michael— Michael Berman, my husband—and he was horrified. His unborn child, on a train for five hours? I said I'd be fine, I said I'd check with the doctor. But you know how men get when you're pregnant . . . They think you're so fragile . . .

"I was ready to give up the whole idea. I mean, I didn't want him to worry about me. It's our first child and it's very important to him. But then he started to act like King of the Universe. 'I absolutely forbid it,' he said to me. 'I *forbid* you to go.' Can you feature it? In 1963, he forbids me?

"Well, you can imagine how much I liked *that*. So here I am. He doesn't even know it, not yet. When he comes home for dinner''— she giggled with great delight—''instead of a nice hot dinner, he going to find a nice cool note. That'll teach him not to bully *me*."

There was only one woman left on line in front of Deena, a jolly fat woman who had kept up a running conversation with her friend in line, punctuated by chuckles. Now she turned and said to Deena, "Whyn't you go ahead of me, dear? I see you're growing."

So they were separated for a few minutes while Cookie waited for her turn at the toilet, enough time for her to think about this chance meeting. They hadn't mentioned their fathers at all, neither of them. Deena must be embarrassed. Uncle Jack had behaved very badly. It was his fault they had to go to horrible Millville. It would be best not to bring it up. It was so good to see her again. Talking about the family feud would only ruin it. She only wished she could tell her parents. But she didn't dare.

The slightest reference to any of the Strausses was enough to set her father off.

She went to the bathroom, and when she came out, Mahalia Jackson was singing. As they walked back to the reflecting pool, the passionate sound of her voice rolled across the lawns, reverberating. Cookie had to stop, to really listen, and they sat down on the grass right where they were. She couldn't understand a single word, there were so many echoes from the speakers. But every single Negro around them was singing along and she realized, with a smile, that this gospel hymn was familiar to all of them, was perhaps an old favorite.

And, suddenly, she was transported back to another grassy field and another magnificent, impassioned voice pouring over her. Paul Robeson, the concert in Peekskill; the overturned car on the road that scared her; the horrible noise when the rocks hit the side of the bus, like the end of the world; her father lying on the bus floor, his head bleeding.

"You know, Deena, there was a concert I went to when I was a little kid, where Paul Robeson sang. Even back then, he was fighting for equal rights for his people. My God, the struggle is never-ending!"

"We had an album of Paul Robeson. *Showboat*, I think."

Just because Deena was related to her, didn't mean that she understood a single thing about Cookie's life. If Paul Robeson meant nothing to Deena but a bit of entertainment, then what did they have to say to each other?

Then Deena leaned over and said, "You know, it's been bothering me and bothering me . . . Who Mahalia Jackson reminds me of. And I suddenly realize— Do you remember ever seeing Earline come to us on a Sunday, right from church?"

The moment she said it, Cookie got a vivid impression of a tall, broad, brown woman, resplendent in a red turban and some sort of bright print dress. "That's right," she said, glad to have the subject changed to something they could talk about.

And then they said together: "Mahalia Jackson looks like Earline Jackson!" And laughed.

After that, they just chatted about the old days. Cookie was dimly aware of a succession of speakers. One of them was a rabbi who said, "I wish I could sing," and that made people laugh. After that, it was a blur of monotonous voices.

Until Martin Luther King. The minute he stood before the microphones, there was an outburst of wild applause and an

outcry of "Hip, hip . . . hooray!" Cookie found herself coming
to her feet, clapping until her hands hurt.

And then he spoke. The entire crowd of thousands hushed
and listened. His voice was deep and rich and measured, and
he spoke in rhythmic cadences that made you want to sway in
time, that pulled you in closer and closer.

> Five score years ago . . . he signed the Emancipation
> Proclamation . . . One hundred years later, the Negro
> still is not free . . . He finds himself in exile in his own
> land . . .

Cookie was mesmerized. She had never in her life heard a
speaker like him. She felt as if she could not move, not until he
was finished. She strained to catch every word, to remember
every word. But she couldn't; there was too much. He had a way
of repeating certain phrases over and over, until they went right
into your brain and your heart. "We can never be satisfied . . ."
"Freedom now . . ." Over and over. And all his people were
swaying to his words and shouting out "Yeah!" and "Yes!" as
if they were in church. It was so marvelous, so moving.

Then his voice got slower and sadder:

> I have a dream that one day this nation will rise up and
> live out the true meaning of its creed: "We hold these
> truths to be self-evident, that all men are created equal"
> . . . I have a dream that one day on the red hills of Geor-
> gia the sons of former slaves and the sons of former slave-
> owners will be able to sit down together at the table of
> brotherhood . . . I have a *dream* that my four little chil-
> dren will one day live in a nation where they will not be
> judged by the color of their skin but by the content of their
> character . . .

Chills ran down Cookie's spine. She had thought, when Mahalia Jackson sang, that nothing could top it for sheer emotional
power. But this—this was unbelievable. She was in the presence
of greatness, something that might never happen again in her
life.

Deena put a hand on her arm and said loudly, "Isn't he the
most spectacular speaker you've ever heard?"

She felt jolted. She turned to her cousin and saw that Deena's
eyes, unlike hers, were not filled with tears of excitement, that

Deena's hands were not tightly clasped. Deena might just as well be listening to *Showboat*, for all that she understood about what was happening.

"Shhh!" Cookie shushed her, pulling her arm away. She didn't care if it was impolite. Deena had to be the only person here who could listen to this man speak and not be moved to tears. Well, she could do whatever she wanted; Cookie Gordon wasn't going to miss another syllable.

When he had finished, and just about everyone was reeling, looking at one another in a mixture of joy and exhaustion, repeating phrases to one another as if they were magical incantations, Deena turned to her.

"Cookie, Cookie. It's been so lovely seeing you, but I must run. I see my group over there and I don't want to lose them." She gave Cookie a quick kiss and a quick squeeze and said, "Call me. Please. Berman. I'm in the book."

Cookie smiled at her, but she didn't answer. She doubted that Deena even noticed. She watched her move away, wondering how she could have felt envious, even for a moment. There goes my cousin Deena, she thought, witness to a great moment in history and she's oblivious!

Chapter Twenty-seven

Thursday, July 16, 1964   Dorothy wriggled in her chair, thoroughly uncomfortable—in more ways than one. First of all, the lights. The lights were unbearably bright and hot. It wasn't hot enough in here, in the middle of summer, they had to bring in three great big floodlights? They said they did. They said, "That's television." Television was also a tangle of cables and wires all over her apartment. Television was being forced to sit in one position for what felt like an hour, and trying to sound intelligent while a camera and a microphone were stuck in your face.

Jonah, on the other hand, was in his element. For the first time in years, he had an audience. He was loving it. Well, she wasn't. As far as she was concerned, the disappearance of those three boys was a national tragedy, not a reason for making a circus.

Just because Irwin was down there, in Mississippi, she and Jonah were suddenly worth listening to. It was suddenly a story, the Summer Project in Mississippi. Not because of what SNCC was doing to fight the injustice down there, but because something horrible had happened. Three young men were missing— for weeks now. It was like the crowds that always gathered around an accident, no matter how gory. That fascination with blood and other people's misery had always disgusted her.

She didn't understand it. If it had been up to her, they wouldn't talk to any reporter, no matter how sympathetic. But Jonah: Jonah saw this as an opportunity to educate the ignorant masses in this country. And maybe he was right.

"Aren't you afraid for your son, Mr. Gordon?" the reporter was asking Jonah.

"Certainly I'm afraid," Jonah said, looking straight into the camera's big blind eye as if he could see all the people who would be watching him later. "But, more than that, I'm proud of him. What he's doing is more important than my feelings. I know what I'm talking about. I'm talking about a section of this country that hasn't changed in thirty years—maybe not in two hundred years.

"I was there in the thirties, as a young man just about my son's age, in a place known as Swamp East, Missouri. There was a strike of sharecroppers there, Negroes and whites together, who moved all their pitiful, poor belongings to the side of the road and set up their homes—if you could call leaking tents homes—right there for passing cars to see. You have no idea." He paused. Dot knew he was fighting tears, as he always had to when he remembered Swamp East. "Brave, intelligent people . . . wanting not riches, not luxuries, but just a decent life. And there they stayed, in spite of the planter autocracy and its buddies the sheriffs. I was there. It was in January. It was cold and bleak. It rained constantly. These people were down to their last handful of beans and still they persevered."

"Terrible, terrible," the reporter agreed, very solemn. "But, the tragic event on the minds of everyone *now* is what has happened to Chaney, Schwerner, and Goodman."

"Of course, of course," Jonah said, frowning. "We're *all* extremely concerned about them."

"Don't you think, Mr. Gordon, there might well be other acts of violence?"

Dorothy closed her eyes and clenched her teeth. The man had no heart whatsoever. How could he say a thing like that to a man whose firstborn son was down there, in danger of being killed every minute of the day and night? That was the trouble with reporters—all they knew was Get the Story, never mind who was suffering, who was frightened, who was bereaved!

Well, thank God, she and Jonah were not among the bereaved, not yet. But frightened and suffering? She would say so. The reporter did not know Irwin. Irwin was the kid who couldn't walk down the street in a small town in upstate New York without getting a bloody nose. Irwin was the teenager who was always ready to start an argument and get beat up for his trouble. Irwin was disaster-prone, as Cookie liked to say.

And this kid was going to be a big hero and register Negro voters, in the heart of Mississippi, the worst of the Southern states! Irwin was trouble looking for a place to happen. And this summer, he was in the worst possible place for it to happen. Never mind how brave, how important, how idealistic! He was going to get hurt, he was *sure* to get hurt, her nudnik. Personally, she was terrified.

"SNCC—Student Nonviolent Coordinating Committee—has been called the Shock Troops of the Freedom Riders," the reporter was saying. "Many of them have been jailed or beaten, or both. And now, we have the growing possibility of a tragic death toll."

He was supposed to be talking to her and Jonah, but he was looking into the camera instead. She hated that, too; it was all such phoney baloney. But when she said that to Jonah, before, when they were arguing about letting them in here, he said, "It's worth it. We'll use him, you'll see, to get our message out to the world."

Now, he cut into the reporter's speech, leaning forward in his chair, his eyes blazing. Like the Jonah she knew of old. "Let me tell you something. There are hundreds of brave young people down there—they've been there all summer, risking their lives every day to register Negro voters—but you don't see any reporters down there, talking to *them* . . . or even coming around to see us, not since the day they first disappeared. Only now, when there's a fear that *white* men have been murdered . . . *now* it becomes news, now it becomes important . . ."

Dorothy could see the reporter's face tighten, noted how his

eyes went quickly to the cameraman. She would make a bet that
this evening on the six o'clock news, if Jonah Gordon was on
at all, this last little speech would be out.

". . . If it weren't for that, nobody would ever hear about
Freedom Summer!" Jonah was finishing what he wanted to say
and the reporter's hand chopped down through the air. Even she
knew what *that* meant: *fartig*, finished, the end, as her brother,
Jack, always said.

"Thank you very much, sir." Again, with the eyes focused
on the camera. He was done with them. "We've been talking to
Mr. Jonah Gordon, father of Irwin Gordon, a twenty-year-old
Boston University student who is one of the small group of New
York City youths who followed Goodman, Chaney, and Schwer-
ner to Meridian, Mississippi . . ."

Irwin squinted through the lens of his camera and focused on
the three half-naked children, their dark brown skin gray with
the ever-present dust, a haze hanging in the air around them. It
was going to be a beautiful shot. The skinny shanks, the raggedy
clothes, the sagging shack in the background, with its sad, sagging porch, the junk in the yard—if you could call a patch of
sunbaked dust a yard—just a glimpse of the tired, thin, worn-
out mother crouched over her laundry tub. When this picture
was printed, a person living a thousand miles away would be
able to smell the dust and feel the heavy heat and see the bleak
treeless emptiness of this place.

"That's enough of the kids, Irwin. God, you must've taken a
million shots of poor little kids. Let's go inside the cabin. We
need to show what passes for a home around here."

I know what we need to show, Irwin thought. You can stop
pushing your weight around, Mr. Harvard University. But he
didn't say it; he couldn't say it. Bob Carter was his roommate
this summer, and his almost constant companion. It didn't pay
to start a fight. But it was getting on his nerves. Just because
Bob went to Harvard, he thought he was smarter than anyone,
especially Irwin Gordon of B.U. Just because Bob was a Negro
and knew how to talk to these people—and didn't feel like an
intruder like Irwin did—he thought he was in charge.

What he said to Bob was, "I took a million interior shots just
two days ago. Remember? Today, we stay outside."

He'd love to tell Bob Carter to get lost. But that wasn't possible, either. The first thing they dinned into everyone's head
during orientation in Oxford, Ohio, last month, was Never Go

Anywhere Alone. So, he never went anywhere alone. And besides, you couldn't pay him to go anywhere alone in this place. This Hell. My God, three guys together had disappeared from the face of the earth. In the distance, right now, he could hear the drone of the helicopters as they circled the area, looking for them. Looking for their bodies, was more like it.

Even the thought of it made him feel sick. He felt sick all the time, really. He was scared to death. He hadn't been prepared for Meridian, Mississippi. That orientation? Just a lot of words. They tried to tell you, they really did. They scared a few of the kids so much that they left! His roommate, Ed, from B.U., the guy who had talked him into this in the first place, he said, "I can't do it, Irwin. I can't do it." And he left.

Irwin and Bob Carter moved across the yard toward the cotton fields that stretched for miles behind the shack. God, what a place! Flat, flat, flat. No trees, no flowers, just the endless, dark green, light-absorbing kudzu vine smothering everything in its path. It was a smothering kind of place, the kind of place you could get lost in and just disappear forever—and nobody would ever be able to find you.

The helicopters were getting closer to them; now you could hear the chop of their rotors cutting the heavy air. Irwin stopped and shaded his eyes, looking up. "If they get close enough, I'll get a couple of shots of them," he said.

Bob Carter shuddered. "Is that all you can ever think about? Your pictures? Man, those copters are—"

"I know what they're doing! I'm very aware what they're doing. And I think a lot about what's going on. A lot. But I happen to think that making a permanent record is just as important as sitting around every night talking nonviolent philosophy and examining everyone's inner motives. That's bullshit! Even those copters are bullshit, Bob. They're not going to find anything!"

"You don't know that."

"And dredging the Pearl River! They've already found a couple of bodies there and who pays attention? Nobody! Nobody even cares!"

Quietly, Bob said, "That's because they were Negroes. Hell, it's always been like that down here. What's a coupla dead niggahs, more or less?" He mimicked the heavy, slow speech of Mississippi with deadly accuracy. "You just finding that out?"

No, I'm not just finding that out, Irwin thought. Condescending bastard! I should tell him my old man was down here thirty years ago, trying to help the sharecroppers get a decent life. And he didn't have any civil rights bill on his side, either, like they do now—well, since June twentieth, at least. He was *really* brave, Pop. Brave and strong.

Not like his son Irwin, who now knew the meaning of the phrase "scared shitless"—who had had diarrhea every damn day since orientation. What was wrong with him? Here he was, in the most dangerous part of the Deep South, doing something he believed in, something that would live after him, something to help his fellowman, all that high-minded stuff.

He should be loving the whole thing. His father would. His father would eat this up. In fact, Pop wanted to join but there were only a few older guys down here for the project and they were mostly doctors and lawyers, a few carpenters. This was a young people's thing. All of SNCC seemed to be kids his own age. But they were different; they weren't afraid.

He grunted another nonanswer to Bob Carter's endless commentary. He was doing a lot of that lately. In his opinion, Bob Carter found his own thoughts too damn fascinating.

"All right," he said. "I've got enough. The helicopters aren't getting any closer. And it's too damn hot to stand out here in the middle of the day, waiting for them. Let's go."

They said their good-byes. They were offered food—they were always offered a share of whatever these people had—but they said no thank you, they had supper waiting for them. "God bless you," the woman called after them. It was unbelievable, how courteous and dignified these people managed to be, in the midst of the most hideous conditions. He should be ennobled by their example, by this whole experience.

But he hated it. Hated it. He walked around all the time, scared out of his mind. He felt guns pointed at his back. He saw enemies lurking in the shadows. He hadn't slept through the night since he got here. He couldn't eat the food; he couldn't live in the grinding, horrible poverty; he couldn't stomach the smells of this place. He wanted to go home in the worst way.

His father would kill him. No. Worse than that, he'd feel let down by Irwin and ashamed of him. Irwin could hear him now: "A son of mine—turn his back on those who cry out for help? Never! Where fascism reigns, in *any* form, it's our duty and our privilege to fight it, in any way we can!" Oh, God. His old man would go on forever! All that same old stuff. But dammit, he was right!

Pop wouldn't understand how a person could get carried away

and make a mistake. He'd never made a mistake, he'd never doubted his convictions. Irwin would never in this world be able to explain to him what happened the day he signed up.

The night before, he'd gone to a meeting and there'd been a Negro there, a young man in overalls who spoke with such fervor. "Your only weapons will be youth and courage," he said. And there was a pamphlet they handed out that said they could *do* something to end the last vestiges of slavery in the South. And then they all sang "We Shall Overcome," linking hands and swaying from side to side, like a human chain, and he desperately wanted to be a part of it. It was the unity, the solidarity Pop had always talked about and dreamed of. And he thought it was *his* dream, too.

It wasn't his fault that the reality didn't match the dream. It wasn't his fault that he didn't have the nerve for it. It wasn't his fault that he couldn't eat and couldn't sleep and couldn't stop being afraid. He looked around at his fellow volunteers and saw that he was different.

Everyone else was strong and courageous, ready for anything. Ready to get beaten up, ready to go to jail . . . ready to *die*! There were a couple of guys here on the staff who had scars, great big welts, from bullet wounds and beatings! The women, even, had put their lives on the line. There were girls who had been arrested and had terrible body searches, who had been beaten senseless! Only Irwin Gordon couldn't hack it!

He knew now that he didn't belong. He certainly didn't belong in the frontlines. He was a coward and a phoney. The only way he could do it without going completely crazy was by taking pictures. He looked at all the ugliness and brutality and humiliation through the lens of his camera and it all became only a composition, a collection of light and shadow, a certain exposure reading. When he looked at this place through the camera, it all receded to a safe distance.

But he *had* to stay. His father! His mother! God, he couldn't leave! There was a drone in the sky that got louder and louder. He and Bob both stopped walking and looked up, squinting against the hot glare. The helicopters. Two of them, hovering very, very close to the ground, hanging suspended in the air. Looking for—Oh, God, it was horrible! It suddenly occurred to him this wasn't a movie about somebody else's life. This was real. At any moment, they might spot three bodies, the bodies of three guys like him, his own age—one of them Andy Goodman, who lived in his neighborhood, who he used to see all the time on the street. In the midst of the down-pressing heat, he shivered.

Pop had come down here in the thirties to work with poor Negroes, just like that woman and her children. Pop had been so sure he could make a difference. He was still absolutely certain of what he believed in.

But goddammit, here it was thirty years later, and not a damn thing had changed! Nothing! The Negroes were still oppressed, still sharecropping, still dirt-poor, still slaves. What was the use of sacrificing your life to ideals, when it didn't do a bit of good in the end? It was so futile!

He wasn't going to do it. He wasn't going to spend his entire life fighting battles that could not be won—and dreaming dreams that would not come true! He was finished! This was *it*. No more lost causes for Irwin Gordon.

If he managed to get out of Freedom Summer alive, never again, he promised himself, never again.

€€€

Chapter Twenty-eight

Thursday, March 25, 1965   Dot came up out of the subway and onto Herald Square, and right away, she saw her group gathered in front of Gimbel's, right across Thirty-fourth Street—a smaller group than they had hoped for, maybe thirty, forty people. But the placards looked good with their bright red and black lettering:

INTEGRATION NOW . . . BLACK OR WHITE, THE VOTE'S OUR RIGHT! . . . EQUALITY FOR EVERYONE.

And she could hear them shouting slogans, even above the din of noon-hour traffic. Did it matter how few showed up, really, as long as *someone* took a stand, spoke up against injustice? And she answered herself: absolutely not.

Feeling a surge of pride, she stepped off the curb and into a sudden icy gust of rain mixed with wet snow—and her little

moment of exuberance threatened to dissolve into the nasty wet
day. *Brrrr* . . . it was so bleak and gray, didn't the weather know
it was already spring?

Well, in spite of the weather, she'd finished all her errands
this morning. The call to the dentist, changing Jo's appointment
for tomorrow—done. Books back to the library—done. The
marketing—done, done, and done. And she'd found a nice piece
of brisket, for pot roast. When Jonah and Dave finally got off
the bus, after that long, exhausting ride from Alabama, they'd
be overjoyed to find a good home-cooked meal waiting for them.
After four or five days of living in circus tents in the rain and
the mud, even her pot roast ought to look pretty darn good!

She'd made sure to leave this hour free for the demonstration;
she'd gotten up at six this morning to do it, too. It was very
important to show support for Martin Luther King's march from
Selma to Montgomery. If you couldn't be there to face the dogs
and the water hoses and Governor Wallace, the least you could
do was schlepp yourself downtown.

She'd planned to go, of course. But then Cookie got the flu
and couldn't even lift her head from the pillow. So Dot told Dave
and Jonah to go to Alabama; she would stay here and look after
Cookie. In any case, there was plenty to be done for freedom,
right here in New York City.

Too bad more people hadn't showed up. But maybe they
couldn't help it. Not everyone got time off from their job, and
even though they'd timed the demonstration for lunch hour, on
purpose, lots of people couldn't make the trip in an hour. She
was lucky. She was lucky to have her job, period. Head Start
was such a wonderful program, and she was happy to be part of
it. And without education, without a degree! They let her take
a personal day for this because they had good reason to feel it
was an important issue.

She stopped a moment to pull the hood of her wool coat up
over her hair. Why she bothered, she didn't know. Her hair was
pulled back in its usual twist, so what could happen if it got
blown or wet? Well, in this weather, her ears could fall off! She
smiled at her own little joke and then quickly looked around.
Jonah was always giving her the business about how she talked
to herself whenever she was alone.

"And you laugh, Dot! I've seen you! There you are, walking
down Broadway all by yourself, and you burst out laughing!"

And she told him, "Hey, I find me very amusing."

She wanted to make him laugh but he only shrugged. "What's the use? The woman is *meshuggah*."

That's what men always said when they didn't understand women. "They're crazy," they said, and, well, maybe they were right! And she laughed out loud.

The light changed and she crossed, waving to Anna and Tanya Dauber who had just spotted her and were gesturing wildly to get her attention. The minute she got to the other side, Anna began talking. Anna tended to talk too much, but her heart was in the right place. "There are so few of us, it's a joke almost, and look at them, out here giving us the business!" She gestured to the corner of Broadway and Thirty-fourth, where two over-weight, middle-aged men, carrying placards, marched back and forth, away from each other, then toward each other, wheeling in military-style. Although tightly wrapped in trench coats and wearing earmuffs, they looked cold and miserable as the wind whipped around the corner and made their signs tremble.

Then Dot read the signs and began to laugh. One said, PETE SEEGER IS A FAG, the other TANYA DAUBER IS A RED AGITATOR.

"Tanya?" Dorothy shot a look at the Red agitator: five feet, one inch tall, dark curly hair, wearing blue jeans and a bright blue parka. "Where'd they get your name?" Tanya, Anna's youngest, was a sophomore at Hunter College.

Tanya laughed. "I made a speech for integration. That's all you have to do to get on *their* list!"

"Some insult!" Anna said.

"Hey, Ma, don't worry. They don't hurt my feelings. I'd rather be called Tanya the Red Agitator by the American Legion than have my name up in lights."

"American Legion . . . is that who they are? Well, all I can say is, they look frozen."

"They should *be* frozen," Anna said. "They should both catch pneumonia and drop dead!"

"Ma!"

"Never mind, Tanya. I don't have to love my enemy."

Now they started marching in a circle. Dot and Anna fell into step comfortably, still talking. "This reminds me of the time we picketed Woolworth's, when they were also doing it down South, remember, Dot? Oh, no, you weren't back yet, that's right. It was 1961. Too bad. It was wonderful, after the apathy of the fifties, to be out demonstrating again—and with youngsters! College kids! It was such a good feeling after being afraid and hiding all those years. I'm only sorry that bastard McCarthy died before I could get my hands on him!'' And she spat her contempt. ''Ben always said . . .'' And then her voice quaked and she stopped, her eyes filling. Her husband had died quite unexpectedly of a heart attack six months ago.

Tanya spotted this and took her mother by the arm. ''Ma, I need you up here, shouting slogans, instead of gossiping with Dot. Come on, your voice can be heard all the way to Times Square.''

Dot was still watching the mother and daughter, so nice, so close, smiling to herself, when a voice she thought she'd never hear again said her name . . . and even before she looked up, her heart began a clamor. Frank. No, no, it couldn't be—but she knew it was. Where did he come from? What was he doing here? And she was looking such a mess! She hadn't even bothered with a touch of lipstick like she usually did, but what difference did it make? It was in the past—and now when she looked up, she was going to be just friendly and casual and say, Well hello there, Frank Green, it's been a long time. She stepped out of the line of the march, preparing herself.

But when she looked up and found herself looking straight into his amused and glittering eyes, she couldn't find her voice at all. So it was he who spoke first.

''I knew it was you from three blocks away,'' he said, and reached out to grasp her hand in his. Even through the woolen gloves, she could feel the warmth of his palm and she knew he could feel her shaking. The harder she tried to control it, the worse it seemed to get. She pulled her hand away, and to her consternation, he laughed.

''Now wait a minute, Dot! Don't get that look on your face!''

''What look? I don't have a look.''

He grinned down at her. God, he hadn't changed, not a bit. A bit gray at the temples, and the smile groove at either side of his mouth had deepened, but other than that, the same. Still heart-stopping. Even as she stared at him, tried to make casual conversation with him, she was aware that some women passing by turned and turned again to give him that interested second look. That hadn't changed, either.

''Yes, you do. Your face says don't touch. Just like when I first met you. You were afraid of me then, too.''

She was at a loss for words. She wished to God he wouldn't bring up the past. She'd put all that completely out of her mind. So she collected herself and smiled at him and said, just as if he hadn't been teasing her, "So, Frank. Did you come to demonstrate with us?"

"As a matter of fact, yes. I just got in from the Coast and someone told me about this."

"Then let's march."

He smiled down at her. "Always in a hurry, Dot. You never did have patience."

Again, she felt flustered, and again, hated herself for it. "So. Long time no see. What have you been up to since . . . ?"

And then she had to stop. Because the end of the sentence couldn't be said. *Since you wrote and asked me to come to you?* She felt herself blushing, and then blushing harder, as he laughed again.

"I've been waiting twelve years to ask you this, Dorothy. *What happened?* Why didn't you answer my letter? I waited a long time, a long, long time."

She had to swallow. "I can't talk here."

He came closer, bending his head so he could speak softly, ignoring the cold blasts of wind that blew his hair across his forehead. "Even after months had gone by, I never could open my post office box without my heart speeding up for a moment because maybe, *this* time, there would finally be word from you."

"Frank," she said, helplessly, "they'll hear. And anyway, it was all so long ago." And then she got hold of herself. How had he managed to put her on the defensive? He was the one who left! He was the one who betrayed Jonah . . . betrayed them all!

"Wait a minute," she said, in a very different voice. "You're the one who disappeared without a word."

"Orders from headquarters," he said. And then, seeing something in her face, added quickly, "No, no. That's the truth. Look. There's a coffee shop. Let's get out of this foul weather. Please, Dorothy, let me buy you a cup of coffee and I'll tell you what happened. There'll be *other* demonstrations."

She hesitated, but didn't they say she who hesitates is lost? She was lost all right. She found herself going with him without a word of protest, without even caring what Anna or Tanya or any of them might think.

The coffee shop was crowded and cozy, redolent of coffee and french fries, its windows steamy. He helped her off with her damp coat and carefully hung it on a hook. They sat in a booth across from each other. Now she *had* to meet his eyes and listen to what he had to say—and she was in dread of what she might hear.

He was silent a moment. Then he said, "You're still beautiful," and once again, she was at a loss. What was he up to? What was he trying to sell? Whatever it was, she wasn't buying.

"Frank. You said you'd tell me what happened. So. Tell me. What happened?"

"All right. The first thing is, none of what you heard about me was true." Oh, sure, Dorothy thought, tell me another. "I know what you're thinking: 'That's what they *all* say.' But I'm telling you, I was sent away on a top secret job by the Party. All these years, I've been underground."

"Frank! Come on. Word gets around. We heard. You were a member of the John Birch Society . . . And maybe you always were. They said you were turning your comrades in to the FBI. And you left," she added, annoyed to feel her eyes filling without warning, "you left without saying good-bye. To anyone. You could have, easily. But you chose not to. Could you blame everybody for believing you were a traitor?"

"Exactly!" he said cheerfully. Then he gave her a sharp glance and added, "Dot, that was my *cover*! I was ordered to leave secretly and not to say good-bye to anybody. It was *supposed* to look suspicious. That way, the John Birchers would trust me. Sending you that letter was a terrible risk, you know. I wasn't supposed to contact *anybody*." He lowered his voice and whispered, "I infiltrated. I was very good at it, they all believed me."

"*We* all believed you, too. How am I supposed to know now—which is the truth and which is the lie?"

He spread his hands. "I'm still a card-carrying member. In spite of everything. In fact, I'm—but never mind. You can see now, can't you, Dot? I had to do it that way just so everyone would think I was a traitor. Unfortunately, for you and me, it worked only too well."

Their coffee arrived in thick white mugs, and while the waitress put them down, he stopped talking. Dorothy was glad for the interruption; it gave her a chance to figure out what she was going to do and say next. The cups deposited, the waitress left and he resumed. "So you see, I'm not the villain you thought I was. Just a soldier doing his duty. Now will you forgive me?" And he reached across the table, taking both her hands in his.

His touch felt wonderful, warm, close, intimate, loving. She had to make him stop. This was no good. Since they'd come back to New York, she hadn't so much as looked at another man. Hadn't allowed herself even one moment of temptation, not one. And now, in ten minutes, she was melting. She had to get out of here, away from him.

"Do you realize what you did to all of us? Jonah quit the Party because of you!" And in answer to his quizzical look, she explained: "They called him in and told him he could have nothing further to do with you, and he said to hell with that. Your friendship was more important to Jonah! Even when the FBI started pounding on our door every day, he insisted you were okay. Jonah went out on a limb for you. Him, you could have told. He wouldn't have said anything to anybody. You know Jonah; he's an ethical man."

"I'm sorry, Dot. I had my orders. Discipline is very important in the Party, particularly when we're surrounded by enemies who want to destroy us. And in the fifties . . . You *can't* have forgotten what it was like, back then."

"Forgotten! How could I forget? Because of that whole business, Jo went into exile—and took all of us with him! Eight years in that hellhole!"

"What hellhole? Where in the world did he take you?"

"Upstate New York. Millville. You can tell by the name, it's the garden spot of New York State."

"But why . . . ?"

"It's a long story. Very boring. Jonah was afraid he'd be deported. And he could have been! It happened. You know it happened!" She laughed bitterly. "We ended up in a dark little flat on a dreary little street in an ugly little railroad town. It was . . . not the best time of my life."

"What can I say? I'm sorry. I'm sorry for all the wasted years. Especially *our* wasted years." He took a deep breath, letting it out with a moan. Leaning forward a little, he said softly, "You want to know how I feel right now?"

She held her breath. No, no. He mustn't.

"I feel exactly the way I felt the first time I saw you."

Damn him for his doing this to her. Because *she* was beginning to feel the same way. Breathless, eager, quivering. She sucked in a deep, noisy breath.

"So. Frank. How long have you been back?"

"Just got in, two days ago. And to answer your next few questions: No, I'm not staying. I'm heading South. I'm not underground anymore. I'm using my own name now and no, Dorothy, darling, I never married."

Dear God, what was the man after? He couldn't still want her, not after all these years. And anyway, he was leaving, he just said so. "Jonah's down South this very minute. In Alabama, on the Freedom March."

"So you're here alone." He smiled.

It didn't matter where she steered the conversation, he managed to bring it around to the same old thing. "I planned to go, but then Cookie—my daughter, you remember her—she got the flu and at the last minute I said I'd stay back with her so her husband, Dave, could go. It was so important to him. Of course, it was important to me, too, I was in all the demonstrations here. But I'm a mother first, so I gave it up and I watch every night on the news—" She was babbling; she just couldn't stop.

He kept smiling at her. "So you're alone," he repeated.

"Frank, quit that!" She was forty-five years old and as flustered as a schoolgirl, all blushes and fluttering heartbeat. And he knew it, he knew it. He was giving her that slow, heated smile, the one that revealed the little dimple just above the right corner of his mouth. His mouth! And now he was rubbing his forefinger up and down the back of her hand and she thought she would never be able to breathe right again.

With a great effort of will, she pulled her hand back, moved herself back, and sat up very straight, like a good little girl, her hands folded in her lap. Now he really laughed.

"The Freedom Riders," she went on. "That's what brought us back. We just couldn't stay up there and do nothing! And then there's Vietnam and the nuclear arms race—stupid politicians! We *had* to come back and *do* something, something that counted. And so . . . here I am."

"Alone," Frank said.

She looked at him. Twelve years. You'd think, after twelve years, there'd be nothing left except maybe tired old memories. You'd think, at her age, she'd know better. He held her gaze, his eyes limpid and steady. Those eyes. She remembered him perfectly, the smell and the look and the feel of him.

She shook her head. "Frank, I have to get home now."

That evening, she was alone in the apartment, curled into a corner of the sofa, tuned to CBS News. In front of her was a tray table with the remains of a frozen dinner. It wasn't very good, but she'd finished it all anyway. Nerves. She hadn't been particularly nervous about Jo and Dave being in Alabama for this march—there were federal troops to protect the marchers.

But an hour ago, while she was still in the kitchen, the news had come over the radio, about those damned rednecks killing that woman from Detroit, Viola Liuzzo. The mother of children. Shot her in the head! The mother of little children. She was driving with a Negro boy who was sitting in the front seat next to her. Down in Alabama, that was reason enough for murder.

You'd never know there had been a shooting, to watch the news report now. They were saying the march had gone well, considering. Very orderly. The camera looked down on a wavy, endless line of people, moving very slowly. They were singing; she knew they would be singing. Whenever there was a meeting or a demonstration or a march, North or South, people were singing.

Today, they had finally made it to Montgomery, in front of the state Capitol. Dexter Avenue, the announcer said. No serious incidents, he said. Good. It was over. Thank God. They were prone to violence, in the South. Why? she wondered. Weeks before the buses were due to leave, the marchers were warned not to dress too differently, not to walk around alone, and especially not after dark. They might get hurt. In the United States of America!

Dorothy shifted on the couch. She'd had a notion that maybe she'd see Jo or Dave on the television. But that was silly. The cameras only went up close to the important people, like Dr. King or Ralph Bunche. All you could see was a mass. Twenty-five thousand people, the announcer said. She got up and wandered over to the buffet, poured herself a little glass of brandy. She shouldn't, she knew she shouldn't but . . . well, she needed it.

The phone rang and she nearly jumped out of her skin. She was so nervous and it was so stupid. Nonetheless, as she picked up the receiver, she could feel her heart thumping against her ribs. Please God, don't let it be—

But it was only Anna, already talking as Dot put the phone to her ear. "Am I dreaming, or was that our old friend Mr. Frank Green in person?"

Oh, Lord! Try to keep anything a secret from Anna Dauber! "You're not dreaming," Dot said.

"So, *nu*, Dorothy? What gives?"

"What are you talking about? He's in town for a day or two and he wanted to know about Jo."

"He has some nerve showing up at our demonstration! How

could you even talk to him? You couldn't *pay* me to talk to that man, the lousy no-good John Bircher!''

''As it happens, Frank's been undercover for the Party. It was all fake, so he could infiltrate—''

''A likely story!''

This could go on all night. ''Anna, listen. I can't talk right now. I'm watching the news from Montgomery . . . Oh, and there's Dr. King! Good-bye, I'll talk to you tomorrow!''

She was glad to hang up, and not only because she was tired of Anna's incessant gossiping. She really did want to hear Martin Luther King. She should have been there, number one. And number two, he was a marvelous speaker. Well, he was a preacher, after all. Listen to the man!

> We are not about to turn around. We are on the move now. Yes, we are on the move and no wave of racism can stop us.

Chills ran down her spine; and on the television they gave a mighty cheer, twenty-five thousand voices yelling out their determination. By herself in her little living room, Dorothy cheered, too, and clapped.

She wished she could be there. Now she wished she hadn't been such a Jewish mother. To be fair, Cookie had told her to go, had insisted that she was on the mend and could very well take care of herself.

''I have hundreds of neighbors, Mom. Nobody's going to let me die on my kitchen floor. Go, go. It's history. I wish *I* could go.'' But no, she had to be selfless and maternal. All right, it was her own fault.

And, let's face it, she might have gone, Cookie or no Cookie, flu or no flu, if Dave hadn't said he wanted to march. Irwin had disappointed his father so badly. Well, Jo should know better than to count on Irwin. But he had been so sure Irwin was going with him, that when Irwin said absolutely not, Jo looked sick.

She herself had been a *little* bit surprised. After all, Irwin had gone down to Mississippi last year for Freedom Summer and he'd even been ready to give up his scholarship at Boston University to stay down there. It had taken her and Jonah together two weeks to convince him that he could do more good in the world if he continued with his education instead. Oh, Jo had been beside himself with pride. At least one of his sons was

going to be a fighter for progressive causes! Paul was so unpo-
litical, it broke his father's heart.

So naturally, Jonah assumed Irwin was eager to answer the
call for the Selma to Montgomery march. When Jo hung up the
phone, he turned to Dorothy, and said in stunned voice. "What
happened to him? Last summer, he was totally committed to
the civil rights movement. Last summer, we had to get down on
our knees to make him come back to school. Now he says he's
got to get pictures together for a show on Boyleston Street. A
show! Pictures! What kind of a life is that?"

Patiently, Dorothy said, not for the first time, "Those are the
photographs he took during Freedom Summer. If the show goes
well, people will buy them or maybe magazines will reprint
them. That's serving the cause."

And when he gave her a disgusted look, she added. "Hey.
You know your son. He doesn't stick to anything. Come on,
Jonah. Remember when he wanted to be Orthodox and insisted
I keep kosher?" Jonah made a rude noise. "Okay, okay. I didn't
like it, either, and I refused. But the point is, you can't depend
on him. Period. He's a nudnik."

So, of course, the minute she said that, he had to stick up for
his firstborn son, call him a lost soul, a man seeking for meaning
in his life, and all the rest of it. She didn't bother responding to
that; she didn't buy it, she didn't believe it, and she certainly
wasn't going to waste breath arguing about Irwin. When Jo saw
that, he stopped talking. That's how it was with them, since they
came back to New York.

Jonah, who had always been so tough and strong and determined, had become depressed in Millville. She understood that
now. She kind of knew it while it was happening, but there was
a living to be made, there was a life—if you could call it that—
to be made, and she preferred not to think about it. Who had
the time! She never allowed herself to add it all up, just went
her own way and did what she had to do to survive.

Then, when she had told him she was leaving with or without
him, he just crumbled, like an ash in the wind. Just gave up.
She had packed, and gotten the kids' things together, and bought
three train tickets to Grand Central Station—and she was really
ready to go without him. And at the very last minute, the night
before their departure, he didn't go to work as usual. And when
she asked him how come, he said, "I quit."

That was all he said. So she had to ask him, "Does that mean
you're coming with us?" And he nodded yes. And ever since

then, she ran the family. He left all the decisions to her. He made a lot of noise, but when push came to shove, they did things *her* way.

And she found she enjoyed being the boss. All the men in her life—Papa, her brother, Jack, Jonah, even Frank Green—had felt free to push her around. Oh, they took care of her, but in return, they also took control of her. At last, she was her own person. Anyway, that's how *she* felt about it. What Jonah thought, he never said—and she never asked.

The doorbell rang. She put down the empty glass and gave herself a look in the mirror over the buffet, taking her time and liking what she saw. Her hair was out of the bun, a shining dark fall, only a few silver strands at the temples. There was a flush across her cheekbones and a gleam in her eye. For forty-five, she looked pretty darn good. Still had that zaftig body that men called Earth Mother. Earth Mother! That's not the way she was feeling! She laughed at her reflection and went to the door and opened it.

When he saw her, Frank's eyes lit up. "Your hair," he said, and then his arms were around her, he kicked the door shut behind him, and bent his lips to hers. Her heart leapt in her throat and she would have fallen, except that he was holding her so tight.

At last, she thought, at last.

€€

Chapter Twenty-nine

Sunday, August 27, 1969   Paul Gordon stood under the marriage canopy, very goddamn close to tears. It was just like a movie, all of it. The big mirrored room with its gilded dome. The white satin canopy embroidered in gold. The double row of fat white candles in their white and gold stanchions, lining the aisle. The glittering rows of guests behind the white satin ropes with their golden tassels. The gold baskets filled with white roses and a lot of other flowers he didn't know the name of. Class. That's what it was: class. Even the rabbi with his white

robe and the huge embroidered prayer shawl and his thick white
hair with the white satin yarmulke . . . It was all perfect.

Steffie had planned the whole thing, right down to the matchbook covers and the flower centerpieces on the tables. Everything was the way she wanted it. She picked the place, the date,
the time, the menu, decorations, music, dresses, even the cum-
merbunds for the ushers. Every little detail. Her colors were
blue and white, so the ushers wore pale blue tuxes and the
bridesmaids, now coming one by one down the aisle, sliding
their feet to the slow, sonorous music, were in identical white
lace dresses with pale blue sashes and floppy wide-brimmed hats
with blue streamers.

Everything was just so. He shouldn't be surprised. After all,
Steffie was artistic; she'd been an art education major before she
dropped out to marry him. Her taste was terrific—it was one of
the things he loved about her. She was going to be a wonderful
wife. He could picture their life right now: a beautiful home,
gracious dinner parties, class friends, great-looking kids, country club, winter vacations in the Islands . . . the whole ball of
wax.

Behind him he could hear, like a strange accompaniment to
the organ, his father's incessant mutter. Not the exact words, of
course, but he could just imagine. ''Waste of money.'' ''Conspicuous consumption.'' ''Starving children.'' ''Outrageous.''
''Bourgeois mentality.'' All that left-wing bullshit.

He'd never forget the weekend he finally brought Steffie home
to New York to meet his parents. He'd put it off as long as
possible. His parents were so different from hers. Sid and Essie
Handleman were live wires, always on the go, full of pep. They
had plenty of dough, and did they know how to spend it! Travel,
the best clothes, fancy cars, servants. How would Steffie ever
understand his irascible father and his kooky mother, with her
homespun dresses and African earrings? But she was such a
good-natured, sweet girl, she was ready to love his family if
they turned out to be little green men from Mars.

But the look on Pop's face! If Paul hadn't cared so much, he
might have laughed. He wished his father wasn't so set in his
ways. So she was a rich girl, the daughter of a rich father! So
what? What was *wrong* with having money, for God's sake? Sid
had worked for it. Nobody had handed out anything to him—as
Sid was fond of saying. Why shouldn't Sid—why shouldn't everybody, Paul Gordon included—be rewarded for their hard

work? He'd never been able to understand that. But you couldn't talk to Pop, not on that subject. He would only give you the Party line.

But he was here, at his son's wedding to that rich girl, and that was the point, wasn't it? Because of Mom, probably. Paul didn't know how, but she'd even managed to get him into a tux. A miracle! But here he was, standing with Mom right behind him—they had walked him up the aisle, one on either side—and Pop was even smiling.

Now the organ stopped playing and there was an expectant hush. Immediately, there was a rustling as everyone turned around in their seats, ready for their first look at the bride. Paul's heart speeded up. He really was in love. Well, of course. That's what this wedding was all about—it was a public proclamation of their love for each other. The rabbi had said that at the rehearsal the other night, and Paul had made sure to remember the exact words.

It stayed absolutely silent for a minute or two. Then, the big crystal chandeliers dimmed and the white satin curtains at the back of the room parted and there she was, standing at the top of the spiral staircase: the bride, in a long white dress, the train arranged in a swirl around her feet, wearing a golden crown, her pretty face hidden by her grandmother's veil, delicate and radiant, and his, his, his: Stefanie Marlene Handleman, beautiful as a princess, loving and adoring, a wife he would always be proud of.

The first time he got to know Steffie, he was sitting in the living room of the A E Phi sorority house at good old S.U., waiting for Bobbie Miller. He was a senior, and it seemed to him like he'd been spending about half of his life the past year and a half, waiting for Bobbie Miller from Fairlawn, New Jersey, known to everyone as the Cutty Sark Queen because her father had exclusive distribution in the greater metropolitan area. He was in his monkey suit, a corsage in a little box on the table next to his chair containing the most expensive orchid in the flower shop, and there it was, wilting as he watched it.

It was a big deal, dating Bobbie. She was president of her sorority, Homecoming Queen her sophomore year, secretary/ treasurer of Panhellenic, and, tonight, a royal pain in the ass. Come to think of it, she'd been a pain a lot lately, breaking his chops over every goddamn thing. Why couldn't he get out of work earlier? Could he shave before he came to see her? Did he

always have to whistle like that? And why weren't they getting
pinned?

He wished he could tell her she was beginning to get on his
nerves. He didn't like a ballbreaker. When he first met her, he
thought she was just full of life and energy. She was a cheerleader type, always on the move, always up, always ready for a
good time. He liked his women upbeat. He liked Bobbie. He
liked going out with her, he liked being seen with her, he liked
going to bed with her. But he didn't like a ballbreaker, and she'd
better watch it.

Tonight, for instance. Why was he sitting here all by himself
in the sorority house, at nearly nine o'clock, while the intrafraternity dance went on without him? He was the president, for
Christ's sake! But Bobbie wasn't ready yet. And why wasn't she
ready? Who the hell knew, with a woman. They'd had this date
for months, so she had no excuse. He'd come a little late, sure,
but no more than half an hour. What the hell was half an hour?
She should have been waiting for him, but Bobbie always said
she had never waited for anyone in her whole life. He knew
Bobbie. She was pissed off because he was late.

Well, screw her! He couldn't help being late. There was a
protest going on—an anti-Vietnam War thing—and it was going
on all across Comstock Avenue, *and* Marshall Street, *and* University Avenue, and just about anywhere else on campus you
tried to drive. They were sitting all over the streets, holding lit
candles and singing and holding up traffic. The one thing they
weren't doing, in his opinion, was stopping the war. Fucking
idiots. He had to drive around and around, and every time he
picked a different route, there they were again. He knew they
thought they were absolutely right, that they thought they were
better than the rest of the world.

Well, they were going to freeze to death. November in Syracuse was no time to sit on the pavement. And they looked
ridiculous, squatting and sprawling there, with their stupid candles blowing out in the wind and dripping all over the place, and
their stupid placards you couldn't read in the dark. And all their
hair. You couldn't tell the boys from the girls: they both wore
their hair in ponytails and didn't shave their legs! He laughed at
his own joke and thought for a moment of stopping the car and
rolling down the window and telling them exactly what he
thought of them and their politics. Nobody paid any attention
to them, not anyone who *counted*. But he knew how left-wingers

thought. They didn't care what was really going on—all they wanted to do was shoot their mouths off and feel superior.

His old man, of course, would be right there in the middle of them, if he was here and saw them. Christ, if his father was here, he'd be giving Paul the business again about being selfish and self-centered and uncommitted and reactionary and wasting his life and all the left-wing bullshit. In fact, there wasn't a doubt in his mind that, at this very moment, his mother and father were doing something just like this, down in the city . . . lying across Broadway or marching up and down Forty-second Street or burning draft cards or some other goddamn thing.

Talk about wasted lives! Just where did his father's politics ever get *him*? He talked so big, but who was he? Just a junior high school social studies teacher, that's all. Never enough money, never time for having fun, no real position: that was Jonah Gordon's life. And he wanted Paul to do the same for the rest of his life! He had to be kidding! No way! Not for Paul Gordon. No, he had a different kind of life planned out for himself.

What you had to do in this life was figure the odds and make the right moves. He had it all mapped out. He was going to make a name for himself at Syracuse—that's why he was in a fraternity, and that's why he was playing first-string lacrosse instead of third-string football, and that's why he was majoring in bus. ad., and that's why he was dating girls from A E Phi. They were a bunch of JAPs, for sure, but that's what he liked about them. They were pretty, they wore great clothes, they had cars, money, position, power . . . all the things he wanted. He was going to marry one of them. He had to marry a rich girl. Oh, he was going to love her; he'd never marry a girl he didn't love. But it was just as easy to fall in love with a rich girl as a poor one. *Easier*, if you asked him. And if her father had a business that had a place for a bright young graduate in business administration, that would be okay, too.

That's why he was cooling his heels in the sorority house tonight. Because Bobbie Miller fit all the qualifications he was looking for. But the longer he sat here and the later it got, the more he wondered whether she really fit into his master plan.

He got up from the easy chair and began to pace. He was beginning to get mad. Here he was, in black tie—his own, dammit, and he worked damn hard to earn the money for it—his roommate's car parked right outside, the perfect corsage, the exact same one she said she wanted and that he bought for her,

even though it set him back twelve bucks. And he was being
kept waiting. With everything just right for the biggest, most
important dance of the year. Where the hell was she?

"Oh, hi, Paul. I didn't know anyone was here."

He turned, putting a smile on his face. It was that cute little
blond soph, Steffie Handleman, the one who didn't look Jewish.

"What are *you* doing home on a Saturday night, Stef?"

She blushed. "Larry and I broke up two nights ago. I was
just coming in to play the piano. I'm sorry. I didn't realize you
were here."

"Don't be sorry. I'm glad to see you. I'm going out of my
mind. I've been sitting here all by myself for half an hour and
I'm beginning to get bored with myself. Play me something on
the piano. I like piano playing."

"I'm not really very good. But I'll sit and talk to you, if you
want."

"That'd be great." What a sweet kid, he thought. A pretty
girl like her shouldn't be sitting home on a Saturday night. Maybe
one of his fraternity brothers . . . Or maybe . . .

She sat down on one of the big sofas and patted the cushion
next to her. "Stop walking back and forth, you'll make me
dizzy. You might as well save your feet for dancing."

He sat down, as ordered. She smelled as good as she looked,
which was pretty damn good. She was wearing blue, the same
color as her eyes. And under the sweater and skirt, he could see
she had a spectacular figure. If he had to keep waiting for Bobbie, he could do worse.

"So how come *you're* here so late, Paul?"

"I'm here so late because, as usual, Bobbie's keeping me
waiting." He almost told her how he had planned to pin her
tonight after the dance and then, for some reason, he decided
against it. Later, he was glad.

"Oh, that Bobbie!" she said. "Honestly!"

"What?"

"Her new policy . . . oops." She put a hand quickly over
her mouth. "I'm bad. I shouldn't have said anything."

He leaned a little closer and gave her the Little Boy Look that
always worked for him. "Come on, Steffie. What policy? I'll
never let her know you told me. Scout's honor."

"I'm sorry, Paul. I can't. I wasn't thinking. And I promised
not to tell. Please don't ask me." Her cheeks were very pink
and she twisted her hands a little in her lap. He had an urge to
reach over and take her hands and hold them tightly in his.

But instead, he patted her shoulder in a brotherly way. "I really would appreciate it. But, well, if you really feel strongly that you can't, I won't force the issue."

"Oh, Paul, you're so understanding. Maybe . . . But no, I just can't . . ." There was a moment of silence, and then she said, in a bright voice, "So, tell me, Paul, are you worried about Vietnam? That you'll have to go? I know a lot of the senior boys are."

"Who, me? Not a chance. I lucked out. I have a number that's so low, they won't get me till the *next* war."

"Don't even joke about another war! This one's bad enough. And I'd hate to think of you being wounded, because I faint at the sight of blood," she said, putting on a Southern drawl. She laughed and blushed, very flustered.

Hey! he told himself. This very cute girl is flirting with you! It made him look at her in a whole new light.

She was so natural, so nice. No cold princess stuff, no high-and-mighty airs, like some girls he could name. Just a regular, friendly, warm, unself-conscious girl, who happened to be extremely pretty, with her long yellow hair and her big, round, blue eyes. And who happened, incidentally, to drive a brand-new, shiny red Austin-Healy. But that wasn't the attraction—that was just a nice little extra. She was so poised and sure of herself, that's what he liked. She was making conversation with him as if she'd known him her whole life. *She'd* never play games, he'd be willing to bet on it. And he liked her sense of humor.

He look at his wristwatch again and got to his feet. "I don't believe that Bobbie!" he said, half to himself. "Quarter to ten! And I'm president of intrafraternity! She knows we have to be there by ten!"

"You're not going to make it, I can tell you that. You might as well take it easy. Bobbie's coming down at ten-thirty and not a minute before."

He whirled around to face her. "Her new policy! Now you *have* to tell me, dammit! It's unfair not to tell me."

"I really shouldn't. But . . . well, it is unfair of her, especially if she knows you're supposed to be there by a certain time and, well . . . It's just unfair, that's all."

"So. Tell me."

"She said tonight that her new policy with you is to make you wait five minutes for every minute you're late."

Swiftly, he multiplied in his head. "But that's two and a half hours! Ten-thirty . . . like you just said."

"Like I just said." She looked at him with sympathy. "Bobbie said you've been late entirely too often this year."

"Oh, yeah? And did she also happen to mention that I have a new job this year and *that's* what's been making me late 'entirely too often'? No, of course not! Well, if she thinks I'm going to sit down here, like her pet dog, and wait until ten-thirty, she's very much mistaken. I'm due at ten, and I'm going to *be* there." He began to smile. He felt really good, all of a sudden, really good. "So do me a favor, okay?"

"Anything."

"When she comes down, tell her that's the last game she ever plays with me. The last."

"Does that mean you'll be on time from now on?"

He gave her a sharp look. Was she kidding, or what? It was hard to tell. Well, either way, it didn't matter.

"Hell no, Steffie." Now he *really* felt good. "What it means is that, from now on, when I come to the A E Phi house, I'll be coming for *you*. What do you say?"

"What do I say? I say, Yes, Paul. That would be lovely." The look of pure delight that spread over her face told him everything he needed to know. How could he have ever thought that Bobbie Miller was a possibility? This was the girl he'd been waiting for. This was It, with a capital *I*.

Now, today, on their wedding day, as she stood there, straight and proud under the baby-pink spotlight, the orchestra began to play "This Is My Beloved," their song, and she began, very slowly, to come down the staircase to meet her parents standing at the bottom, one on either side of the pale blue runner. She looked like an angel, floating in the air, ethereal, fragile, and so lovely. He made himself a solemn vow right then and there that he would always love her and take care of her and be good to her, and damned if his eyes didn't fill up. Well, if a man's eyes couldn't fill up a little at his own wedding, when could they?

His father-in-law, Sid, had become teary just last night at the rehearsal dinner, when he made his toast to them. "My little girl is going into very good hands," he said, and then he choked up and had to stop and blink a lot, and Essie had to finish making the toast for him.

". . . And we're very happy about it." And one of Steffie's millions of cousins—she had more relatives than anyone he'd ever known—leaned over and whispered, "Happens every family gathering. He starts to cry, she finishes up for him." The cousin laughed and so did Paul. God, what a wonderful big family he was getting!

Now the music stopped, as Stef reached the very bottom of the stairs, and there was a small, total silence. And then, the familiar strains of "Here Comes the Bride" started and she was on her way down the aisle, to him. It was all going to happen! He wanted to laugh with his happiness. He'd made it! He'd made it! This was the beginning of the life he'd always wanted. One small step for man, a giant leap for Paul Gordon!

Chapter Thirty

Sunday, September 20, 1987   Jack Strauss looked around him with obvious pleasure. "One thing you have to say about Elaine," he remarked. "She has taste."

His wife, sitting next to him on one of the oversized gray leather couches, patted his hand. "There's more than *one* good thing you could say about Elaine."

He waved her off. "Why do you always assume I'm picking on her? I think this apartment is gorgeous, it's like a palace! There! How's that?"

Sylvia smiled, shaking her head slightly. "What am I going to do with him?" she asked the ceiling, which she noticed had recently been repainted cream dragged with a peach glaze. Very nice.

"What are you going to do with me? The same as you've always done—take good care of me and then give me a hard time."

"What do you mean, give you a hard time? I'm being very nice to you! You're nervous, that's what it is," she decided. As he began to shake his head in denial, she added, "You're so nervous, I can't say a word without you jumping down my throat."

"Nervous? Me? What, are you kidding? Hey, it's not the king of England coming, it's only Jonah Golodny."

"Gordon."

"See? You just did it again. So who's the nervous one, huh?"

"Not nervous, Jack. Just . . . anticipating. Think of it: all those years we haven't seen Jo or Dot or their kids. And now, their *children* have children. It's been such a long time—and we didn't part on the best of terms. Let's face it. We're both a little on edge."

He growled something she couldn't make out but knew meant the end of this particular topic. Okay. She didn't mind. It wasn't her favorite subject. It certainly wasn't *his*, not by a long shot.

For years, she had been . . . what? . . . ashamed, that's what. Ashamed that a charming, outgoing, lovable man like Jack could be so cold, so unforgiving, so rigid. And so cruel! She still remembered with pain the day Deena—before she was bat mitz-vah so she wasn't quite thirteen—found an old snapshot of her-self with her cousin Cookie and Uncle Jo and brought it to the dinner table, all excited. She'd handed it to her daddy and he just ripped it in two, and handed her back the part of the photo that showed only her.

She'd never forget, not as long as she lived, the look on Deena's face: shocked, unbelieving, as if she'd had the wind knocked out of her. Sylvia hadn't felt so different, herself. An intelligent man, acting so childish and vindictive! And the worst of it was, he didn't think he'd done anything out of line!

All those years, he'd refused to soften his position, and all those years, she and the girls had known better than to even mention the names of his sister and her family in front of him.

If Jack Strauss had one big fault, it was that he couldn't for-give, couldn't say I was wrong. The words just stuck in his throat. Oh, he might make peace with you after a fight, but in his own way—he'd bring presents or he'd plan a nice evening out or something like that. But never a discussion. The subject would be dropped forever and you'd *never* hear those words. He didn't know *how* to apologize.

Meeting with Jonah today was going to be very tough for him. If she was nervous at all, it wasn't about seeing Jonah and Dorothy after all this time—she was really looking forward to that—it was her worry about how Jack might behave. He was a good man, her Jack, and he had a hundred friends . . . but you just never knew what might set him off.

She regarded him, slumped down into the soft cushions, pre-tending to read a magazine. Which was hilarious, considering it was the latest issue of *Elle*—in French, yet! And he didn't have his glasses on, anyway. He still looked damn good for a man his age, seventy-one, who had had one pretty big stroke—not to mention a couple of little ones. His color was still good . . . Well, he kept his tan under the sunlamps at the club, but even under the tan, he wasn't *schvach*, old-looking, like so many of his buddies. A little thinner than he used to be, maybe, but when she asked Jack's doctor, he said that was all to the good.

"Better than most men his age," he said, "carrying a big belly around all the time. Don't you worry about Jack," he'd said—and so she didn't worry, not like she used to. She kept an eye on what he ate and made sure he didn't miss his walk every morning. He was fine, he was really okay, even talking lately about buying a condo in Phoenix for vacations.

He still wouldn't look at her, so what was she doing, sitting here doing nothing? She got up, smoothing out the slim skirt of her silk polka-dot dress, giving herself a quick look in the mirrored wall in back of the sofa. Also not bad. Eight point seven on a scale of ten, she'd say. Still fairly trim, still standing up straight, still good-looking if she did say so herself. Mr. Peter gave a good haircut and she was very glad she'd decided not to cover the gray; now that it was nearly all white, she really liked it.

She drifted into the dining room, where the caterers' people were setting up. What were they thinking, putting a chafing dish there at the end of the table where God forbid someone could brush against it! A chafing dish belonged safely in the middle and she'd already said something about it. But Elaine had given her a look and raised her eyebrows and put a finger to her lips.

All right, it was Elaine's house and Elaine's caterer and Sylvia was only a guest—she wasn't allowed to open up her mouth. Elaine told her, "Sylvia, when I hire professionals, I let them do everything their way—yes, Sylvia, even if they fold the napkins the wrong way, even that!—because that's why I'm paying them. To do all the work, however they choose to do it, and allow me my freedom."

She'd been more than brisk, she'd been almost rude—and in front of the help, too. That was another thing Sylvia would never do. But, never mind, today was the day for forgiveness.

It was very quiet in the apartment because Elaine had sent the kids outside to play touch football or something. And then she and Howard and Deena had made themselves scarce, somewhere in the back of the sprawling apartment. They knew it was bound to be awkward, those first few minutes, for the "old folks."

Sylvia headed back to the living room, where she could see her husband had given up all pretense of reading and was sitting with his head thrown back, his eyes closed. His mouth had fallen open, and for a horrible moment, her heart stopped. And then she noticed his foot drumming silently on the thick carpet and the terrible fear dissolved instantly and was forgotten. She sat down next to him. "We're very lucky, Jack," she said.

"About what, this time?" He didn't move, or stop tapping his foot, but he opened his eyes and slid a glance in her direction.

"Our family. We can be very proud of our daughters, and our grandchildren are all dolls, each and every one." She gazed out into the distance for a moment. "Noel, of course, is special."

"Sylvia! Shame on you. No favorites, remember!"

"For every phone call from the rest of them, Noel calls five times. He calls more than *all* of them put together."

"Why not? We were like second parents to him when he was little. Elaine thought nothing of running right back to work in the *shmatte* business and leaving the baby with you. Remember how he called you Mommy?"

"Agh, he was only doing that to tease Elaine. And it was only for a month or two. Besides, I loved having him around. He was such a bright little thing. Remember how you used to take him out in the park to throw a football around, took him to baseball games?"

"War movies, too. He loved them, especially with airplanes. Well, you know, with a father in the ladies' underwear business, a man who's . . . well, not quite a hundred percent masculine, if you know what I mean . . ."

"Jack!"

"Well, I didn't want to take any chances. And Noel turned out good, didn't he? He's smart, making a lot of money, and he likes girls." His tone was definitely triumphant.

Sylvia couldn't help laughing. "Jack, darling, let me remind you. No matter what you thought, so does his father."

Now he turned to face her. "Sylvia, I love you."

She felt a blush beginning. "You just found out today?"

He reached over and took her hand in his. "Oy, Sylvia, stop with the smart talk for once, would you? A day like today makes you think about your life. When I picked you, I picked a gem. No matter what happened, you always stuck by me. Through thick and thin. You're the only one, the only one in my whole life, who's always been loyal to me."

She pulled her hand away from his, pretending she had to tuck a wisp of hair behind her ear. She didn't like it when he talked like this; it made her feel uneasy. It was morbid. And it brought up the past.

But, of course, once he got started, there was no stopping him—never mind how it hurt anyone else. "Sylvia, I'm not getting any younger, I almost died—"

"You didn't almost die, Jack. Dr. Kopmar said—"

"I don't care what Kopmar said, I don't even care what Dr. Marilyn said, I know I almost died, period, *fartig*, finished. Why else do you think I agreed to this . . . this reunion thing? This major production?"

"You agreed because your daughter Deena asked you to do it."

"My daughter Deena! Between you and my daughter Deena, I've been talked blue in the face all summer! You'd think nobody had ever had a cousin before, in the history of the world! According to my daughter Deena, if I didn't agree to see Jonah Golodny . . . excuse me, Gordon . . . I was a monster!"

He made a face and, at the same moment, pushed himself off the couch with a grunt. She didn't want to, but she couldn't help noticing all the little signs that he was not quite the man he used to be. Especially today, for some reason. Now he walked over to the window and stood there, looking out over Central Park, like he'd forgotten she was there.

And then suddenly he spoke—to her? She couldn't tell. "It was this time of year, Mama died," he said. "Every Rosh Hashanah, I think about sitting *shivah* in that crummy little apartment. I'll never forget it. Jonah wouldn't come until the very last day, and then he wouldn't say the prayers, just stood there like a goy, like he didn't know what he was supposed to be doing! Wouldn't pay for a taxi for his wife—she had to schlepp herself and the baby all the way from the Bronx to Brooklyn all week. To her own mother's *shivah*! The schmuck!"

"Jack! Some reunion we're going to have, if this is how you're thinking! And anyway, you know they didn't have money for taxis."

"I offered to pay. But that stubborn SOB had my sister so brainwashed, she couldn't accept. I tried to reason with her—"

Sylvia let out a hoot. "Some 'reason'! You could be heard at the other end of Brooklyn! But never mind. It was a difficult time. Everyone was upset."

Jack said, "You have only one mother, and when she's gone,

that's it." There was a moment of silence and then he said, in
a very different tone, "So he did us a big favor and finally
showed up. Did he have to talk politics? Henry Wallace! Another lousy Red! And everything I said to him made Dorothy
cry. Agh! I'll never forget it. And anyway, where are they?
They're late!"

"Maybe this was a mistake," Jonah grumped, and Dorothy
swallowed her irritation. Ever since they got up this morning,
he'd been voicing his doubts and talking himself out of them.
Sure enough, she didn't even have to answer; he answered himself. "But, look, it's now or never and whatever'll be, will be.
At least I'll see the children and the grandchildren. Probably
spoiled rotten, the whole bunch of them."

"Jonah! You haven't even seen them yet! And already you've
decided what they're like. Maybe his grandchildren are left wing,
you don't know."

"Left wing!" Jonah laughed and then lost his breath and
began to cough. She hated when that happened, and it was happening more and more often lately. "That would be the day! A
fitting punishment for that self-centered bastard." Again he
coughed, and again she found herself holding her own breath
until he managed to catch his.

Had he really changed so drastically in the two days she was
up in Boston with Cookie? It seemed impossible and yet, with
cancer, anything was possible. Probably, being with him every
day, she just hadn't noticed how much he had declined in the
past couple of months. Maybe she hadn't wanted to notice.
Whatever.

At any rate, when she came back from the trip and he met
her at the door, she felt like someone had kicked her in the
stomach. He looked so frail, all of a sudden, so stooped. She
just stood there staring at him for a minute. And then, quickly,
she gave him a big smile and began to talk about Michelle and
how pretty Harvard was, never mind it was an elitist school for
the wealthy. She could only hope he hadn't noticed her initial
shock.

Since that moment, she was fighting tears constantly. She
woke up with tears in her eyes. She brushed her teeth and looked
in the mirror and her eyes filled. She heard a silly song from the
forties, on the radio, and had to turn away. Why? Why? She
couldn't figure it out. She had thought every strong emotion
between them long gone. She had cast her lot with him, for

better or worse, and she thought she had already lived through the worst . . . She thought she had used up all her tears. In a way, he had died in Millville. Something between them had certainly died there, and she had mourned for years. If anyone had asked her what they were doing together now, she would have said, Making the best of a difficult situation, that's all . . . Keeping each other company in our old age.

But no, it wasn't that simple, after all. Here she was, watching him die again, only this time it was forever, and this time she couldn't do a thing about it. She couldn't grab ahold of him, the way she did back then, and drag him back into the world of the living. She was helpless to do anything but watch it happen.

"If you're still so angry with him, Jo, then why are we doing this?"

He gave her a sharp look. "I thought you'd be thrilled to see your beloved brother once more."

Quickly: "I am. Of course, I am."

"Yeah. Of course. But you haven't had one good word to say about it. Too much trouble. It'll tire me out. Why does it have to be at Elaine's? Why not a quiet little meeting between me and Jack? . . . Always some little *kvetch*. That's not like you, Dorothy."

She looked at him, amazed. He was so quiet, seemed so vague, and then, out of nowhere, he was reading your mind. She licked her lips and took in a breath. "It must be the time of year. I always feel sad this time of year. I find myself thinking about my mother. Not just because she's gone. But she had such a wasted life! Always in a housedress, always *kvetching* a little under her breath, because you couldn't ever say anything out loud in that house, not with *him* there. God, you were hardly allowed to *breathe* in that house, never mind having a thought of your own!"

A bit breathless, she went charging on. "When we sat *shivah* for her, I swear to God, I noticed a strange thing. People said they were sorry, and then, not another word. No one mentioned her name. It was so sad. She was nobody. It was as if she had never existed. It was awful, just awful. I didn't even want to go after the first day. But Jack insisted."

"I remember that week, too," Jonah said. "What did he care, that you had to schlepp all the way from the Bronx on the train every day? He had to put on a big show of grief because that's how your brother does everything. Appearance above all, that's Jack Strauss! A piece of torn black ribbon pinned to his

jacket, like everyone else? That wasn't enough for *him*. Oh, no.
He had to have the lapel of his best suit torn, so he could show
everyone how his mourning was the *real* article! Yeah, I remember.''

"He made me feel that I didn't love her enough or mourn her
enough," Dot mused. "All his friends—no, never mind the
friends—every person he ever did business with, they all came
by. I remember them, all alike in their blue suits, awkward, not
knowing what they were supposed to do. But Jack only kept
count. The last day, he told me exactly how many people had
come, how many cards, how many phone calls, how many trees
to be planted in the new state of Israel in her memory, how
many dishes of food brought, how many this, how many that,
and, of course, how much it cost. Not to mention the brand-
new Sylvania television he was going to buy Pa so he wouldn't
be lonely.''

"The TV—yes, that I remember," Jo said wryly. "All that
money spent for a big box with a little picture—when so many
people in the world were still starving, still digging out of the
ruins of Europe, trying to stay alive!''

"Never mind the television! Yes, it was a *shandah*; but the
real shame was the way Pa sat in the corner, rocking back and
forth, weeping. Weeping! I ask you! And saying she was an
angel come down to earth! An angel come to earth . . . *really*?
He never said a nice word to her in her whole life, never. He
put on a show for his audience and it was all a lie, every bit of
it.''

"Is it any wonder your brother's that way? I never could stand
that—''

"It's forty years ago, don't excite yourself. And Jack's *nothing*
like Pa. I'm sorry I brought it up. Let's forget it, okay?''

"I ask myself—why did I want so badly to make it up with
him? What are we doing this for?''

Patiently, Dot said, "I asked you that same question, about
a hundred times. Not ten minutes ago, I asked you again. Now,
all of a sudden, you're wondering?''

"You know what I think?" Jonah said. "I think you've been
a lot happier without him butting into your life. I think that
secretly, you don't really want to see him! That's what *I* think!''
He gave her a triumphant smile.

"That's ridiculous!" But she did not look at him. Did he
suspect something? Did he *know* something? But he couldn't.

And then, thank God, they pulled to the curb and the cabby

turned around and said, "Here we are." And it was finished.
For now.

❦❦❦❦❦❦❦❦❦❦❦❦❦❦❦❦❦❦❦❦❦❦❦❦❦❦❦❦❦❦❦❦❦

Chapter Thirty-one

Sunday, September 20, 1987   The doorbell rang. You'd
think they hadn't been sitting for half an hour, waiting for it, the
way they both jumped. Sylvia got to her feet and said, "Come
on, Jack! It's them!"

"Elaine'll get it."

"No, she won't. Don't you realize? We've been left alone to
say our first hellos in privacy."

"What are you talking about—left alone?"

Sylvia looked at him and shook her head. "Men!"

The bell rang again and she pulled him by the hand. "Take
it easy," Jack grumbled. "They're not going anywhere."

"Aren't you excited? You haven't seen Dorothy in nearly forty
years, for God's sake!"

"I'm excited, I'm excited. You want me to have a stroke,
right here and now?"

"Jack! You promised—"

He spread his hands, grinning like a naughty little boy. "So
nu, Sylvia? What are you waiting for? Answer the door already!"

She gave him a look and went, with him trailing behind her.
As the bell pealed for the third time, she opened the door. And
had to fight herself, not to gasp out loud. Jonah! Oh, my God,
she'd never have known him, if she'd passed him in the street.
He looked shrunken. He was so thin, so stooped, so lined, so
. . . frail-looking. In her mind, Jonah was still a vigorous, in-
tense, angry young man, his light eyes snapping and his hair a
bright copper. He was old! Of course, she should have expected
it—they were all of an age, and didn't she have her own share
of wrinkles and gray hair?—but somehow, she had managed to
forget they had all aged. And, shame on her, how could she
forget he was a very sick man?

And then that familiar voice, rather deep for a woman and absolutely unforgettable, cried out, "Sylvia! Sylvia! It's so good—" Sylvia got a quick glimpse of the highly colored, vivid face, still pretty, still youthful. And then she was enfolded in an embrace, surrounded by the remembered scent of lemon verbena. Tears pricked at her eyes. Dorothy was instantly familiar to her, yet they had not seen each other for half a lifetime. Craziness! Absolutely meshuggah. How had she let it go on so long?

She pulled back and said, "So? I got the impression you didn't age. Let me check. Uh-huh, I was right. You're still as cute as ever!"

Dot laughed. "Look who's talking. You look like a million bucks, Sylvia." They were standing a bit apart, their hands clasped together, both fighting tears and both smiling broadly, the two men forgotten.

Then Jack's gruff voice: "So? You want to stand in the hall all day? You maybe don't want to come in to a decadent Capitalist palace, Golodny? You want to go in the service entrance? Go ahead. We'll wait."

"Same old Jack. And the name's Gordon."

"I beg your pardon. Mr. Gordon, please come in—and Mrs. Gordon, how about a hug for your big brother?"

They embraced, and when Sylvia sneaked a look at him, she saw his eyes glittering. Jack was not a man who cried easily, either.

Jonah still stood hesitantly in the doorway. Jack cleared his throat. "So . . . uh . . . will you shake my hand? And maybe come in now? Look, Jo, in three days, it's Rosh Hashanah, the New Year. We're supposed to forgive and forget and start with a clean slate. So what do you say?" He stuck out his hand.

"I say, men of reason and goodwill don't need a superstition to tell them when to forgive and forget." But his hand went out.

"Still an anti-Semite, I see. Well, what the hell." They shook hands briefly. "Come in anyway."

"Why not? It's been a long time. Water under the bridge." As the door closed behind him, Jonah added, "Tell me something. You really believe a guy with a white beard is sitting up there in the sky with a big book and he's going to open to the page with your name on top and judge you? Every September, you think this really happens?" He didn't exactly smile, but his lips twitched a little. Jack made a dismissive gesture.

"No. no," Jonah went on. "I'm serious, Strauss. *Do* you believe in God?"

"I believe in Rosh Hashanah. I'm a Jew."

"But do you believe in God?"

"What does God have to do with it?"

Jonah burst into laughter and Jack struggled visibly for a moment with annoyance. Sylvia quickly said, "Together two and a half minutes and already you're disagreeing. Come. Let's go in. Jack, pour four glasses of champagne and let's have a toast to this reunion."

They all headed into the living room—Jack protesting that they weren't arguing they were just talking—but no one paid attention, and Sylvia just patted his arm and repeated, "The champagne, Jack. The champagne."

But when they entered the room, there was already a big silver tray on the coffee table with a bottle in the cooler and seven glasses in a circle around it. And in a kind of loose circle around the coffee table, Deena, Elaine, and Howard.

Sylvia couldn't help wondering what Dot and Jonah were thinking as they were introduced. They hadn't seen her daughters since they were kids, and here they were, two elegant, self-assured women, mothers themselves, and beautiful. Yes, she decided, if she were meeting these two women for the first time, she'd be very impressed. Elaine *was* a little heavy, but she was a large woman, very imposing and, as always, beautifully turned out, a real head-turner. Today she was wearing a silk outfit in a glowing shade of garnet, with huge garnet and pearl earrings Howard had found for her in an antique store the last time they were in London. Deena, of course, was dressed in the very latest style. She'd always loved clothes, and luckily, she could wear anything. The skirt she was wearing was one of the new really short ones, almost a miniskirt, and Sylvia did not approve. But she had to admit that her beautiful daughter had the legs for it. Even Howard, not the handsomest of men, looked distinguished with that little Vandyke beard, like a diplomat.

"Welcome!" Elaine said, and took a step or two forward.

And there was Jack, more or less pushing in front of her, putting his hand on Elaine's shoulder and saying, "This is Elaine, my eldest, you remember her . . . But she was a *pitsel* the last time you saw her, *now* she's the female Donald Trump with her own publicist and a car with a driver."

He was beaming in his pleasure. Elaine, Sylvia noted, was not. She was trying very hard not to show it, but she was be-

ginning to boil. He always did this to her; he would never learn.
Oh, God. She opened her mouth to say something that might
shut him up, but it was too late. He was already going on. "And
how about this apartment? Gorgeous, huh? *House and Garden*
wanted to do a big story on it, but Howard wouldn't go for it.
My son-in-law, Howard Barranger . . ." He made a sweeping
gesture. "Would you believe he's a college boy? But first he was
a millionaire. Only in America!"

Howard opened *his* mouth, but it didn't do him any good,
either. Deena was grinning in a devilish way. She knew her
daddy. Unlike Elaine, though, she was able to take him as he
was, and be amused. He was a lot more nervous than anyone
had realized; he couldn't seem to stop talking.

"Every bit of furniture in this room is either custom-made,
like those two leather couches, or authentic antiques. See those
two chairs by the fireplace? They're on loan . . . do you believe?
on *loan* . . . from an antique dealer in London. He sent them
so Elaine could live with them for awhile before she decided to
buy. It's another world—"

"Daddy!" It was Elaine and Deena, objecting in unison. Jack
broke off, looking a little startled.

"What? Did I tell a lie?"

"Nobody cares about my furniture. Let us say hello, for God's
sake. Hello, Aunt Dorothy, and hello, Uncle Jo." Elaine stepped
around her father, pretending to laugh, and hugged each one.

Jack went right on. "And, of course, you'll meet my youngest, Marilyn. She's a doctor—that's right, an M.D. They're driving down from Vermont, that's where she lives, so they're not
here yet—"

This time it was Deena who decided to interrupt. She hugged
her aunt and uncle and then said, "You can guess who I am,
just by the process of elimination. We middle children are always forgotten! Just kidding, Daddy. I know you were just saving
the best for last. Elaine is a tycoon, Marilyn is a doctor. I'm
Deena and I'm divorced. That's *my* major accomplishment."

"Deena!" Jack objected. Turning to Dot and Jo, he said,
"Deena has four children. Her oldest, Nat, is also a doctor.
Well, almost. He's a resident, in Colorado. Colorado! I ask you!
I said to him, 'Nat, stay in New York, meet a nice girl. *Then*
you can go to Colorado.' " He looked around, as everyone
laughed. "He laughed, too! But how many nice Jewish girls are
there in Boulder, Colorado?"

The doorbell rang just then, insistently. Jack turned as if to go, and Elaine said, "Daddy. Sit. Howard will answer the door."

He sat down, almost in the exact center of the sofa, spreading his arms across the back. "That'll be Marilyn now, my daughter the doctor. Excuse me for bragging, but how many men can say that?"

Tersely, Deena said, "Hundreds. Probably thousands."

But Jack went on, as if she hadn't spoken. "You've heard the joke about the nun who goes to heaven and gets to meet Mary and Joseph and she asks them how they feel, to have their son become the Savior. And *they* say, 'To tell you the truth, we were hoping he'd be a doctor.' " He laughed hugely at his joke.

Elaine said, "The way *I* heard it, it was in the manger—and Mary and Joseph were crying and one of the Wise Men asked them why and they said, 'To tell you the truth, we were hoping for a girl.' "

Jack spread his hands, saying, "What can I tell you? I'm surrounded by liberated women."

There were voices out in the hall, coming closer. But it wasn't Marilyn who came in. It was a woman with curly red hair and a big smile. Sylvia wouldn't have known who it was, except that Deena ran to her, crying, "Cookie, Cookie!" They embraced with such easy familiarity. An arm around each other's waist, they stood together, beaming with delight.

Sylvia felt an emotion she at first couldn't name. And then she had it: envy. She was jealous of their closeness. She'd never had a friendship like that; and she'd never felt really close to her sisters, either. But why not? It struck her suddenly that she'd been taught not to trust other women. Other women were the enemy. Other women were the competition. Other women might get *him*.

And other women did, that was the truth. For all her being careful, for all her being on guard, what good had it done? It hadn't saved her from that particular heartache, had it? Like the man said—just a few minutes ago—water under the bridge, so forget it.

Look at the two of them, the two cousins, so happy at what they'd accomplished. It really was their idea, this reunion, and good for them. She should have thought of it herself. Well, here they were, and so?

Look at Cookie, what a cutie! But, really, a redhead with that milk-white skin should never wear purple. Made her look washed out. Maybe if she brightened her makeup a little . . . She had pretty legs, even if she was overweight—someone should tell her to wear her skirts shorter. Well, if she had picked an outfit that was a little . . . smarter . . .

It was with a great deal of satisfaction that Sylvia looked once again at her own two girls. She had done a good job with them; they both had wonderful taste.

Now came the hugs and the kisses, exclamations of delight— and, finally, introductions to Cookie's husband and daughter. Cookie came first to Sylvia, which gave Sylvia unexpected pleasure, and then went to greet Jack. The daughter, Mickey she was called, was very striking—tall and vividly dark, slim, nicely dressed. Another smart one, from what Deena said. A Harvard student, like Nat. Such a nice girl. She gave Sylvia a nice warm hug and kiss, no holding back, then passed on to Jack, who, of course, turned on the charm. He could charm the birds off the trees when he wanted to.

The husband, Dave, hung back. Another quiet one, like Howard. A vague, pleasant expression on his face, he stood very patiently, waiting for all the tumult to simmer down. He was very dark, even darker than Jack. He was very nice-looking, this Dave, but he looked closed off somehow. And when Cookie turned and said, "Oh, and everybody, meet my husband, Dave Adler," he moved forward to shake hands, but he still didn't warm up much.

Then Jonah said, "My son-in-law, the hero," and went on to tell them all a long-winded story about Dave and the city of New York. She couldn't follow all if it, but she got a definite impression that this was a man who was a fighter. Frankly, she found it hard to believe. She kept looking at him, trying to see something in that dreamy, almost vacant expression that revealed a core of toughness. It must be: he'd done it and they'd fired him, and he'd fought it and they'd had to take him back. So it must be. But she couldn't see it.

Now, of course, they needed more glasses. And more champagne. Sylvia moved off toward the dining room to get them and was stopped by a young man from the caterers carrying a loaded tray. Well. They knew how to do *something* right. When she got back to the living room, everyone had sat down except Deena and Cookie.

"We all hid in the kitchen," Deena was saying. "In case, when they first saw each other they started to throw punches, we wouldn't be in the middle."

And Cookie looked around in mock inspection and said, "Well, everyone's still in one piece."

"Wait. The day is young yet."

"Well, I planned to be here to hide out with you. But Michelle wanted to wait for Uncle Win. You have to understand my brother Win. This is a Win Gordon doll. Wind him up, he comes late."

Everyone laughed. So. Surprise. The drab-looking Cookie was funny, just like Deena and Elaine.

It wasn't so funny, Cookie thought. Actually, it was damned maddening. She'd promised Deena they'd be early, and her wonderful, cooperative, and dependable family had made her late. She was pissed.

It all began at the breakfast table. Out of nowhere, Win announced he was going to the Statue of Liberty "for an hour," to take pictures while the light was right. Well, forget it. An hour to Win was whatever he felt like. And it never entered his mind that maybe he ought to either be on time or call.

Cookie wanted to leave at eleven without him. But Mickey wouldn't hear of it. "Mom, that's so rude!" she said, looking down her nose and sneering a bit.

For the first time in years, Cookie wanted to smack her. But she didn't, of course. She used sweet reason. "Don't you think your uncle is being rude by keeping us waiting?"

Michelle's chin came up even higher, if that were possible. "Win is an artist, Mother. He can't be expected to fit into *your* rigid schedules."

Rigid schedules! Cookie had always prided herself on being flexible, had *always* arranged and rearranged her life to accommodate her children and their ever-changing interests: ice-skating, Boy Scouts, museums, art classes, you name it. And now she was accused of being *rigid*? She could only stare in astonishment at her daughter.

And then Dave, damn him, instead of supporting her, only said, "Hey, what's the big rush? You waited thirty-seven years and you can't wait another few minutes?" She was ready to slug *him*, too.

"Listen, Ma, you want to get there early, go ahead. I'll wait for Uncle Win," Michelle said, giving Cookie one of her wide-eyed smiles.

Damn it. Cookie wanted them all, her whole family, to get there together—as Mickey knew very well. Jon was still being stubborn and had announced he was going to come later. And now Mickey wanted to separate herself, too. This was a very special occasion and they knew it! Why was everyone on her case?

The doorbell pealed. "That'll be Marilyn," Uncle Jack announced.

"His daughter the doctor," Deena explained. "I'll go."

But before she could move, the door opened, and in came three young persons in their twenties—plus Win, loaded down with his cameras—and all laughing.

Win gave Cookie a jaunty wave from across the room. He'd never apologize . . . hell, he didn't know there was any *reason* to apologize. Other people's needs simply did not interest him. "We all got into the elevator together, never realizing we were related," he was saying.

"Until we all came to the same door," Noel added. "So we had our reunion in the hall."

"This is my son the Wall Street tycoon," Elaine said. "Noel, darling, come in and meet all your relatives. And introduce me to your Uncle Irwin, please."

The four of them all came in together. The smaller of the two girls, Zoe, was a clone of Deena. The other daughter, Judy, must look like her father. Cookie couldn't help but note that when she got to her mother, she coolly offered a cheek to be kissed, and didn't allow Deena to really embrace her. Aha, *another* hostile daughter. Maybe it was catching.

No question Noel was a Strauss! He went straight to Jonah and Dorothy, crouching at their feet, smiling at them as he chatted. Cookie found herself fighting tears. What a nice boy. He saved his mother for last, giving her a loud smacking kiss on her cheek, and said, "So now can we eat?"

"Noel! You just got here!" But Elaine was laughing as she said it. "You know where the food is." To the others, she added, "He's always hungry. He's been hungry for twenty-one years."

Noel turned then, without a beat, and said to his newfound cousin Mickey, "Come on, you look hungry, too. Beautiful, yes. But also hungry." Michelle gave him a brilliant smile.

"If you stay in here," he went on, "they'll talk you to death. And then you'll *never* get anything to eat." As the kids walked out, Cookie noticed that her sullen daughter was suddenly all smiles.

Win hadn't yet taken a seat and he still didn't, even when

invited by Howard. "Not yet," he said. "First, I have something to show you. Something special, I think."

He reached into a big envelope he was holding and handed around some half-dozen copies of an eight-by-ten photograph. Cookie took hers. It was obviously a copy of an old family portrait, with its little cracks and creases.

Cookie gazed at the picture. There she was, a plump baby, probably not even a year old, not what you'd call beautiful, very fair and nearly bald, held by an unbelievably young, unlined, pretty Dorothy, her face turned slightly toward the child in her arms. And that had to be baby Deena, with a full head of dark hair and sucking her thumb, also held by her mother—God, Sylvia was gorgeous then. Uncle Jack stood next to his wife, an arm around her, but smiling straight at the camera, very sharp in his double-breasted suit. The striking young woman in WAC uniform was obviously her aunt Yetta, a serious expression on her face, her hair rolled neatly into a pompadour. All three of the young women wore their hair in the same style, and Yetta had her smart little overseas cap perched in the middle.

And there, on the other side of the picture, next to her mother, was Pop, dressed in his one good blue suit—he didn't approve of fussing with clothes—with a plaid shirt and a knit tie. They all looked so very young.

Her grandparents sat on a bench, in front, with a very chubby, very overdressed Elaine standing between them.

"What year was this?" she asked, and her father immediately answered, "It was 1944."

Jack said, "Are you sure? I thought 1945."

"Don't worry, I remember very well what year it was. 1944."

"Yes," Sylvia said, "it had to be because Deena and Cookie are still babies. In '45, they were toddlers already. No way you could have got either of them to sit still that long."

"Wouldn't it be nice," Cookie said, "if Aunt Yetta was here, today?"

"With all her assorted children?" There was something judgmental in Uncle Jack's voice.

Dorothy apparently heard the same thing. She leaped to her sister's defense. "Absolutely! They're family, too!"

Aunt Sylvia reached over and patted Dorothy's hand. "Thank you, Dot. You saved me the trouble of saying it myself." She gave her husband a meaningful look.

Proudly, Win said, "I found this picture buried in a box of

old papers. I had to make a negative first and *then* I made all the prints. I did it for you, Pop.''

''Yes? Well, it's a nice picture, but that was a day I'd rather forget.'' Win's face fell and his father immediately added, ''I told you. I like the picture. I appreciate the thought. But that day . . . oy . . .''

''That day,'' Dorothy put in, ''your *zayda* was at his worst. He managed to insult everyone in the room in the first five minutes. Including the photographer.''

''What are you talking?'' Jack demanded. ''Pa was okay until Jonah here started up. Don't you remember? Your husband didn't want his picture taken. And Pa made a joke, that's all, a little joke.''

''Some little joke: 'What's the matter, Jonah, you think maybe the FBI will find you? Don't worry, we won't put it up in the post office.' '' Dorothy's voice was tinged with remembered anger, and Jack quickly rejoined, ''It was just a joke. He was always joking.''

''Look at those three little girls, so adorable. And here they are today . . .'' Sylvia's voice was overloud. She was obviously changing the subject.

''And still adorable,'' said Elaine. Everyone laughed.

''Someone else here,'' Sylvia said archly, ''is hiding in this picture.'' She looked around and, when nobody responded: ''*You*, Irwin. You're in the picture. Your mother is pregnant!''

''It doesn't show.''

''How could it? I was only in the third month. But, let me tell you, I was so sick. Every morning *and* every evening. Even before you were born, Irwin, you were *noodging* me.''

Win's face tightened, just for a moment, and then he shrugged and gave a little laugh. The room was so quiet that the caterer could be heard giving instructions in the kitchen. Cookie searched for something to say, something light, anything that would break the silence. As far back as she could remember, her mother had never let up on Win, never. Enough, already! The man was forty-three years old, for God's sake!

Sylvia saved the day. ''Didn't your mother get sick right after this was taken, Jack?''

''I think she already knew, and that's why she insisted on this picture being taken. It was so unusual for her to dig her heels in about anything. She must have known.''

Dorothy said, ''All day today, I've been thinking about her.''

''Yes, me, too. You girls, you don't remember your grandma.''

Deena said, ''We were too little. But I remember *Zayda*. I was so afraid of him. But every time we went there, he gave me a quarter.''

''Your *zayda* was not an easy man,'' Jack said wryly. ''To put it mildly.'' He paused. ''Ma's funeral, we had hundreds. At Pa's, forget it! Of course, my sisters had both run away from home. You couldn't find either one of them, not when the going got tough!'' He laughed but it sounded hollow.

Dorothy sat forward, frowning. ''You know why I wasn't there. We had to stay in hiding . . . anyway *Jonah* seemed to think so.'' In his seat next to her, Jonah turned a startled face, but she refused to look at him.

''Yeah, that's how it was . . . all on my shoulders, both my sisters gone, you hiding up there in Yehupetz and Yetta running around Europe, a regular hippie!''

Elaine laughed and said, ''Daddy, there was no such thing as a hippie until the sixties!''

''You don't know your aunt Yetta! Anyway, there I was, all alone sitting *shivah*—''

''I want everybody in this room to know,'' Jonah interrupted, ''that there won't be any of that superstitious crap when *I* die . . . Cookie, don't look at me like that. I shouldn't say anything? Listen, I'd better talk now because at the funeral, it'll be too late.''

Jack went on, just as if Jonah had not spoken. ''So I sat there, all by myself, trying to explain to all the yentas from the neighborhood how my sisters, the twinnies, had both disappeared into thin air, and neither of them married—''

In unison, Cookie and Win cried: ''Not married!'' which made all the others laugh rather nervously. Cookie said, ''You're not married and you never told us?'' She wasn't particularly shocked by this news—lots of her parents' friends hadn't bothered to get married. But to keep it a secret . . . !

Jonah gave a massive shrug. ''What difference does it make? It was an ideological decision. We didn't need the state to tell us we could be man and wife!''

''At least you could have told *us*!''

''Everybody in my day knew you Commies believed in free love!'' Jack laughed.

"Free love!" Jonah echoed. "That's a laugh. Believe me, it cost plenty!"

Dot spoke to her brother: "So we didn't have a rabbi say words over us. You think maybe it'll last anyway?"

Again, the doorbell rang. "That'll be Marilyn," Elaine and Deena sang out in unison.

"She's a doctor, you know," Deena added, giving her father a look.

"All right, all right, I get it. I brag too much about my children. Do me something!"

What a sweet man, Dorothy thought, watching Howard as he ran to get the door. Quiet but in his own way a mensch. Like Cookie's Dave. You'd never know what a brave and forceful man Dave was, just to sit and chat with him. If you sat and had a chat with Dave, *you* did all the chatting. Unless you got him started on his work; then he really opened up.

A slender blond woman who must be Marilyn strode into the room, followed by a man holding a baby. She looked so different from her sisters: fair where they were dark; pale where they were vivid; unmadeup and definitely not New York. She was wearing faded denims that looked years old and sturdy leather sandals, nothing high-style. She looked so plain. Cookie should tell her about Bloomingdale's. What a difference a little blusher and mascara could make with these very fair women. But a doctor . . . maybe it didn't matter to her, maybe she was too busy to think about it.

And that was her husband—it had to be. And the sweetest little baby, a bright little thing with a fuzz of yellow hair, his head turning to see everyone, his eyes wide and intelligent.

Marilyn came first to them, to her and Jonah, her smile radiant. That smile changed her whole face. "At last! Uncle Jonah! Aunt Dorothy! What a pleasure! And this is my husband, John LaSalle, and our son . . ." Her husband was tall and skinny, too skinny if you asked her, and so dark he looked foreign. He had those sleepy-looking heavy eyes. She wondered why a girl smart enough to graduate from medical school would pick a hick like this.

"Ho-ho!" Jack cried. "My son-in-law's ponytail is gone. Let me tell you, the first time Marilyn brought him home, I said to myself, 'What is this guy, a Red Indian?' I swear, hair down to here . . ."

John LaSalle smiled benignly upon his father-in-law and said,

"Yeah, I guess it looked pretty strange to you. But your cigars looked pretty silly to *me!*" Dorothy looked at him with new respect. She had to be so quick to judge?

Out in the hall, there were shrieks and hoots from the kids. A minute later, everyone could see why. In came the whole gang of grandchildren, pushing in front of them a tall, bearded, heavyset, handsome young man.

"Will you look at this guy? Mom, look. Saul grew a thousand feet!"

"Grannie! Papa! Look at this beard! Look at these muscles!"

Saul grinned self-consciously. "Sisters!" he explained to the world at large. "Hi, Mom."

Deena, eyes brimming, was already on her feet and holding out her arms to him. "Look at me, " she said, "crying like an idiot. You'll be happy to know, Saul, that I'm not weeping at the way you look. You look *wonderful.* Judy, Zoe, stop that carrying on! He looks fantastic . . . yes, including the beard! Marilyn, you have created a monster."

"Not Dr. Strauss, but Dr. Frankenstein?"

The children all hooted at this and Noel put his arm around his aunt and said, "Hey, Moo, that was *funny.*"

This made everybody laugh like crazy, and Saul turned to the Gordons and said, "Old family joke."

Marilyn laughed. "My sisters have such mouths on them, I was thirty-two before I could get a word in edgeways. And then everyone stared at me and said, Hey, that was *funny*, like they couldn't get over it! They haven't got over it yet!"

More laughter. Then the three of them, Zoe and Judy and Noel, all together, said, "Hey, Moo, that was *funny!*"

Then there was a cry from Jack, so loud that the baby jumped in his father's arms, his lower lip beginning to quiver. What now? Dorothy thought, but when she turned, he was pointing at John LaSalle and they were both laughing, so it couldn't be anything serious.

"An earring!" Jack was saying. "What the hell are you doing with an *earring*? Isn't that supposed to mean you're gay or something?"

"Gay? John? Daddy, honestly!" Deena peered at John's ear dramatically and then burst into laughter. "John, show them."

Well, it was a tiny gold Jewish star. Dorothy didn't know what she thought of that.

"What kind of statement does that make, John?" That was Elaine.

"I've converted."

Well, after that, there was no other conversation for a while. Jack and Sylvia had to know all the details, of course. John and Marilyn were very calm about it and Dorothy had to agree with their attitude: what was the big fuss? It was a free country; people could believe whatever they wanted. She did cast an eye to her Jonah, who was apt to say exactly what he thought about organized religion. But for once, he was just listening.

And when she began to listen, too, she understood why. John had converted because of the *Havurah* in their town: people who had decided they didn't need a rabbi to lead them or a fancy temple; that they could gather in fellowship in one another's homes to pray and meditate and share a meal and their thoughts. It sounded a lot like the Coops. Not the prayer part, maybe, but the support, the closeness, the banding together for a common cause. And Jonah—he was so interested in every word, so absorbed in the conversation. It was wonderful; he'd forgotten his pain.

Just then, four waiters in white jackets came in carrying trays of such wonderful-looking hors d'oeuvres: caviar, sturgeon, smoked salmon, pâté, don't ask! And more glasses of champagne, or juice or liquor or anything you wanted. She couldn't help herself—every time one of the waiters came around, she took. She took for two, in fact, and gave to Jonah. And he actually ate with an appetite. That made her feel very good because lately, she wouldn't tell Cookie or Win, but lately he wasn't too interested in food. But who could resist these savory little tidbits?

"Don't fill yourselves up, folks," Jack announced. "This is only the first course. In the dining room is the *real* food."

Dorothy happened to be looking at Elaine and she caught the swift look she exchanged with Deena. She knew exactly what her niece Elaine was thinking. She'd never noticed before how much Jack was like Pa: taking over his daughter's house, his daughter's food . . . he thought he owned his children.

"This is enough food for us," Jonah said. Dot turned quickly. There was something in his voice. "*More* than enough," he continued. "With all the hungry people—never mind in the rest of the world—right outside the door, right out there on Central Park West, people are starving. We should all do without a meal a day to feed the hungry."

Marilyn, who had taken a seat across the room, swiveled to

listen to him, her face alert. And when he finished speaking, she got up and came over to them.

"You know, Uncle Jo, we actually do something like that in our little town. Once a week, our *Havurah* gets together with two local churches, for a simple supper of bread and soup. And we all contribute the money we would have spent on a normal dinner, to buy food for the poor. Not only that, but I've started an Urban Gleaning Program—"

"What's that?" Jonah was all ears. This was the kind of talk he thrived on. Who would have thought you'd hear this, coming from a daughter of Jack's?

"All the restaurants and resorts contribute all their leftover food. Nothing gets thrown out unless it's inedible, and nothing is wasted. John owns a ski resort, you know, and just our leftovers are enough to feed three families. It's very exciting. And let me tell you, as a doctor, it's a pleasure to see some of my patients eating properly for the first time in their lives."

"And from the tables of the rich, too!" Jonah chortled. "Marilyn, you're my kind of people."

He looked much more animated than he had in months! So many of their friends had turned away, afraid of his cancer. You'd think they could catch it just by saying it! One day in the supermarket, she saw Lil Lubliner, a friend since the old days, and Lil pretended to be picking out apples, when you could see she already had a big bag of them in her wagon. Another one who couldn't face it, couldn't deal with it!

Didn't these people realize now was the time Jonah needed his friends, more than ever? But as he failed, the visitors became fewer and fewer. Old friends! Close friends! And here was this young woman who had never even met them before, and she was terrific. Bless Marilyn. She was just what the doctor ordered, excuse the pun.

Again, she gave him that wonderful, unexpected sunny smile. "Uncle Jo," she said, and bent to put a kiss on his cheek, "I think this may be the beginning of a beautiful friendship."

Chapter Thirty-two

Sunday, September 20, 1987   One o'clock and all's well,
Sylvia thought, walking down the hall to the kitchen. So far.
Everyone in the living room was sitting around schmoozing,
picking at the remains of the appetizers. They were all waiting
for Paul and his family to show up before starting lunch. They
were awfully late, but as Dot just said, "When you drive on the
Long Island Expressway you have to start yesterday to get here
tomorrow."

So they'd wait! Nobody seemed to mind. Elaine and Deena
and Cookie had gone off together to Elaine's room, giggling
over something or other. Howard and Dave were deep in a conversation about whistle-blowing and personal responsibility and
President Reagan, sitting by themselves over in a corner.

As for Marilyn, she was so taken with Jo and Dot that she
hadn't even heard her own baby fussing. It was John who tended
to him, while Marilyn, leaning forward eagerly in her chair,
kept asking questions about the Spanish Civil War. So Jo was
an activist! So were a lot of people. What was the big attraction?
He hadn't accomplished anything so great in Spain; they still
lost. But that didn't stop him from going on and on about it—
fifty years later! Didn't he know most people could care less?

She knew that's why Jack had picked himself up and taken
baby Caleb for a stroll around the living room, to the big windows overlooking Central Park. He had had enough of Jo, and
anyway, Jack loved this baby. Well, they both did. They had
thought they were finished with babies. Who knew Marilyn
would go and get married at thirty-six . . . and then have a baby!
In my day, Sylvia thought, it was considered *scandalous* for a
woman to be pregnant at such an advanced age. But thank God,
not nowadays. Otherwise, they wouldn't have this adorable little
boy to squeeze and play with.

Jack had held him up at the window, kissing that rosy little
cheek over and over, and then he said, "See that park down
there, little man? I had that made for you." And he laughed. "I

told them: 'No buildings! Jack Strauss's grandson needs a lot of room to run and play.' ''

Sylvia, watching them, couldn't help smiling. It was exactly what he had always told Deena and Elaine when they were little girls. The same words, even! The same laugh, the same hugs and loud kisses. They had believed him. Why not? He was Daddy. Would Daddy lie?

She remembered well the day Elaine found out it was not really *her* park, but that it belonged to everyone. The tantrum! You wouldn't believe! She had almost killed Peggy, the little kindergarten friend who told her. God, it was all so long ago, so long ago! Sylvia's eyes misted over.

And that's when she got herself out of there. They could all sit around—*she'd* see what the caterers were doing in the kitchen. So it wasn't her house. Elaine wouldn't even think to check. You couldn't depend on hired help. No matter how good they were, if you wanted it to be perfect, you had to supervise. But no use trying to tell Elaine anything. She'd just roll her eyes and sigh.

As she walked down the hall, she could hear the chatter from the den, where all the kids were. Didn't sound like a football game; they must be just talking, catching up. It gave her a good feeling. Families should be in touch with each other. These past thirty years . . . well, that was a *shandah*. But thank God, it was over now and everything was fine. She stuck her head into the powder room to make sure there were enough guest towels. Further down the hall, she straightened out a picture on the wall. At least now, they could start moving ahead and forget those wasted years.

With her hand on the kitchen door, ready to push it open, she stopped. If everything was going so well, why did she have a strange little knot in the middle of her chest? On the *surface*, everything was fine. But somehow it didn't feel right . . . as if they were all pretending and even the smallest thing might burst the bubble. Never mind. She went into the kitchen.

Just as she thought: the waiters were all sitting around Elaine's kitchen table, smoking and eating Elaine's food. And they didn't even turn around when she walked in. She was about to give them a piece of her mind, when in came Elaine, full-speed ahead.

''I knew I'd find you in here, Sylvia.''

''Excuse me. I'm not allowed?''

''It's all right, you know. I *told* them to have their lunch now.''

"Did I say a word?"

Elaine did it again—rolled her eyes and looked disgusted. "Never mind that. Look at *this*."

The *this* was Irwin's photograph. "I saw it already."

To her shock, tears slid from Elaine's eyes and rolled down her cheeks. "Elaine, what's wrong?"

"All my life," Elaine said in a shaky voice, "Daddy's given me such a hard time about my weight. Eyeing my plate all the time, counting every mouthful, commenting on every piece of clothing!" She stopped, taking in a deep breath.

Sylvia gave a quick glance at the help but none of them seemed to have heard anything. "Just *look* at this picture, Syl. Look at Aunt Dot, look at my grandmother . . . They're built like me, both of them. *Just like me*."

"Yes, of course. There's a strong family resemblance."

"That means *he* knew it. And still, he ridiculed me!"

"Elaine, what's to cry about at this late date? You're a beautiful woman, with a wonderful husband who loves you and I'm sure has always been faithful, you have a handsome, smart son, you're rich, successful!"

Sylvia put a hand on Elaine's arm and this seemed to calm her. The ugly flush began to fade from her cheeks and she closed her eyes, obviously pulling herself together.

"Look, Elaine, darling," Sylvia pleaded, feeling rather desperate. What a time for a tantrum! "Put it out of your mind. You have guests. And don't mention this to your daddy, okay? Take my advice, Elaine, go into the bathroom, throw some cold water on your face, and fix your eyeliner. There's nothing like fresh makeup to make a girl feel like a new woman."

Elaine pulled away and squared her shoulders. "What you mean, Sylvia, is there's nothing like fresh makeup to hide a girl's pain from the world."

"And what's wrong with that?"

"Nothing, Sylvia. Nothing." She turned and walked back out.

A minute later, Sylvia left, too. She'd better make sure those two guys weren't wrangling again.

Well! Talk about surprise! While she'd been in the kitchen, a young couple had arrived. He was tall and slim, with a head of auburn hair, like his grandfather's used to be. Cookie's Jonathan, without a doubt. And *she*! She was tall and slim, with very dark skin, dressed in a white jumpsuit. Oh, she was stunning! But very black, very definitely black.

Sylvia was as liberal as the next person, but it was something of a shock to suddenly be confronted in your daughter's living room with a black guest. But nobody would ever know, not from *her*! And with a warm smile and an outstretched hand, she went to greet the two young people and welcome them to her daughter's home.

Oy, Dorothy thought, as she watched her sister-in-law come in, Sylvia's in shock! Didn't anyone tell her about Sonora? But give credit where credit is due, she thought. The look was gone in three seconds and she greeted Jon and Sonora just as if she wasn't shocked.

Jack hadn't carried it off nearly so well. He'd hardly been able to mumble "hello" and had immediately turned back and pretended to join in Jonah's conversation with Marilyn and her husband. Too bad for him; his loss. Sonora was lovely, very smart, very talented, an architecture student. What kind of a threat was brown skin? Could it kill you? Was it catching? Shame on him!

As soon as Jack saw Sylvia, he brightened up. "Sylvia, darling! Come in and rescue me! These people are talking Commie talk. They're going to start a revolution on Central Park West!" Poor Jack, Dot thought, he was really out of his element.

They all laughed, even Jo. But she could tell he was bristling. "You know what's wrong with you, Strauss? You're stuck in the Dark Ages. You haven't changed any of your outmoded ideas. Not even after McCarthy? Nixon? After *Reagan*, for God's sake?"

Marilyn laughed. "Daddy, change an idea? Don't be silly. One thing about Daddy that will never change is that he'll never change."

From the doorway, where she stood with Cookie and Elaine, came Deena's voice: "Hey, Moo. That was funny."

"Funny, maybe. But not very nice," Jack complained.

"Let me tell you something, Marilyn," Jonah said, ignoring his brother-in-law. "Back then—when I was a boy, so you can imagine how long ago *that* was—people were going hungry, people were jobless, homeless, hopeless. The Capitalist system had failed—hold on, Strauss. That happens to be a fact." He gestured to the doorway. "Ask Dot. She could tell you. Hell, ask Cookie!"

Cookie held her hands up. "She could, but she won't. She's staying right out of *this* discussion." And she walked away.

Jonah waved her off, saying, "Go, then. Some daughter!"

He turned back to Marilyn. "Like I was saying, the Capitalist system had failed, and the Great Depression just proved it. Even *you* have to admit that, Jack.

"And Marilyn, when poor people needed help, not just fancy phrases, but real action, the only ones who stood up for them, organized them, marched with them, and got them what they deserved—be it a meal, heat, medical attention, rent relief—the *only ones*, Marilyn, were the Communists. You're surprised! You were brought up to believe that Commies are the enemy, that they want to take over the world!

"But all we ever wanted was a fair shake for everyone, black or white—or any other color for that matter. All we ever wanted was a new kind of society where there wouldn't be haves and have-nots. It was a beautiful idea. And, believe me, Marilyn, back in the old days, millions of people—people like you and me—joined the Party. You have to understand how it was, then. There was no other alternative."

"Hah!" Jack said. "There was one other alternative I can think of. You went out and got yourself a job, any job!" He smiled, very pleased with himself, and sat back in his chair as if to say, And that ends the discussion, period, *fartig*, finished.

Jo gave him a tight smile. "Sure. If you happened to have a father-in-law who had a business and took you in—that also was a good alternative, isn't that right?"

"What are you trying to say? That I didn't work hard? I worked plenty hard, believe me!"

Sylvia quickly went to him, soothing him, giving him a warning look. "Let it go, Jack. We all know how hard you worked."

A clatter came from the hallway, mixed with voices overlapping and a lot of laughter. They came tumbling into the room—Saul, Mickey, Noel, Judy, and Zoe—elbowing each other out of the way, having such a good time. Both Sylvia and Dorothy smiled at them, with an identical look of indulgent love, and then caught each other at it and winked.

"Mom, you'll never guess!" Michelle cried.

From across the room, Cookie looked up from a photo album and said, "I'll never guess what?" Hooray, she thought, Michelle was treating her like a human being again. No more sulks.

"Noel's a fabulous bridge player! And he's been teaching me and it's *such* a fascinating game! How come you never played bridge?"

Cookie couldn't help but notice the high color on her daughter's cheekbones, the sparkle in her eyes. She also couldn't help noticing that Noel was giving her the eye. Mickey hadn't been this excited—about anything—in a very long time; and she was pretty sure it wasn't all about bridge, either.

She never got a chance to answer Mickey's question because Pop got there first. "Bridge!" he said with obvious disdain. "A card game! A waste of time, a meaningless activity!"

"Grandpa, don't be so arbitrary. Not every minute has to be spent on the barricades. Bridge isn't a dumb card game. It's challenging and takes a great deal of intelligence."

Marilyn spoke up. "Oh, I don't know. When I was in college, I knew some pretty dumb girls who were marvelous bridge players . . . excuse me, Noel."

"It's okay, Moo," Noel said with a charming smile. "I know I'm not a dumb girl."

Cookie eyed him. He certainly was an attractive young man . . . and actually only a second cousin to Mickey. And then she said to herself, You yenta! What are you thinking of? Mickey just met him today and she's obviously charmed and why not? And you, you typical Jewish mother, are already thinking marriage. Don't be a jerk!

Mickey continued to battle Jonah. "That's beside the point. My grandfather thinks that if you're not committed to changing the world, you're not worth talking to. Well, there are other things besides politics, Grandpa. There's the life of the mind! There's creativity! There's excellence! And if you express yourself through painting or playing bridge or watching sunsets, who's to say it's not of value!" She stopped, her face pink with feeling, breathing a little hard.

"Excuse me!" Jonah said. "Did I ever say you shouldn't watch a sunset, Mickey?"

And before she could answer him, Marilyn said mildly, "Your grandfather's been telling me about his politics, Michelle. I find it all fascinating. I had no idea any of this American Communist movement existed! I'd never heard of the Coops before! I never knew about the Smith Act—"

"Wait," Jonah interjected. "I haven't got to McCarthy yet."

Jack rose up from his seat. "Oh, no, you don't! Not in my daughter's house! Come on Marilyn, stop egging him on . . . save the political discussions for another time and place, preferably when I'm in Palm Beach."

Cookie watched her father, wondering if he was going to rise to this juicy bait. He did open his mouth; she could guess he was about to make some crack about the idle rich. But instead, it was Mickey who spoke up.

"He'll tell you about McCarthy!" She stood very tall, her chin set stubbornly. "But will he tell you about Stalin?" She sent a defiant glare in her grandfather's direction.

"What—tell about Stalin? I'll tell her about Stalin! What's to tell? Everybody knows he was a monster!"

"Oh, Grandpa! You didn't always think so!"

"So? I could learn. In fact, Miss Wise Guy, I learned all about Stalin before you were born . . . and not from a book, either!"

"Come on, Grandpa. When I took Communist World in high school, we had a big argument."

"What I told you then—and I still say it today—is, just because Stalin was lousy, that doesn't make the whole Communist movement lousy. Just because the *man* was crazy, it doesn't discredit the ideas—"

"Sounds like old times around here!" Everyone turned to the sound of this new voice.

"Paul!" Cookie cried, jumping to her feet. "How'd you get in? We didn't even hear the bell!"

They were coming into the living room smiling, Paul and Steffie—and right behind them, their three girls, all slicked up for the occasion. Steffie, as usual, was perfectly turned out, in a silk outfit that probably cost a week's wages. Paul grinned unself-consciously at everyone in the room, expecting everyone to love him, which everyone always did. It struck Cookie suddenly that they looked as if they belonged to Uncle Jack's side, not theirs. Especially in this setting. They looked exactly right in this setting, like they belonged here.

Paul walked further in, totally at ease. "How'd we get in? Magic! How else?" He turned. "Uncle Jack! Aunt Sylvia! What a pleasure! After all these years, how nice to see you again! I've never forgotten the wonderful chocolate cake we always had at your house. I hope you brought some today. . . ?"

Sylvia was enchanted by him, that was obvious. "This is a catered affair, I'm afraid. But don't worry, Paul. You'll come to my house and I'll make it for you. And this lovely lady must be your wife."

Cookie looked on with great interest. Uncle Jack and Aunt Sylvia were very taken with Paul and his family. And why not? To the casual observer, they were a picture-book family. She watched Paul bend a bit to give Jack his best manly handshake, doing his usual adoring-husband routine, holding Steffie around the waist and giving her tender looks; and she wondered idly what Uncle Jack would say if she told him the truth.

Of course, she wouldn't. She put an arm around each of her cousins and said, "These lovely ladies are Elaine and Deena." As she watched, Paul turned, his arm still around Steffie, and stood gaping at Deena, thunderstruck. Cookie couldn't believe that everyone else didn't notice. She began to chatter nervously about Elaine's business and Deena's plays and Steffie's interior decorating and God knows what-all, anything to fill up the void as Paul struggled to regain his equilibrium.

And then the moment passed. She couldn't have said for sure how long it had lasted, but their eyes unlocked and now they were shaking hands and acting like normal people. But Cookie knew. She knew it had really happened. And Steffie? She slid a glance in her sister-in-law's direction, but she seemed just the same as always: smiling, gracious, ready with social chitchat on any subject.

Nevertheless, Cookie kept an eye on her brother—while the wine was being poured, all during lunch, and even later, when they all came back to the living room for demitasse and liqueurs, half-listening to a Pete Seeger album Noel had dug up from somewhere in his room. She noted, for the millionth time, that Deena and Paul couldn't seem to keep their eyes away from each other, the way they managed to give each other information—ostensibly talking to others but really giving each other messages. And they had managed to sit down next to each other on one of the big couches.

Paul was leaning forward, supposedly telling his uncle Jack about the closet business, being funny and charming and saying, "Call me Mr. Hanger," with never a glance in Deena's direction. But he couldn't fool his sister. He was showing off. She knew who was supposed to be impressed—and it wasn't Uncle Jack.

It was perhaps half an hour later when Jack stretched and stood up and announced that it was time to take pictures of the grandchildren. Win had just come back up from taking pictures in Central Park—just in time to have his uncle Jack press him into service. "Aha! the right man for the job!"

"For what job?"

"Pictures, of course. What's a family gathering without pictures?"

And Dorothy added, "You don't remember you've had a family gathering, unless you have pictures of it. At my age at least."

"Exactly!" Jack agreed. "So, come, Irwin. Here's my camera . . . What're you shaking your head? You don't like my camera? It's only a Minolta Maxxum 9000, the very best, but all right. You don't want to use my camera? So, take yours. I'm sure it's a good one."

Win kept shaking his head. "I don't take . . . snapshots," he said brusquely. "I'm sorry. I'm a professional. If you had a friend who was a doctor, would you bother him at a party for a quick appendectomy?" He gave a huge shrug and a little laugh. "Same thing!"

"Irwin, you can't make an exception for your uncle . . . on such an occasion?" Dorothy's voice tried to be sweet but failed.

"Leave the boy alone," Jonah said. "He's talking professionalism."

"You call it professionalism . . . I call it *nudnikism.*"

They all went down the hall then, including the Minolta 9000, off to take pictures of their grandchildren. And that left the middle generation gathered in the living room: Marilyn and John squeezed into the big chair next to the baby's car bed; Deena, Paul, and Steffie on one couch; Howard and Dave on the other; and Win sprawled on the floor, as usual, with his long legs stretched out under the huge coffee table. Cookie stationed herself on the arm of another chair where she could see everyone.

"What was the name of that little town you all grew up in?" Deena asked.

"Millville," Cookie said.

"Millville," Deena echoed. "How quaint."

Cookie and Win and Paul all laughed. "Quaint it ain't!" Win said.

"When I think of Millville," Paul said, "I get cold. I see the river, frozen over. I see snow. Lots and lots of snow. My feet were always cold."

"Well, you never would wear your galoshes," Cookie said. "Stef, does he wear them now?"

"Are you kidding? He won't carry an umbrella no matter how hard it's raining. He won't wear a hat in the coldest weather. That's my Paul."

"Better you had cold feet," Paul said with a laugh, "than to be caught by the big kids wearing *galoshes.* They'd make your life miserable. They'd call you a mama's boy till August fifteenth."

"Well, there was *snow* till August thirteenth," Win said, and the three of them laughed.

"Come on, no tall tales. What was it really like?"

"What tall tales?" Paul was enjoying himself immensely. "Sometimes you had to make tunnels through the snowdrifts to get to school."

Deena clasped her hands together and said, "Like a village on a Christmas card. Icicles hanging from the roof, drifts of snow, kids ice-skating . . . I've lived in New York City my whole life—I even went to college in New York . . ."

"God, I'd almost forgotten the snow we had. We always had sleds—some of the kids even had toboggans—and, oh, God, the snow forts and the snowball fights—"

"Yeah," Win put in. "And all the Irish kids put rocks in their snowballs. Remember that?"

Dave laughed. "Sounds like the Bronx."

"The Bronx was heaven," Win said. "Millville? It was the armpit of the world; probably still is."

"That whole time in Millville," Cookie explained, "we had to live a lie. I could never admit what I really believed or what I really thought, not to anyone outside the family. And I could never admit to my parents how lonely and frightened that made me."

"Why not?"

"Why not?" She paused a moment. "It wouldn't have made any difference. I knew they would never have understood my pain."

Paul looked at her with some surprise. "Pain? I don't remember any pain. Early on, I learned to stay away from that political garbage. I could see where *that* got you: exactly nowhere. Pop was totally political— Do you ever remember him talking about any subject without bringing his politics into it? And was he a happy man? No, he was not!"

"He changed in Millville," Win said.

"Well, I can't remember him before Millville," Paul swiftly answered. "What *I* remember is how he always talked about the Soviet Union as if it were a dreamland come true, how his friends in the Coops had made the trip and had come back talking about everyone smiling and hugging them and kissing them and giving them flowers, love everywhere. Those were my bedtime stories. When I say Soviet Union, I can see the tan wallpaper on my bedroom walls, the ruffled curtain at the window.'' Paul stopped talking for a moment. Nobody moved or spoke.

"The day Khrushchev made his speech—when he exposed the horrors of the Stalin era: the purges, the gulags, the executions—I walked into the kitchen and found my father sitting there, not speaking, not moving, not making a sound, just tears pouring endlessly down his face. I went up to him, I was scared to death, and I said, 'Papa, what is it?' I thought—I didn't know what to think. I'd never seen him like that, never. He was the strongest man in the world to me. But I was too scared to leave, so I climbed into a chair and waited.

"And after I don't know how long, he finally spoke to me. 'Just like the Tzar. So nothing changed. Nothing. It was all a lie.' He never looked at me. He may not even have known I was there."

Again, Paul stopped talking. Everyone in the room was silent. Then he shook himself and gave a little laugh. "Sorry. I didn't mean to go on and on. I just wasn't used to him showing any kind of emotion, I guess. I remember him always buried in the newspaper, hardly speaking a word, or with his chair pulled up in front of the radio staring at the wall, always listening to the news . . . not the kind of guy to come out and throw a ball with you, not the kind of guy to show up at a game to cheer you on, either. Even if you were the star quarterback, written up in the *Millville Gazette*."

"Be fair, Paul." Cookie leaned forward. "Pop wasn't the kind of guy to throw footballs around at the best of times. And Millville was far from the best of times for him. He was wretched and depressed. That's why you remember him so silent."

"So, like I said, politics didn't look so great to me. I wanted to have *fun*."

"Yeah," Win said. "It was easy for you. You were always outgoing and athletic and you didn't look Jewish so they left you alone. But me, with this *punim*, that was a different story. They gave *me* a bloody nose . . . every goddamn Easter Monday! 'Christ-Killer!' They'd chase me down the street, screaming at me. 'Dirty Jew!' " Win's voice began to shake.

"Win, for God's sake, why didn't you ever tell anyone? Why didn't you tell *me*. I had no idea—"

Win held up a hand. "Cookie, Cookie. Don't get so emotional. It was a long time ago."

Deena stood up and said brightly, "I know what let's do!

Let's all have a drink. Maybe now isn't a good time to talk about the bad old days.''

"I'll drink to that!'' Paul said.

His laugh sounded forced to Cookie. She looked at Deena and Paul looking at each other. And then she saw that Steffie had reached out and was holding her husband's hand—and her blood began to boil. It was time she and Deena had a little chat.

"I'll go with you to get the wine,'' Cookie said cheerily, and Deena gave her a big warm smile, as if nothing at all were going on. What a phoney! So she was waiting for the great love of her life to magically appear? Okay! But if Cookie had anything to say about it, it wasn't going to be Paul Gordon!

<hr />

Chapter Thirty-three

Sunday, September 20, 1987   "Bad old days . . . that says it, all right. No matter how hard I tried to make it good for them!'' Dorothy's voice shook a little.

Sylvia put an arm around her shoulder and pulled her gently away from the living room entrance. Dot should have minded her own business. Your children's memories should be private, that's how *she* felt.

"So they didn't like it up there. It was no bed of roses for you, either. You did what you had to do . . . what any good woman would have done. You followed your man wherever he had to go.''

"Ah, that's the question. *Did* he have to go?''

"What do you mean?''

"I mean, why he felt he had to take us to that horrible place!'' She hid her eyes with one hand.

"Dot, Dot. Don't torture yourself. What's the use? It's all so long ago.''

"I never knew. Isn't that awful, Sylvia? I was their mother and I never realized how bad it was. Oh, yes, I knew they felt a little left out, that it was hard for them to hide what we believed in, that our family life left something to be desired.''

"You made the best of it. Come. We'll get a cup of tea, you'll relax, you'll feel better."

Dorothy gave her a tremulous smile, but this time she began to walk down the hall with her. "They picked on Irwin. And so did I . . . You want to know something, Sylvia? I never liked him."

"Bite your tongue! Of course, you liked him. He's your child."

Dorothy shook her head. "You can have a child you never really like. I *love* him. Of course. How do you not love your own child? But he's *always* irritated me, right from the very beginning. I know that doesn't excuse me. I should have protected him."

"If he didn't tell you, how could you know? You're not a mind reader!"

"I should have asked questions." She paused. "Whenever he came home with a bloody nose, I figured he asked for it. Shame on me!" Again she hid her face in her hands, weeping.

"Oy, Dorothy, don't cry. Take my advice—don't think about it anymore. Oh, I know, it's easier said than done. But come on, try. There's hot coffee and tea in the dining room. Let's go have a nice little schmooze like we used to. Wait."

There, at the other end of the dining room by the windows, were Cookie and Deena, talking so intently they were completely unaware of anything else.

"Doesn't that bring back memories?" Sylvia said in a whisper. "Come on, let's not disturb them. They're having such a nice talk."

As they continued down the hall, she reminisced. "Remember how they used to go behind my brocade drapes with a box of cookies and make themselves a little apartment and tell secrets and write letters to us?"

"Of course, I remember." Dot was smiling as she recited: " 'Dear Sylvia, I hate it when there aren't any Mallomars—' " Dorothy paused and laughed. "Mallomars . . . *that*, she could spell!"

As she and Cookie stood near the window in the dining room, Deena had a sudden memory: sharp, vivid, complete down to the chocolate smell. "Remember, how we used to run away with Mallomars and play our-own-house behind the drapes in my dining room? We were so sure nobody could see us, that we were invisible behind the drapes.'' She giggled. ''Of course, we forgot about our feet.''

She was feeling so good. First of all, it was so good that the reunion was working out. The kids, especially. They were acting as if they were old friends. And Daddy and Sylvia and Jonah and Dot were really enjoying one another—even the little fights and digs were part of it all. And, of course, Cookie, with whom she felt so close. For the first time since her divorce, she didn't feel all alone.

And she was falling in love—correction, she had already fallen in love—and it was the most fantastic floating feeling, like having your veins filled with champagne! The second best thing about it was keeping it a secret, hugging it to your heart, not sharing it with *anyone*.

''Your feet, my dear Deena, are still showing,'' Cookie said. She was unsmiling, even a bit grim.

''I beg your pardon?''

''You and Paul. Do you think nobody noticed? It's so obvious! Look. This is very difficult for me. I've been so happy to get to know you again and to have this reunion finally take place. But, really, you can't start up with my brother, you can't! Deena, he's a married man.''

How could Cookie have seen anything? There was nothing to see. He hadn't touched her. All they had done was look at each other a little, smile at each other a little. And he had leaned over to get a napkin at lunch, and he'd murmured, ''Nice perfume,'' very low in her ear and her heart had nearly stopped. But nobody had heard him, and if they did, so what? All he did was comment on her perfume.

''You're crazy,'' she said to Cookie. She didn't owe Cookie any kind of explanation. Nothing was going to come of it. Yes, she had been immediately attracted to him. She'd been trying to figure out a way she could talk to him alone. But still, she hadn't *done* anything. ''I'm not quote after him unquote.''

''Deena, give me a break, okay? I know what I see. Plus, I know my brother Paul. Deena, listen. I'm not accusing you of anything, really I'm not. But Paul . . . well, Paul's a flirt and it's not a good idea to take him seriously.''

Deena felt herself flush. Dammit. ''I've been known to do a bit of flirting myself.''

''Hey, what I saw today was different. Look, Deena, aside from everything else, Paul owes everything to Steffie. His wife—

the one sitting next to him, looking at him adoringly. Remember her? Well, she's been an angel, sticking by him through thick and thin. She loves him and believe me, he loves her. He'll never leave her.''

"Okay, I find him attractive—and I will admit he seems to find me attractive, as well. But probably nothing's going to happen so let's not fight. I don't want to fight with you. Let's get the wine and go back to the living room and forget all this, okay?''

"What do you mean, 'probably'? Probably's not good enough for me.''

She was panicked, but she mustn't show it. "Hey, Cookie, nobody asked you.''

Cookie took in a deep breath. "Listen to me. Please.'' She hesitated. "You wouldn't be the first.''

"What's *that* supposed to mean?''

Cookie shook her head, looking sad. "My brother Paul is a wonderful man in many ways, but he *is* a womanizer. Don't look at me like that, this is not easy for me. I'm only telling you because I don't want *either* of you hurt.''

"You're way out of line, Cookie. What I do—with *any* man— is none of your business!''

"Don't you *care*? For God's sake, Deena. What I'm telling you is that running after women has always been a game with Paul—that's all, just a game.

"But a few weeks ago, he called and told me that suddenly he saw what he was doing to his life. He told me he'd made many terrible mistakes, he was desperately sorry, he had come to see that Steffie and the girls are the most important thing in his life. He'd come so close to losing it all! He said he was finished fooling around.

"And now *you*. I can see how attracted he is. So *you* have to be the strong one. I'm asking . . . I'm begging you to leave him alone. Please. Promise me.''

Deena wanted to tell her to shut up and mind her own business. It wasn't up to her to protect Paul. He was a grown man. But she could see there was no talking to Cookie; she was too emotionally involved. Deena was going to have to calm her down and end this conversation, which wasn't doing either of them any good. She put a nice conciliatory look on her face, and took Cookie's hand.

"I'm sorry," she said. "I do appreciate your concern. I really do understand that you're only trying to help. You've become very dear to me and I certainly don't want to do anything that might jeopardize our relationship."

"I'm sorry, too." Cookie gave her a hug. "It's probably none of my damn business. But, hell, I care about you both."

"I know, I know," Deena murmured, thinking You're right, it's none of your damn business. And furthermore, if you think I'm just going to give up something so exciting and full of possibility, you're crazy. I'm going with it, whatever it is. And if I have to lie to you, so be it.

And then she said, with a smile, "Cookie, you want my promise? You got my promise."

The help was long gone and the kitchen was empty. Sylvia bustled about, filling the teakettle, turning on the gas, finding two cups that pleased her, making the tea, putting out a plate of cookies.

"This is like old times!" Dorothy played with a cookie, crumbling it into little bits.

Sylvia sat down across from her. "They were good times, weren't they? I remember when you moved up from Washington, I was so pleased. At last the kids could be close to one another!"

Dorothy smiled. "It was 1947," she said. "A long time ago . . . and yet, it seems like it all happened yesterday. Remember our Sundays together? The kids playing on the floor. The Sunday papers scattered all over the place. You and me in your kitchen over a cup of tea, just like this."

"Yes . . . and the men, arguing, always arguing."

They both sighed. Then Sylvia said, "Who knew they'd keep us apart for almost forty years?"

"*We* knew. We knew that sooner or later it would come to that. We were smart enough to realize that it was more than two men having friendly political arguments after dessert."

"You're right. We pretended. But in those days, didn't we all pretend, all the time? For the sake of the marriage, for the sake of the children—isn't that what we told ourselves?"

Dorothy looked down, licking her lips. After a moment, she said, "There's one thing I always thought wasn't pretending and that was our friendship."

"What do you mean, *thought*? Of course, it was real, it still is. Look at us, sitting here talking together just as if we'd seen each other only yesterday! Dorothy, listen. I loved you like a sister. Better, God should forgive me, than I ever loved Helen and Ruthie.''

"Then what happened? The last time I saw you, do you remember?" Sylvia nodded; of course, she remembered. "Just before the children and I left. You came to my place that time. I opened my heart to you and you—you turned your back on me. When I needed you the most!''

Sylvia couldn't look her in the eye. It was true. She stared at the floor, twisting the big diamond ring Jack had given her on their twenty-fifth, turning it around and around while she tried to get her jumbled thoughts into order. How much could she tell?

"Dorothy, you're right. I did not give you the comfort you deserved.'' She stopped. She could feel the tears piling up behind her eyes. She pulled in a deep breath and went on. "You know your brother—how he needs attention from women . . . how he loves to charm them . . . how he can't resist flirting with them . . .'' No, she couldn't do it, she couldn't.

There was a look of pity on Dot's face, and that, she couldn't bear. No, she couldn't do it, she couldn't. But she owed Dot something. "When you told me about your . . . situation . . .'' Another breath. "When you told me . . . that you had a lover . . .''

"Frank," Dorothy said.

"Yes. Frank. When you told me about him, I had just . . .'' No, she couldn't. "Look. Jack always had other women—" Dot looked stricken. "I'm sorry, Dorothy, but it's true.''

Dorothy said, "I was only thinking: how terrible for you.''

"At first. But I learned to live with it. He always came home to me, he always said he loved me, he loved his children. We had a good life.'' She cleared her throat.

"Well, you did the right thing. Because look, he's still here and that's all in the past. You and me, Syl, we're survivors.''

What to say? Her eyes kept filling. She hadn't thought of this in ages and it was harder than she had imagined. She willed her voice to stay steady, even as she looked at Dot through a blur of unshed tears. God, this was impossible. The years of keeping everything inside was a weight pressing in on her chest.

She held out her hand for silence and said, "Dorothy. Wait. That's not the whole story. I always figured, if you marry a handsome hunk like Jack, with women always after him, going along with it is the price you have to pay to keep him. In those days, weren't we taught they need, we don't? So when he ran around a little, I put up with it. But . . .'' She stared into the eyes across the table, the troubled, questioning eyes that looked just as young as ever. ''Dot. He has a son.''

Dot threw her hands up with a sharp cry, just as if she'd been struck. ''No!'' she said. ''Oh, no!''

''Now you know. The day I came to visit you, I had just found out.''

Again, Dot cried out. ''Oh, Sylvia, I'm so sorry! I didn't know. Why didn't you tell me? You could have told me!''

''I couldn't.''

''But—but he didn't *love* her, he couldn't have. He was always crazy about you!''

In spite of herself, Sylvia began to cry. ''Jack Strauss wanted a son more than he wanted anything. And when she gave him a son, there was no getting rid of her, ever!

''You don't know what it was like. He didn't send her away. He kept her as his personal secretary and when the boy grew up, he took *him* into the business.''

Dot made soothing noises, but Sylvia waved her down. ''All right. I made up my mind to hold my head high, no one should know. But that day when you told me, it was still raw—and every word out of your mouth pierced my heart like a knife. Dorothy, you shouldn't know from it . . . It was the worst thing I've ever lived through, seeing that baby for the first time, worse even than my miscarriage!''

''If you'd only told me! Sylvia! I would've talked to him, I would have made him do the right thing!''

''Dorothy. You don't remember how, in your eyes, Jack Strauss could do no wrong? I couldn't tell you anything bad about him.''

There was a long silence. Finally, her head turned to look out the window, Dot said, ''I'm sorry. Jack was more than just a brother to me, he was more like a father. I owed him. No one will ever know how much I owed him. Now I see I was *too* loyal to him, much too loyal. You have no idea. Oh, my God, what did I do to everyone, me with my so-called loyalty?''

Sylvia was alarmed. What was she talking about? *What* had she done to everyone, that she should look so anguished? She opened her mouth to ask just as the kitchen door was flung open, slamming against the wall, and in they walked. It was Jack, of course—who else opened doors that way? And Jonah with him.

''So *here's* where you disappeared to!'' Jack started, and then frowned. "What's the trouble, here? You both look like you lost your best friend."

"It's nothing," Sylvia lied. "What are you doing away from the football? Is the game over?"

"Too much noise from the kids," Jack said, and at the same time, Jonah said, "Football! Who cares about a senseless game where grown men knock one another down?" And Jack said, "At least on that, we can agree. How's that?"

"How's that?" Sylvia said with some asperity. "That's a miracle." She was being sarcastic, but they just found it very funny. "As long as you're here," she added, "I suppose you won't turn down the offer of a cold drink."

Their answer was to each pull back a chair and sit down. She shook her head at them. They were sitting there, both of them, waiting for her to wait on them! So what else was new? She got up and went to the fridge.

While she got the glasses of iced tea ready, those two guys kibitzed without mercy. Not too much ice, two slices of lemon, isn't there any Sweet 'n Low? where's the rest of the *ruggaleh*? so what's taking you so long? She wasn't afraid to answer them back, and there was a lot of good-natured laughter.

But not from Dot, she realized as she brought the two glasses to the table. Dot sat very quiet, very silent, very serious. She hadn't pulled herself out of her mood, not at all. It was worrisome.

"At last, my iced tea. What took you so long?" Jack joked.

And Jonah said, "Maybe you'd like my cane, Sylvia? I don't use it, but Dorothy insists I take it everywhere. So I take it. But I don't use it."

Sylvia sat herself, still with her eyes on Dot. "Keep your cane. A skateboard is what *I* want!"

And then, out of the blue, Dorothy said, "We've been talking about the past. All those memories—" She stopped and sighed.

Jack quickly finished her thought. "All those wonderful memories. When we were all young and our children were just kids. All day long, I've been looking at them, all grown up, their kids nearly grown up . . . And here's my Marilyn with a brand-new baby boy. At lunch, I looked around . . . I'm telling you, my heart was full. Reminded me of all those wonderful Passovers and Hanukkahs and Thanksgivings. I can't tell you, the way it makes me feel. If only Ma and Pa could be here, to

see it all, to see us back together again, three generations . . .
a beautiful thing. I wish they both could have lived to see this
day. They would be filled with joy!'' He beamed.

"Jack Strauss, what in God's name are you talking about?''
Dorothy was sitting straight up in her chair, her eyes wide open,
staring at him in disbelief. "As you damn well know, Pa would
be just as he always was: angry. He was never satisfied, not one
day in his life. As for Ma, she'd be wringing her hands, *kvetching* about everything.

"Stop making up fairy tales! The Passovers and Hanukkahs
and Thanksgivings *I* remember were not so terrific. In fact, I
remember one particular Passover when you and Jonah fought
so bitterly over Israel that the kids all began to cry. You don't
remember that everyone left the table—who could have an appetite, with *that* going on? And then you wouldn't speak to me
for a week and told Sylvia she shouldn't, either. There was
always something . . . always something!

"You men with your orders! I sit here and listen to you telling
Sylvia how to put an ice cube in a glass! Always giving orders
to us! 'Don't talk to this one. Don't be friends with that one.
Believe this, don't believe that.' Your laws and your rules all for
your benefit, and to hell with the rest of us! Even your classless
society, Jo—the women and the children are second-class. You
get to call the shots, we get to obey.

"*Both* of you! You've never stopped trying to push me around
and make me behave! Your constant arguing and carrying on!
Ever since I first met Jo, I've been torn into pieces by the two
of you!

"No wonder it was finally just too much for me! I'm sitting
here and I'm feeling so guilty! And you, Jack. You come in here
and start with your stories. I can't take it. I just can't stand it
one more minute!''

"Dorothy, you're not making any sense,'' Jonah said. As for
Jack, he sat there with his mouth open, with nothing at all to
say, for a change.

"Dorothy, listen,'' Sylvia said. "You know Jack—he likes to
remember only the good. Don't we all?''

But Dot only looked more frantic. "You, too, Sylvia? Are
you all determined to rewrite history, so that everything comes
out good? Do you think that hiding the truth makes it disappear?
It doesn't. When you hide the truth, any truth, it stays there,
and festers, like a terrible boil!''

"For God's sake, Dorothy!'' Jonah said with a frown. "This

is no time for self-indulgence. What's past is past, what's done is done. Isn't that why we're here today?''

"I'm not talking just to hear myself talk, dammit! So *listen* to me! I did a terrible thing! I convinced myself it was for the best, but I was wrong! It hurt all of us!''

He reached over to her and took her hand. "You never did a terrible thing in your whole life,'' he said.

"Oh, really? Well, listen to me, Jo. I'm to blame for everything, the whole mess.''

"What are you talking about?''

"The night you came home, after you quit your job. Remember? You threatened to turn Jack in, you said they'd put him in jail. I ran out of the house. I walked and I walked and my head was spinning. What to do? It wasn't an easy decision, believe me. I didn't want to hurt you, Jo, but, you know, it wasn't only Jack you'd be hurting, it was his whole family! How could I let that happen, when it was in my power to prevent it? My *brother* . . . So I went into the candy store and I called Jack and I warned him.''

Jonah's face reddened. "The same old story! No loyalty to me!''

"Don't start with her, Jonah!'' Jack pounded the table with a fist. "I deserved her loyalty. At least I always protected and took care of her . . . which is more than I can say about certain other people, not mentioning any names!'' They glared at each other. "And furthermore, if a building inspector had come after me with an 'anonymous tip,' you think I'd need a phone call from Dorothy to clue me in? You would have been the first person I suspected!''

"It's always haunted me! I've always felt that none of this would have happened if I hadn't made that call.''

"Well, that's crazy, Dot.'' Sylvia stood up. "Seems to me your call made no difference whatsoever. Didn't you tell me the FBI was always around, always after you? So what was the big deal about your phone call?''

"Right after I called Jack, they began to come upstairs, knocking on the door. He must have called the FBI.''

"Well, for your information, lady, I didn't. And for *your* information,'' pointing a finger at Jonah, "I never used faulty material, either!''

A sound from the doorway brought all four heads around. They were standing there: Paul, Marilyn, Deena, Cookie, and

Steffie. When did *they* appear? Dot wondered. How much had they heard? Let them hear it all!

"The two of you!" Jack went on, his voice rising. "I can't believe what I'm hearing—that you would think for one minute I would have done anything. I was angry—with reason—but a fink, I'm not, and never have been!

"All I did was fire you, Golodny, and for damn good reason. That's a crime, in this country? *You* were the criminal! *You* belonged to the Communist party! *You* were dedicated to the violent overthrow of our government! You were the traitor!"

"Daddy!" Deena cried. "Stop it!"

Jonah turned to Jack, his eyes blazing. "This whole reunion was a crazy idea! A whole day! When was I ever able to spend more than two minutes with this guy without wanting to puke?"

Cookie stepped forward. "You, too, Pop! You think Deena and I planned this just to hear you fight?"

But Jonah was not about to be stopped. "As a matter of fact," he went on, "I feel like puking, right now!"

Jack was on his feet, shaking a little. "You talk like that in my daughter's house? To me? Who do you think sent money all those years? Yes, that's right, up there to *Gurnischtville*, No-whereville!"

"I never wanted anything from you, Strauss. Tell me how much. I'll write you a check."

"Pop!" Two voices, Paul and Cookie both.

Now Jonah turned to Dot, his eyes narrowed, and his voice suspiciously mild. "You took his money? You never told me?"

"Lay off!" Jack shouted. "I was always there for her—even when you took her up there away from her family. And if it wasn't for me, your children wouldn't have had winter coats!"

"The hell you say!"

"Jack! Please!" That was Sylvia. "Enough already!"

"I'll say when it's enough!"

"It's more than enough, Jack. Let it go," said Dot. "I'm sorry I said anything. But I was so afraid Jack would let the cat out of the bag today, that he'd say something about my phone call . . ." Tears leaked out of Dorothy's eyes and she let them crawl down her cheeks. "And in the end, it was *me* who opened my big mouth!"

"That's it," Jonah announced, getting to his feet. "We're leaving. Come on, Dot. I knew this would never work!"

Cookie ran to him. "Wait, Pop! Don't leave! We're here to reconcile, not to fight! Look how nice it is for all the kids. And they're loving it! They want to be a whole family again. And, Pop, so do we!''

"That's right, Pop," Paul put in. "Don't leave this way."

"Daddy, say you're sorry . . . please say you're sorry."

Everyone began talking over everyone else, making such a tumult that the rest of them came into the kitchen to see what was going on. And through it all, Jonah: stubborn as ever, shaking his head no, no, no.

"Me? Say I'm sorry? Let him say *he's* sorry. He started it!" Jack said.

"You schmuck!" Jonah looked as if he might explode. He began to shake violently.

Suddenly, Marilyn was at his side, holding his arm and beginning to walk him out of the kitchen. "That's enough for one day," she said quietly.

A sudden and absolute silence fell, and it was through this unnatural quiet that Jonah and Marilyn started out of the kitchen. Cookie and Deena both looked stricken, Irwin and Paul looked blank, and Elaine was asking Sylvia what the hell happened. Everyone seemed stunned, uncertain of what to do next.

Dorothy looked at Sylvia, who stared back at her with sad, liquid eyes, but didn't make a move or speak.

From the doorway, Jonah said one word: "Dorothy." Dot looked to her brother. Jack met her eyes briefly, then folded his arms across his chest and deliberately looked away.

So she went. What else could she do?

❦❦❦❦❦❦❦❦❦❦❦❦❦❦❦❦❦❦❦❦❦❦❦❦❦❦❦❦❦❦❦❦❦❦❦

Chapter Thirty-four

Sunday, September 20, 1987   For a few minutes, it was a tableau: everyone standing or sitting precisely as they had been before Dot and Jonah left. Then Elaine gave a little grunt of exasperation and began to storm around her kitchen, throwing things into drawers, banging cupboard doors, shoving chairs back under the table. She picked up the big bowl of fruit, looked at it, and then slammed it back down onto the table.

The group standing in the doorway shifted as Howard came hurrying in, a worried frown between his eyes. "What's going on? We shoot some pool, Dave and Jon and me, and we come out to rejoin the group and we find Dorothy and Jonah on their way out. Nobody would say. What happened?"

"Daddy happened," Elaine said grimly. "What else?"

Jack snorted, glaring at his daughter who refused to acknowledge him. He turned and stormed out without another word.

"Jack!" Sylvia called to his departing back as he stomped away. "Where do you think you're going? Jack! At least let me get my pocketbook!" Her head turned to him, then back to Elaine, then back to where he was fast disappearing down the hall. "Elaine. I know he's not the easiest man in the world, but do you *have* to start up with him all the time?"

Deena shot her sister a look that would have killed if looks could kill, ran out, and they could hear her calling "Daddy! Wait!" as she trotted down the hall after him.

There was an uneasy silence for a moment. Then Elaine, in a very calm voice, said, "I knew this would happen. From the very beginning, I said to keep it simple, let the two of them meet somewhere, let them work it out. But my sister Deena had a fantasy of some kind of love feast. Forget reality! Forget objectivity! Agh!" She dismissed the whole thing with a downward chop of her hand that was an unintentional and exact imitation of her father. "It was a stupid idea," she finished.

"Then I'm stupid, too," Cookie said. "Because it was *my* idea, as much as it was Deena's. And there's no reason it shouldn't have been wonderful. After all, we're a family. Aren't we? Supposedly?" With the last words, her voice began to wobble.

Paul made a face. "Aw, come on, Cookie. What's the big deal? That's what families are for—so you have someone to fight with." He laughed.

"Baby brother, you better start realizing that people get hurt by what other people do."

"More Meaningful-Life talk! Do me a favor, Cookie! Don't tell me how to live!" He dropped his eyes and turned away, brushing by his wife, who was just coming in. She put out a hand to him, but he shook his head and hurried on; and a minute later, they all heard the sound of the bathroom door across the hall slamming shut.

"Ah, the bathroom," Howard said lightly. "Sanctuary." Everyone laughed, relieved to have the subject changed.

Win said, "Exactly! When we were kids, it was our hideout. Well, of course, it was . . . it was the only room in the house with a lock on the door."

"Which you used all the time—to read comic books!" Cookie said.

"I had to. They weren't allowed, remember?"

"Is that where Paul learned it?" Steffie put in. "I always thought it was so funny. Whenever he gets upset, he just goes right for the bathroom, locks himself in, and talks to himself in the mirror until he's calmed down."

"Oh, sure." Cookie was finally able to smile. "God, he's been doing *that* since he was six or seven."

Another ripple of subdued laughter, even though there was still tension in the air. "You know what we all need?" Howard said. "We all need to get into the living room where we can be more comfortable," and he smiled at the quick and positive response from everyone.

Deena closed the front door as her parents left, and she stood there, fighting off tears. But she was disappointed, terribly disappointed. Elaine would *never* let Deena forget this—this *debacle*, not as long as they lived. The anticipation of thirty or forty years of Elaine's condescending comments made her stomach hurt. It wasn't *her* fault those two old men couldn't let anything go, not even after all this time, not even for the sake of their supposedly beloved children and grandchildren.

The grandchildren . . . thank God they'd missed the whole thing. They were shut up in the den, totally engrossed. Even from here, she could hear their laughter, their excited voices. Even over their music which, as usual, was playing at the decibel level of a jackhammer. She smiled a little. At least their generation had had a genuine reunion.

God, Daddy was impossible, sometimes. He couldn't even give her a nice kiss good-bye. Sylvia had just rolled her eyes as if to say, You know *him*. Yes, she did know him and she loved him; but, really, did he always have to have the last word?

Oh, well. Deena drew in a deep breath, for the tenth time that day. Back into the breach, she supposed. Let's try to salvage what we can of this day. Time to rejoin the others in the kitchen.

But the kitchen was empty. Well, okay, she'd get herself a glass of wine and go find them. She went to Elaine's fancy new wine cooler and opened the door, peering in.

She didn't hear his footsteps, but suddenly she knew he was there, standing right behind her. Her heart began to thud. She did not turn around.

Very quietly, he said, "Keep on doing what you're doing. I have to talk fast. I want to see you."

Now her heart almost stopped, but she kept her voice neutral. "You want to see me? Well, here I am."

"Deena, don't do that. All I want to know is—am I making it up or is it real?"

Deena felt as if she were shaking all over. But when she looked at her own hand—the neatly manicured nails with their pale pink polish and the one chaste star sapphire ring—they were perfectly still. At this moment, with just a few words, she could change the course of her life. It was scary. But it was exciting. It made her feel alive. She should deny it, she should say You're making it up. But, even with her back turned, she could see him. She knew how he was looking at her; he'd been doing it all day; she knew his eyes were smoky with desire. There were waves of heat coming from his body; she could feel it. And he had a scent about him that made her weak at the knees. She stood very still. She had to or she would shatter into tiny pieces.

He was waiting. "It's real," she said.

He sucked in a deep shaky breath. He was smiling; she knew he was smiling. He lowered his voice further. It shook a little, and she shivered at the sound. "I'll call you," he said, and she wanted so badly to turn and say, Now. I want you *now*. She could hear the sound of both of them breathing.

"Oh, there you are, Paul, honey!" Deena nearly jumped out of her skin. She had forgotten anyone else existed in the world. Especially Steffie. Especially her. The slightly nasal, artificially bright, loud voice rasped her nerve endings. "Oh, hi, Deena."

Deena turned, a smile ready on her lips.

"Oh, wine! Terrific! I'm dying for a glass of wine!"

"Sure thing!" Deena heard herself echoing Steffie's chirpy tone. "I was just going to open this. Chardonnay okay? Good." And she turned back, busying herself, opening the bottle, taking down glasses from the wooden rack overhead, acting as if this were just any ordinary moment in her life. How easily Paul turned to his wife, smiled easily at her, and easily said, "Hey, look at this, Steffie. Elaine has one of those Hammacher Schlemmer wine coolers we keep drooling over in the catalog. Come here and take a look at it. If you like it, I'll get you one."

How could she have forgotten he was married? It was obvious

that these two people with their heads close together, examining the cooler, their bodies touching unself-consciously, shared a marriage, shared a history, shared a life. As she finished pouring and prepared to turn to them, she decided she wouldn't see him. She couldn't compete with all of that.

She put a pleasant, impersonal expression on her face, not quite looking at them. Steffie was touring the kitchen, chattering about the glass racks, the Garland range, the Zero King refrigerator, and, "oh, look, Paul, a built-in wok . . . and, oh, look, Paul, that nice white steel shelving, like they have in the deli . . . this is such a gorgeous kitchen . . . I wonder who did it?" On and on and on.

When Deena finally allowed herself to look at Paul, he wasn't paying his wife the least bit of attention. He lounged against the counter across the room, his eyes fixed on Deena. And that look on his face! She stood absolutely still, feeling like a butterfly that has been impaled. He didn't move, not a muscle, just held her gaze until she felt she was drowning.

Forget forgetting him! She had been waiting her whole life for something like this to happen to her.

As Steffie turned, Deena held out a filled glass and smiled right into her eyes. "I'm so glad you could come today," she said. "Otherwise, I would never have met you."

Chapter Thirty-five

Saturday, October 24, 1987   Paul sat in his office, staring at the telephone on his desk. His hand went out to pick it up; he pulled it back. It went out again, and again he thought, No, how can I do it? Dammit all to hell! He was an executive, the president of a company. He ought to be able to make a simple decision and act on it.

Having had that thought, he reached out for the phone again—only this time, he did it. He dialed Deena's number. She'd gotten him to promise to see her tonight. A Saturday night! He couldn't do that! He couldn't even remember how she got him to say it.

Dammit. Damn *her*! She had to be so seductive, he couldn't resist. But he had to. No way could he leave Steffie on a Saturday night to go see another woman. Not even Deena.

Dammit! Just a couple of weeks ago, he'd been feeling so terrific, feeling so good because he'd really lucked out this time, with this lady. It was too bad he couldn't tell anybody about it, but these meetings had to be Top Secret. Not even his best friend Steve. They always had traded stories, but not this time. Not this lady.

He had come into the Heights on this particular Wednesday afternoon to meet her and they had strolled hand in hand down Monroe Place; the beautiful old brownstones with their little gardens in front; bluestone sidewalks; big old trees making dappled patterns on the pavement, their leaves just changing to red and gold. The whole scene just reeked of money and position.

He sneaked a little look at Deena, who was chatting easily as they strolled along. She was so cool and elegant. She took it all for granted. She'd always been a rich girl. And it showed. She was class!

When he glanced over, he caught her gazing at him; and she gave him that special smile. It always excited him, the way she smiled at him. He knew what it meant. That was her best bedroom smile. But in the meantime, she was talking about how she had to drop in at Simon the shoemaker and did he mind? And maybe they'd pick up a few things to nibble on at Moishe's bagel bakery, it was only down the block. And all the time, he knew damn well what was in her mind. Talking cool but thinking hot.

Christ! He still had to pinch himself. She was a class act, head to toe. He thought it every single time he saw her. Today, she was wearing slacks and a silk shirt and a snakeskin belt: the very latest, the very best. Her shoes he knew cost a hundred and fifty dollars, because Steffie had a pair just like them.

They went up her steps, kind of snuggling into each other, and as she unlocked the front door, she let herself lean into him. He could smell her perfume. It was sophisticated, just like everything about her. She opened the door and there was that big wide foyer, hung with paintings, a large statue of a nude woman standing by the entrance, surrounded by big trees in Chinese porcelain pots. He loved this house. It was class, too, like her, like her clothes, like her style. This is what he thought he was getting when he married Steffie. Stef came from a rich family—

she grew up in a big white house, with a big green lawn, and a big golden retriever. That's what he wanted, all of it. And when he got it, it was good. Steffie was good. She was a wonderful woman and made a beautiful home. But nothing like *this*.

This was . . . elegant. WASP elegant. *Understated*, that was the word. The Oriental rugs all antiques, and not necessarily in perfect condition. A little shabby: that's what people had when they were absolutely sure of themselves. The first time he walked in here and saw her furniture, how simple it was and how nothing really matched anything else, he realized how flashy his office was. And maybe his house, too. Steffie had very good taste, she always spent a lot of money on their home. But, next to Deena's, it looked cheap.

"Wait right here," she said.

"What do you mean?" But she wouldn't tell him, wouldn't take no for an answer, wouldn't let him kiss her. "Just wait," she said. "Have a little patience." So he sat himself down on the church pew in her hall, while she ran up the stairs, giggling.

A few minutes later, she was still giggling when she called down to him to come on up. She greeted him from behind the partly opened bedroom door, smiling that sexed-up smile. "Come on in," she said, and he had to inch his way in sideways, saying "Why are you hiding behind there?"

And then he saw. And he nearly dropped his teeth. She was dressed in what looked like all her jewelry. Period. Nothing else. Just smooth bare skin and millions of necklaces, bracelets, and glittering belts, wound around her arms and legs and breasts, and, oh, Christ, between her thighs! He was instantly ready. If she wanted him, she didn't have to ask twice! What a turn on! But when he reached out for her, she backed off, saying, "Uh-uh. All look-a, no touch-a. First, I undress you." And goddammit, she did. Took off all his clothes, slowly, folded them neatly, put them in a nice little pile next to the wall. When he was naked, she backed off, gave him the once-over, and laughed, so damn pleased with herself.

He lunged at her—well, who wouldn't?—but she pushed him away. "No, no, Paul, not yet. Now *you* undress *me*."

And that meant he had to find every fucking clasp, on every fucking piece of jewelry, when all he really wanted to be doing was fucking, period. And in the meantime, fumbling around with those tiny little safety catches, he had to keep touching her. As he lifted a gold chain from around one of her breasts, he brushed the nipple and it became erect. Well, of course, he went right for it, but she backed off, grinning at him, saying in a teasing tone of voice, "Not yet, Paul. I said undress me, and that means *everything*."

The last thing, a rope of pearls, just wouldn't come open. By this time, he was nearly crazy, and he had an erection that was going to explode. So he grabbed the necklace and he yanked. Pearls went flying all over the place and both of them began to laugh, and in a minute, they were all over each other . . . and then they fell onto the carpet together, still laughing, and they were still laughing when he pushed into her, into that delicious, warm, wet tightness.

Later, they lay together in the bed, Deena's head on his shoulder, perfectly at peace. Her eyes were closed and he thought she might be falling asleep. Usually, he fell right to sleep as soon as he came, but with her, he didn't have that luxury. He didn't have the time. He always waited a decent interval, of course, but he had to get up, get dressed, and get himself home before it got late.

He liked leaning against the piles of soft pillows, a quilt pulled up over them, looking past the foot of the bed to the fireplace. She actually had a fireplace in her bedroom! And another slightly worn Persian rug on the floor. And polished wood paneling and leather-bound books. The first time he came to see her, he said, "My God, it looks like a library from an English estate," and she laughed and said, "It *was* the library, when the house was first built. Nobody put bookshelves into bedrooms then. But it was always my favorite room in the house and as soon as Michael got out, I did what I always wanted to do."

This was the best room he'd ever been in. It was dark and cozy and . . . high class. Take the portrait of her, hanging on the other wall. It was a beautiful oil painting, huge, in an ornate gold frame. "Deena at twenty-one," she explained. "Daddy insisted."

"It's great," he said. "Why don't you hang it in the living room?"

"It was in the living room, while I was married. Michael insisted."

Something in her voice told him she found the idea of a big painting of herself hanging in the living room in poor taste. It made him wince, inside. His dream had always been to have a big house and a family portrait done in oils over the sofa in the living room. To him, that said the man of the house had made it. And he had one: him and Steffie and the girls. He had always been very proud of that painting. But the minute Deena wrinkled her nose at hers, he couldn't help but wonder whether his painting wasn't just a little ostentatious and nouveau riche.

He'd already stopped wearing his heavy gold ID bracelet and gold chain around his neck because Deena had said something. Oh, not about *his* jewelry . . . about some guy they passed on the street, who was really loaded down. "Sleazy Long Island," she muttered. "All that gold."

He gave a glance at the clock on the bedside table. Almost six! Christ, he was going to be so late! It was time to get a move on. She hated him to leave. Well, he wasn't crazy about it, either, but it had to be done. This was wonderful fun, but come on, he was a married man.

He bent and put a kiss on Deena's warm smooth shoulder. "You know what, babe? When I'm a little old man, I'll always remember this room."

Now her eyes opened. She pushed herself up on one elbow, and eyed him. "How about when you're a little old man, you nudge me in bed and tell me, 'I still remember that room.' "

Oh, no! Not her, too! They had such a good thing going. What the hell was she doing, trying to put the manacles on him! Christ, was she going to ruin this by getting emotional? And here he was, thinking she was so damn sophisticated! What the hell was he supposed to say to that?

Nothing, he figured. She shouldn't have said it, dammit. But she had said it, and now he was going to have to move fast to fix it without turning her off. So he kissed her and nuzzled her a little bit, rubbed her back and tucked the quilt around her like she was a little girl. And finally, he could feel all the tension just ease right out of her body and he breathed a secret sigh of relief, off the hook again.

But now he felt her trying to reel him in again. It was tempting, it was damned tempting. But he couldn't allow it. He hadn't expected this kind of excitement, not at his age! But demanding a Saturday night was crap! No woman was going to push Paul Gordon around. Her phone rang once, twice . . . Christ, she *had* to be home!

When the phone rang, Deena picked it up figuring it was one of her kids, and gaily sang out: "Talk to me!" But it was Paul. She smiled happily. Obviously, things were *really* changing. He usually didn't bother to call her when he was on his way over. Saturday night! Saturday night! Since she was eleven years old, she had known the special meaning of The Saturday Night Date. She had won a major victory.

She'd just finished laying out the costumes for their own private Halloween party. She would be a harem girl with a black bra and panties and a *lot* of chiffon scarves and tinkling jewelry. He, of course, would be her she**ik**. For him, she had a white caftan and the ropes and tassels from her old silk drapes. All week, she'd spent every spare moment finding exactly the right things. It was going to be so good. She'd piled every pillow from the living room onto her bed and she had even managed to rig up some Paisley sheets to make a tent. Down in the basement, she'd found one of those pierced tin lanterns from her Spanish provincial period, back when she was first married. Into it went a dim soft-pink lightbulb, and when she turned it on, it was absolutely perfect. Like sunset on the Arabian desert. She chortled happily to herself now.

But instead of saying something sexy to her, like he usually did, he just blurted out, "Deena, I can't do it. I can't see you tonight."

"Oh, Paul!" She wanted to *cry*!

"Look, I'm sorry. I really wanted to. I really was going to. I suddenly remembered this dance I have to go to . . ."

"Suddenly?" She was so angry. "You're really trying to tell me you didn't recall this dance until just this minute?"

"That's right." His voice had a hard edge all of sudden. Oh, really? He was going to be angry with *her*? "See, I was working with my accountant all day. You know how it is with accountants . . ."

"No, I don't."

He sighed. "Well, the way it is with accountants, Deena, is that they take a lot of time."

"You promised."

"Deena, please don't. I hate standing you up, honest."

"You're the one who said Saturday."

"I forgot, but there's always this big Halloween dance at the club. We go every year. The girls, too."

"You promised me." Dammit, he couldn't do this to her! Wasn't it bad enough she had to take his wife's leavings?

Now his voice sounded like steel. "I also promised my family, Deena."

She found herself crying. She didn't want to, dammit, but she couldn't seem to stop it. "Don't talk to me about your wife, Paul."

"I never lied to you. I never pretended. You knew from the very first that this was all we'd ever have."

"You've certainly said some very different things to me."

"In bed, Deena. Hey, don't play games with me, okay?"

"Please, Paul. I'm not playing games. But . . . it's so important to me. Can't you come over later, maybe?"

"No."

Well, two could play *that* game. "Okay, Paul. Whatever you say. But if you don't see me tonight, you're not going to see me ever again."

"Okay. That might just be the best idea—"

His voice was so grim, so distant. She found herself shaking. No, no. No! He mustn't be saying what he was saying! Frantic, she cut into his words, making her voice sound cheery and calm. "I didn't really mean that, Paul. It was just that I was so disappointed. I understand your situation. So we won't have this Saturday. That's okay. I can wait."

"Don't wait for me, Deena."

Her mouth went dry. "What do you mean?"

"You know what I mean. You've made it very clear to me tonight that this is not good for either of us."

"It's good for me . . . it's so good for me."

"All right, then, not for me. It's not good for me. This is the hardest thing I've ever done, but the time has come to say good-bye."

"No! Don't say that!" She could not get hold of a coherent thought.

"Deena, don't make it any harder. I've made up my mind. It's over. Good-bye, Deena." His voice faded at the end; she could barely catch the last word. And then there was a click and he was gone.

She sobbed with relief when the phone rang the moment she hung up.

"Oh, Paul—"

There was a strange silence on the other end and then an all too familiar voice, edged with ice, said, "Funny you should say his name since he's the reason I've been trying to get you for three days now."

Sylvia! Of all the damn times! And . . . *what* had she just said? Christ!

"How the hell did you find that out?"

"You talk to your mother like that?"

Deena took in a deep breath. In a much different tone, she repeated, "Sylvia, how did you find out?"

"Never mind how I found out. But as a matter of fact, Elaine saw the two of you together. At Top of the Sixes."

Deena almost groaned aloud. Oh God! The one time they had taken a chance and gone out! And it had been *her* idea . . . worse, she had insisted and pestered and nagged until he finally said okay, okay, they'd go have a drink in Manhattan . . . but it had to be a big place, with lots of tourists, so they could get lost in the crowd. Some lost!

"Sylvia, listen. I can't talk to you right now."

"Oh, yes, you can, Deena Berman—so you just keep still for a minute while I give you a piece of my mind. Deena, you're killing your father."

"Sylvia, give me a break. That line went out with Noel Coward. And my name is no longer Berman, in case you'd forgotten."

"There's nothing funny here, Deena. What you're doing is wrong . . . What you're doing is against nature. Are you listening?"

"Do I have a choice?"

"No. You're hurting other people and you'll end up hurting yourself most of all. Deena, give him up."

The words drove into her chest like a hurled knife and she doubled over sitting there on the edge of her bed. Give him up. He was gone! He was out of her life! She knew; she had heard that finality in his voice.

"I'm sorry I have to talk to you this way, Deena. Normally I wouldn't butt in—"

Deena began to laugh in spite of herself. She'd love to make this a tragedy, but it looked like her mother was going to turn it into farce.

"You're still my child. I don't care how old you are. Give him up, Deena. That's the only way. The man has a wife, he has three children, he has obligations. He'll only hurt you in the end."

"Sylvia, please, you don't understand. I love him."

"Love. Is that what they're calling it these days?"

"Ouch."

"Deena . . . I'm sorry . . ."

"Say no more, Sylvia. Okay."

"Okay?"

"Okay. I'll give him up."

She understood her mother's stunned silence. Sylvia would

suspect such an easy victory. So she crossed her fingers and said, "I've already done it. This very evening. It's over."

"Truly?"

"Absolutely. Scout's honor. Over. Done with. *Fartig*, finished."

Another pause. Then, in honeyed tones, "As long as you're being so sensible, maybe you'll do your daddy a favor and allow a certain gentleman to take you to the synagogue dinner dance in December."

"Which certain gentleman I used to be married to did you have in mind, exactly?"

"Deena, darling, you were happily married for so many years! Give him a chance!"

What the hell. "Okay, Sylvia. This time. I'll go to your dinner dance with Michael. But I don't promise to like it."

"All we ask is, give him a chance. He still wants you, Deena."

That didn't sound so bad. At least *somebody* wanted her! But as soon as she hung up, the tears started again. What a damned fool she was! She'd been so sure of him, so sure he was crazy about her, and then he'd been able to give her up so easily! Oh, God, it was unbearable! She had nobody, nobody at all. She was horribly, utterly alone!

<hr/>

Chapter Thirty-six

Friday, November 7, 1987   Cookie walked around the apartment, in the beautiful silence—no television yammering away, for a change—and reveled in her elation. Yes, *elation*: there was no other word for the lighthearted, light-headed fizziness that bubbled through her. She was alone, blessedly alone, and it felt so *good*.

She picked up today's *Times* and *Post* and *Daily News* from where Dave had scattered them next to the couch and put them in a neat pile on the coffee table. She picked up three dirty glasses and two empty soda cans, and brought them into the kitchen. She picked up two pairs of running shoes and his dumb-bells from the dining area. And then she went into the bathroom and put everything back into the medicine cabinet—where it damn well belonged, dammit!—and actually slid the mirrored door shut.

Dave had left, maybe an hour ago, to take Mom and Pop up to Vermont. They had been invited to Marilyn's for the weekend plus a couple extra days. Pop had been so excited. He was crazy about Marilyn—"The only sane member of that family," he called her. Dave was driving them, and he had more or less asked Cookie's permission to stay the entire five days. "Would you mind an awful lot?" he said.

"No, really, no, Dave. I'm so relieved to know you'll be with them, in case . . ." She couldn't say anymore and her eyes filled and he patted her hand.

Her eyes filled again, now, just recalling it. God! Best not to dwell on the awful inevitable. She wiped off the bathroom sink—he never did, never—and took a tissue to pick up all the black hairs. No matter how many times she asked him not to brush his hair over the sink, he did it. Now she looked around the bathroom with satisfaction. At last, it looked the way it should. And, what's more, for five days it was going to stay that way.

For five days, she was going to see what it felt like to live alone. She'd *never* been on her own, not really. From her father's house to her husband's, just like she was supposed to. Well, she tested herself, how do you feel about being all alone for five whole days? And the answer came instantly: What, are you *kidding*? It was going to be fabulous. She had a whole long list of things she was going to do for herself. Take a bubble bath—for hours, maybe. Eat whatever and whenever she felt like it . . . even in the middle of the night. Oh, and *wherever*, too, in case anyone wanted to know. She had taken three Dorothy Sayers books out of the library and she planned to read them all. She was going to be too busy to miss anyone.

Oh, hell. Who was she kidding? She was *glad* he'd gone with her parents, because if he hadn't, she might have sent him to the moon.

She was so damn mad at him! More than mad, she felt be-trayed. Two nights ago, she came home late from a meeting and she could tell, the minute she dragged herself into the bedroom and he looked up from the TV, that he was dying to tell her something.

"I've got something to tell you," he said. She was very proud of the fact that she did *not* say, Yes, I know. She just put an expectant look on her face, receptive but calm. Inside, her heart was going pitty-pat. He was actually going to confide in her, without her having to dig it out of him! So he had finally heard her!

"I've just spent the evening with Jon," he said proudly. "Four hours."

"Oh, wonderful, Dave! You mean—?"

"Yup. We made up."

She waited. And then realized that he was finished. She *was* going to have to dig and fish. "What happened? Did he call you?"

Again that proud look. "Nope. I called him. Ever since the reunion, I've been thinking about . . . you know, the trouble between us. I saw that two perfectly okay guys can get stuck in an attitude and then there's no way to fix it. So I decided . . . one of us had to give in and it was going to be me. You know how stubborn Jon can be."

Cookie stood there, torn and feeling foolish. She was glad and she was furious. Glad because she'd been agitating for a peace treaty for lo these many moons. Furious because, goddammit, she'd begged him and pleaded with him all this time! And he'd been going around for days—thinking about it and making up his mind what to do—and had made a date with Jonathan . . . and all without even the tiniest hint to her! Why was she always left out of the whole process? And even now, he begrudged her the details!

On, hell, what was wrong with her? He'd done something she'd been wanting. And instead of feeling good about it, here she was, pacing back and forth in her neat, empty living room, mumbling to herself, making herself angry all over again.

She took herself into the kitchen and peered into the refrigerator. Nothing appealed. And then she knew exactly what she was hungry for: peanut butter and banana on Wonder bread. It was one of her favorite comfort foods from childhood, Paul's, too. God, the thousands and thousands of peanut butter and banana sandwiches on white bread that she had made in that Millville kitchen! She could still see the worn linoleum on the counter, the late-afternoon sun slanting in through the window . . . could recall like it was yesterday how Paul used to wheedle and beg, how he would promise her anything, if she'd just make him another. "I'll be a good boy, Cookie. I'll be extra good!"

Paul and his promises! she thought, biting into her sandwich.

They didn't have any more meaning today than they had when he was four and didn't know what he was saying. He'd never grown up, apparently. Still single-mindedly going after whatever he wanted at the moment. Still making promises to her that he had no intention of keeping.

He'd sounded so sincere when he said he was going to be faithful from now on. He'd been near tears and she'd felt so sorry for him. Well, forget sorry! He was the same self-indulgent, spoiled little boy he had always been. If a pretty woman smiled at him, he was off and running.

Once, years ago, the first time he'd confessed to her, she had put her hands on his shoulders and looked deeply into his eyes, and she had asked, "Paul, darling, why? You *know* you're handsome and lovable."

He had smiled wryly and said, "I guess I don't . . . otherwise, I wouldn't keep trying to prove it, would I?"

And now the same old story. A couple of weeks ago, he'd called her—"just to touch base," he said. She had a feeling it was something more and it was. He needed to confess to her. He and Deena had been carrying on an affair, ever since the reunion! He had promised. Deena had promised. And they had both lied! A pox on both their houses!

She couldn't remember the last time she'd felt so betrayed! Who could she trust, anyway? And then, when she told Dave about it, he just found it amusing. *Amusing!*

"Hey, they're both consenting adults," he said in that off-hand way she hated. "And it's none of your business." She started to answer him, but he had already turned away and gotten very busy looking for his running shoes. End of topic.

She couldn't talk to him about *anything*. So who did she have? She might just as well be alone permanently! The person who was supposed to be her closest intimate, her best friend, her ally, never wanted to "get involved," always wanted to stand somewhere off on the sidelines, observing from a safe distance.

Dammit! She stood in the middle of her living room and wondered what she wanted to do. She had no idea. Make another peanut butter and banana sandwich. That's how women made themselves fat—and that's *why* women made themselves fat, too. What was *wrong* with her?

Well, she wasn't going to find out in the next ten minutes. But neither was she going to stay here and spend the evening feeling sorry for herself. So much for Cookie the Independent Woman Who Loves to Be Alone! Hey, it was a beautiful evening, the night was young—even if she wasn't—and she was out of here!

Outside, she paused on the steps. Which way? Which way did he usually walk his dog? Oh, Cookie, you are shameless! You can't take a walk in the evening without hoping—You're as bad as Deena, waiting for a man to come along and make life worthwhile.

You're as bad as your brother Paul, she berated herself as she set off down Columbus Avenue, knowing full well that he always ended up with the dog on Columbus to get his ice cream. You're as bad as Paul, on the prowl. And then she told herself to stop that. It was ridiculous. Paul would sleep with anyone, anyone at all. Not she . . . She felt her thought stumble and hesitate. She stopped walking. Then she made herself continue; it was time to stop tiptoeing around those years. She knew damn well what was in her memory—she just didn't like to look at it. No, she wasn't like Paul, not now. But *once* she was, oh, yes . . .

Johnny Carstairs, seventeen years old, his long black hair slicked back in a DA, his Lucky Strikes rolled up in his T-shirt sleeve, driving around town in his father's Studebaker. Oh, God, how she loved him. He was so handsome, he was so tall, he was so sure of himself. He was captain of the basketball team and president of his class. He was a big wheel.

And she was fifteen-year-old Cookie Gordon, with not much going for her except being an A-student. And large breasts, of course. She got a lot of attention for those breasts, a lot of boys wanted to take her riding in their father's car and feel her up. And sometimes she went. Usually she went. She liked it. She liked the look they got when they saw her coming down the street to get into the car. Eager and excited. And excited is exactly how they always got. It felt so powerful, being a girl who could make boys act the way they did. They panted and they groaned and they pleaded with her to let them do this and please do that to them. And they got all hard, and they put her hand on it and said, "You're driving me crazy, Cookie." And she got to say yes or no. Sometimes, if she was in the mood, she said yes.

But Johnny was different. She loved Johnny. He was so special, and here she was, sitting in the front seat of the car, his hands under her sweater, undoing her bra with practiced fingers. Practiced because for weeks now, they'd been coming out to the abandoned cemetery road to neck, once or twice a week, whenever he could get the car—and he always wanted her bra off, first thing. He loved her tits; he said so, all the time.

She felt so lucky, being with Johnny Carstairs, the BMOC. She'd had a crush on him for so long. The first time he asked if she'd go for a ride with him, she almost fainted with happiness. It would have been nice if he'd asked her to have a Coke at the drugstore; she knew enough not to dream about a real date, to a dance or a movie, but a Coke or something would have been nice. She knew why he wanted to take a ride with her. The other boys had told him, "Cookie Gordon puts out." She knew it. She didn't care. It felt so good, so close and warm and nice. So she had a reputation; so what?

This night by the Catholic cemetery, with a full moon shining down on the gravestones with their carved babies and angels, they both got terribly excited. When he unzipped her jeans and pushed down on them, she helped. Her panties came off with them, and while the pant legs were still on, he took out his erect penis and shoved it into her. She couldn't move her legs, but instead of feeling trapped, she felt twice as hot. "Baby!" he was saying. "Oh, baby, baby, baby!" And he was holding on to her breasts tightly, breathing hard, his eyes tightly shut, pushing, pushing, hard and big and hot inside of her.

It didn't take very long, maybe five minutes. And it was over and he was kissing her gratefully, collapsed over her. Only then did she realize she was very cramped and uncomfortable. But she wouldn't dream of pushing Johnny Carstairs away from her. She stayed where she was, his weight crushing her and her poor head jammed against the door handle.

Finally, he pushed himself up, struggling to turn himself around in the tight space, laughing a little at their strange contortions. "Makes you wonder," he said, zipping up his pants and settling himself back behind the wheel, "how we got into that position in the first place. Well? Next stop, your corner."

She remembered forever, the sinking feeling in her stomach. What had she expected? She knew what the score was. He took her out for a ride, she put out, and now he was taking her home. Not even home. A block away. She'd walk that block to the house, all by herself, like always. That was the part she didn't like, the alone part, afterward. She knew from her reading what happened when people were in love. Long-stemmed roses, walks over the moors arm in arm, long tender looks. Not being dropped off on the street, ten o'clock at night, and having to sneak back upstairs. That wasn't love.

Would anyone, she wondered, ever love her? Probably not, not if things kept going the way they were. And in the meantime, she'd keep going out for rides in cars.

On the corner of Cannon Street, he pulled the car over. "That was nice," he said, and gave her a kiss. Cookie held her breath. Was this it, or maybe . . . ? And then he said, "Monday night? Seven o'clock?" And she said yes even as she was thinking that it was a school night and she was going to have to make up a very good lie to get out of the house.

Poor little thing, Cookie thought. Poor little unhappy girl that I was. And why, Cookie Gordon Adler, have you taken a job, so carefully chosen and competed for, a job in which you spend long, exhausting, hopeless days with adolescent prostitutes? *Duh*, I dunno. Oh, sure. Tell me another!

It was so long ago, it didn't even feel real. But it must have felt very real back then, because when they came back to New York in '61, she remembered vividly her decision, made on the train, sitting next to the window, watching the Hudson River widen and narrow and widen and narrow, that she wasn't going to do that anymore. She had a chance to make herself new, to be whoever she wanted to be. And she wanted to be a virgin and save herself for her husband, just like all the other nice girls. So, when she met Dave, she had long ago rewritten history and was a blushing virgin bride.

Pausing on the corner, across from the ice-cream shop, she laughed at herself. Virgin bride! What a laugh. But he never knew and he never would.

A girl jogged by, just as the light changed, wearing a T-shirt that made Cookie laugh out loud. It said IF WE CAN SEND A MAN TO THE MOON, WHY CAN'T WE SEND THEM ALL? Right on, sister! Then maybe the women of the world could get down to business, instead of spending all their time wondering about men, and worrying about men, and thinking about men. As she was doing right now, of course, planting herself where she was almost sure to maybe possibly bump into Phil Mitchell, perhaps.

She crossed the street thinking, Life is peculiar. I spend every single working day trying to convince my charges that they have to live their lives for themselves, not be focused on what some *man* wants, be he father, boyfriend, or, God help us, pimp. And here I am—

"Say, lady," said a familiar voice. "Would a nice ice-cream cone bring a smile to your face?"

Cookie regarded Phil Mitchell, standing there before her, complete with dog, a sweet, rather goofy smile on his face. He was a nice man: he was a very nice man. And she was a lady who needed a nice man. And then she opened her mouth and said, "No. No, thanks."

He was surprised—but not nearly as surprised as she was! She'd thought this is what she came out for. He quickly put on a smile and said, "Aw, come on, Cookie. You can pick any flavor you want!" And when she shook her head, he went on: "Where've you been? I've missed you. The poor dog is so tired because I keep taking her out for walks, hoping you'll 'accidentally on purpose' bump into me."

She knew this was meant to be charming. She was not charmed, however. In fact, with every word, she found herself becoming more and more set against him. She wasn't exactly in the mood to go jumping into bed with a guy who always waited for her to read his mind. If he was so interested, why the hell didn't he call her?

She gazed at him. She'd love to get laid but no, not by him. In a world full of people jumping in and out of bed, saying, "I can't help myself," and "I need," and "I want," and "I got to have," count me out. Not me, not again. And anyway, he was just another Dave, another passive guy waiting for her to make all the moves, waiting for her to be the aggressor, waiting for her to give him permission. No thanks, she already had one of those at home.

"Excuse me, Phil. I have some things to do. See ya!" He got a hurt look on his face. But she was determined not to feel guilty. To hell with it. She turned abruptly and marched herself across the street, toward home.

What was she thinking of, anyway? Going to bed with Phil Mitchell was just the same as screwing Johnny Carstairs in the front seat of his father's Studebaker. Oh, yes, it was—exactly the same and for the same reasons. And even as she was thinking this, she was hesitating, thinking if she turned around right now and ran back, she could catch him before he got out of sight.

Don't do it, she told herself. Don't do it. Go upstairs and eat chocolate pudding, and read your mysteries, and stop this nonsense. You have a perfectly good husband. You picked him, as much as he picked you and maybe more. Why did you pick him? You picked him because he was calm and quiet, and sweet and good-natured. You picked him because he was idealistic and he understood your background. You picked him because he was good-looking and when you were dating him, all your friends said how handsome he was. You picked him because he didn't try to get into your pants, like the other boys, and that felt romantic and normal—and that's what you wanted more than anything else, more than love, even.

She thought of Dave. He really looked terrific for a man his age. He was still a handsome man. And he was a good husband. He came home, he never fooled around, she'd never had a moment's worry about his fidelity, never. What the hell was the matter with her, that she was so *kvetchy*?

He was a nice, easygoing man. When everyone else was becoming uptight and feeling crazy, he was calm and collected, ready to do whatever had to be done, telling the rest of them to take it easy. Yes, and on the other hand, that laid-back attitude meant he didn't care if he was late, it didn't bother him if he left things lying around, he forgot to pay a couple of bills from time to time . . .

Stop that! Cookie said to herself. Stop it this minute! What's a pair of Nikes left on the floor in front of the couch, compared with infidelity, for instance? What's a couple of dunning letters, compared to constant criticism? Most of her married friends would give their right arm to have a man like Dave—and several of them had said so.

As she let herself into the building, a wave of gratitude swept over her. What an idiot she was, she thought, as she got on the elevator. She had a bright, faithful, decent husband who loved her. She should be on her knees, thanking whoever, instead of carping about nothing.

No, better than that, when she got this way she should remind herself of Sharon and Nancy and Carol and her other divorced, separated, and otherwise on-the-loose friends. Not one of them was happy being single, not one. And yet, every one had chosen it, had been positively euphoric at the time. "Finally, I'm rid of him and all his shticks." That sort of thing.

But in the end, all they could think or talk about was men: how they couldn't meet any, how there weren't any good ones out there, or straight ones, or decent ones, or unmarried ones. Had they all forgotten how miserable they were when they were married?

She asked that question one evening when they were all sitting around her dining table eating take-out Chinese, talking about men, and complaining about being single. And the answer they gave her? "Easy for *you* to talk. You have someone." As if the answer to all their problems was having somebody.

When she got into the apartment, she marched straight down the hall to the bedroom. In a funny way, she missed the sound of the TV. She missed Dave. Maybe her friends had been right, after all. Even playing at being single for a day was proving more difficult than she had imagined. For whatever reason, she really loved him, in spite of everything. Or something.

She sat down on the edge of the bed. Too bad he was gone; if he were here, she could tell him how she felt. She could kiss him tenderly, and apologize for her short temper, and they could make love and feel close.

She picked up the phone. She'd call him at Marilyn's. She'd tell him over the phone. When he left, she had been so cool and casual, so uncaring. Now she was sorry for that.

She dialed, she said all the proper bright and cheery things to John, who answered, and waited, her heartbeat actually speeding up, while he called Dave to the phone.

"What's wrong?" he said, without preamble.

Cookie chuckled. "Nothing's wrong, darling."

"Then why are you calling?"

She felt put off, somehow. He was spoiling it. Here she was, filled with love and tenderness, and even regret—and he sounded annoyed, as if she had interrupted him. All her tender feelings were beginning to dissipate.

"I'm calling because I was out for a walk and I thought about you and I missed you."

Silence. Then, awkwardly, "I . . . miss you, too. That's why you're calling, to tell me you miss me?"

"That's right." She could hear her voice tightening. "That's why I'm calling—to tell you I miss you. Is there something wrong with that?"

"No, no, it's fine. But I've only been gone a few hours."

All gone, all, all gone. One more try and that was it. "I was thinking how much I'd like to see you right now." She felt so damned awkward. How could that be, that her husband could make her feel so self-conscious? Deep breath, very deep breath. "I wish you'd jump right back in the car and drive down."

"You've gotta be kidding, Cook! I just got here! And it's only five days. In five days, you'll see me."

The surge of red-hot anger took her by surprise. She almost couldn't talk. Her throat felt totally constricted. So much for romance. So much for reawakened feelings. So much for the whole damn thing.

At last, she had her voice. "Dave," she said, "I don't think I want to live with you anymore." And she hung up before he had a chance to answer her.

<hr>

Chapter Thirty-seven

Friday, November 7, 1987   Dave hung up the phone and swiveled around, a puzzled look on his face. Dot hadn't heard him say good-bye.

"What's the matter?" she said.

He turned to her but he wasn't really looking at her, and his expression did not change. "What was *that* all about?" he asked of nobody in particular.

"Dave. Has something happened?"

Like a man in a trance, he said, "She says she doesn't want to live with me anymore. Out of nowhere!"

"What are you talking about?"

He repeated it, tonelessly: "Cookie's leaving me!"

"I don't believe it! You must have heard her wrong!"

He shook his head. "That's exactly what she said. And then she hung up."

She loved Dave, but he had a bad habit of giving up too easily sometimes. "Give me the phone. I'll dial. You talk."

Dave gave her a bleak look. "It's no use," he said. "I know Cookie."

"That's not the Cookie *I* know!" The Cookie *she* knew did not drop bombs without warning. The Cookie *she* knew did not suddenly announce to her husband that she was throwing him out. If she could put up with him while he was having all those problems, what could have gotten into her *now*? It was crazy! It was not like Cookie at all.

Meanwhile, there he sat, in Marilyn's kitchen, looking shell-shocked, shaking his head. Just sitting there, shaking his head.

"Dave, call her back."

"She hung up on me!"

"Never mind what she did. Call her back. *Talk* to her!"

"No. She hung up on me. And she meant it. I know Cookie." He sat for a minute, chewing on his lip, and then he said, "But, Mom, *why*? Our troubles are all over now! I told Cookie, we can take a trip now, we can go anywhere . . . to China, if she likes. She's always wanted to take a trip to China. I don't understand."

Dorothy regarded her son-in-law, biting her tongue not to say too much. He heaved a big sigh and his shoulders sagged—and his face got that sad hangdog look. Another one! What was the matter with these guys? They were ready to take on the whole world for their principles, but let their wife say one little word and they were ready to give up. Look at him! Forty-six years old, his wife hangs up on him, and he's totally depressed!

It was an old familiar story, to her. Wasn't Jonah the same kind of man? Everyone said how well he was doing, considering. Well, they ought to know how many times a day she bucked him up. He got so excited about their invitation up here, he was so eager. And then, when it was planned, he got nervous and worried and said he probably shouldn't take such a long trip, it was too much trouble, he didn't think he could sleep in a strange bed, don't ask!

She knew she had to convince him. She had to talk her heart out until he finally agreed that yes, maybe he'd give it a try. He *expected* it from her. Well, why not? She'd always done it.

When they came in, an hour ago, he wanted only to go lie down, and Marilyn said, "Aunt Dot, go into the kitchen. There's a pot of tea waiting for you and my own homemade brownies from a mix. I'll get Uncle Jo settled." And she took him away to the living room.

Well, she had had her cup of tea and her brownie, and Marilyn had come in to make sure she had everything she needed, and Jonah called out for her, for Marilyn—for Marilyn!—and away she went. Dot didn't know exactly how she felt about that. On the one hand, it was nice to have him calling for somebody else; she was plenty tired. On the other hand, how come all of a sudden he didn't need her? And then she scolded herself. Dorothy Gordon, quit that! You should be grateful you're able to sit and have a quiet cup of tea for a change.

So she sat and she rocked a little in the rocking chair. It was nice, it was relaxing. Marilyn's kitchen was old-fashioned and a little worn around the edges. But there were crisp curtains on the windows, and pots of geraniums blooming, a hooked rug on the floor, and space for a rocking chair and an old sofa. Very nice, very comfortable.

Like an old dog, Dave shook himself and pushed himself out of the sofa. "Come on, Mom. Let's go in and see how Pop's doing. He should be rested by now."

"And Cookie?"

"Ah, I'll let her cool off. You Gordon women are sure full of fire—and at very unexpected times." He laughed a little and Dot wanted to say, Schmuck. Your wife is trying to tell you something. God knows she doesn't tell me much, but even from the little she says, *I* can tell she's not very happy lately. If I were you, she thought, I'd find out what's wrong and I'd do it *now*.

"You're just evading the issue," she said.

He laughed. "You're right, you're absolutely right!"

Thank God he wasn't *her* problem. Her problem was in the living room, *kvetching* and moaning and wanting his own bed.

Surprise! Oh, no, he wasn't. Her *kvetcher* was *singing*! It was a song from the civil rights movement, one she hadn't heard since the sixties. "Go Tell It on the Mountain." And his audience of one sat at his feet—literally, at his feet, on the rug—entranced.

Dot stood at the doorway in wonderment. This was a very different Jo than the man who had hobbled in from the car, earlier. This was a very different Jonah than the man she'd been living with the past few weeks! Marilyn must be the original miracle worker.

When he finished the song, Dorothy and Dave clapped, and Marilyn turned. "I was just going to get you two. After the third verse. Did you have a nice rest?"

"I did. And I see I'm not the *only* one."

"Yeah, yeah," Jonah said. "I got my second wind. Marilyn got me talking about the old days and I was just starting to tell her about Freedom Summer."

"I'm so eager to hear all of it," Marilyn said. "The Coops. Millville . . . you know, Millville isn't far from here. I could take you down, or John could. It can't be more than an hour away."

"Agh, Millville!" Jonah waved it away. "That's boring! You don't want to hear about Millville! The civil rights movement—now, *that* was something. The things that went on, not only down South!"

Dorothy stopped listening. He always liked to just slide by those years in Millville, as if they'd never happened.

"Enough for now, Jo," she said. "You'll have all weekend to tell Marilyn everything."

Marilyn laughed, consulted her wristwatch, and said, "Yes, and anyway, I have to check the oven in about five minutes. John left me written instructions. He's the cook around here, but he's busy right now." She gestured to the big bay window. There was John raking leaves, with little Caleb in a baby carrier on his back.

"So, Aunt Dot, how's the rest of our family, since the re-union? I know you had lunch with Sylvia . . ."

"Oh, yeah?" Jonah turned to give Dot such a look. She gave it right back. "It's news to me," he said.

Dot ignored him. "Yes, we've seen each other a couple of times," she told Marilyn. "We wised up. The last time those two stopped speaking, we went along. We thought we had to. Now, we know better."

Jonah gave a grunt of disapproval and Marilyn laughed. Good, she could find it funny if she wanted to. Dorothy knew better.

"How about Cookie and Deena? I know they were thrilled to rediscover each other."

There was an awkward silence. And then Dave said, "It's not Deena and Cookie who are thrilled . . . it's Deena and Paul."

"Excuse me? Did I hear right? Are you telling me they're *seeing* each other?"

"Yeah," Dave said wearily.

"My sister Deena! Self-indulgent, as always."

"It's the same with Paul. Gimme, gimme, that's him," said Jonah. "I failed with Paul. Everything I taught him: down the drain!"

"Jonah!" Enough, Dorothy thought. Paul might be a Capitalist, but he was *their* Capitalist. He was their son, and Jo could stop complaining about him in front of a stranger. Sorry for the word *stranger*, she thought, but we only met Marilyn a short time ago. Even though Jonah has fallen in love. "We don't know anything about them for sure," she went on. "I say we should drop the subject."

Marilyn got up. "You're right, Aunt Dot. It's none of our business. I have a good idea—let's eat. Yes, you too, boys," she added, as John and the baby came in, smelling of fresh air and dried leaves.

Dinner was a simple but delicious meal of shepherd's pie and corn bread. Dot told John how much she liked it, and he said, "It's an old LaSalle family recipe. I'll tell you the secret ingredient later, when no one else can hear."

Now she had to laugh. "The secret in my family, young man, is *gurnischt helfen* . . . which means it won't do any good to give *me* secret ingredients because I can't cook. Tell him, Jo." She had been watching Jonah eat with pleasure. He'd been picking at his food a lot lately.

Now he turned with a smile and said, "You make a helluva pot roast, Dot." He winked at John and added, "Every night, she makes it."

" 'Practice makes perfect,' " Marilyn remarked.

"Hey, Marilyn, that was funny!" John said, and pretended to duck. "Sorry, sorry. But I didn't want you to miss Saul too much."

"The kids have discovered each other," Dorothy said.

"They're not carrying the old baggage," Marilyn said. "They can just enjoy one another."

"Their own family reunion!" Jonah snorted.

"Never mind!" Dorothy told him. "They're doing their own thing. Mickey told me on the phone, they're all going to sleep on the floor of her room. All of them!"

"Talk about sleeping on the floor!" Jonah put down his spoon and smiled reminiscently. "That summer, on the Selma to Montgomery march, believe me, we slept wherever. A floor was already a good bed. A *mattress* on the floor, that was luxury!" He laughed.

"That was the big march, wasn't it? With that horrible sheriff?"

Jonah laughed again. "Which horrible sheriff? Those years, the South was *full* of them. We used to wonder what zoo they escaped from. Yes, that was the big one. A call went out, all over the country. Everyone who believed in equal rights for the Negro should come down and join in this march. And everybody came. Even ministers and rabbis got down from the pulpit for that one!" He shook his head.

Dorothy interrupted. "Even ministers and rabbis were liberal—and you know it, Jo. My God!" She gave him a look. "You forgot, maybe, that the Reverend Martin Luther King was the leader of that march? The civil rights movement started in the Southern black churches!"

Jonah held up his hands in surrender. "You're right, you're

right.'' And he turned back to Marilyn and John. ''The weather, you wouldn't believe. We were walking in mud up to our ankles. You ever try to march with about ten pounds of muck on either foot? It's not fun, believe me. But we had a noble purpose, and when you're working for something bigger than your own selfish needs, you can do anything. Anything.''

''Aunt Dot, were you there?''

''No, no. Cookie got sick and I had to stay with her—''

''So *I* could go,'' Dave put in. ''And I've always been grateful because . . . well, I hope this doesn't sound too melodramatic, but it changed my life.'' He leaned forward, the words tumbling out, for a change. ''You have no idea what it felt like, marching side by side with thousands of other people, all of us totally committed to the same ideal, the same goal.

''We knew it was dangerous, we might be killed. But this was too important not to do. It was an extraordinary experience. On that march, I decided I would never sit back and accept things that were wrong.''

''And you haven't.'' Jonah applauded. ''So what happened to my son Irwin? He was like that once! Marilyn, the boy spent all of Freedom Summer in the worst part of Mississippi. That was '64. I was filled with pride. I was scared for him, of course, but I fought in Spain and it made a mensch of me!'' He paused, breathing with effort. He looked a little pale; he'd gone on too long, as he tended to do lately. All right, he wanted to get everything said before . . . But he didn't know when to stop, and now he was tired. Well, she could talk, too.

''Funny how you have three kids, and you're the same parents to each of them and yet, they come out so different,'' she said. ''Paul never was interested in any of this, not for a minute. Irwin, yes, for a minute. Cookie's the one who's always been active. Am I right, Jo? Sure, I am. As a matter of fact, she met Dave on the bus coming back to New York from the March on Washington.''

''That's right,'' Jonah put in, and began to cough. When would he learn to take it easy? ''Cookie and Dave are two of a kind. They knew they'd have a good marriage, right from the beginning.''

Abruptly, Dave pushed his chair back and stood up. ''Who thinks 'good marriage' at the age of twenty? I couldn't get over her! She was so natural, so easy to talk to, and, come on, Pop, we're grown-ups here, she was very sexy . . . all that curly red hair and that figure!''

He stopped and began to smile. "If you'll excuse me, my wife and I have had a misunderstanding and I think I'd better drive down and fix it."

"Now? It's past eight!" That was John.

"Yeah, I think I'd better. I won't be able to sleep, anyway. I'll be back for Mom and Pop . . . whenever they want." And off he went.

They all kind of sat there for a minute or two, nobody quite knowing what to make of this . . . except for herself, Dot thought.

"She hung up on him, earlier," she explained. "It'll be all right."

Marilyn leaned forward and put a hand over one of Jonah's. "You look a little tired, Uncle Jo. Don't argue with me— remember, I'm a doctor." She laughed. "We have many days to talk. John will go upstairs with you. And we ladies will stay behind and do the dishes."

But after the men left and could be heard climbing the squeaky stairs, Marilyn made no move to start doing dishes. She sat right where she was, her hands folded on the table in front of her, looking at Dorothy and smiling gently.

Dot had a funny feeling, all of a sudden. And then when from upstairs the baby began to cry, Marilyn held up a hand and said, "John will get him. He's probably thirsty." And she leaned forward.

"Aunt Dot," Marilyn began, in her compassionate, careful, doctor voice, and the anxious feeling got worse. "Aunt Dot, I think you're tired, too. You do a good job of acting strong and cheerful, but I understand what you're going through."

The gentle tone brought tears to Dorothy's eyes. She quickly said, "Look at this! Tears! Yetta always turned on the waterworks, not me!"

Marilyn shook her head, smiling a little. "It's okay. You can cry. This is very difficult."

"Yes, but you know, it occurs to me that all he needs is a change. Ever since he got here, he's been like a new man. I was just thinking at dinner—"

Something in Marilyn's face stopped the words. "Aunt Dot. Listen to me. It's wonderful, yes, to see Uncle Jo having a good day. Yes, I agree. He's been quite lively and I know how good it must make you feel. But you must start thinking about the future, about what you're going to do—"

"About what I'm going to do *when*?" She hated that lovely,

warm, gentle smile, hated it because she knew what it was saying—and what it was saying, she didn't want to hear.

Marilyn reached over and took her hand. "About what you're going to do when Uncle Jo is gone."

"Aren't you rushing things a little?"

"Please, Aunt Dot. Try to hear me. It's never too soon to start making plans when someone is so ill."

Dorothy shook her head stubbornly. She didn't want to hear this, didn't want to think about it. "Time enough, when it happens. But it isn't going to happen so fast . . . I don't care *what* you think, Marilyn! You're not even his doctor!" And then she had to stop talking because she was choking on her tears.

Chapter Thirty-eight

Sunday, January 17, 1988   The meeting room in Cookie and Dave's building was already beginning to fill up and it was only ten o'clock. Dave had set the time to start at eleven. Dorothy stood by the entrance, feet together, shoulders back, head high, willing herself to stay in control.

This was a memorial service for Jonah, and she wasn't going to spoil it by crying or carrying on, the way some women did. Cousin Ida threw herself on her husband Jesse's casket at the cemetery and shrieked, "Take me, too! Take me, too!" The idiot. Jesse hadn't given her a moment's peace in forty-two years; she should have been happy to be left alone, for God's sake!

Ah, here was Anna Dauber—and a few others from the old days at the Coops. How nice! Dorothy embraced each of them, heard each of them say how sorry they were to hear about Jo. "I'll never forget how he used to jump up on a chair at meetings whenever he wanted to give a speech." Nice of you to remember, nice of you to come. Some neighbors from their building, not good friends, so just a handshake. The doorman, the elevator man, Marcos the super. A wonderful man—when Jonah really got bad and had to stay in the hospital bed, Marcos

checked in three times a day to see if she needed something.
An angel. And Anna still here, next to her, waiting patiently.

"Anna, you want to talk to me?"

"I just wanted to say . . . someone's coming this morning
you haven't seen for a long time and I want to prepare you."

"Oh? Who's that?"

Anna's voice lowered. She smiled a very little smile. "Frank
Green. I don't have to ask if you remember *him*."

Dorothy knew what she was getting at. It was annoying, all
this coyness. But she wasn't going to tell Anna she'd already
heard from Frank and knew he was coming.

"If you'll excuse me . . ." she said, turning to greet a group
of Cookie and Dave's friends.

And after them, for a few minutes, thank God, nobody. She'd
been standing here for an hour, greeting people. Her feet hurt
in her best black shoes. She eased one foot free so she could
wiggle her toes. Over a hundred had already come in—not to
mention Jonah's bag lady, who somehow got her wits together
enough to show up. And if you were the wife, you had to wear
your good shoes even if they pinched your toes. Soon, she'd sit.
Right now, she was waiting for her brother and sister. And Sylvia, too. She should be at the door to greet them. It was only
right. This was no ordinary occasion. In honor of that thought,
she eased her poor aching feet back into her shoes.

Everything was just like Jonah wanted it: plain, simple, no
frills, no flowers. Not even a candle. In his last weeks, he and
Dave worked out the whole thing together.

"I don't want a big production. The only reason I'm allowing
a memorial at *all* is because Dot wants it. Yes, that's right, Dot.
It's for you." After an hour of discussion, he agreed there could
be a poem, if someone wanted it. Singing was all right; on the
Left, singing was a part of everything you did. But nothing
schmaltzy. "A good union song. A good civil rights song. You
know the kind of thing I mean, Dave."

She missed him. He'd only been gone a month and already she
found it too quiet, too empty when she came back into the apartment. She didn't know what to do with herself: argue with the
radio? She wasn't going to make up stories, that they had had
the perfect marriage. She wasn't going to kid herself. There had
been plenty of problems. There had been plenty of times when
she had asked herself how she ever got herself into this life. But
it hadn't been all bad. He had been an interesting companion.

She pictured him the way he was that day in Rock Creek Park, the first time she ever saw him. Such a handsome fellow, with his blazing red hair and his beret tilted at a rakish angle and that little limp and the cute smile.

They had both known, from the very first minute, that they were meant for each other. He was a very exciting person to her, the young Jo, full of energy and high spirits, ready for anything! The man knew what he was born for, what he was fated to do with his life. That was wonderful to her, who was the shy sister, never sure of herself, always hanging back, always following Yetta's lead.

When she cast her lot with him, she thought their life was going to be a grand adventure. It hadn't exactly been on a grand scale, but an adventure? Absolutely. And now, suddenly—or so it seemed to her—the adventure was over. Finished. Her eyes burned and filled and she turned to the wall, blinking, willing the tears not to fall.

She was just getting herself under control, dabbing at her eyes with a tissue, when she heard her brother Jack's voice as he came down the hall. Giving orders, as usual. But it made her smile through her tears, and today, she could use a few smiles. The last time she'd seen him was a couple of weeks ago. He came to sit with Jo, when Jo really began to sink, and she never got to really *talk* to him. Sylvia, she'd talked to a lot—over the phone mostly, although Sylvia had come over toward the end, a couple of times a week.

Here he was, Jack, in a dark blue suit, a little stooped, a little faded, but still a man and a half. Suddenly she remembered him, age thirteen, a bar mitzvah boy, standing up at the *bima*, so grown up all of a sudden, his face scrubbed, with a very serious expression, his hair slicked back, still with the wet-comb marks in it, and wearing his first suit, a dark blue suit, just like today. She had a sudden realization that, somewhere deep inside that aging man standing in the doorway, his arms outspread, was still the young boy she had so idolized.

"Jack!"

He came to her and gathered her to him, holding her tight. She began immediately to cry again. Dammit, she couldn't keep leaking tears all morning! She had responsibilities. She had prepared herself for Jo's death, she knew that he *wanted* to die. It was better than suffering. All through the end, she hadn't shed a tear. So, why now?

When Jack let her go, his eyes were wet and he was blinking rapidly. "Dorothy. What can I say?"

She patted him on his arm. "You're a rock, Jack."

Now Sylvia came to her and embraced her. She didn't speak. She didn't have to; there was nothing left to say now. What a good friend. *She* was really the rock. Jack tended to spread his hands and ask, "What can I say? What can I do?" Sylvia just said it and did it.

They let each other go and looked at each other, and she saw Sylvia's face crumple and, in a minute, they were in each other's arms again, bawling like a couple of kids.

Good, Cookie thought. Mom is finally crying, really letting go. She'd been so controlled, so brittle, these past few weeks. Cookie knew why she had to do it, but at the same time she couldn't help thinking that if the break didn't come soon, it was going to be devastating. Let Mom cry her heart out. *She* would take care of things.

She had seen Deena coming in, and her first thought was to hide until Deena had found a seat. And then she said to herself, Coward! What are you thinking? *You* haven't done anything! Sooner or later in the course of this day, she was going to have to deal with Deena. She might as well get it over with. It wasn't such a big deal to say hello to her cousin. Was it?

She tapped Deena on the shoulder and stuck out a hand, to show she wasn't about to hug and kiss. But Deena ignored the signal.

"Oh, Cookie, I'm so sorry. He was such an interesting man. And it's so hard to lose your father," she said, putting her arms around Cookie, forcing a hug. And then, as it turned out, it felt good. Cookie hated being mad at people; it hurt her stomach. Maybe, just maybe, she and Deena could be friends again. Maybe. If she could ever trust her again.

In the meantime, let them talk about nothing. "I'm so glad you came, Deena. Look at our mothers—they're so fond of each other, even after all the years of separation."

"Some things don't change," Deena said. "But sometimes people do stupid things, not realizing how they might affect others."

Talk about code messages! Was Deena going to tell Cookie the whole thing? Cookie knew only what Paul had told her. "I'm not seeing her anymore. I ended it," he had said abruptly one morning on the phone, not bothering to say who the "she" was. She had opened her mouth to answer, when he added, "I never want to talk about it again." She'd like to know what had happened.

But it was going to have to wait. Here came Sam and Nelda—and look at that—half a dozen of her kids from the center. But not Barbara Ann. She didn't like *that*; something had to be wrong. But now was not the time. After the service was over, she'd corner Sam and find out. Later.

"There are some of my charges," she said to Deena. "And that tall black dude with them is my boss. I'll introduce you."

"*Those* are 'your' kids?" Deena began to laugh, covering her mouth quickly. "Oh, God, I somehow imagined . . . I don't know, but I have a feeling the picture in my mind was more middle-class, more like the kids *I* work with."

Cookie gazed upon her runaways and had to smile at "middle-class." Not quiet. Four girls wearing six pounds of makeup and twelve pounds of junk jewelry among them, dressed in the proper black clothing, which is all most of them owned, anyway, but hair in four or five improbable colors. And the boys? Similarly outrageous. She loved them all.

"They do kind of look like hookers, don't they?" she said. "Well, sad to say, they are. *Used* to be. I hope."

Her group came over to her, the kids all a bit weepy, but managing to mutter their self-conscious "sorry's." Sam gave her a big hug and she clung to him for an extra moment. And then Nelda, who murmured in her ear, "The hours they took getting ready! You wouldn't believe it! And then, I ended up wiping off half the makeup."

Cookie gazed at them: fidgeting, uneasy, self-conscious, out of place, not knowing exactly what they were supposed to do. But here for her. And that's what mattered right now. Dammit, she had been so totally under control, and these half a dozen pathetic kids were going to make her cry.

And then they all turned to the clack of high heels, the sound of a husky female voice, the smell of a wonderful, exotic perfume. Down the hall, heading right for them, sailed an older woman, the very essence of the word *glamour*, her long fur coat open and billowing in her wake, her formfitting black dress relieved of starkness by a simple sunburst of diamonds the size of a small dinner plate. Her snow-white hair had been cut into a curly cap and she was beautifully made up. This vision swept right by Cookie and Deena and went straight to Dorothy.

"My poor baby sister!"

"Oh, Yetta! You told me it would be hard, but you didn't tell me it would be like this!'' She burst into tears and began to sob into the befurred shoulder. Aunt Yetta—for that, indeed, was who this personage was—murmured nonstop and patted her sister's back.

Cookie was surprised by the pain she heard in her mother's voice. She had had no idea. If she thought about her parents' relationship at all, it was that it was a comfortable arrangement. She knew The Bad Time in Millville had been bad for them, too, but they seemed to have put that all behind them. They had been a bit contentious, to be sure, but any *passion*, Cookie had thought, was long gone. Her mother's cry of anguish astonished her. Life was full of surprises, wasn't it?

''Who in the world is that?'' Sam asked.

''That, Sam, is my mother's twin sister Yetta, fresh from I don't know, either her Tuscan villa or maybe her pied-á-terre in London. She *is* quite something, isn't she? Well, she's the Family Character.''

''So that's the famous Yetta,'' Sam said.

Nelda gave Cookie an amused look. ''And I thought your *mother* was so young-looking! But your aunt! No wrinkles, no sags, no bags! I'd like to know her secret.''

''At last count, three face-lifts.'' Cookie laughed. It felt good to laugh.

It had been a long haul with Pop, and filled with tears. But, she reminded herself, Pop had said, ''I want jokes and laughing.'' He'd said it about a thousand times.

They'd put a hospital bed in the living room for him, and that's where he spent his last few weeks. He lay peacefully, his eyes usually closed. You'd think he was sleeping, but if he heard you come in, without opening his eyes, even, he'd begin giving orders.

''And another thing: none of that slow, sad music.''

''And another thing: no long faces from anyone. I want people to think of the good times.''

Then he'd open his eyes, so he could address you by name. ''Cookie. You listening?''

''Yes, Papa. I hear and I obey.''

And him: ''Don't get fresh. I'm not gone yet.''

She laughed, remembering. ''The last time Yetta paid us one of her flying visits, Pop rolled his eyes and later, after she'd gone down to the Village or uptown to a jazz club—she was always going out, we never knew where she found all these people all the time—he said to Mom, 'With all those face-lifts, if your sister laughs out loud, her eyebrows are going to fall off!' ''

Deena eyed her aunt. "I hope *I* look like that when I grow up. *Whatever* it takes." She turned, as a broad hand descended to her shoulder. "Oh, hi, Daddy. Where'd you go?"

"I checked in with Dave, to see if he needed me to do anything. And look: I turn my back for one minute, and Yetta appears. Tomorrow, I'll turn my back and zip! She'll be gone. That's Yetta!"

"I hope she'll stay longer than that," Cookie said. "I'd like to get to know her, finally. God, she's been wonderful. She's called Mom from Italy, and then from the Balearic Islands, and then from London—every single day since Pop really started to fail."

"Yeah?" Jack eyed his sister as if he'd never seen her before. "Yetta did that? I knew she called, Dorothy told me, but every day? That had to cost her plenty! And all these years, I've been thinking of her as just a crazy artist who knew how to screw in four languages."

"Daddy!"

"What? Oh." He focused suddenly on the little knot of teenagers standing near him. "Sorry. Pardon my French. But Yetta would be the first to tell you the exact same thing!" He laughed. "So let me go say hello to my sister the stranger."

The little group began to disperse, all but Deena. Deena, apparently, wanted to talk.

"I really do admire her," Deena said. "She always has done exactly what she's wanted."

"So do you, it seems to me."

Deena flushed. "Me? I'm a coward. I've always done the conventional thing . . ."

Cookie raised an eyebrow. "Oh, really?"

"Yes, really. I married young, had a lot of kids right away. I never worked. I never went anywhere on my own, I was a good little wife . . . the whole ball of wax." She laughed a little. "Even my divorce was the done thing by the time *I* done it! Not like Aunt Yetta. She was a liberated woman—and she didn't need the world to tell her it was okay."

"Some would say she was promiscuous," Cookie said. And then, realizing how harsh that sounded, she quickly added, "Not me. The thing about Yetta is, she's always been open, honest, right up-front. She never felt she had to sneak around."

"Exactly! Exactly! She wanted to screw in four languages?

She screwed in four languages. She knew about personal freedom before it got popular.''

Cookie looked at her cousin for a moment. Should she say it? If she didn't, then *she* was the coward. It was time to be bold. So, boldly, she said, "Tell me. Where do you draw the line between your personal freedom and another woman's husband?''

Deena winced. "You don't have to worry about it anymore. It's over.''

"I know.'' Cookie was sorry she had opened the subject. She was mad at Deena, yes, but she didn't want to lacerate her. It must have been a first for Deena, getting dumped.

Deena's voice became sad and thoughtful. "I knew I had to. No matter how badly it hurt, I just had to do it.''

What? Cookie thought, flabbergasted. Who did Deena think she was kidding? She couldn't even look at her cousin. More lies! She wished Deena wouldn't.

And then Deena interrupted herself, saying, "Oh, hell! I'm lying, I'm lying. He dumped me. And—'' She stopped talking, biting her lip and obviously fighting tears.

"Oh, Deena, don't. I know it hurts, but it's for the best.'' She stepped close and put an arm around Deena's shoulder.

Tearfully, Deena looked at her and said, trying for a smile, "Look at us. You're comforting *me*, and you're the one who's lost your father.'' Now they hugged, *really* hugged. God, she was so tired of dealing with everyone's *mishegaas*!

"I remember Cookie and Deena when they were two little girls who tiptoed into the guest room one Sunday noon to watch me sleep!'' Cookie smelled Aunt Yetta's wonderful scent before she turned to the sound of that typical Strauss voice, the rather husky voice that could be heard for a mile. "And when I woke up, they told me stories about all the other people who let them climb into bed and sing good morning songs. Hello, Deena, more gorgeous than ever. Hello, Cookie, my darling girl. I'm so sorry, more sorry than you can ever know. He was a cutie, your dad. I remember the first day they met. I had to drag her to that picnic—she didn't want any part of my weird, left-wing friends! Next thing you know, it's a whole lifetime, gone like a dream.

"Well, he lived by his beliefs. There aren't too many men who take that opportunity . . . who have the intestinal fortitude, as we used to say in the army. Your mother told me you were especially close. Agh, it's so hard to lose someone you can really talk to. You know, when I lost *my* father, I was then in Paris, I think, and it was meaningless to me. I didn't even come back for the funeral. I was always . . . devil may care, in a way. Saying there was no use worrying about death because you'd never know it, once it happened to you. But last year, Mauritzio died, and it was so different. I still miss him. Look at me: I'm crying. I cry all the time. It's amazing!''

Cookie gazed at her aunt in wonderment. Yetta never changed. A nonstop talker. Opinionated, candid, insightful, sensitive. All in her own peculiar way, of course. Nevertheless, she made Cookie feel better.

"Yetta, you're sweet. I'm so glad you're here. Especially for Mom. You have no idea how much your phone calls helped."

Yetta smiled. "I haven't always been such a good sister. So this time, let me do it. Before *we* go, me and my twin.''

"Bite your tongue," Deena said.

Cookie wished they could all just stand around and schmooze like this and never mind the memorial service. She was dreading it. But it was close to eleven, time to sit down, and she said so.

She glanced over, wondering if her mother needed her; but Yetta had already taken care of that and the two of them were walking arm in arm down to the front row of chairs, with Jack and Sylvia right behind.

And that was it. Cookie looked around, checking everything out, and then she, too, went down to the front row of folding chairs and sat between her children, stopping first to kiss Win and then Paul.

There was a podium up front and behind it, a table with the stereo. Dave stood up behind the podium and gazed out over the room. In a minute or two, the hum of low-pitched talk had dwindled into attentive silence.

Dave said, "We are here today to honor the memory of Jonah Gordon, who was born Yonah Velvel Golodny in Ekatrinaslav, in the Ukraine, in 1920. He came to this country at the age of ten, and lived in various southern cities until the age of sixteen, when he took himself to New York. He was outraged at the way black people were treated in the south. At a very early age, he dedicated himself to the principles of equality, brotherhood, justice, and the dignity of the workingman.

"We here all know he was an ardent Communist and union man. Therefore, we will begin this memorial with a song he chose himself, just a few weeks ago, a song he sang hundreds and hundreds of times."

He turned and started the tape, and the room was filled with the stirring words of Joe Hill's "Solidarity Forever." In a minute, half of the audience was singing along.

*They have untold millions that they never toiled to
     earn . . .
But without our brain and muscle, not a single wheel can
     turn . . .
We can break their haughty power, gain our freedom when
     we learn
That the union makes us strong.
Solidarity forever
Solidarity forever
Solidarity forever . . . For the union makes us strong.*

Dave's head was thrown back and he sang with complete unself-conscious fervor. Cookie watched him, smiling a little. When Dave was totally engaged, he was totally engaging. That's what she found so appealing about him all those years when she considered herself happily married.

The minute she'd hung up on Dave that night, she'd been full of satisfaction. But that feeling didn't last more than ten seconds. While she was still sitting with her hand on the receiver, her heart began to thump wildly, as if from fear. It felt like a great yawning pit had opened beneath her feet.

What the hell was *this* all about? She'd been waiting for more than three years to tell him that very thing: "Dave, I can't live with you anymore." So how come she felt so lousy? How come she wasn't jumping up and down with delight? How come she wasn't busily packing her things? Or his things? What was the matter with her? What she desperately wanted to do right now was pick up the phone, dial that number in Vermont, and tell him there had been a terrible mistake, that she hadn't meant it. But she *had* meant it. Hadn't she?

She got up then and marched herself straight into the kitchen. When in doubt, eat, right? What was there that was gooey enough or sweet enough or slippery enough to obliterate her anxiety? Aha, Dave's Dove Bars. Three thousand calories each. A Dove Bar should be fattening enough to make her feel better!

So she took out a Dove Bar, chocolate ice cream no less. When Dave Adler picked out a goodie, he didn't stint. The first bite was heaven, but by the third, she was already feeling a little overdosed on chocolate so she rewrapped it—how could a person put a Dove Bar into the garbage can?—and shoved it back into the freezer, next to Dave's Ben & Jerry's Heath Bar Crunch and Dave's Kit Kat bars. And damned if she didn't begin to leak tears. Oh, she was going to do just wonderfully as a single woman, wasn't she? When the sight of her husband's beloved treats lined up in the freezer could move her to tears! What might happen if she caught a glimpse of his running shoes or his television remote?

All that time, those three years since she first composed her exit speech, she'd been waiting, so as not to desert a sinking ship. And now, here was her moment, and all she could do was stand at the refrigerator, crying.

She went out for a walk. She came right back. She made herself a Weight Watchers frozen entree. She couldn't eat it. She turned on the television. She turned it off. She picked up a book. She put it down. She picked up the phone. She put *it* down. She walked around, she sat down, she walked around again, she picked up the phone again, she hung it up. All in all, a perfectly wonderful evening.

Around eleven o'clock, she got the bright idea to get out the bottle of vodka. She poured herself a half a glass and put ice cubes in it and took a swallow. Yuck! It was strong, and it didn't even taste good. Who said vodka had no taste? On the other hand, once it went down, it spread a nice warm feeling all through her. She filled the glass with tonic and that was better. So she took another gulp. And another. Better and better.

At one-thirty A.M., she was feeling no pain at all. So that's what they meant when they said that! All her anxieties, and all her fears, and all her indecision, all just kind of melted into a cozy fuzzy blur. She turned on the stereo then; God, she hadn't done that in ages and ages. But she needed suddenly to hear Barbra Streisand sing sad love songs. The record was called *Memories*. She went through the records. Carly Simon's *Torch* . . . she'd forgotten they had that. Ahmad Jamal. Frank Sinatra. Maybe Frank Sinatra?

But no, she wanted Streisand; singing about endings, memories, how it used to be, singing about throwing him out, ending it, love gone bad. *That* was the kind of song she was in the mood for. Nothing too happy or hopeful, not in her present frame of mind.

But why? She was being absolutely ridiculous. That's what Dave would say, if he could see her like this! And then, that thought made her cry—that Dave might never see her again, not in any shape!

There was an emptiness somewhere in the pit of her stomach, a huge, boundless, endless black hole. Suddenly she saw the maroon and green living room in Millville, the scratchy upholstery, the faded flowered draperies. She heard her mother's voice, she could smell the ever-present pot roast cooking on the stove. Johnny. She saw him, as sharp and as clear as if it were yesterday. Saw herself, running down the dimly lit stairs, running down the street to the next corner, putting herself into the deepest shadow, waiting for those familiar headlights to turn the corner.

She didn't want to remember that time! She didn't want to think about it. All those boys, all those cars, all those hands on her breasts and her thighs, the wriggling and the squirming and the fogged windows. No. She had put that all behind her. She stopped doing it so she'd never again have to have that horrible feeling that she was about to fall down into a big black hole, where she would disappear forever.

She shook her head, very hard, to clear it. Long ago, she'd forgiven herself for being so bad, for being so needy back then. Marrying Dave had felt so safe. She was sure there would never again be that abyss. *Dave!* What had she done? What crazy, terrible thing had she done to herself tonight?

She listened to "You Don't Bring Me Flowers." And "Memories," with its haunting refrain. By the time Streisand began "The Way We Were," the last song on the record, she was singing along and sobbing. That song, from that movie, with all its left-wing reverberations, was just too much for her. She wept and wept, happily, and she kept putting the needle back onto that groove, listening to the same regretful words over and over and over.

And that's what she was doing, sitting cross-legged in front of the stereo, half-potted, crying and singing along, missing Dave, when the door opened and there he was, like someone she had conjured up with her thoughts: her husband, Dave Adler.

She was up like a shot and flinging herself at him before she even had a chance to think about it. She threw her arms around his neck. She could tell he was amazed and astounded because it took a couple of beats before he put his arms around her. She knew what he was thinking. He was thinking, *Huh?* He was trying to figure out what happened to the ice-cold woman who had been so nasty to him on the telephone a few hours ago.

She kissed his face and his neck, still crying and laughing all together. "I'm so glad! I'm so stupid!"

He held her away a little, so he could look at her. "Which one?" he said.

"Both, both, both!" She pulled him close again. He felt so good to her, so good and familiar and, yes, beloved. How was it she had missed knowing what love felt like? This is what it felt like.

She clung to him and he kept patting her back and murmuring dumb stuff, like people did. "There, there. Now, now. It's okay, it's okay."

Then she heard him give a jaw-cracking yawn and she suddenly realized, my God, he's been driving and driving . . . for *hours*!

"Oh, God, Dave. You must be exhausted."

"I'm not exactly fresh as a daisy." His little quirk of a smile. "But I had to see you."

What a cute guy! She'd let herself forget what a cute guy he was. She grinned at him and he gave her a slightly embarrassed grin in return. He looked a bit awkward, a bit pleased, a bit relieved, a bit shy.

"You really drove five and a half hours, in the middle of the night, just to see me." He nodded. A man of few words, her Dave. "I hope you realize," she said to him, "how romantic that is."

"Well . . . I want to keep you."

"Oh, yeah? Well, let me tell you. You can have me, you can keep me, in fact, you may *never* get rid of me." All her ghosts receded and disappeared.

Well, here they were, still together. Nothing had really changed between them. He hadn't changed, not really. The things she hadn't liked about him before, she still didn't like. But now she knew that she needed him, needed to be married to him. Maybe one of these days, when she had some extra time, she'd go back to her shrink and try to find out why.

But in the meantime, he'd been the proverbial rock these past weeks. All the time Pop was getting weaker and weaker, Dave was there. Toward the end, if Pop had to be moved, Dave lifted him, carried him, as tenderly as a baby. It brought tears to her eyes this very minute, remembering. Dave had done it all, was doing it all.

"This will be a very informal service," Dave was saying now. "A few people have told us they'd like to speak—I know I would—but anyone who feels moved to say a few words about Jonah, please feel free to do so."

He paused for a moment, then cleared his throat a little and said, "Jonah Gordon was my father-in-law, but he was much, much more. To list every way in which he influenced me would take all day, so I won't.

"Jo was my mentor and my role model. We believed in the same things. When we marched together in '65, from Selma to Montgomery, Alabama, I saw that he *lived* what he believed. He didn't just sit around talking about it, writing letters to the editor, and signing petitions—although you who know him know he did plenty of that . . .

"Jo Gordon put his body where his soul was. When the civil rights movement needed people, he didn't hesitate for one minute. He volunteered. And marching with him, my admiration grew. He showed no fear, he was the first one to start a song when our spirits were low and our feet were wet, he set such an example to the younger people—to all of us—that I promised myself that I'd always try to live what *I* believed, no matter what the cost. Just as he did."

He waited a second or two and then said, "Cookie?"

Cookie got up and went to the podium. She had a card palmed in her hand, where she had scribbled a few lines about Pop. Her heart was pounding and she could feel her throat closing up as tears flooded into her eyes. Dammit.

"I loved my father—" she began, and could go no further. The tears were spilling down her face and her lips were trembling so badly, she could not form another word. "Sorry," she whispered, and then broke down completely.

She felt Dave's arm around her shoulder, felt his hand patting her, heard him murmur, "It's okay," and then she went back to her seat. She sat back down, next to her mother, who took her hand and squeezed it wordlessly.

"I'm sorry," Cookie finally managed.

"He'd understand."

Cookie sat, flooded with memories, like watching a movie go by in fast forward—too many images, too fragmented. And then it stopped, almost at the end. She had been sitting with him by his bed, as she did for a couple of hours every day. They would talk, sort of. He'd be his old self for five or six minutes, carrying on about Reagan, or what was happening to Solidarity in Poland, or the moral fiber of the country which was, of course, going to pot. And then he'd stop all of a sudden, and drift into one of his hallucinations.

The oncologist had explained it all to them: that the drifting off into the past was part of the process. There were medications that would stop it, but Pop didn't want any medication, none at all. "It's so nice," he told Cookie. "I'm visiting with old friends, long dead. I saw my father and my mother in the shtetl. It was somebody's wedding and everyone was dancing. I was small. I could tell I was still a child because I had to look way up to see my father's face."

It frightened Cookie, usually. It was a dramatic indication that he was dying and she didn't want any dramatic indications. She didn't want him dying, period. So she always said, "Pop. Come back." And he always heard her and he always said, "Okay. Here I am."

But this one day, when he drifted away, he laughed out loud. She gathered up her courage and asked him, "Papa, where are you?"

"Dneiperpetrovsk. Our house by the river. With my brothers and sisters . . . Tanya, Nunya, Mischa. It's so good . . . Mama. On *Mamushka*'s lap."

He smiled so happily, it brought tears to Cookie's eyes. Then he began to sing, very softly, a Russian song, one she hadn't heard since she was a little girl, a lullaby. Oh, God, he really was going to be gone forever. And part of her childhood would disappear with him, forever. Tears began to pour down her face, slipping out of her eyes and down her cheeks. But she smiled. And so did Pop. That she wanted to remember: the two of them holding hands and smiling together.

She looked up, expecting Win or Paul to be next, but it was Uncle Jack. He stood there in his dark blue suit, a handsome elderly man, looking very serious. He waited a few moments.

"My sister Dorothy and Jonah Golodny had a hot romance," he announced. There was a ripple of laughter. Cookie looked over at her mother, who was blushing and laughing. "No, no," he said, "that's not a joke. That's how it was. Once they met, you couldn't keep those two apart—and believe me, I tried!" More laughter.

"We never did get along, me and Jo, we were too different. We came from different worlds and we believed in different

ideas. During his lifetime, I called Jonah every name in the
book—and some *not* in the book, and believe me, he returned
the favor!

"We were not exactly friends. We never really respected each
other's opinions, but—" He stopped suddenly, paused, tried to
resume, and, finally, reached into his breast pocket for a handkerchief and blew his nose at length and noisily. Then, he went
on: "Goddammit, I miss him. This was a real man!" He paused
once more and then repeated, "A real man!" and sat down.

In his seat, on Mom's left, Paul shifted a bit and recrossed his
legs. Nice speech, he thought. At first, he hadn't liked it . . .
What did Uncle Jack mean, they never respected each other?
But then, thinking about it, he decided Jack hadn't meant anything by that and that, in fact, he had been remarkably open and
honest and Pop came out looking good.

He wasn't going to talk. He couldn't. He already told Dave
he wasn't any good at this sort of thing, this emotional kind of
stuff. He wasn't feeling very much grief, that he could tell; but
you never knew. What if he got up there and broke down, like
Cookie did? That was okay, for her. But he didn't want his girls
seeing him out of control.

He watched as his brother went up, leaning forward on the
podium. Irwin, the firstborn son and always favored because of
it, and look what a loser he turned out to be. Paul made himself
a bet that Win would say something political. For a long time,
he'd just followed blindly in Pop's footsteps and then, suddenly,
it was all photography.

"My most vivid memory of my father," Win said, "is on a
subway . . . no, wait, make that three subways. The Broadway
local, the Broadway express, and the BMT. It was a Saturday,
or a Sunday, and I couldn't have been more than six or seven,
and he was taking me all the way from the Coops to Ebbets
Field in Brooklyn to see the Dodgers play. What an adventure!
We always listened to the Dodger games on the radio because
they were the ball club of the working class." He paused to
allow people to laugh a little. "But to see them! I could hardly
believe my luck. And to this day, I can't even remember who
they played, only that they won. Of course, they did, the same
way we would win over the evils of capitalism one day."

He smiled as everyone laughed again. Look at him, Paul
thought, he speaks so well, he looks so good, but . . . Christ,
what a wasted life! He didn't catch all of it, but then Win began

to talk about some book he was going to do, a book about the Old Left, a book that "will make sure that, even though Pop is gone, what he stood for will not be forgotten."

What bullshit, Paul thought. Working on a book, huh? Ask *me* what that really means. It means I'm going to be stuck supporting him forever.

Earlier, before they came in for the service, Win had hit him up for a couple of thou. He'd asked for five hundred and Paul, for some goddamn reason—maybe because it was a memorial service and he was feeling nostalgia—he said, "Five hundred won't keep you going long. Tell you what: how's three thousand?"

"Gee, thanks, Paul." That goofy smile—it hadn't changed since Win was a kid. And then he said it: "Now nobody in the family will have to worry about me for a while."

Paul had stood there, staring at his brother, wondering what planet he was living on. What made him think he was everybody's top priority? What a screwed-up, self-centered bastard! And how about the brother who always handed over the money with a smile, no questions asked? How sane was *he*?

Not very, he answered himself. In fact he felt *very* crazy at this moment in time. Here he was, sitting between his mother and his wife, both of them holding his hands, both of them leaning against him, both of them crying a little.

And all he could think about was Deena, sitting somewhere behind him. He could feel her presence like an electric current running right through him. Dammit, he'd made himself a solemn vow he was going to forget her, he was never going to think about her again, she was *dangerous*. He'd been very careful not to look directly at her. He'd kind of nodded in her direction when she and her parents first came in.

And then the three of them came over and he had to say hello to her, he had to lean over and kiss her cheek. Jesus! He thought he would go right out of his mind. He could smell her perfume. Her hair brushed his cheek. And he wanted to grab her and run away with her. He dreamed about her all the time. It woke him in the middle of the night and he always checked Steffie guiltily, looking to see if she was awake, as if she could read his mind while he was dreaming. He was a crazy man.

He shook his head, and Steffie squeezed his hand, thinking he was grieving, probably. She couldn't be more off the mark. He was feeling nothing for Pop, nothing at all. Why can't I feel anything? he asked himself. My father is dead. Dead. Dead.

Dead. He silently repeated the terrible word, pounding himself with it, waiting for pain . . . or sorrow . . . or regret. *Something*.

Then, Cookie's boss, Sam, got up. Paul expected a nice little speech, but Sam said, "Jonah Gordon fought hard for the rights of black people in this country . . . so, in his honor, I'd like to sing a song from the movement, an old inspirational we always sang when we weren't sure we'd see each other again. It's a song of farewell." And he sang, in a rich deep baritone clotted with tears:

> *This could be the last time,*
> *This could be the last time,*
> *May be the last time,*
> *I don't know . . .*
> *This could be the last time,*
> *I don't know.*

Now, at last, Paul was able to cry.

Deena was trying very hard to look out of the corner of her eye without anybody noticing—especially Sylvia and Daddy—trying to get just a glimpse of Paul's face. But it was no use; she could only see his hair and his gray-suited shoulder. And his wife and mother, one on either side, both leaning into him. She was so jealous. She knew she shouldn't be, that it was childish and ridiculous and stupid and crazy. But she was, anyway.

When would this pain stop, if ever? She hated it. It was going on much too long! She should be over him by now; she should be seeing other people. Well, she'd tried. She'd gone to the synagogue dinner dance with her ex, as promised. But it was just no good. Nobody was any good!

Cookie's boss stopped singing and there was such a deep and absolute silence in the room, it rang in her ears. She hadn't even really listened to him. She was not in good shape. Well, she was going to have to get over this. *He* wasn't hurting, that was for sure.

A new voice came booming from the back of the room. "I was Jonah's comrade for many years. I'd like to speak."

There was a rustle and a low murmur as everyone turned. A man strode up the aisle, a man in his seventies, his craggy face deeply lined, his broad shoulders slightly stooped in the tweed jacket. But handsome! The looks of a matinee idol.

* * *

Dorothy watched Frank Green march up to the podium in his definite way, and turn to survey the room. She'd seen him do *that* at more than one rally, a million years ago! Look at him. Except for the lines in his face and the gray in his hair, he was the same firebrand. He certainly hadn't lost his looks. Oy, Dorothy, what a thing to think at your husband's memorial service.

However, she couldn't help but think it, since Frank had been around already, making big hints that now she should come with him to California, that they should live together. What was she saying: "big hints"? He'd asked her outright. "Dorothy, come with me now. Haven't we waited long enough?" And shame on her, she hadn't given him the definite no he deserved.

Jonah not even cold in his grave—except, of course, he wasn't *in* a grave. He'd been cremated, just as he wanted, and his ashes scattered in New York Harbor, by the Statue of Liberty. Dave had taken the Staten Island ferry, late at night, and he'd done it.

"Jonah Golodny—that's how I knew him—was my comrade," Frank began. "We were innocent and idealistic young men," he said, leaning his arms on the podium, looking completely relaxed as he spoke to this roomful of strangers. "We both heard Spain's cry of anguish and each of us answered it, although I was on the West Coast and he was living in Washington.

"And so, thousands of miles from home, on the battlefield, we met . . . We had both been wounded, me in my shoulder, and Jonah in the leg. We were trying to move across an open field while half a dozen Fascist planes strafed us. We didn't know each other, but that didn't matter. We half dragged, half pushed each other to safety.

"I said we were idealistic. The Communists were the *most* idealistic of all the idealistic young people of that time. We wanted to change the very shape of this society, to make it what it was supposed to be from the very beginning: a country where every single person, regardless of class, regardless of race, or religion, or anything, had the exact same chance to a decent life.

"I see here many people who were young in the sixties . . . hippies, maybe." There was a ripple of laughter at this. "You think *you* had a counterculture! *We* had a *real* counterculture. Our whole lives—work, play, romance, hobbies, beliefs, activities, relationships—everything was within the left-wing movement. You didn't need anything else.

"We had such a strong feeling that we were the future of this country. We were so sure that what we were fighting for was what every person wanted: peace, freedom, unity, equality!

"His whole life, Jonah was true to these ideals and principles. He never faltered. He fought for the sharecroppers in Missouri in the thirties, and then he had to go back to march for those same civil rights for our black brothers and sisters in the sixties. As I said, he never faltered in the good fight.

"Was Jonah ever a rich man? No, he was not. Did he have a high position with a title? No, he did not. Was he famous? No, he was not. But don't mourn Jonah's life. He exemplified the spirit of the Left. They call it the *Old* Left now, but I think of it, as he thought if it, as *The* Left—plain, simple, definite, the original. The only."

He waited for another murmur to subside and then he pushed himself upright. Dorothy thought for a moment that he might salute; that's what it looked like. But he only recited a poem, in stirring tones:

> *Mourn not the dead . . .*
> *But rather mourn the apathetic throng—*
> *The coward and the meek—Who see the world's great*
>   *anguish*
> *And its wrong*
> *And dare not speak.*

Into the utter silence, he added in a more normal tone of voice, "So mourn not Jonah Golodny. He *did* speak. He was indomitable."

Dorothy's eyes filled, and her sister, Yetta, who was watching her closely—almost too closely—immediately put her arm around Dot's shoulders and gave her a comforting squeeze. She wanted to say, No, Yetta, you're wrong this time. I'm mourning the years lost . . .

Oh, yes, she thought, indomitable. What a nice-sounding word. Strong, high-minded, powerful. If you don't think what it means to live with it.

It means scrambling and scampering around, twisting and bending and contorting yourself, always trying to accommodate yourself to his principles, his ideals. Let them ask her about it and she'd tell them: she was *tired*. Too damn tired, now that she thought about it, to start taking care of another principled idealist! Frank was very different from Jonah, but Frank was just like him, too. So sure he was right, undeviating, rigid, demanding that the rest of the world change to suit him.

Yes, Frank was the one true love of her life, no question. But not again. No. Even though it was tempting to think of living in the California sunshine, orange trees in the backyard, a handsome, intelligent man for her companion, and who knew? maybe her lover. Tempting, yes, but no, no, thank you.

No more bending to a man's will. Never again. She was so weary. The end with Jonah, the end that everyone else thought was so peaceful, so right, such a blessing . . . they didn't know. Only Marilyn, of all of them, knew what she, Dorothy, knew.

A month ago, it was, maybe a little more, maybe a little less, she couldn't remember anymore. But, about a month ago, Jo asked her to sit by him. He took her hand and, for a change, he opened his eyes and looked right into hers and said, "Dorothy, I've spoken with Marilyn."

She waited while he caught his breath. These days, every little effort tired him out. She waited and she waited. And then she said, "Yes? You spoke to Marilyn? And?"

"I asked her for something. For a pill."

Dorothy knew what he was referring to. But it chilled her so, she tried very hard to pretend she didn't understand. "What kind of a pill? A painkiller? Something to stop the hallucinations?"

"Dot. Come on. You know."

She knew. God knows he'd talked about it often enough. Even before the cancer got so bad. "When my time comes," he always said, "I don't want to hang around, dying forever, making a nuisance of myself to my family. When my time comes, I want to go when *I* want to go."

"Jonah, we don't always have a choice."

"We have a choice if we agree to do this for our partner."

And, of course, she told him to bite his tongue, his time hadn't come yet. But he made her promise. She had to agree with him. What was the sense, if you were old and dying, of being hooked up to machines that kept you alive—if that's what you were willing to call it—suffering, maybe unconscious, certainly of no use to anyone, including yourself?

So that day, she sighed, and then she said, "Yes, I know what you're talking about. You're telling me that Marilyn gave you enough pills so that if you take them, you'll—" Funny, wasn't it? They'd both prided themselves on speaking plainly: tell the truth, call a spade a spade and all that. But when it came to the point, she could not say the word *die*. She choked on it. *He* had to be the one to say it.

"I'll die. That's right. I told you, Dot. When my time comes, let me go before it gets messy. Go into that drawer, the one where I keep all my important papers."

She went. There was a plastic vial of bright-colored capsules right on top of everything. She brought it over to him. "These?"

He looked, he smiled, then he closed his eyes again, nodding. "Those. Please put them in my hand and bring me water."

She sat, staring at him, her heart pounding suddenly. "Not now!" she said, and began instantly to cry, without volition. "You can't mean *now*!"

"Give me your hand, my darling Dorothy. Bend over and let me kiss you. Dorothy, listen. You've always stood by me, even when it got tough. So this is a little tough. So don't let me down."

"Jonah, I can't! I can't! I thought I could, I really did. But . . . I just can't!" Why now, she thought, why now, all of a sudden? And then she saw a ripple of pain go down his body, saw him tense against it, give in to it, let it move on—and all without a sound, without even a grimace, just the arching of his poor wasted body as the pain moved down.

"Jo, Jo," she said, still weeping. "You've been fooling us all, haven't you? You've been in terrible pain—how long?" He made a gesture that said as plainly as words that it didn't matter. "For a long time," she answered herself. "Only now it's gotten too bad to hide anymore."

"That's right. So, Dorothy. Please." The faintest whisper . . . It would be so easy to make believe she'd never heard it.

She didn't know how long she sat there without moving, clutching that plastic cylinder in her hand as if she could will things to change. How could she do it? How could he ask her to do it, to take the responsibility for ending his life? But was this any different than it had always been? All the years they'd lived together, he had asked the impossible of her, and she had always done her best to do it for him.

So in the end, she pried open the cap, poured them into her hand, then put the capsules in his palm and folded his fingers over them, and handed him the water glass with the bent straw for bedridden people. And watched with pounding pulses as he put the pills in his mouth and sipped at the water and swallowed, once, twice, five times in all.

She was crying harder than ever, wishing she could pull those pills back out of his throat, knowing that was silly, that was stupid. Was the man not an adult, capable of making such a decision? Who was she, after all, to say no? Was she in pain, was she riddled with disease?

She took the glass from him and carefully put it down on the side table and took both his hands in both of hers. After a moment, he said, "Dorothy. Thank you." She was no longer capable of speech; she was clogged with grief. And then he said, with a little smile, "If I should die before I wake, tell my children good-bye." And in a little while, he gave a moan and he was gone.

What would all these people sitting here today, she thought now, think of her if they knew? She hoped they would understand. But, whether they did or not, she didn't care. She had promised him and she'd done it. Frank called Jo indomitable. What about her? Jo had had the principles; she had made the home, and brought up the children, and worked by his side and followed him—and did as he asked, most of the time—brought him back to life, and, finally, helped him die. That's what she called indomitable. The women of this world, they were the ones who did all the tough stuff. Yeah, Dorothy, so you're indomitable. So that and a buck will get you on the subway. You're alone, he's dead, and you're here without him. And you're lonely.

Again, she began to cry, almost against her own will. It wasn't so simple, was it, this grief business!

Then Cookie whispered in her ear. "Mom. Look. The kids." And she lifted her head to see all her grandchildren standing together up front with Jack and Sylvia's grandchildren. They all had their arms linked. It was beautiful. She wiped her eyes and pulled herself together because this, she didn't want to miss.

They sang:

Turn, turn, turn, a time to be born, a time to die . . . A time to kill, a time to heal, a time to laugh, a time to weep . . . A time to dance, a time to mourn . . . A time of war, a time of peace . . . A time to love, a time to hate, a time for peace, I swear it's not too late.

About the Author

Marcia Rose is not a real person. She is *two* real persons—two women who met as young mothers twelve years ago and suddenly found themselves writing novels together.

Marcia of *Marcia Rose*, comes from a long line of redheads, hotheads, and marathon storytellers. She has two beautiful daughters, aged twenty and twenty-two, and lives in a co-op apartment in Brooklyn Heights, NY. She enjoys everything life has to offer.

Rose of *Marcia Rose* is witty, sly, and quite athletic. She has been married for twenty-seven years—to the same man!—lives in a 100-year-old house in Brooklyn Heights, and has two beautiful daughters, twenty-three and nineteen. She likes to ski, garden, and talk.

Every word of every Marcia Rose novel is spoken aloud, as they work side by side at the word processor. After so many years as a team, it no longer comes as a surprise when they think of the same thing at the same time, in the same words. What *is* a surprise is that writing books is still so much fun!

ALL FOR THE LOVE OF DADDY	SBN 32991-0, $4.95
ADMISSIONS	SBN 31269-4, $3.95
CHOICES	SBN 29151-4, $2.95
CONNECTIONS	SBN 30458-6, $3.50
SECOND CHANCES	SBN 31918-4, $2.95
SUMMER TIMES	SBN 31854-4, $3.95

All Ballantine Books by Marcia Rose are available in a bookstore near you, or call toll-free

1-800-733-3000

to order with your American Express, MasterCard, or Visa. To expedite your order, please mention Interest Code "JOB 30." Postage charges are $1 for the first book, 50¢ for each additional book.

To order by mail, send check or money order (no cash or CODs please) to: Ballantine Mail Sales, 8-4, 201 E. 50th St., New York, NY 10022.

Prices and numbers subject to change without notice. All orders subject to availability of books. Valid in U.S. only.